PACTUM

PACTUM

BY NICHOLAS TAYLOR

Pactum

Text copyright © 2012 Nicholas Taylor

Somnium Press, LLC

ISBN-10: 1938387023

ISBN-13: 978-1-938387-02-9

www.NicholasTaylor.co

Dedication

This book is dedicated to all of the friends, family and readers in my life who read and encourage my writing. Without your love and support none of what I do would be possible.

Other Titles by This Author

The Legon Series
Legon Awakening-Legon Ascension
Legon Restoration

CONTENTS

PROLOGUE

BILLY LANNER stepped out of The Gaylord Street Bar and Grill, the warm August night air scented by a handful of smokers standing outside chattering. Billy turned left, his shoes scraping loudly on the gravel as he started searching for his car. He wasn't drunk, he'd only had one beer, but he still looked around to make sure there wasn't a pig parked nearby looking to fill his DUI quota for the month.

Billy played with his phone, posting status updates on various social sites and checked out what a few of his friends were up to. He slowed, hearing a car door open. He looked up the street and froze. A man was looking inside the back seat of Billy's car. His heart began to pound, *You idiot you knew this would happen!* He turned, walking away and trying to step softer, cursing the gravel on the street and the late hour. There was almost no one around; the smokers were back inside the bar. He thought about ducking back in, but decided whoever it was at his car would just wait for him outside the bar until last call. Billy heard a distant car door shut; his car door, no doubt. He glanced over his shoulder and sure enough a figure was walking quickly in Billy's direction. He swore under his breath, turning left down Mississippi. As he rounded the corner he broke into a jog, panting, not for the first time wishing he was a runner. *Keep focused, moron* he told himself.

His legs started to burn just a bit as he hung another left on York, aware of a sound from behind him. *Does he just want to talk?* Not likely. If Billy was lucky he'd just get beaten up, but if Billy was lucky he'd have never been found out in the first place. The late hour meant that no lights were on in the little brick houses he passed. He saw plywood covering the window of a small home to his right. He ran around back, breathing hard and dodging heaps of wood, the house was obviously under renovation. Billy found the back door and turned an old knob. *Finally some luck!* The door swung open and he entered.

He closed it softly and tiptoed his way to the front room, thankful that the shiny hardwood floor didn't creek. He sat down in a closet, bringing his knees to his chest, a little plume of sawdust rising and catching in his throat. He tried rather vainly to calm himself. What was he going to do? Out front he thought he heard movement, the light sound of grass being walked on. Billy made sure his phone was on silent, knowing whoever it was wouldn't be able to figure out where he was if he could keep quiet. And then he noticed it…a panting sound followed by a deep growl.

God no, not one of those! There was a sniffing sound at the edge of the plywood window and Billy moved deeper in the closet, praying in earnest for the first time in years. There was a snort and then nothing. Billy breathed out softly, and then heard the back door click shut.

A deep, raspy voice called out, "Billy…Billy, I can smell you Billy," it chuckled.

Billy's eyes stung as sweat dripped into them, his mouth dry as parchment. *Don't run, that's what it wants, it wants the sport, don't run, don't run, don't run…*his ears were pierced by a howl. Deep in Billy's brain, instinct took over. Fight or flight were his options and his terrified mind knew only one response to a wolf's howl. Billy bolted from the closet without thinking.

There was a guttural growl behind him and he turned to see two glowing eyes higher than his own and a flash of white teeth. Pain exploded on Billy's left side as claws raked his ribs sending him flying.

Billy hit the floor twisting his ankle, his weight buckling the joint, taking him to the wood floor. He hit, landing on his side, the air knocked from him as the pain from his other side flared. He tried to crawl away, his rational mind only a faint whisper telling him it was all over, the scared animal in him reaching for safety.

Billy cried out as claws sank deep into his leg.

DETECTIVE ALISON KAUR set her latte in her cup-holder, shut her door and put on her seat belt. She looked up to see two teenagers dressed in ratty hoodies in an alleyway exchanging a bag and money. Alison un-clicked the seat belt and a voice in her head said, *You aren't on vice anymore, it's not your problem.* What was her problem was the crime scene she was supposed to be heading toward, the one with a stiff, not a couple of kids with grass. She re-clicked her belt and started the car.

She turned out into morning traffic on Alameda, hanging a right on University, thinking about a world without rush hour. She looked around, seeing everything. Her uncle had told her this would happen when she decided to become a cop: you see everything. Like the kids at the coffee shop, or now the hookers getting off a bus from a long night's work. Next to her a woman was texting, not looking at the road, and further up someone wasn't wearing his seat belt. Another lady was dabbing at a bruise under her eye with makeup. This was just another morning drive. She saw the good around her too, like the young girl gazing at a diamond ring on her finger, though good didn't seem to hold the same effect on Alison. She knew most people didn't see what she did, it wasn't their job, but it was hers. Well not everything, just homicide. She moved forward, turning on Mississippi.

She drove up York and got out of her car, sipping on her latte. On the right-hand side of the road was a small two-story house with taupe bricks that was undergoing a renovation. She ducked under yellow tape and greeted one of the many uniformed officers.

She gave him a once-over. "You look a little worse for the wear, Charley," she said.

Charley smiled grimly. "Yeah, and you will too in about five minutes ma'am, it's…ah…pretty bad in there," he said.

"Peachy."

She took deeper sips on her coffee as she walked up the lawn and porch. She gently pushed open a red front door to a scene of organized chaos. CSIs were fluttering around the front room of the house dusting for prints and snapping pictures of everything. She turned and winced.

"What happened here?" she asked in disgust.

Alison was far from being squeamish, but the mess in front of her made her stomach turn. Blood pooled around a corpse whose head lulled against half-finished drywall. Gore spattered the drywall like someone had been spraying a hose, the droplets soaking into the material, the body of the victim shredded.

"Pretty nasty, isn't it?" a voice asked.

She turned to her partner, Sean Hughes. His sandy hair was carefully disheveled, his tie just barely loose, the picture of what every city girl thought a trendy detective should look like. His blue eyes seemed unaffected by the remains before him.

"Yeah, it's bad," Alison said in response. "What do you think?"

"Do I look like an ME to you?" Sean asked, sardonic.

She ignored him and spoke to a CSI examining the body. "What do you think?" she asked.

He looked up, his face distorted by a plastic shield, his voice slightly muffled, "We'll have to wait for the official autopsy, but I'd say blood loss." He pulled at some of the man's tattered clothing. "Not too many deep wounds here on the chest and abdomen." He paused, "I think it was a dog that did it. I haven't seen an animal attack like this before, and I've been doing this for some time detective. At any rate, this cherry wood floor is ruined." His tone was almost sullen for the lost flooring.

"Animal attack? That's what this is?" Sean asked, irritated. "Why are we here? We are homicide detectives not animal control! Why were we called here? And wood floors are resilient, sand it and stain it with something other than our stiff's blood and it will be right as rain," he said.

"Does he look like dispatch to you, Hughes?" Alison asked in the same sardonic tone he'd used a few minutes ago.

"Funny. So, do you know why we are here?" he asked, a bit more respectful this time.

Alison looked at her phone. "The vic's car was found down the street from here and this isn't his home, and unless Fido can open the back door or ransack cars I'd say this is a homicide."

Sean cursed, "Freak used a dog as a murder weapon, that's just wrong."

The CSI was back to work, holding a little device that looked like an electric razor over one of the many wounds on the victim. He paused, "Detectives, I think I know what did this…"

"What?" Alison asked.

The CSI held up the device. "There's Vis residue here."

"Vis?" Sean asked.

The CSI rolled his eyes. "Yeah, Vis or magic; it matches that of a Werewolf."

A cold feeling crept into Alison's veins. "Are you sure?" she asked, her voice a little weaker than normal.

"Sorry ma'am, but I'd say so."

SEAN HUGHES shook his head. He hated magic. All it'd done was cause problems since it'd come out in the open three years back. He leant over, picking up a blood-soaked wallet from the floor. He flipped it open in a gloved hand and read the victim's name.

"So why did the big bad wolf attack Mr…William Lanner here? He sure doesn't look like Red Riding Hood, now does he?" Sean asked the CSI.

The CSI scowled, Sean didn't care for CSIs either; they were all just geeks on power trips as far as Sean could tell.

"I don't know detective, I guess that's for you to figure out, now isn't it," the man said icily.

"Thanks, we'll be on our way," Alison said, giving Sean a look. "Let's walk the house."

She led him away, both of them looking around for any clues they could find.

"Ya know, maybe if you weren't such a dick to the folks in the lab they might not hate you," she said. "Just sayin'."

Sean snorted. "Yeah, I know I shouldn't be so hard on them, but those nerds just get on my nerves. I never liked the smart kids."

"Really, that's what has you so on edge? Hmm, and to think I thought it was because magic was involved," Alison said.

She was dead on, but he wasn't going to admit it. Instead he walked into the kitchen of the house, the back door ajar. Another geek was dusting for prints but Sean would be surprised if they found anything of use. A month ago Sean had been forced to sit through a lecture about magic; about Wolves in particular. They didn't leave prints, not due to any skills per se but because they didn't have normal fingers. He walked out the back, trying to find anything of use but couldn't. They gave a few orders to the CSIs on site and he turned to Alison.

"Shall we check out the car?" he asked, bored.

Alison agreed and added, "Did you catch a ride down here?"

He said he had and followed her to her car. Mr. Lanner's car wasn't far away. Sean tried not to bother the nerds as they worked and went to the trunk of the car and looked around.

"What do you think it was looking for?" Sean asked, looking into the trunk, the fabric was torn apart, metal was turned up in areas. He leaned in, Alison next to him, looking at bent metal. "Man, what kind of freak can do that?"

"Bright side is maybe it cut itself on something tearing the car apart," Alison said.

Sean breathed out, the lab would find more but he said, "We have to tell the Sergeant about the magic."

Alison looked serious for a moment, "Rock, paper, scissors?"

Sean won, sparing him from having to tell Sergeant Montoya that the department would need to contract with witches and wizards. But he could hear the Sergeant swear, even with the phone to Alison's ear.

"He sounds chipper today," Sean noted.

Alison smiled brightly. "Yeah the picture of joy, we have to go back in when we are done here, Sergeant said not to follow any leads until he contracts with Mages."

"I hate magic," Sean complained.

They spent a few more hours getting anything done they could before having to leave. Sean sat in the passenger seat as Alison drove down Colfax back to the station. Alison stopped on the way back to get another cup of coffee.

"That junk will kill you, ya know," Sean pointed out.

"How is coffee going to kill me?" she asked with a chuckle.

"OK, so for most people it wouldn't but you drink what, like a gallon a day?" Alison opened her mouth to respond and shut it. Sean laughed, "Ha! Yeah, what you got to say to that one?" he taunted.

Alison smirked, "Whatever. Like you're one to talk."

"What? I don't even drink coffee," Sean said.

She pointed at him, "But you have enough product in your hair to style a beauty pageant! That junk must be soaking into your brain."

"Really? That's the comeback? I use too much hair gel? Wow, it's a good thing you're good at catching killers because comedy…not happening."

They continued to talk trash as they entered the station and made their way to their floor. They came in the office laughing and for just a moment forgetting the morning. That changed when they entered the office. Everyone was silent, all either standing or sitting, looking at the Sergeant's office.

Inside, the Sergeant was talking to a girl with brown hair and thin features. Sean came up next to someone he didn't know. "Is that the witch?" he asked.

The man's face reddened. "Yeah that's it," the man said softly.

Sean looked at the woman; she glanced out into the office from behind glasses. She looked uncomfortable.

HEIDI DECOR looked out of the office window at the gathered police officers outside in the neat rows of desks. None looked happy to see a Mage in the office. She turned back to Sergeant Montoya. He was a little short for a man, maybe 5'7" and in his early fifties, his hair short black bristles. His dark eyes looked up from his paperwork. She focused more Vis into her glasses, reading his emotions. Fear, anger, curiosity and even awe were visible. Fear and anger were the strongest emotions. Part of her figured he wanted to kick her out. She didn't blame him, normal humans had only known about Mages for a few years. Most people still hung onto their silly superstitions, and after all, her kind had killed many people in the recent years. No, she didn't blame him or any of them for not wanting her around.

The Sergeant looked out his window. "No one wants you here," he said as a matter of fact.

She looked out again using Vis this time, true no one wanted her there. She saw murder in the eyes of one man and wondered if she shouldn't have taken Gabriel up on his offer to come with her to the meeting.

"You requested a Pactum, not us," she pointed out, not letting her own fear color her tone. She could affect the Sergeant's emotions, she could affect everyone's but that was against the Pactum.

"Pactum?" he asked.

"Yes, the Pactum or contract, if you will; it's our agreement. You requested this meeting, didn't you?" she asked.

"The mayor thinks whenever magic is involved in a crime we should contract wizards and the likes," he hedged.

"Mages, we are called Mages and it's not magic; it's called Vis. Your mayor is right, Werewolves are some of the most dangerous Mutari. But be that as it may Sergeant, you contacted the North American Pactum Guild and requested this meeting. If you do not want to contract with us, you are not obligated to do so."

He waved his hand. "Like I said I don't have a choice, now in our Pactum here it says that we owe you half upfront in gold or silver minted bullion. Do you want that now?" he asked.

She frowned. "Don't you want to talk the terms of the Pactum?" she asked.

He shook his head. "Nope, now do you have something to take this with?" he said dumping a handful of coins on his desk.

Heidi placed the coins in a velvet pouch and then looked out at the people in the office again. Cops or not, some of them would like to hurt her, and Mage or not she was no Paladin; she couldn't take them. No, she wasn't going to add any more incentive for them to hurt her.

"My people will take it tomorrow," she said.

"People? As in more than one?" he asked, not looking happy.

"Yes people, as in two of them. Your Pactum is with Gabriel, and his sister Faith will be assisting him." She stood. "Now, I think I should be on my way, thank you for your time Sergeant."

He walked her to his door and pointed the way back to the elevators. She made her way across the office, fighting the urge to panic as she received cold glances. A portly man standing next to a rather well-groomed one stepped in her path just a bit. She stopped. His emotions were boiling.

Before the man could speak, a woman with long brown hair came forward. "My name is Detective Kaur, let me show you out," she said, leading Heidi safely through the office.

ALISON KAUR walked the Mage out of the office before turning back to find Sean. She found him standing with the man who had blocked the Mage.

"What was that?" she demanded.

"What?" the officer asked.

"Are you trying to get us a bad mark with the Pactum Guild?!" a different voice said.

Alison turned to look at Steven Lee, the head of the crime lab.

He went on, "What was your plan? Take a swing at a Mage? What would that do?"

"I wasn't gonna do nothin', besides who cares if we get a bad mark with this guild of theirs?" the man said puffing up.

"I do!" Sergeant Montoya's voice rang. "Don't be stupid here, people, Denver is one of three cities contracting with Mages on a regular basis. The Mayor's office has made it clear we aren't to screw this up! Now Hughes and Kaur get in here," he said closing the subject.

Alison walked into the Sergeant's office with Sean in tow.

"You're going to have two Mages with you tomorrow and until you solve this case," the Sergeant said.

"Sir…" Sean started.

"I don't want to hear it Hughes, we don't have a choice. I don't like it either. Any questions?" he asked.

"What is their role?" Alison asked.

"They are here to protect you from other Vis users only; they won't assist or get in your way. You don't even have to talk to them if you don't want to, got it?"

"We are getting babysitters?" Sean asked.

The Sergeant changed tack, sitting down and motioning for them to do the same before he spoke. "Look…I've talked to other departments with experience with Werewolves…and you two are my best people. This year Denver has already lost four people to Wolves alone. I'm not happy about the Mages being here, but I have to admit they could be handy to have around."

Sean calmed down. Alison knew that Sean was a bit of a hothead but he deeply respected the Sergeant as did she. "We won't mess up sir," she said.

"Yeah I know. OK, what do you have so far?"

Sean spoke, "One victim, a William Lanner, friends knew him as Billy. He was a white male in his early thirties. He was a CPA with a clean record, other than that we don't know yet."

"The victim's car was ransacked and the killing took place a block away, so I think it's safe to assume this wasn't a random act of violence," Alison added.

The Sergeant looked off into the distance. "No, it's not. Let me know when the drug screen comes back. I want to know why a Wolf was after this guy and looking around in his car."

"What are you thinking, Sarge?" Sean asked.

"Well, from what we know Werewolves don't attack at random. For centuries Mages have kept them along with all the other magical races in check, but now that magic is in the open…and, I don't know about you, but having a Werewolf as an enforcer sounds like a good plan to me."

"Right sir," Alison said.

They talked for a while longer before they were dismissed. Alison spent the rest of her day profiling William Lanner's life.

ONE

ALISON KAUR strolled in to work, a latte in one hand, her tablet in the other. Her case had already made the front page of the online edition of the paper. She read through, seeing the handiwork of the Public Affairs office. Alison didn't have a lead yet, but according to the article the police were hot on the trail of a suspect. There was no mention of the killer being a Werewolf, though. She turned the tablet off as she exited the elevator. She walked to her desk, seeing the message light blinking demandingly on her phone. She put her bag down and set her coffee on her desk.

"Kaur," the Sergeant's voice said.

She turned to see him poking his head out of his office. "Come in here when you get settled. If you see Hughes, tell him the same," he said disappearing back in his office.

Sean came in, setting his things down at the desk across from hers.

"Didn't you wear that shirt yesterday?" Alison asked.

Sean smiled. "That I did. Since you're in different clothes, I'd wager your night wasn't as good as mine."

She rolled her eyes. "Montoya wants to see us."

Sean joined her as she walked into the Sergeant's office. He sat behind his oak veneer desk. Across from him were two people. A man stood in his late twenties, wavy hair a dark brown, almost black. His face was strong, his body fit, his rich brown eyes had a warmth she couldn't pinpoint. Next to the man was a small woman probably in her mid-twenties, her chin-length hair the same color as the man's, her green eyes framed by an elfin face. They were both attractive but the girl was by far more radiant. If she wasn't so short she could have been a model. Alison continued her assessment of the two. Both had on black overcoats despite it being August. The man wore black slacks and a white button-down shirt with the top two buttons undone. The girl had on a short skirt, leather boots coming up past her knees. She too wore a white button-front shirt, showing off just a hint of cleavage.

All this Alison absorbed, in the space of a few moments. Her mind processed. *Brother and sister, both athletic, the girl is attractive and knows it but doesn't want to flaunt it too much. She's probably smart though, and based on the bored look on her face, she thinks this work is below her. The man is harmless; he is in shape but too relaxed to pose a real threat.* As usual for Alison, this head-to-toe assessment registered immediately in the databank of her brain without conscious thought or effort.

"Detectives, let me introduce you to the Mages you'll be working with," the Sergeant said.

The man stood up and extended his hand to her. "Hello, my name is Gabriel Decor and this is my sister, Faith Penn," he said warmly.

"Detective Alison Kaur. This is my partner Detective Sean Hughes," Alison replied shaking his hand.

Gabriel offered Sean his hand, Sean didn't take it. Gabriel just shrugged. His sister stared off into space.

"Right." the Sergeant said. "I was told to give you the deposit," he said to Gabriel.

Gabriel took a velvet bag that clinked. Faith held out her hand to him.

As Gabriel looked in the bag and smiled, Alison saw Faith's foot pull back. "Ouch!" Gabriel said. She continued to hold her hand out and Gabriel rolled his eyes. "Honestly, make one bad investment and no one lets you live it down," he muttered, handing her the bag.

"Is everything all right?" the Sergeant asked.

Gabriel smiled. "Yes. My family thinks I make bad decisions on money, so I'm not allowed to take the deposit," he said sheepishly.

Faith snorted. "You lost five thousand dollars in gold on a horse race with a horse that had never won a race in its career."

Gabriel shook his head. "I really thought he was just holding back. I mean, Erin even said it was a good bet…"

"She said only a moron would bet on that horse."

"Which I thought was code to make everyone around us think the horse was a bad bet but really she knew he'd win. Oh well," he turned his attention to a dumbfounded Alison, "so should we go over the Pactum?"

"Um, yeah," Alison said.

She led Gabriel, a frosty Faith, and a reluctant Sean back to her desk. Sean scowled and Alison prayed they'd find William Lanner's killer quickly.

Alison sat on the edge of her desk, Sean next to her. "So what do we have to go over?" she asked.

Faith pulled some folded papers out of a shoulder bag and handed them to Gabriel.

"Thanks," he said handing some of the papers to Alison. "This is the Pactum. In it are both sides' agreements. This top page outlines payment and time frame. You have a Pactum with us that will last as long as this case is open, or until the Werewolf is killed, brought into custody, or its name is cleared. While in our care, when you are on the clock, I am to protect you and Mr. Hughes from any and all Mutari and Mages," he said.

"Wait, Mutari?" Sean asked.

Gabriel nodded. "Yes, Mutari. They are people affected by Vis, or magic as you call it. For example, the Werewolves are Mutari. So are Vampires, Trolls, Succubi, Elementals, Shape Shifters, Banshees, Goblins, Wraiths, as well as Fairies if there were any alive."

"You mean all those things are real?" Sean asked incredulous.

Alison was surprised too. She'd heard of a few on the list and rumors of others but she had always just chalked up most of the rumors to legend. "How many Mutari are there?" Alison asked.

Faith took the Pactum from Gabriel. "The number of Mutari are irrelevant, my brother will protect you from all of these while you are on police business. At the end of the Pactum we will take the rest of our fee. Should Gabriel be killed during the Pactum, you are not required to pay the rest of the fee," she said flatly.

"And what if we don't pay?" Sean asked.

"Then we tell the Pactum Guild that you violated your Pactum with us," Gabriel said.

Sean laughed. "What, so we don't shell out and you tell mommy and daddy and that's that?"

Gabriel took a moment. "Yes, in effect; however, should you not hold up to your end of the Pactum, you will receive a bad mark on your record with the Guild. Since you haven't done much business with the guild yet, this would likely result in Mages either being unwilling to work with the city of Denver or charging higher prices with upfront payment."

"So nothing, really," Sean snorted.

"The latter is far less likely to happen. You would probably be unable to contract with Mages, leaving Denver completely open to attack from Mutari and Mages alike," Faith said again with a flat tone. "But do as you like."

SEAN HUGHES eyed Faith. She was smokin' hot; he'd give her that, but she was a Mage. Who was she to threaten a cop? Who was she to even walk into the station thinking she could act however she wanted? Faith was back to looking passive, not a hint of emotion on her face.

Sean was distracted by Alison. "Look, you two might be here on contract with the department, but Detective Hughes and I have a job to do. This is our investigation and we are in charge, understood?"

Gabriel smiled. "Of course, I won't get in your way."

Sean sized Gabriel up. He was in shape and carried himself with confidence but aside from that he didn't seem all that amazing. Sean figured the Mages were ripping the department off; these two couldn't protect anything. He noticed a bulge in Gabriel's jacket at his hip.

"What's with the coat?" Sean asked trying to get Gabriel to show what was causing the bulge.

Gabriel shrugged. "Think of it as a uniform, but also," he said opening his jacket, "it covers Iram here." He fingered the grip of a sword.

"You have a sword on you!" Sean spat.

Gabriel nodded. "Yes, a Katana to be exact."

"I'm going to need you to hand that over. Only cops carry weapons here," Sean said sternly, his own hand edging toward his service weapon.

Gabriel frowned, letting his jacket cover Iram again. "I'm sorry, but that won't be happening."

"Really? Do you want to make a bet on that?" Sean said stepping closer to the Mage.

Alison stepped between the two men. "Hold up Hughes," she turned to Gabriel, "he's right; hand the sword over," she said in a kinder tone.

Gabriel didn't look uncomfortable in the least bit as he shook his head. "Detectives, I am not required to remove my blade," he held up his hand as both Detectives opened their mouths to speak. "If you read the Pactum you will see that indeed I have more discretion with my weapon than most law enforcement," he said calmly, holding out the Pactum.

Alison read the spot Gabriel pointed at. "Keep it hidden if you don't mind," she said.

"Of course."

"Hughes, come on, he's right," she said. "We have work to do."

"Right," Sean relented, not happy at all about some crazy wizard with a sword.

GABRIEL DECOR found a chair to sit in and slumped down. Faith sat down next to him. They exchanged a look before her eyes closed. He watched as Detectives Kaur and Hughes started talking about their plans for the day. Gabriel made sure he looked like he was staring off into space as he scanned the room and focused on what the Detectives were talking about.

Alison was rattling on about looking into William Lanner's finances, in some attempt to track down the Wolf that killed him. Gabriel tried not to smirk as the Humans strategized. If they weren't so cheap, Faith could find the Wolf by the end of the afternoon, but Denver was unwilling to pay for more than protection. In a way he didn't blame them; making a Pactum with Faith would run triple what the city had paid for Gabriel.

He flexed his Vis, checking the wards he'd placed on the office late in the night. They were all untested; nothing had used Vis on the building in the night. He cast wards around Alison and Sean, though he didn't care about either of the Detectives; he was just doing his job.

ALISON KAUR ran over the facts in her head before speaking. "Right, nothing popped up in William's finances, but he was a

CPA, so if he was involved in anything shady he'd have kept things hidden, which makes a dead end there."

"Looks like the ME is done with the stiff," Sean said looking up from his computer. "Shall we?"

Alison smirked. "Nothing like the smell of morgue first thing in the morning."

Alison stood, noticing Gabriel and Faith immediately fell in step behind her and Sean as they left the office. The Sergeant said they were on contract to protect her and Sean, but she still didn't trust them and found herself glancing over her shoulder every few steps. A few times Gabriel caught her eye and smiled warmly.

They rode the elevator down to the basement and the ME's office. Dr. Scott Partington, the ME, was inside sitting at his desk.

"Detectives," he greeted them formally. "Ah, and you two must be the witch and wizard I've heard nothing about," he said in an awkward attempt at humor.

"Mages," was all Gabriel said, his voice light and kind.

"Mages, ah well yes, I suppose that is the politically correct term now, isn't it?" Dr. Partington asked.

Alison always found visiting the ME to be an adventure, not due to any thrills or danger but just that Partington was one of the oddest people she'd ever met. She never knew what he was going to say and he had the most twisted sense of humor.

"Doctor," she interjected.

"Right, right, your friend Mr. Lanner," he said.

Partington led them to a table where a body lay, covered in a white sheet. "Is it OK for the Mages to see the body?" he asked.

"They can but don't need to," Sean turned to Gabriel and Faith. "You two can wait outside if you like."

The Mages said nothing, not moving. Sean's jaw tensed but he didn't say anything further.

Alison turned her attention back to the doctor who was watching Sean talk to the Mages like he was watching a movie. "May I?" he asked.

"Please," Alison said.

Dr. Partington pulled back the sheet, revealing Mr. Lanner's corpse.

The doctor cleared his throat. "In the report, the CSIs theorized that the cause of death was blood loss. Indeed, Billy boy's mechanism of death was exsanguination caused by lacerations to the body, in particular his chest and torso. He also sustained a broken left ankle and two broken ribs." Partington placed a gloved hand on Billy's chest, drawing their attention to a cut, "As you can see, the wounds were not deep in most spots."

"So it took him a while to die?" Sean asked.

Dr. Partington frowned. "Yes and no. From the body we can see that the wounds were caused rather rapidly, and with the amount of wounds he sustained, I'd say Mr. Lanner was severely hemorrhaging and would have lapsed into unconsciousness quickly." Dr. Partington moved down the table and adjusted Billy's left leg so Sean and Alison could see his calf. "The only abnormality here is that there are bite marks all over Mr. Lanner's calf and lower leg. Some were caused premortem but most were postmortem. Swabs of the wounds show large amounts of Werewolf Vis residue. Mr. Lanner was quite the chew toy, I dare say."

"Thank you doctor, is there anything else you can tell us?" Alison asked.

"Yes. The ribs were broken not by a fall but with impact. The Wolf 's claws dug into the bone. That coupled with the bite marks says that the creature you are after is very strong and based on the condition of William Lanner's remains, I'd say the perpetrator is very aggressive."

"Thanks, Doc," Sean threw over his shoulder as they walked out.

SEAN HUGHES and Alison brought all the information they had into a small conference room. Sean didn't comment on Gabriel and Faith seating themselves in the corner, and at least Faith was nice to look at. Sean laid out the crime scene pictures on the oak veneer table, neatly organizing them. Alison put some magnetic clips on the whiteboard and hung some notes and a picture of Billy Lanner in the center.

She sipped at her coffee. Sean's habit was gum. He started in on a stick and the rhythm of his chewing had a meditative effect.

"Skimming," Sean said in a matter of fact voice.

Alison cocked an eyebrow and Sean explained, "Think about it. The tox screen came back clean; the only thing in his system was some alcohol and prescribed anti-anxiety medication. If he wasn't doping, what would a CPA get into trouble with?"

Alison started pacing. "Right, if he was in deep with a gambling debt or something like that he'd still be alive. Dead men don't pay. Which leaves us with: he either ripped someone off…or it was a random act," she finished.

Sean turned to a stifled chuckle from Faith. "What are you laughing at?" he asked.

Gabriel answered. "Detectives, please forgive my sister's rudeness it's just…ouch!" Faith elbowed him and gave him a stern look. "The sooner they solve this, the sooner we are done here."

"It's not in the Pactum," she said pointedly.

"No; it's not regarded in the Pactum, but it's not excluded," Gabriel said.

"Are you two going to include us in this conversation?" Alison asked tartly. "If not, my partner and I have a killer to catch."

"Fine," Faith said and then spoke to Alison and Sean, "in point of fact you have a killer to find, but it will be Gabriel who takes them down."

"Only if the suspect fights back as a Werewolf," Sean said.

"Which he will," Faith said. "And of course it's a he; there are very few female Werewolves. I laughed at your comment about it being a random act, Detective Kaur. While I'm sure you were just saying that to put every possibility out on the table, let me assure you that this was not random. Werewolves don't kill at random. They are still too scared of Mages," she nodded to Gabriel.

"Werewolves are some of the most dangerous Mutari. They are not very common and are very expensive to hire," Gabriel said.

Sean didn't like the Mages but they were the experts. "So that means Billy pissed off the wrong people."

"And if having a Werewolf on staff isn't cheap, that means someone with resources was behind it," Alison continued.

Sean walked over to a table and picked up some papers as Alison spoke. "Do we have traffic cams in that area?"

"Already on it," Sean said. "If Billy's death was planned, then the perp would have shown up hours before stalking his victim."

"I'll canvass the neighborhood," Alison said and then added, "Come on Gabe, I'm driving."

Gabriel and Faith followed quickly behind Alison as Sean went back to his desk to find videos.

ALISON KAUR walked out to her car, Faith and Gabriel in tow. It was midmorning and the August sun was already blazing. At her car Alison removed some sneakers and a baseball cap from her bag. Her blouse was lightweight and she had on jeans, so she wouldn't get too hot, but the Mages...she looked them over. "You two are going to get heat stroke," she said.

Gabriel smiled kindly. "Not likely. Would you like me in the front or backseat?" he asked.

She thought for a moment, wondering why he didn't offer to let Faith sit up front, but decided not to comment on it. "Front."

Alison made her way through the traffic, her eyes naturally scanning around her. *Mugger in the alley, fake hobo panhandling,* the list of people ran in her head. Gabriel looked out the window with a bemused expression.

"What do you like to listen to?" she asked, feeling obligated to make small talk.

"Anything but rap," he said, not adding anything else.

She couldn't read the two Mages. Gabriel seemed friendly enough but mostly just didn't say much. She figured that he wasn't all that diligent at what he did, but at least he was nice on the eyes. As for Faith, Alison couldn't tell if she was all there, but when she spoke she seemed knowledgeable.

Alison turned down Mississippi, parking at the corner of York. The sidewalks were shaded by trees that had been planted before Alison's parents were born. Little old-fashioned houses ran along the street in a neat row, small yards in front. She got out of the car, put her Denver Police Department name tag around her neck and made sure her badge was in plain sight.

"I'm going to canvass the area, which means that I'm going to be knocking on a bunch of doors and talking to people. I don't want you two making people uncomfortable," Alison said.

Faith rolled her eyes. "Yeah, I'm sure the house wrapped in police tape and you with a shield around your neck will inspire ease in the people living around here."

Alison changed her assumption about Faith. There wasn't anything wrong with her mind, she was just rude.

Gabriel rocked on his feet. "Thanks for that, Faith. What I think she's trying to say is that people are already on edge, but I promise we will be on our best behavior."

"Whatever," Faith rolled her eyes again, which promptly went out of focus.

I'm beginning to see why Sean hates magic. Alison walked up the sidewalk to a small home made of dark red brick with flowers out front. Wrought iron covered the windows and doors; it was decorative and effective. The houses in the area went for a ton of cash but the neighborhood still wasn't completely safe. She knocked on the door.

"Who's there?" a timid voice called from inside.

"Detective Alison Kaur with the Denver Police Department ma'am, may I have a word?"

Door locks slid out of place and the bright white door opened to reveal a lady in her eighties, short wispy hair around her head like a Q-tip. "Well hello there, officer," she looked over at Faith and Gabriel, "and who are your friends, dear?"

Alison didn't let the Mages answer. "This is Gabriel and his sister Faith. They are here as consultants…"

"You are a lovely girl, aren't you?" the lady said to Faith.

To Alison's eternal amazement Faith blushed. "Thank you so much, you're so sweet and can I say how nice your tulips look," Faith gushed.

"Is that scones I smell?" Gabriel sniffed the air.

The little old lady giggled. "Why yes my boy it is, that's a good sniffer you have there, would you like to come in and try some? And thank you about the flowers dear, you're too kind."

"We don't want to put you out Miss…" Alison started and stopped at a stern look from the little old lady. "Yes, we would love some scones."

The little old lady beamed. "Perfect, I'll put some tea on. Do you mind Earl Grey?"

"There are other kinds?" Gabriel joked.

The little old lady tittered.

Alison sat on a soft couch with a flower pattern and took out a pad of paper while Faith made small talk with the little old lady. The Mages' new friend was named Grace. Grace plopped herself down on a chair and watched as Faith and Gabriel bit into their scones. Alison was not offered a scone or tea.

Faith closed her eyes. "Hmmmm, Gracie, this is so good, you have to give me the recipe, my sister-in-law will flip!"

Grace beamed. "Oh thank you so much dear, I'd love to give it to you. Such a charming girl." She turned watery blue eyes to Alison. "So Detective, how may I help you?" she asked.

"Ma'am, were you home the night of the fourteenth?" Alison asked.

"Why yes, I was," Grace answered and offered Faith more tea. Alison still had none. She tried not to get annoyed, telling herself she didn't want hot tea on a hot day anyway.

"Did you hear anything around one AM?" Alison asked.

"Well why would an old woman be up at one in the morning?" Grace asked sweetly.

Alison breathed out and tried not to get frustrated. "There was a murder up the street. Did anything wake you up?"

Grace grimaced. "I wish I could help you but I was asleep in my room. Even if I had been awake, that murder happened several houses down and my hearing isn't all that good anymore. Perhaps someone else heard something," she said.

"Thank you," Alison said and handed Grace her card. "If you hear anything, please give me a call."

Alison stood and the Mages followed her lead.

"You two aren't leaving too, are you?" Grace sounded dismayed.

"Sorry but yes, we have to; we are here to help the police," Gabriel said.

Grace nodded. "Well, you two keep yourselves safe and I'm glad you're on the case. I dare say…" she looked at Alison's card, "Detective Kaur can use all the help she can get."

Alison walked from the house, back stiff.

The next two doors Alison knocked on no one answered. After those came a procession of people inviting Gabriel and Faith into their homes. Alison was treated with the mild distrust and disdain every detective was used to. As for Gabriel and Faith…

after 20 houses that went exactly the same way Alison rounded on Gabriel at her wit's end. "I thought you weren't going to interfere with my investigation!"

Gabriel looked taken aback. "I'm not, and I haven't asked anyone a single question about the death of William Lanner."

Alison ground her teeth. "No, but you've charmed yourself with everyone around here! This is taking forever and we should be done by now!" she said gesturing angrily at the rest of the block.

"Alison, we are being polite and I've found today to be very informative," Gabriel looked stung.

Alison wanted to say something ugly but chose not to; instead she took a deep breath and counted to ten, and then looked at Faith who again looked bored, not paying attention to the conversation at all. Alison took another deep breath and this time counted to thirty.

"I need something to eat. Come on," she said.

She walked around the corner and into a gas station. She grabbed a snack while Gabriel and Faith wandered around looking at magazines. The kid at the counter gawked at Faith in her short skirt, long jacket and boots. Alison thought the kid was about to drool. She held out a picture of William Lanner.

"Any chance you've seen this guy?" Alison asked. When the kid whose nametag read "Ben" didn't answer she said, "Hey hey, pay attention!"

"O-ah sorry there officer," he looked at the picture, "yeah, that's Billy; what did he do this time?"

This time? Alison perked up, "What do you mean 'this time'? Do you know this man?"

Ben's head bobbed. "Yeah sure do, he comes in here all the time and he's always with sketchy people. Billy's good with numbers, I think he's an accountant or somethin'. Hey, would you like to support kids with developmental disabilities?" Ben asked motioning over to a display.

"No thank you. What else do you know about him?" Alison asked.

"Sorry to ask - I just have a quota, ya know? Ummm, right Billy, well I don't know much about him...are you sure you don't want to donate? It's a real good way to help out kids and it's only five bucks, officer."

Alison scowled, pulling out a five and slapping it on the counter. She'd been extorted for more getting information before and at least this was a good cause. "Are you sure you don't know anything?"

Ben smiled, triumphant. "Well now that I think about it he did look a little worried the other night. I think he pissed some people off. Can I interest you in a slushy, officer?"

"Cherry please," Alison growled.

Faith came bobbing up. "Ooo can I have one too?" she asked Ben, smiling so big Alison could count all her teeth.

Ben turned redder than the cherry slushy. "Hi there, who are you?"

"I'm Faith. My brother is working with the detective here," Faith said making a face when she pointed to Alison.

"Oh yeah, that must suck, do you want a pretzel too?" he asked.

"Yes thank you," Faith said.

Alison didn't know who she disliked more, Ben or Faith. "Anything else, Ben?" Alison asked.

"Oh yeah, he came in here with a wad of cash he had me turn into money orders," Ben said and then to Faith, handing her the drink, "It's on the house."

"That's sweet, thanks Benny," she said walking off.

Alison turned but Ben stopped her, "Hey, that will be three bucks for the slushie."

SEAN HUGHES looked at more video and wondered if Alison was having a better day. His phone rang, *speak of the devil.* "Hughes," he said.

"I got a lead for you. I need you to check the cameras at the intersection I'm at."

Sean took down the information. "Any idea on the time?"

"William Lanner was at the bar at eight, so check around then."

Sean checked and sure enough he watched Billy Lanner's car come in around seven thirty. He watched as Billy filled up with gas and went inside looking tense. He came back out and threw something in a trash can before driving off. Sean was about to tell Alison to go dumpster diving when another car came into the video. A tall man with a white wife beater and short cropped hair got out of a car and pulled something out of the same trashcan Billy had been at.

"Got him!" Sean said. "I found our perp, he was in a black sedan. I'll see if I can make out the plates."

"I'm coming back in," Alison said and hung up.

Sean noted that she sounded a bit testy.

TWO

ALISON KAUR walked into the office at a fast clip. She was so focused, she didn't even think about the Mages behind her. She had her killer she knew it.

"Hughes," she said.

He was just as keyed up as she was, "The plates belong to a Ramon Tabor, twenty-five-year-old male living around Washington and 5th. Records show him working at a dry cleaners."

"Have we called the employer?"

"They're closed, but Ramon's latest online post shows him home alone," Sean said with a smile.

Alison sat down at her desk, making sure she had her ducks in a row before talking to Sergeant Montoya.

"OK, what do we have?" she said to herself. "We have him following the vic, but do we have enough for an arrest?"

"I don't think so. What's our motive?" Sean asked.

"Do you need one to talk to him?" Gabriel asked.

Alison turned on him. "Gabriel, this isn't the time."

Gabriel looked serious. "Do you need a warrant to talk to him?"

Alison shook her head. "No, but to make an arrest or to go into his house I need one, or at least probable cause."

Gabriel laughed. "Well, you'll get that."

He had their full attention now. "How so?" she asked.

Faith rolled her eyes and sighed. "Please...he's a Wolf! Knock on the door and say who you are; he'll attack and there you go: probable cause. You can talk to him all you like, if he lives."

"If?" Sean asked.

Gabriel still looked uncharacteristically serious. "Yes, as is the case in our Pactum, if Ramon uses Vis and turns into his Wolf form, you are to leave him to me. I can guarantee you he will take his Wolf form, I know you two are very good at what you do, but please listen to me when I tell you that you cannot handle a Wolf . When this goes down, get out of the way. If he's not alone or you are too close I may not be able to protect you."

Alison was about to say something when Sean put his hand on hers. There was a look in his eyes she didn't like. "Right, you're in charge once he changes. I won't get in your line of fire and neither will Alison. It's almost seven, he'll probably be home now," Sean said.

Alison stood. "Sean, can I get a moment?"

Sean nodded. Faith and Gabriel stayed put as Alison took Sean into a room. Before she could speak he said, "I know what you're gonna say and look, magic is their job, right? Plus, we have our orders."

"How can you all of a sudden trust them, Hughes?" Alison demanded.

Sean turned red. "I don't Alison, but we have orders. One of the things I learned in war was that the chain of command is there for a very good reason. If the Sarge doesn't want us taking on a Werewolf, then I say let these two nitwits get themselves killed."

She recoiled. "You're going to let them die to prove we don't need them?"

"We don't Alison, and the mayor needs to see that; but we have to do as we are told."

Alison didn't like this plan at all.

"We'll run it by Montoya, OK?" Sean said.

"Fine," Alison said flatly.

They walked into the Sergeant's office. Sean knocked on the door. "Sir, do you have a moment?"

"Come in," was the reply.

Montoya looked them both over. "What is it?" he asked suspiciously.

"We think we've found William Lanner's killer, and we want to go and talk to him. The Mages have told us that when we contact him he will take his Wolf form and attack us."

"OK,"

"Sir, Sean wants to let Gabriel get killed to prove a point," Alison said.

"I figured as much, what is Gabriel's take on this?" Montoya asked.

"Well sir, it's kind of his idea really, he said if we need probable cause, that when our suspect attacks, we will have all the cause we need." Alison admitted.

Montoya looked down at his desk for a moment and then back up. "Let's see what Gabriel can do."

Alison gawked, her mouth opening and closing like a fish out of water. She didn't know what to say.

"Look Kaur, it's his idea and they are supposed to be the experts, and either way this fight is gonna happen, whether it's when you question the suspect or when you try to bring him in."

Alison walked out of the office, the back of her neck burning. They approached the Mages, who looked ready to leave.

SEAN HUGHES knew that Alison was pissed. She didn't like the Mages, but she wasn't going to risk anyone's life. In a way,

Sean respected her for that, but like Montoya had said, this fight was going to happen at some point anyway.

Alison walked up to Gabriel. "OK, we are going to try this. I'm not happy about it. Try not to get killed."

Gabriel smiled. "Thank you for your concern detective, but I assure you that I will be fine. If a Werewolf manages to kill me, then I shouldn't have been alive to begin with."

Sean had to give it to him, maybe it was balls or maybe Gabriel hadn't seen action, but he looked completely at ease.

Sean and Alison put on police vests which Faith eyed with amusement. They loaded up in Alison's car and she drove down Colfax to Washington and then down to a strip mall just north of Tabor's house. Sean called dispatch and asked them to send two squad cars to a fast-food joint a few blocks away just in case they needed backup.

They got out of the car, Sean feeling tense as he always did before taking down a perp. They walked down Washington, Gabriel almost taking the lead, and Faith staying just back a bit. Sean found it odd. It looked as though she wasn't going to help him at all. *Mages and their Pactums*, he shook his head.

The houses in the area weren't in the best condition. They soon came to a run-down one story with a waist-high chain fence.

"I thought Wolves were expensive?" Sean asked Gabriel, nodding at the dilapidated house, its white paint peeling from age and wear.

Gabriel chuckled darkly. "They are but that doesn't mean he's being paid with money."

Gabriel gestured for Sean to walk up the path to the front door. Sean stood right in front with Alison off to the side, her hand firmly gripping her Glock 40.

Sean knocked on the door. "Denver Police Department, open up!"

There was nothing. No wild animal sounds, no sound of running feet, nothing.

Gabriel and Faith exchanged a glance, Faith looked confused and then Sean heard her say softly, "Nothing."

"Maybe he isn't home..." Alison said.

"No," Faith said.

Sean turned to see Faith with her eyes closed, they opened and she pointed. "Window."

Alison looked apprehensive but peeked into the window, she cursed loudly.

"Sean, the door!"

Sean didn't need any further prompting. He kicked the door hard, the door jams wood splintering as the door opened, banging against the wall. The force made the knob stick in the drywall.

Sean ran in, drawing his .40 and sweeping it in front of him. Adrenaline rushed in his veins, years of training helping him keep his nerves in check.

Alison ran past him and Sean followed her into the room, seeing what she was after. Ramon Tabor lay in bed, blood staining the sheets. His throat slit open, the gaping wound oozed blood. Alison didn't bother checking for a pulse. Instead she pulled her phone from her pocket to call it in.

ALISON KAUR walked the small house that belonged to the now deceased Ramon Tabor. She and Sean kept everyone out of the house for almost an hour before letting the CSIs in. Now the small space flashed with camera bulbs and people moving about.

Ramon was only in a pair of boxers in his bed. A CSI ran a black light over the bed. "Well at least he had a good night before he died," he said. "There are fluids on the sheets." The CSI pulled out a device for checking for Vis residue, and it lit up showing two signals. "Looks like our Wolf friend's Vis and that of a Succubus."

"A Succubus?" Sean asked.

Alison looked at Gabriel whose head was shaking. "What?" she asked.

"He's not in his Wolf form," was all Gabriel said.

Alison didn't feel like questioning him so instead she spoke to the CSI "And his cut?"

"No Vis; it's all Human. The sheets are pretty dry from the day's fun; Ramon was killed hours after intercourse."

"So the Succubus didn't do this?" Alison confirmed.

The CSI said he didn't think so.

"Thanks," Alison said.

She walked out of the house with Sean and the Mages. "Well, it looks like your obligations with us are done," Sean said.

"Yes they are. All we need to do is pick up the rest of the payment and we will be on our way," Gabriel said.

The night was muggy for August and the hour now very late. They walked up the street back toward the strip mall, Alison thinking about what a waste of money the Mages had been. Gabriel was next to Alison walking casually when Faith spoke. "Danger."

Gabriel stopped cold, his hand flying and stopping Alison before she could register that something was wrong. "I feel them too," he said.

"What's going on?" Sean asked with a hint of concern.

Faith and Gabriel were looking to their right, down an alleyway. "Mages," Faith said.

"There isn't a Seeker?" Gabriel noted.

"A Seeker?" Alison asked.

To their right, two figures materialized from the dark, both holding swords. Alison went for her gun, her hand stopped by Faith's. Alison turned to the girl who gave an almost imperceptible shake of her head. Alison looked back at the two figures. One was a short girl in her early twenties with long blond hair. She carried a broad sword, and her long white coat rustled as she walked. Just behind her was a tall boy, his sandy hair disheveled. He too held a broad sword and wore the same white coat. A memory of that morning, when Gabriel told her that his and Faith's coats were like a uniform, popped in her head.

Gabriel was in front of Sean, Faith and Alison as the other Mages calmly made their way forward. Gabriel's head turned back toward Sean, his voice soft as death, "Stay put."

Gabriel stepped forward a few steps, causing the other two Mages to stop.

"Hello there," Gabriel said, his voice back to his normal tone. "How may I help you this fine evening?"

The boy answered with venom. "You can get out of the way unless you want to die. We have business to conduct with the pigs you're guarding."

"And that business would be?" he asked, his voice still warm.

"To kill them," the girl said.

"Ah," Gabriel said nodding his head. "I thought you might say that. Well, this is awkward, isn't it? You see I am under Pactum to protect these people and I'm sorry but I cannot allow you to hurt them while under Pactum."

"Pactum? You're one of those morons?" the boy said, and Alison found herself getting mad. *How dare this kid speak that way to Gabriel?*

"Am I to take it that you two are not under Pactum this evening?" Gabriel queried.

"We are not," the girl said. "I respect your Pactum, but you must see this would not be a fair fight. There are two of us and one of you…"

Gabriel nodded again. "Yes, yes this wouldn't be a fair fight, indeed."

Alison wondered why Faith wasn't stepping forward. The blond girl was right. Was Faith going to let her brother die?

"And there is no convincing you otherwise?" Gabriel asked hopefully.

The girl shook her head.

Gabriel lowered his as if sad. "Very well then, may I have the honor of knowing who I am fighting?"

The boy laughed. "You are old-fashioned, aren't you?"

"Keith!" the girl spat. "Forgive him." she said. And then in a strong voice, "I am Tracy Hope, my sword is Dolor."

Keith laughed again. "Fine," his voice became sarcastic. "I am Keith Spencer and let's see, my sword is named, hmmmmm… Bob," he laughed. Tracy didn't look impressed.

"And who are you?" she asked.

Gabriel's hand moved to his sword. Alison heard the metal as it was unsheathed; his voice rang strong and confident. "I am Ark Third Seat Gabriel Decor, my blade is Iram," he finished with Iram in his right hand held to the side.

Alison felt a knot in her gut form, why wasn't she doing anything? Why wasn't Sean? Alison turned to Faith. "Aren't you going to help?"

Faith looked into Alison's eyes. "Of course not; I'm a Seeker, not a Paladin and my brother is an Ark," she said not offering any other explanation.

Alison watched Keith and Tracy moving to flank an unmoving Gabriel. Tracy looked concerned, which Alison found odd.

Keith thrust his hand forward. "AERIS!" An orange ball blossomed in his palm, flying at Gabriel who still did not move. There was a flash of light, orange slamming into a wall of amethyst. Gabriel still didn't move. Tracy's face showed fear, Keith's anger, "Fine! USQUE!" this time a small brown sedan glowed orange, lifting in the air. Alison staggered back in amazement.

A small hand grasped her arm. "Gabriel told you to stay put," Faith said, without a hint of her normal malice.

Alison looked to Sean, his face white as a sheet.

Keith laughed. "Block this!" he barked. The sedan flew at Gabriel. Alison reached forward vainly, trying to pull Gabriel to safety.

As soon as the car started moving, clarity came to SEAN HUGHES' mind and with it time slowed down. No longer was he trying to make sense of what was in front of him. He stood stock still as the car flew at Gabriel.

Gabriel slashed Iram through the air. "Vis caesa." A thin ribbon of lavender left Iram, hitting the car in the center to seemingly no effect. "Pars," Gabriel said. The ribbon of color illuminated to purple. Still, as if in slow motion, Sean watched as the car split in two along where Gabriel's spell had hit. The two pieces separated, landing a good ten feet on either side of Sean, Alison and Faith with a grinding clang of crunching metal and glass.

He looked to Alison, her face a pale mask of terror. When their eyes met, time resumed to normal speed.

GABRIEL DECOR waited for the car to hit the ground with a grinding crash before turning to look back at the two detectives, one in awe, the other in stupefied fear. He spoke to Faith. "I've got this." She nodded understanding that she was not to assist.

Gabriel turned back to the other Paladins. Tracy didn't look all that shocked, though she did look apprehensive. Keith, on the other hand, looked appalled that Gabriel had deflected two attacks. *I told you I was an Ark,* he thought.

Tracy didn't look to be a moron like her companion, but still Gabriel didn't want the fight to last long. Keith obviously didn't care about what he damaged; Gabriel would deal with him first.

Gabriel tapped into his Vis, power rushing into his body. He closed his eyes, feeling it infuse him, Vis saturated the air around him, too faint for the other Paladins to see, but with it he could see them perfectly. They were like silhouettes, their bodies a sharp contrast in Gabriel's cloud of Vis. Tracy and Keith's own Vis left a shadowy wake that Gabriel could see without effort. Had they had a Seeker, he wouldn't have been able to do this. *Stupid.*

Gabriel opened his eyes letting Vis flow from his body, as he was wrapped in a cocoon of amethyst light. Tracy's eyes hardened, her grip on Dolor visibly tightening, her corneas turned emerald and her body burst with green Vis, licking around her like translucent flames. Dolor's edge glowed with Vis. Keith's eyes turned orange, his body enveloping in a smaller cocoon of Vis. *He can't control his Vis output yet.* Keith wouldn't take Gabriel long and he could focus on Tracy, giving her the respect of fighting one on one.

Gabriel pushed with Vis, sending himself in the air, power gushing into Iram. He poured Vis into his body and mind, making time slow and his mind race, his limbs tensed with Vis-induced strength. His eyes and ears became stronger. Keith was rushing up at Gabriel with his sword pulled back. Gabriel swung Iram out with a casual flick. Metal clanged as the two swords glanced off each other. Gabriel twisted Iram, moving himself to the side to parry a thrust from Tracy.

Behind him, Gabriel could sense Keith, his sword's silhouette rushing at Gabriel's back. Gabriel waited until the last moment, *Celeritate.* He moved out of the way from Keith's attack coming alongside the young man at the speed of lightning. Gabriel flexed Vis in the back of his right hand swinging it at Keith's exposed side. "Rumpo," he said as his hand met Keith's side. Gabriel could feel the thin layer of wards around Keith buckle and with it the effects of his shattering spell. Gabriel's hand didn't even register the breaking ribs beneath his touch. Keith cried out, turning away from Gabriel and exposing his back. Gabriel brought the butt of Iram's handle down on Keith, this time his shoulder blade making an audible crack. Keith's orange Vis faltered a bit as he plummeted back to earth.

All this happened in the space of a few breaths and Gabriel moved out of the way of one of Tracy's attacks, Iram catching the edge of Dolor in a block. He blocked a few more blows from Dolor before finally using Iram in an attack. Gabriel lashed out at Tracy, swinging at her left side. She barely blocked Iram and then said, "Celeritate," becoming a green blur as her speed increased. Within the mist of Vis and using his increased senses, he again swung Iram to where Tracy would be. She tried to avoid the attack, twisting in the air. Iram cut a shallow wound into her arm. She didn't make a sound, but dropped to the ground.

Gabriel did likewise, Tracy between him and his group. Tracy looked scared but determined. She growled, rushing at him with Dolor held high in the air. Iram rang as Gabriel deflected Dolor, both blades infused with Vis to the point of being near unbreakable. Gabriel sidestepped, still not putting much in the way of effort into the fight. Tracy twisted, swinging at Gabriel who dodged, leaving her front completely open. Gabriel brought Iram up in a slashing move to cut Tracy in half.

Vis-enhanced as she was, Tracy saw the attack coming and also saw that there was nothing she could do to stop it. Gabriel brought the sword up and looked into her eyes. He believed if you took a life you should, if possible, give the person the respect to look them in the eye as you killed them. Tracy's deep blue eyes shone with fear, the look on her face that of sorrow. Gabriel leaned backwards. He didn't know why he did it. He saw something in her eyes - she wasn't ready to die, she wasn't committed to the fight. Iram still hit her, slicing up her left side to her right shoulder.

She fell back in a gasping scream and hit the ground hard, blood spraying.

ALISON KAUR couldn't feel her body, she wasn't awake… there was no way what she was seeing was real. The Mages moved so fast. Gabriel slashed the girl Mage and she fell down hard, blood spraying from her chest.

"Focus!" Gabriel barked at the woman.

Tracy gasped and choked, her body thrashing, but she slowed

some and Alison could see an emerald sheen over her wound which stopped the bleeding.

Gabriel turned his head over his shoulder to Keith, who was rising and picking up his blade.

"Healing your ribs was a waste of energy," Gabriel said in an ice cold voice. "You should have saved what little Vis you had. Numbing them would have been smarter. Even had you not wasted any power at all you cannot hope to defeat me," Gabriel said as a matter of fact. "You have two options here. Your companion is gravely injured; she will not last long. You can use what little power you have left to rush her to a Healer and you can both live, or you can waste your life attacking me. In that case you will die, and with you Tracy. It is your choice Keith Spencer, death or life."

Keith looked like he was going to pick the former but a moan from Tracy stopped him.

"Life," he said sheathing his blade, no air of vibrato in his tone.

Gabriel only nodded, pulling a rag from his pocket and wiping down Iram's crimson edge and sheathing it. Keith flashed orange at Tracy's side, picking her up. "This isn't over," and then glowing brightly, sped away in the direction from which he came.

Gabriel smiled. "I'm sure it's not."

"You let them get away?" Sean asked half in fear, half in anger.

"You do not have prisons that can hold them and Tracy will die if she does not see a Healer," Gabriel said.

"Why didn't you kill them?" Faith demanded in shock.

Gabriel looked at her, the sternness in his gaze faltering. "Keith was hardly worthy of it and without a Pactum, they may decide that killing the detectives here isn't such a good plan after all. Besides, we are not under Pactum to kill, just to protect until we get back to the office."

She squinted at him, puzzled. "That explains Keith, but

Tracy was worthy of you killing her, why did the great Ark Gabriel Decor spare her life?"

Gabriel looked down, deflating. "I don't know…"

Sean was missing something. "What's an Ark? And before I heard one of you say something about Paladins and Seekers."

Faith turned to him, her normal disdain absent. "I am a Seeker; Gabriel a Paladin."

"I thought you were Mages?" Alison asked in a shaky voice.

Gabriel walked over to her, putting out a hand. Alison recoiled from him, fear pulling her away. She had been wrong about him; he wasn't harmless, and he was everything people feared about magic.

His voice was soft his eyes looking earnestly into hers, "Alison please, you are in shock. We need to tend to you."

"So are you a Mage?" she asked, holding on stubbornly to her question.

Gabriel looked put out. "Yes I am, just as you are a Human, and you are a Detective right? That is your job, not your race. I am a Mage - that is my race. My job is that of a Paladin; we are warriors," he explained. "Now please Alison, we need to get you something to drink."

SEAN HUGHES let Gabriel lead Alison away and turned his attention to the people starting to come outside. People in the area weren't dumb; they knew to keep their heads down when they heard loud things at night, but now most would assume the coast was clear and they would come out to have a peek.

Sean got on the radio and asked for squad cars to come and make sure people got back inside.

"Decor," Sean said. Gabriel turned to him, looking surprised by the use of his last name, "What do we do about the car Keith cut up? And do we need to scrub this for evidence?"

Gabriel looked at the car. "Sadly I don't think Keith left his insurance information. I dare say the damage will be for the city to take care of. As for the crime scene, there is no evidence that needs to be collected."

"OK," Sean said.

He didn't care for magic, but care for it or not Gabriel had just saved his and his partner's lives, proving he was willing to risk his own. In Sean's book, that didn't mean he had to like Gabriel, but respect him for his skills; that he did have to do. Sean also owed Gabriel now, and Sean didn't forget things like that.

Sean got things straightened out before they returned to the station. Sergeant Montoya was waiting for them. He was in a pair of sweats looking like he'd been asleep, which he probably had been. Alison sat down at her desk still looking frazzled. Before Montoya could talk a woman walked in.

HEIDI DECOR walked into the police station at way too late of an hour for her liking, but Gabriel had fought two other Paladins. Whether Sergeant Montoya liked it or not, they were going to need a new Pactum, unless he wanted his people dead by morning. Heidi cast her gaze around the nearly empty room. She didn't need Vis to see that Alison Kaur was not handling the night's events well. As for Detective Hughes, he was obviously flustered, but keeping his head straight.

Montoya scowled at her, his expression sour. "What are you doing here?" he asked.

"We told her about tonight," Gabriel said.

Montoya moved his scowl to Gabriel. "And why did you do that?"

"While our Pactum covers protection from all Vis users, that Pactum ended as soon as I walked into your station," Gabriel explained.

"We aren't safe anymore?" Alison asked her voice small.

Faith placed her hand on the woman's shoulders. "Pactum or

no, we will not allow you to be harmed in our presence."

Alison gave Faith an odd look. Heidi used Vis to view Alison's emotions, seeing that they were a tangle of fear and now extreme confusion. Heidi decided not to ask about their day.

"Sergeant, I dare say you will want another Pactum. If I understood Gabriel correctly, the Paladins who attacked your people tonight seemed quite determined," Heidi said. She didn't want to make threats or use fear mongering to get a deal, but the Sergeant needed to know what he was up against.

Sergeant Montoya chewed his lip. "How do I know this whole thing isn't a scam? Your lot may have planned that attack to get more money out of us."

"I can inform the Guild that you want another group of Mages if you do not trust us," Heidi said.

Detective Hughes shook his head. "Sarge, this isn't a setup; that was a real fight. I trust Decor here," he said indicating Gabriel.

"Fine," the Sergeant relented. "How much is this gonna cost the taxpayers?"

Gabriel walked over to Heidi, leaning in to whisper to her. "No charge," he said insistent.

Heidi eyed him. "What? Why?" she asked.

"What are you two whispering about?" Montoya demanded.

"My brother-in-law here thinks we should do this job for free," Heidi said incredulous.

"Not free just no charge; our expenses should be covered but other than that..." Gabriel said.

Heidi turned to Faith. "Faith? What's your take? You'll be actively involved."

Faith looked at her brother. "If that is what Gabriel wants, I'm fine with it."

"And why do you want this?" Kaur asked, her voice sounding more confident.

Gabriel looked serious. "Mages work in teams, a Paladin with a Seeker. Tonight we were attacked by two Paladins and unless Faith and I missed something, there was no Seeker."

"What are Seekers and Paladins?" the Sergeant asked.

"Paladins are warriors, Seekers find things as their name implies, and they hide things like Paladins, and people as well," Heidi explained.

"So you want to do this for free because they didn't do things by the book?" Montoya asked skeptically.

"We have worked this way for thousands of years. To not have Seekers is either reckless or somehow a strategic value. I'm not sure which one it is in this case. Whatever my reasons, you are getting a deal; trust me, Sergeant. These Mages were going after your people because of the case they are working, a case I dare say that goes deeper than a CPA skimming. Paladins don't give up."

Heidi could see Montoya's emotions turn, settling on calm. "Fine, what do I have to sign?"

"Are you OK with this?" Gabriel asked Heidi.

"Do I have a choice?"

"Yes, of course you do, and this may take everyone, at least Erin and James," he said.

Heidi thought for a long moment. "If it's going to take everyone, I can waive the charges for you and Faith, BUT we will still need to work something out Sergeant, I cannot commit my whole team at no charge for an undetermined amount of time."

The Sergeant took a moment. "Alright, do we need to do this now?" he asked.

Heidi pushed Vis to her glasses, everyone including Gabriel was tired, only he was staving off fatigue with Vis. "Yes, I will come by in the morning. As for tonight, Gabriel, do you mind making sure the detectives are safe?"

Gabriel nodded. "They should be - Tracy was hurt badly as was Keith. Even if they aren't alone, my name should stay their hand for at least a few days."

THREE

ALISON KAUR woke from a shallow sleep. She was still in her clothes from the previous day and her mind refused to wake up completely. Defused light made its way past her curtains. A glance at her alarm clock showed it to be 9:30 am. Alison never slept in but after the night before…she still was in shock. She replayed the memory in her head again and again of Gabriel cutting a car in half. Fear and shame were battling inside her. Fear of what Vis users could do, and shame about how ineffective she'd been after the fight kept her pinned to her bed.

Alison sat up in bed and swung her feet off the side, her normally soft carpet having no effect on her socked feet. She stripped down, stumbled into her bathroom, turned on the light to look in the mirror, and saw circles under her eyes. *Keep it together today Kaur,* she told herself. She turned the shower on, steam filling the room. She thought better of the hot water and turned it to cold. She stepped into the bathtub/shower and stood just outside the stream of freezing water. Her gut clenched, an involuntary action, her body fearing discomfort. She took a deep breath and stepped forward. Instantly her fatigue vanished as icy water pelted her body. She gasped a few times with shock as her heart raced. She reached out and turned the hot water back on.

It didn't take her long to get ready for her day, the cold water having woken her up by jolting her system. She stopped and got her usual cup of coffee as she made her way into the office. When she got there, the station was a buzz of activity and she fell into a familiar step. People were giving her and Sean's area a wide birth, which Alison figured was due to Gabriel and Faith. When she made it to her desk she was mostly right. Gabriel and Faith were present with their black overcoats. Gabriel was once again in slacks and a white shirt. Faith was boasting another mini skirt but had opted for strappy heels instead of boots. With them was another woman in her mid-twenties with long bronze hair and blue eyes, she was fair skinned and thin. She wore a white dress with red polka dot's that made her looked like little Miss Susie Homemaker. The woman looked a little uneasy and kept shooting furtive glances at Faith and Gabriel.

Gabriel saw Alison and smiled tentatively at her. "Good morning, Detective," he said.

He probably remembers what a freak you were last night. She tried not to look scared of him as she answered, "Morning Gabriel, Faith."

Faith smiled. "Morning." Then her face went slack, a bored look crossing it. The night before Faith had been kind, almost loving when Alison was having a hard time, but was that over now?

Gabriel gestured to the woman with them. "This is Erin Penn, our sister-in-law and Healer. She will be helping us today."

"Healer?" Sean came around Alison and set down a folder on his desk. "Paladins, Seekers, what else do you guys have?"

Erin smiled warmly, almost excited. "There are Healers," she said indicating herself. "Builders, Enchanters and Contractors. Heidi is our Contractor," Erin supplied.

Getting information out of Gabriel and Faith hadn't proven to be easy, but with Erin...

"And what is it you do as a Healer?" Alison asked the chipper girl.

"Mostly as my name implies, I heal people and animals; however, I can do many other things. Like for example, examine the corpse of Mr. Ramon Tabor."

"What, our people can't handle it?" Sean asked sarcastic.

Erin shook her head. "I mean no disrespect Detective Hughes, but I will be looking for signs of Vis on him. The tools your Medical Examiner has cannot do as detailed an analysis of Vis as I can. And may I add, you look rather dashing and handsome," she turned to Faith, "not a pretty boy at all."

Sean rounded on Faith. "You said I was a pretty boy?"

"If the shoe fits," Faith said before going silent again.

Alison had a hard time not smiling, she liked Erin. She seemed harmless, but Alison wasn't going to let that lull her into a false sense of security. She'd thought the same about Gabriel and she had been dead wrong with him.

"And what's with the silent treatment?" Sean demanded. "You were talkative last night."

"Detective," Gabriel said. "Please do not take Faith's silence as rudeness; she is a Seeker," he held up a hand, "which we will explain later but now we need to go over the Pactum."

"Fine, what do we need to cover this time?" Alison asked.

"Heidi and Sergeant Montoya met early this morning and came up with an agreement." Gabriel handed her a folded bit of paper as he explained, "Again I will be in charge of protecting you, but this time Faith and I will be playing an active role and we will be assisting you in the investigation. Should it be needed, others from our team will assist. As we are dealing with other Mages, you and Detective Hughes will need to carry trackers." He pulled two objects from his pocket. One was a necklace that he handed to Alison, and the other a watch he gave to Sean. "These are enchanted to allow us to easily find you in case of an emergency; also should you feel any strong emotions, Faith and I will be notified so as to determine if you are in danger."

Alison looked at the necklace; its simplicity fit her personality and looked like something she would pick for herself. Sean's watch also looked like something he would wear. The Mages had done their homework.

Gabriel went on, "I will also be coming over to your homes to place defensive spells called wards; Faith will be doing likewise."

"Hold up!" Sean said. "You want to track me and mark my house?"

"Yes," Faith said. "Detectives, this is very important, even though we did not encounter a Seeker last night I can assure you that Tracy and Keith have one they are working with."

"And how do you know that?" Sean asked still agitated.

She shrugged. "Simple, I cannot find them," she said and her eyes slid back out of focus.

"Sean, these measures are as much for your safety as ours. With other Mages, Faith and I will run a higher risk of getting injured; if we are spread too thin, we run the risk of missing something. Also, if Faith and I are too late to save you…"

Alison spoke. "Yeah whatever, what is your part in the investigation?" she asked wanting to know what was going to be getting in her way.

"We will take the Vis side of things, with Seekers in the mix I dare say we will still need to do things in the manner you are used to. However, Faith and I will be able to give more in the way of resources to you and your people and Erin here will also be a guide. I would rather that if there needs to be any surveillance, you leave that to us. Faith's husband James has many handy objects when it comes to surveillance."

SEAN HUGHES listened to Gabriel talk. He didn't like the idea of being tracked, but he also didn't care to have another car thrown at him either. He should have known that Faith was married, the hot ones always were, and it was good to see that there was at least one thing in common with Humans and Mages. He wasn't sure what to make of Erin; she was cute and friendly, which was nice but she didn't look like what he thought a Healer should be. When he thought of magic he still pictured people in cloaks with pointy hats, not a girl who looked like she'd walked out of some home care magazine for soccer moms.

"So what's with Faith's attitude?" Sean asked earning a glare from Faith.

"What? When you're talking to people you're charming and friendly but the rest of the time…" he accused.

"You did say when we met that you didn't want us around, correct?" Faith pointed out.

"Well yeah…" Sean started.

"And your Sergeant told Heidi the same, so why would I go out of my way to 'charm' you as you put it?" she questioned.

Faith was right, Gabriel had tried to be nice but had only been met with hostility.

Before Sean could try to defend himself Gabriel spoke, "Faith is a Seeker, meaning she finds people, things, or whatever as we've already said; she also hides things as well. Being a Seeker takes a lot of concentration. The reason Faith doesn't talk much is because she is working. At almost all times she is looking for trouble or hiding us in case trouble is on the lookout for us."

"Do not fret, Detectives, once Faith has this area secure with wards and other spells I dare say she will be quite charming," Erin gushed and looked at Faith. "Won't you," she added sternly.

Faith rolled her eyes. "Fine but being polite goes both ways," she said before zoning out again.

"So how long does this Pactum last?" Alison asked.

"Unlike our last Pactum there is not as much of a limit. Your Sergeant agreed on a bit steeper price in exchange for us to not be as limited to this case. We are in essence on loan permanently to your department. If at the end of this case, or during, for that matter, one party decides they do not want to participate anymore; that is their choice. Also, if you have other cases that you are working, we will be happy to help; however Faith's Seeking role in those cases will come into question, as the rate for Seekers is normally rather high."

Sean didn't care to think about the cost behind that. "OK, so what else do we need to know?" he asked.

Faith's eyes came back into focus. "I need to more fully explain my role in this," she said. "My job takes a lot of my focus; I am primarily trying to get past the Vis of other Mages, other Seekers to be more to the point. Other Mages can use Vis to find and hide things but they are no match for a trained Seeker. It is my job to keep Tracy and Keith from being able to easily find you. However, that does not mean that they won't be able to find you. I can create a safe house that they would not be able to find on their own, but should they have a talented Seeker with them there is no guarantee. Gabriel said before that you two will have to do much of the leg work in a standard manner. This is due to the fact that Tracy and Keith do have a Seeker."

Sean perked up. "Then how come you could find them last night?"

"They didn't have one last night or at least not with them. I suspect they either figured that you two would be unguarded or that two Paladins would be enough to scare away any protection you might have had. However, shortly after our encounter last night I stopped being able to track them, which means they now have a Seeker or they went back to a safe house. Either way, we will have to follow clues instead of using Vis. But I can still be of assistance, if we are looking for Humans or Mutari that are not under a Seeker's protection - I should be able to find them without issue. Also, I will try to break whatever wards their Seeker has, but once again there is no guarantee on that."

"How fast could you find someone?" Sean asked.

"Without a Seeker it would only take a matter of hours," Faith explained.

Alison chuckled. "Well Faith, if that was the case, then I don't think the FBI would have such a huge wanted list now would they?"

Erin giggled. "Detectives, the FBI has that list because they either don't want to pony up and pay for Seekers or more likely if they did that, there wouldn't be much need for the FBI, now would there?"

Alison looked dumbfounded for a moment and then like she was going to argue but chose not to say anything. Sean figured he knew what she was thinking. He, like she, wanted to disagree with Erin but couldn't because he knew it was true. The FBI might come out and say they didn't use Mages to hunt criminals due to the cost but the reality of it was if Faith was even half as good as she was saying, then the bulk of the FBI, CIA, NSA, DEA, ATF, and every other agency would be rendered near worthless within a matter of months. Sean didn't see the heads of those organizations putting themselves out of a job. On the flip side, it would give Mages too much control of Human affairs which could cause other problems. *Stop,* he needed to focus, he could think about the unseen political and social impact of magic later.

ALISON KAUR listened to Faith's explanation, wanting to disagree with her, but she couldn't. She also thought about what the girl had said at the beginning of the conversation.

Alison hated to admit she was at fault but had to do it. "Thank you, Faith and Gabriel…" she paused not wanting to say what she needed to. "And you are right, politeness does go both ways. Gabriel, you have tried to be friendly from the word go and Faith…well I mistook your silence for rudeness, and I apologize. You are here doing a job and I should have been more respectful of that," she said looking away. Just because she was saying 'sorry' didn't mean she had to make eye contact.

When Alison lost it, Faith had been exceptionally kind to her which made her feel that much more guilty for her behavior.

"Not to worry," Gabriel said. "Erin?"

Erin looked at him and then bobbed on the balls of her feet. "Oh yeah, can I take a gander at the dead guy?" she asked and added with a smile, "I made muffins – they're in the break room."

"Homemade muffins?" Sean asked perking up. "Kaur you want to take them to the morgue? I'll secure those muffins!"

Alison rolled her eyes. "Call if you need back up. OK, come on, Erin, let me take you to see Mr. Tabor's body."

Alison led the Mages through the halls, earning glances from other officers. Some looked curious but most just looked distrusting. Undoubtedly news of the Mages fight had made it to every on and off duty officer in the state. Alison was sure that by lunch even all the retired cops would know about it. She entered the morgue, cold and sterile. Dr. Partington was poking around the pale corpse of Ramon Tabor.

He looked up at Alison. "So I understand that I am to wait on the autopsy of our friend here."

Alison gestured to Erin. "Yes, this is Erin Penn, she is with the Mages we are under contract with. She will be doing her own inspection of the body."

Alison wondered if this would upset Partington, but instead he looked excited. "Are we going to be using Vis?"

Erin nodded. "Yes we are, do you mind?" she asked pointing at the body.

Partington stepped back. "By all means, may I ask questions?"

Erin smiled warmly. "Yes of course, may I do the same during your investigation?"

"Of course."

Erin stepped up to the body, pulling a long, polished stick from a pocket.

"Is that a wand?" Alison asked looking at it.

Erin brandished the wand, which looked like something from a movie. "Yes it is, most Healers use them, why?"

"I just didn't know that they existed in reality, is all."

Gabriel spoke. "Mages will often use objects to focus Vis; Healers use wands a lot of the time. In many cases the object is not special in anyway, however certain materials and construction can affect the performance of a tool. Most Mages find that making their own tool is the most effective way," he explained.

"Do you have one?" Alison asked curious.

Gabriel rested his hand on Iram and smiled.

Seeing the blade made Alison uncomfortable, so she changed the subject. "What are you looking for, Erin? I thought we determined that it wasn't a Mutari or Mage that killed Tabor."

"Yes, but he was with a Succubus prior to his death, and I have a theory," Erin said.

She leaned over the body, running her hand just above Tabor's skin. "Hmmm, that's what I thought," she whispered and then held her wand tip just above Tabor's groin. "Vis," she said. A pink glowing ball popped into existence where her wand was. "I told you I'd explain, so here goes. I think that Tabor was drained of energy by the Succubus and was unable to take his Wolf form. Gabriel had the same thought, but I'm going to confirm it. I am placing spells above chakra points to test his Vis flow. Even though he's dead, I will be able to see how strong his Vis was prior to death," she said and then proceeded to light up his belly and other points, ending above his head. Erin muttered a few things Alison couldn't understand. "Yes, he was drained, and severely I might add. His heart is almost completely fried. I would say he was all but crippled when she was done with him. She'd have been careful about it, but once she had a good hold on him…" Erin said.

"And you're sure it wasn't the Succubus that killed him?" Partington asked. "And what do you mean his heart?"

Erin nodded. "Yes, had it been her, she wouldn't have needed to cut his throat - she wouldn't have let Vis go to waste, but she made killing him easy to do. A child could have over powered this man. As far as the heart goes, do you understand how Vis is produced and works, doctor?"

"It comes from our cells doesn't it?" Partington answered.

Erin smiled warmly. "Yes, all living things produce Vis; it's our life force. Mutari can use Vis in various ways as can Mages. Most of these powers, if you will, come from using excessive amounts of the Vis the person produces. In the case of Werewolves and a few other Mutari, only one organ in their body produces the extra Vis they use. For Werewolves, it's their heart. So when the Succubus started to drain Mr. Tabor, the cells in his heart tried to make more Vis to keep him alive and to keep the rest of his body from being drained. Strong though a Wolf may be, a Succubus can drain energy faster than a Wolf can make it. Plus with the extra Vis, a Succubus would be very strong."

The doctor looked thoughtful for a moment. "So Tabor knew what was happening to him?"

Erin frowned. "Yes, he would have been near paralyzed, feeling his life being sucked from him." Erin looked back at the body, "Even had someone not come in and killed him, it would have taken him weeks to recover, though it's possible that his heart was so strained he may not have lived."

Alison was amazed by what Erin was saying.

"Can you get me a sample of the Succubus' Vis?" Faith asked.

Erin placed her wand around Ramon's lips, they glowed a pink that converged into a small drop of color. She held it out to Faith's waiting hand where she placed the little dot of color.

"Thanks," Faith said.

Alison and Faith left Erin to Dr. Partington, finding Sean still in the break room with other people. There were no muffins left.

"What did you find out?" he asked.

"That we need to find this Succubus. She had something to do with Tabor's death," Alison said.

"Did we get DNA? Maybe we'll get lucky and get a hit," Sean said.

"That won't be necessary," Faith said. "I'm running a search; unless she's being protected, I'll have her location within an hour or two."

"Do you think she has protection?" Sean asked.

Faith shook her head. "Not that I can tell. I can find her, I'm sure."

Montoya walked up to them. "Gabriel, I have your payment for your last Pactum and three silver Eagles for today as per our new Pactum."

Gabriel took a velvet bag. "Thanks," he said and handed the bag to Faith after fishing out a coin. It was a one ounce American Silver Eagle which he pocketed.

"What's that about?" Montoya asked.

"The gold you pay for the week is our fee, but each day you are to give one ounce of silver for every Mage on the job, and like all payments it has to be in minted bullion," Gabriel said.

"I know that, but why did you take a silver one?"

"That is my per diem for the day; the other two are for Faith and Erin," Gabriel said.

"So you really only work for gold and silver?" Alison asked.

"Yep," was all Gabriel said.

GABRIEL DECOR thumbed the coin in his pocket, looking forward to more steady work. It wasn't that his family was broke; far from it, but he was hoping that this could turn into a steady gig. Other Mages had them; they had stable work and steady pay, albeit lower than regular Pactum rates, but a place to go every day, friends to make.

Sean was still a jerk but better somehow, like he respected Gabriel. He could tell Sean was just a jerk by nature so Gabriel didn't hold it against him. Still, the respect was nice. As for Alison, she was trying to play it cool but Gabriel could see she was uncomfortable around him and Faith. He used slight amounts of Vis to read the tenor of her emotions, trying to keep from making her more uncomfortable.

Alison was looking at paperwork. "I'm going to head back to the crime scenes and see if I can find anything new and canvass the area."

"You aren't going to wait and see what Faith comes up with?" Gabriel asked.

"Of course I am, but William Lanner was killed by Ramon Tabor who was killed by a Human after he was drained by a Succubus. That's not a group of random coincidences. Unless I'm mistaken, both Ramon and William's murders were hits. We need to find a connection and find out who was doing what. And unless this Succubus knows everything, then we have a lot of work to do."

"Gotcha," he turned to Faith. "You coming?"

"No, I'll stay here unless you think you'll need me," she said.

"I don't think we will."

"I'm sticking around too, I'm going to see if I can find a paper trail," Sean said clacking away at his computer.

Gabriel turned to Alison. "Looks like it's just us," he smiled.

ALISON KAUR waited until noon before leaving the office. This was what most people would find to be the boring part of her job, but she fed on it. As they got ready to leave the station Alison asked Gabriel if he wanted to stop and get something for lunch.

He pulled a small card from his pocket, pressing his thumb hard on it before talking to her. "Yeah, do you mind if I stop and get some cash first?"

"Where?" Alison hedged.

"I just need to see a changer; there is one off of Sixteenth."

Alison shrugged. "That works. I thought we'd pick something up in the mall anyway. What's a changer?"

Gabriel smiled. "You'll see. This works great. Hey, do you mind if I see if Faith and Erin want their per diem changed over?"

"Yeah go for it," she said.

Once out of the station they walked the short distance to Sixteenth Street with all of its shops and eateries. Gabriel led her to a jewelry shop just off the mall. They walked inside, the door dinging. A college kid looked up from the corner over a pile of homework. Alison noted that he wasn't watching the shop at all. Gabriel walked up to the counter to where a wizened old man with glasses looked up at him. "How may I help you?" he asked as Alison pulled up next to Gabriel.

Gabriel placed three silver coins on the counter. "I need to change 3SE to D."

Alison had no clue what that meant but the old man seemed to as he held out a card that looked like the one Gabriel had earlier. Gabriel held it, pressing his thumb down on it. The old man smiled. "Thank you, one moment," he said taking the coins, looking at them intently and walking into the back room. He came back with a small stack of cash.

He noticed Alison's look of confusion and then turned his gaze back to Gabriel. "Human?"

"Aren't you?" Alison asked.

The man smiled. "Hardly."

"Mage?" she tried.

"Goblin," Gabriel said.

"Oh…" she wasn't sure what to say. "Is that boy a Goblin too?"

"You're awfully nosey," the man said though not unkindly.

"She's a cop," Gabriel said.

"Ah I see," the man said. "Well then, officer, allow me to explain more," he pointed to the boy. "He is not a Goblin but a Troll. He is protection; not that I need it. I take it your Mage friend here didn't tell you what anything meant, did he?"

"No he didn't," Alison said.

The man nodded sagely. "That's typical. We are a private lot, we Vis users. He changed over three American Silver Eagles, or 3SE. The number three is the ounces, the first letter is for silver and the last is the coin, in this case Eagles, and he changed it for D which is dollars."

"Ok, so do you change for other currencies?" Alison asked.

"Yes of course, the Vis world works in gold and silver so Human currency doesn't mean much to us. We use what is convenient for the area we are in. Here we trade in Dollars, Euros, Yen, you name it. Now is there anything else I can do for you two?"

"That will do, thanks," Gabriel said pocketing his cash and steering Alison out.

Once they were out of the shop Alison spoke to Gabriel. "You didn't seem all that friendly."

"He's a Goblin, I don't trust them."

"Why not, what can they do?" she prodded.

"Goblins are able to examine metals and gemstones, they can tell how pure they are and work with them. They are like the bankers of Mutari and Mages; they are the backbones of the Vis economy."

"You have bankers?" Alison wondered.

"Yes and no, Mages don't need them per se, but Mutari do if they want to deal with Mages. As for Mages, we use them as a matter of convenience. Though neither side keeps their gold with the Goblin guilds, we do change gold and silver over and many Goblins trade in Vis-related objects."

"What was that card?" Alison asked.

"Mine told me where a branch was, his told him if I was in good standing with the guild. Is there a specific place you wanted to eat?"

Alison stopped questioning Gabriel during lunch, happy to finally be finding out more about the Magical world, even if it was just banking.

 FOUR

ALISON KAUR'S feet hurt after walking up and down Ramon Tabor's street all afternoon. She didn't have much to show for her efforts other than that Ramon kept to himself and had lived on the block for about four months. The dry cleaner he worked at said that he showed up on time and did his job. Back at the office, Sean only found a spattering of phone and financial records.

"Seems like a lot of dead ends," Gabriel said.

Alison shrugged. "Nah, it always seems that way at the beginning of an investigation. Don't worry; something will break and from there things will move. Any word from Faith? I thought it wouldn't take her this long to find the Succubus."

Gabriel looked concerned. "It shouldn't have, it's possible that a Seeker is hiding her."

"Does this happen a lot?" Alison asked.

"What?"

"Ya know, dealing with other Mages?" she asked.

Gabriel thought for a moment. "In a way, yes. We live with our teams for the most part, or we live close to each other. It's rare for Mage groups to know where another lives. Even after Mages retire, we keep to ourselves, generally speaking; it's just safer that way. So in that regard, yes; we are always playing a game of cat and mouse, though most times Mages aren't actively looking for others. Well, at least not in years."

Alison wanted to know more but the look on Gabriel's face said that he wasn't going to be forthcoming. *That's fine, earn his trust.*

Gabriel stopped for a moment, placing a finger against his ear. "Faith has found the Succubus."

SEAN HUGHES drove down Colfax, Erin next to him, while Faith sat silently in the back seat. Erin looked out of the window, humming to herself.

"Do you drive?" Sean tried to make small talk.

She looked at him. "Yes, I can, but I don't find the need to that often. Did you like the muffins?" she asked.

Sean looked ahead, had he liked the muffins? Heck yeah he did. "They were alright."

"Good," Erin chirped.

Sean hung a right on Gilpin Street, taking them into Cheeseman Park.

"Where to?" he asked Faith.

In his rear view mirror, he could see her scowl.

"What's wrong?" he asked, tense. The last time she'd looked like that Gabriel cut a car in two.

"It's odd, I'm getting a vague idea of where she is, and now that we are close, it should be easy to find her despite the park," she explained.

"Despite the park?" Sean questioned.

Erin giggled. "Come now Detective, Cheeseman Park is ranked as one of the most haunted places in America."

"What? You mean all that crap is real!?" he asked shocked.

"Don't worry Sean, Erin and I won't let the big bad ghosts get you," Faith poked.

Erin giggled again. They were messing with him, weren't they? Ghosts weren't real…but he'd heard stories about the park, knew guys who wouldn't go in it at night…"Where am I going?" he demanded.

Faith pointed. "Park by the pavilion."

Sean pulled into a small lot next to the pavilion, catching himself looking nervously around the park. *Don't be a wimp, Hughes; they were probably messing with you about the ghost thing.*

FAITH PENN got out of the car and looked around. *She should be close.* Another car pulled up and Alison and Gabriel got out. Erin came up next to her. "Where is the Succubus?" she asked.

"She should be close to here, but I'm having a hard time locking down a location," Faith said.

"Right," Gabriel parted his jacket and let his hand rest on Iram's handle.

"What's going on?" Sean asked firmly.

Faith's gaze swept around her. She looked at the pavilion with its white pillars and open air set up, *nothing there*. She moved onto a grove of pines next to a walking path. Faith started toward the trees without commenting on Sean's question.

"Decor?" Sean asked.

"She's looking. The park is hard to track in; there's already too much Vis," he explained.

Faith felt Gabriel take a step next to her in defense. She could sense Vis pouring from him; he was looking for danger. Faith stopped by the grove and scowled. "I can't get a lock on the Succubus. Hmmmm, Gabriel can I get a hand?"

"What do you need?" he asked.

"Push out a mist of Vis."

He didn't question but did as he was asked. Faith let Vis run down her right arm deactivating a hiding spell she had on a small crystal ball. It hung in a small clasp from a chain connected to her wrist. She released the ball. It hovered just

over her palm. She focused Vis into the ball and closed her
eyes and instantly she could see with the ball. The area was
alight with the natural Vis of all living things. Radiating from
Gabriel was a lavender mist, it extended from him, covering
the other Vis in the area. It illuminated the trees and at their
center it faltered for just a moment. "Got it!" she said.

Faith opened her eyes looking to where the disturbance had
been. "Lux," she said. A wave of yellow Vis rippled from her
in all directions. The air in the grove twinkled, the light from
the area warping. The air shimmered and then the figure of a
woman on the ground came into view.

ALISON KAUR watched Faith's glass ball with apprehension.
In front of them in a grove of pine trees, a body materialized.
Alison rushed forward, forgetting about Faith. Alison jerked
to a stop, Gabriel's hand like iron around her arm. The sudden
firmness of his grasp almost made her gasp. She turned, her
face flushing an angry red.

"Stop!" he said firmly before she could speak, his other hand
on the grip of Iram. "She's dead, let us clear the area."

Gabriel stepped forward, passing Alison. Erin trotted up next
to her. "Alison, you can't rush around Vis," she said maternally.

Alison watched as Gabriel walked forward extending his
hand. "Vis," he said softly. A ripple of energy extended from
his hand, pushing out past the pines. "There's no web," he said
and looked at Alison. "Forgive me but I had to make sure it
was safe for you to enter."

"Thanks," Alison said, glancing at Erin's worried visage.
"And thanks for the tip, Erin."

Alison walked forward into the pines with caution. In the
center of the trees lay a woman in a short tight skirt, heels, and
a low cut blouse. She lay on her back, brown hair fanning out.
Alison stood over her pale body looking down on what was

once the girl's face. The right side of her head was caved in, blood, bone and brains leaking out onto the soft ground.

"Baseball bat?" Sean said next to her.

Erin came up to the body pulling out her wand, muttering to herself in Latin. "There's no Vis on her head."

"So a Human did this then, right?" Alison confirmed.

Erin shook her head. "No, there is no Vis around her head, but this girl was a Succubus. Her whole body should leave Vis behind and it does, all but her head. There is no Vis around her lips which should be where the most is." Erin peered at the girl more closely, holding her wand near where the girl's face and skull were caved in. "Impressio," she said. A pink cloud flowed from her wand tip around the wound, becoming solid like a mold. Erin held her wand up, the Vis mold of the girl's face coming with it. Erin turned the mold around, muttering to it, refining its shape until it resembled that of…

"A hand?" Sean said incredulous. "There's no way someone's hand could do that kind of damage."

Gabriel spoke. "Yes it could. Remember what Erin said about the Vis?"

"Yeah…why?"

"Do you remember what I did to Keith?" Gabriel continued.

Sean's face darkened. "Yeah, you broke that guy's ribs with the back of your hand, so a Paladin did this?"

Erin shook her head. "No, though any Mage could have with the size of the hand and the type of death. I'd put my money on this being the work of a Troll."

"That seems more likely than a Mage," Faith said picking something up from the ground. "A Mage wouldn't have needed an enchanted object to hide the body."

SEAN HUGHES was getting sick and tired of finding dead people. He rounded on Faith. "I thought you said you could find this girl in a few hours? It took you all day and now she's dead!"

Faith gave him a stern look, she opened her mouth to talk, but was cut off by Erin. "Actually, she's been dead most of the day; I'll be able to give you an exact time of death when we get her back to the lab."

Sean clenched his jaw. "Fine."

Hours later Sean sat at his desk after getting ripped into by Montoya about having another murder. The Mages were out somewhere with Alison. Erin came up to Sean, shooting glances around the room at the other cops, uncomfortable.

"Umm, detective?" she said timid.

"What is it Erin," he said not bothering to mask his irritation.

"I have a time of death for you."

"OK, so let's have it!"

She flinched. "10:46 am," she spluttered.

Sean rolled his eyes. "It's not possible to get down to the minute, Erin…"

"Actually it is," Faith's voice came from behind.

Fantastic, everyone is back. Faith came into view with Alison and Gabriel, her small features a mask of concern. "Did you say 10:46 this morning?" she confirmed.

Erin seemed a bit more comfortable. "Yep."

Gabriel looked serious. "And what time did we task you with finding the Succubus?" he asked Faith.

"About 9:30," she said.

"What's going on? I am so sick of you people not telling us what is happening!" Sean blurted out.

"Relax, Hughes," Alison said then to Gabriel, "but he's got a point."

Faith was looking around now as was Gabriel. "What are you two doing?" Alison asked, her own tone coloring with annoyance.

"The station is bugged," Gabriel said as a matter of fact. "That Succubus was killed to stop our investigation or at least slow it down." He looked to Erin. "Can you please call James? I think we are going to need his help."

"Bugged? Impossible," Sean was insulted.

Faith muttered a few things and then held out her hand. From the ceiling, what looked like a marble fell into her hand. "Impossible huh?" she commented.

Sean looked at the marble in her hand. "What is that?"

"A listening device I'm sure, but it may also transmit images, it's hard to tell," she said pocketing the marble. "We will have to sweep the building for others, but I dare say we will miss a few."

"So what you are saying is that Succubus was killed because of us?" Alison asked.

"Think about it," Faith said, "whoever was listening in on our conversation this morning knew that you were going to have a Seeker looking for that girl, right? If we found her alive, she could trace back to whoever ordered the kills of the other two victims."

ALISON KAUR needed another cup of coffee. "So how did a bug get in the station? I thought you two had wards or something on the building," she said with just the hint of accusation.

"Some yes, but we have more to do. My guess is after I fought Tracy and Keith, the bugs were planted," Gabriel explained. "My wards are for Vis users but not normal Humans…"

"What, so you're saying a cop is on the take?" Sean asked angry.

Faith rolled her eyes. "Because that would be a first," she snorted. "Maybe it's a cop or maybe not, there are a lot of people who come in this place, and it's possible if not probable that they didn't even know they had the bug on them."

"But everyone who comes in here is searched; it's a government building," Alison pointed out.

Faith looked a little exasperated. "Searched by Humans...I had to use Vis to find this bug; I'm sure there are others that I haven't or won't be able to find."

Alison shook her head, trying not to think of the ramifications of a police station being bugged. "Fine what do we do?"

"We will have James look around for more bugs, but we need to make sure the other Mages aren't able to find out about the investigation. Do you have a conference room that we can have exclusive use of?" Gabriel asked.

"I'm sure that can be arranged, what do you want with it?" Sean asked.

"We'll make it a clean room," Faith said. "Gabriel and I will both place powerful spells and that will make it impossible for others to listen in on us, and also restrict who can enter the room."

Sean left to go make the arrangements for a room. Alison decided to work on her reports and try and make sense of things. She opened up a file folder.

"Maybe this isn't a great place," she commented.

She looked up to Gabriel who smiled at her. "Sorry," was all he said but after a moment he added, "Want to get some coffee and maybe a scone?"

Alison got out of the chair. "You had me at coffee Gabriel, you had me at coffee."

The two of them left the station, walking out into the August heat. The setting sun turned the sky orange, casting the buildings of downtown Denver into sharp shadows. The streets teemed with end of the day traffic, business men and women walked along talking on cell phones or trying to catch buses. Others were gathering at restaurants, quickly filling up outside seating.

Alison and Gabriel walked to a coffee shop on Sixteenth.

"I got it," Gabriel said.

Alison didn't argue, taking the cup of hot liquid gratefully. Gabriel ordered something and got himself a scone. The shop was trendy, not ultramodern trendy, but retro. College kids sat at two small tables with laptops and stacks of books piled haphazardly on the edges.

Alison and Gabriel sat next to a window with a view of the mall.

"What are you thinking about?" Gabriel asked her.

What was she thinking about? A triple homicide? No, those happened more often than people thought, but something was bothering her…

"What do we do now?" she said almost to herself.

"I don't know, collect evidence? I have a few contacts we could use," Gabriel started.

"No," she turned to him. "I mean us…society. Gabriel I've seen things in the last two days I've lived most of my life knowing weren't possible…how are Humans supposed to fit into all this?"

"Magic, you mean?"

She'd never heard him call Vis that. "I thought it was Vis?" she jabbed using humor to try and push him away.

Gabriel smiled warmly. "It is Vis, but you Humans," he said emphasizing the word Humans, "seem to be more comfortable with calling it magic. I think it helps you to not take it seriously," he mused.

Alison looked back out the window. "Yeah magic, how do we manage this?"

"I don't know, Alison. We Mages tried to keep Vis from you for thousands of years, perhaps though this time will be different."

"This time?" she prodded.

Gabriel smiled again. "Yes, this time. There was a time when we were in the open and it didn't work out so well, but maybe now with there being so many Humans and with your technology and whatnot, things will work better this time around."

"You don't sound convinced," Alison said.

Gabriel locked eyes with her for a moment and then looked away. "That I'm not…" he said in a whisper.

Gabriel placed his finger to his ear. "James is at the station; we'd better head back."

SEAN HUGHES watched as Alison and Gabriel came back in the station. Next to him was a pissed off Sergeant Philip Montoya, along with Faith and her nerdy-looking husband, James. The guy had shaggy black hair and a thin build, totally not what Sean pictured Faith's husband to be.

"So James, what is it you do again?" Sean asked.

"I'm an Enchanter," he said.

Sean snickered. "Is that how you landed Faith? Did you 'Enchant' her?"

"I'm not in the mood for dumb jokes Hughes," Montoya said, "How was your break Detective? Was it nice?" he added acidly to Alison.

"Sorry sir," she said.

"Decor, I hope to hell you have an explanation for this," Montoya added to Gabriel.

"Oh, I thought while we waited for James we could have some coffee. After all, with your office being bugged I didn't think Detectives Kaur and Hughes should work on the case," he beamed.

Sean wasn't sure if Gabriel was trying to make the Sarge more pissed off or if he was just that socially stupid. Sean's bet was on the latter.

Montoya's face reddened and a vein on his forehead popped out but he didn't yell. "Not the coffee," he said in a growl, "my station being bugged!"

Gabriel flinched away from Montoya. "Oh right, well I'd said after I fought the other Mages I assume they bugged the station. Didn't Sean tell you that?"

Yeah, Decor was a social misfit, but on the bright side, Sean figured seeing him get torn into would be good entertainment.

Sadly before the Sergeant could lose it, James spoke. "I wouldn't take it as a slight on your station, Sergeant. If anything it's a compliment. The other Mages figured you'd have the foresight to hire a Seeker, and they were right to think that, weren't they?"

Montoya looked to James, Sean, Gabriel, Faith and then to Alison. "Kaur, solve this case so we can get these pricks out of my station."

That was it? Sean had gotten yelled at for way less than that.

As Montoya left, Alison said softly, "Be careful Sean, the Sergeant said he wants 'these pricks' out of the office and he does call you a prick at least twice a week."

James turned to Faith. "What's a prick?"

"It means you're a great guy James. OK, what do we need to do?" Sean asked.

Faith eyed Sean coolly and spoke to her husband, "Honey, it's a rude thing to call someone, though in the case of Detective Hughes I think it fits." She spoke to everyone else, "I'm going to clear the conference room and Gabriel and I will place wards on it. As for James, he'll sweep the office and place a few counter bugs of our own that should hinder the other Mages."

FAITH PENN walked away from Hughes and the others with Gabriel to the conference room. It wasn't large, with a table in the center covered in cheap veneer. Gabriel shut the door behind him with a thump. Faith breathed a spell, making a fine silver chain around her wrist visible; at the end of it was a crystal ball in a clutch. She held out her palm. *Dimittere,* the clasp let the ball loose to hover above her palm. The ball pulsed yellow.

"I'm going to sweep," she told Gabriel.

Faith closed her eyes, focusing on the ball. Vis filled her, flowing from every cell in her body flowing down her slender arm and into the crystal ball. Her spell formed and she spoke, "Ostende te ad me." She opened her eyes. The ball enveloped in a yellow flash. Flaxen rays rushed out into the room, casting the room in sharp contrast. Faith focused the spell, pushing it just into the wall material. She felt resistance and flexed her Vis. A paperclip on the table shook and glowed violently. Gabriel stepped forward picking up the clip, "Adolebit." The clip vanished in a burst of amethyst flames. Faith felt the resistance to her spell vanish. Before releasing it she altered it rapidly, trying to find other objects.

"It's clear," she said releasing the Vis. The room went back to normal. "Should I cloak the room before you add your protection?" she asked.

Gabriel nodded and again Faith went to work with the crystal ball. She infused the space with energy, placing wards and other enchantments. After an hour she pulled a metal block the size of an egg from her pocket. It was one of James', she charged it with Vis allowing the enchantments inside to activate. She placed it on the table.

She looked to her brother. "You're up."

Gabriel's eyes didn't close as hers had, his focus so strong that spells the likes of which he was going to use now didn't tax his concentration. Not for the first time Faith felt herself shrink.

"Textus," was his simple command. From his right hand thick lavender strands of Vis spun out like a spider's web. The strands connected themselves to walls, chairs and even the floor and ceiling. When they touched they expanded into even more complex webs, the thick strands dividing themselves to fine gossamer strands. Faith watched as Gabriel imbued the bits of web with different attributes. The web faded, disappearing from sight when Gabriel was done. Faith knew it was still there. Only a few strands activated, waiting to be touched so they could in turn activate the rest of the web. For Sean and Alison, they would enter the room not even seeing the webs, but for those not welcome, should they enter, entrapment or death awaited. Faith had placed spells on the door, making it so no Human would willingly enter the room unless they were welcome. Gabriel's trap was for Mutari and other Mages, a trap that was one of his specialties.

ALISON KAUR followed James around the station making sure he didn't get into trouble. He was walking around the office running his left hand over objects and muttering to himself. On occasion Alison would see a slight glow of red coming from his hand and he would stop and pickup an object.

"Don't you use a wand or anything else, like the others?" she asked. She didn't distrust James, well not completely, but she didn't trust him either. She also wasn't thrilled about having bugs in her office.

"Oh I use an amplifier, yes," he commented holding his left hand up wiggling his fingers.

"What is it?" she asked not seeing anything other than his wedding band, and then it clicked. "Your ring?"

He smiled. "Yep, most Enchanters use rings or amulets for their work, though the latter is rarer these days." He went back to wondering around the office.

James seemed to be more talkative than his wife or brother-in-law so she thought she'd take the opportunity to find out more about the Mage world. "So why a ring?"

He didn't look up this time when he answered. "No reason really, though I find having something on my finger to be more useful when I'm working on something. I find it keeps both my hands free."

He was back to her desk, pulling pens and clips from his pockets. "Can I get your house and car key by chance?" he asked.

"Sure," Alison said reluctantly giving him her keys.

He started to mutter again and the keys shone ruby for a moment before he gave them back to her. "Thanks."

"What did you do?" she asked.

"Hmmm?"

"To my keys?" she asked again.

It seemed to take James a second to figure out what she was talking about. "Oh, right. Well, while we have a tracker on each of you, and my wife and brother-in-law will place wards on your house, there is a small chance that someone could be waiting for you when you get home or in your car. In that event, the spell I placed on the keys will notify both you and us."

She couldn't say that the Mages weren't thorough.

Faith and Gabriel stepped out of the conference room.

"OK, we are done. If you and Sean want to go in there and work on the case, you won't be listened in on," Faith said.

Alison called Hughes over. "Come on; let's see if we can get some work done today."

They walked into the conference room which didn't look any different than it had earlier in the day.

Faith and Gabriel came in with them, along with James.

"OK what have you figured out?" Alison asked the Mages.

Faith spoke first. "Well, I found a lot of bugs if that's what you're asking. There were only a few in this room. As for the rest of the office, it's safe to assume that even after James' inspection that some are still here."

"He missed some?" Sean said frustrated. "What are we paying you for?"

Faith's eyes narrowed. "The bugs won't last forever and I dare say that whoever placed them in your office can do it again. Also, whoever made the bugs was skilled in the extreme; it was very hard for me to find the few I did."

"I found a handful," James said. "Some were pretty easy to find and others weren't."

"How many did you find?" Alison asked.

"About forty," James supplied.

"Forty!" Sean spat. "That's a little bit of overkill, don't you think?"

James shrugged. "Well, considering the differences in them, I think it's safe to say that there are several groups of Mages listening in on the office."

Alison felt her mouth drop open "How many are we up against?"

Gabriel spoke. "Not many; I'm sure. If it's any comfort, it's unlikely that all the Mages are the ones we are looking for. I'm sure some of the bugs are other groups that have been hired to listen in on the Denver Police Department."

"Yeah, I feel real comforted knowing that there's been a bunch of freaks listening in on me," Hughes said acidly.

Alison wasn't going to think about that right now. She waved her hand. "Fine, whatever. Do you have any ideas on how to find this Troll that killed our newest vic?"

Gabriel perked up. "I do, actually. I have an informant who might be able to identify the victim. And if we are lucky, she will know who her guard was."

"Guard?" Sean asked forgetting to add his normal tone of disdain.

"Yes Guard. Succubi don't have pimps to find them clients and to take care of problems. Instead they hire guards, normally in the form of a club of Trolls. The Trolls will have someone from the club go with them when they are changing cash for gold or silver and also to protect them if needed."

"How is that gonna help?" Sean asked.

Faith rolled her eyes. "The victim didn't have defensive wounds, which meant she knew the Troll who killed her."

"So it was her Guard who murdered her," Alison said nodding. "Right. OK Gabriel, where do we find this informant?"

FIVE

ALISON KAUR and Sean were going to go with Gabriel to see his informant. It was dark when they left the office, the night giving much-needed relief from the heat.

"Where are we headed?" Sean asked.

"It's a bar by the campus," Gabriel said.

Alison drove Gabriel, with Sean following in his own car.

They pulled in front of a college bar, Gabriel turning to Alison. "I will let her know we need to talk. Meet me at the diner."

"Why can't we go with you?" Alison asked.

Gabriel shook his head. "She's working and I don't want us to interrupt her night. I'll let her know we need to talk and she'll come to us. Don't worry," he said smiling.

Alison and Sean went to the diner and waited at a table for Gabriel and his contact. Sean and Alison looked over the menu morosely. It didn't take long for Gabriel to come back in and sit down across from them.

"She's coming," he said.

The door opened and a beautiful blonde entered. She was about 5'3", thin with a figure that made Alison's self-esteem take a small hit. She looked around the diner, coming up and sitting next to Gabriel. Her blue eyes pierced the detectives. Sean adjusted himself in his seat. The girl, whoever she was, was dressed in a mini skirt and tight shirt.

She eyed the two detectives and turned back to Gabriel. "Why Human cops?" she asked.

"I have a Pactum with them," Gabriel said and then pointing to Sean and Alison added, "This is Detective Alison Kaur and Detective Sean Hughes. Detectives, this is Mandy Stafford."

Alison extended her hand. Mandy took it with a firm but gentle grip. "It's a pleasure," Alison said and then asked, "How did you know we were Humans?"

Mandy looked over at Gabriel who just nodded. Mandy spoke to Alison, "I'm a Succubus." Not really answering her question. Then to Gabriel, "Sorry Gabriel, but it's a busy night. What do you need? I'm kind of in a hurry."

"You're a whore, aren't you?" Sean said bluntly.

Mandy looked at him. "Yes, I'm a whore; good work, Detective."

For the first time since meeting Gabriel, Alison saw irritation flash across his face.

"How much of a hurry are you in?" Gabriel asked Mandy.

"Does it matter?" Sean asked.

Most detectives had several hookers they used as informants. Alison had a few of her own. They were a great source of information and in return Alison would provide them with a modicum of protection and a free pass for soliciting sex. Sean, however; hated hookers for some reason Alison had never learned.

Alison shot Sean a look. Mandy was Gabriel's CI, not his. "Hughes, give it a rest," she hissed.

"What? Why? So the whore doesn't lose the opportunity of stiffing a few guys out of some money?" He looked at Mandy, "We could just arrest you for solicitation."

Gabriel's eyes narrowed and his voice became ice. "That's enough, Sean."

Sean looked at Gabriel. "Or what?"

Gabriel's appearance became darker. The warmth and innocence he seemed to possess melted away. In its stead were dark cold eyes, a set jaw, his look one of someone who not only would kill but had done it many times before. Images of Gabriel fighting the other Mages flashed in Alison's mind. Coupled with the look on his face, Alison felt a very real fear about the man sitting across from her. Sean shifted back in his seat; Alison could see fear cross his face as well.

"Sorry; I was out of line," Sean said.

Gabriel turned back to Mandy. "How much of a hurry?"

Mandy didn't seem bothered by the exchange at all. She paused. "About two days."

Alison didn't know what Mandy was talking about but Gabriel seemed to. He nodded and then to Alison's surprise, he leaned his face into Mandy's and kissed her. She kissed him back and Alison thought she heard the girl make a slight gasp. When they pulled away she looked down. "Thanks, you didn't have to give me that much."

"I know, but maybe you can take some time off," he said.

"So are you two an item?" Alison asked.

Mandy chuckled, "No, I'm a Succubus."

Alison was confused.

"Succubi need Vis from others to survive. I didn't pay her with money but with Vis," Gabriel explained.

Mandy smiled. "Yeah, about enough to last me a week; thank you. Well, now that my night has cleared up what do you need to know?"

Alison took out a picture of the latest victim and handed it to Mandy. "Do you know this girl?"

Mandy raised her hand to her mouth. "That's Hannah. Gabriel, what happened to her?"

"Troll," he said. "We think it was one of her guards."

Mandy shook her head. "No, no that can't be. There's no way a Troll club would break a Pactum like that," she insisted.

"Mandy, Hannah didn't defend herself…" Gabriel said.

"Is it possible that Hannah thought her attacker was a Human? Maybe a John?" Alison asked.

Mandy shook her head again. "She knew it was a Troll. She knew the same way I knew you were Human."

"A Succubus can read someone's Vis; they can tell if you're a Human or Mage or any type of Mutari," Gabriel supplied.

"Why would a Troll do that?" Mandy asked.

"From what little I've read on them, aren't Trolls kind of violent?" Sean asked.

"Yes, they are and they are very hard to hurt, but you don't understand; you don't hurt someone you have a Pactum to protect," Mandy said.

"It's true. I've only seen a Troll hurt a Succubus their club has agreed to protect on a few occasions. In all those cases the club would find the Troll responsible and kill them," Gabriel said and added, "Troll clubs have been guards for thousands of years. If a club breaks a Pactum by hurting its clients, they would lose business."

"Whoever Hannah's was will be losing it now," Mandy said.

"How so?" Sean asked.

"Well, I haven't heard of a Troll getting taken out by any club lately. The clubs are pretty good at being open with that stuff; it helps to inspire confidence in them," she explained. "But even if they don't know who's responsible, the club will lose business. Hannah's friends will talk about that club. Soon everyone will know what club it was and that they don't protect their people."

Gabriel nodded. "You're right; that club is done. They'd have lost business even if they killed the Troll responsible right away, but now? They're done."

"So?" Alison asked.

"So now we need to find the Troll who did this, or at least his club. If the club is in on it they must be getting paid a pretty penny. If the club isn't, then we need to work fast, before they find the Troll and kill him, and before we have a chance to ask questions," Gabriel said.

"I can ask around, I should be able to find out what club did it," Mandy said.

"It wasn't the one you use?" Sean asked.

"Nah, Hannah and I used different ones."

GABRIEL DECOR said good bye to Mandy, joining Alison and Sean on their way back to the station. Sean was getting on his nerves. He looked over at the man. Sean had backed down when he saw that Gabriel was mad, which in the end was all that mattered.

Back at the station they were greeted by Faith, Erin and James, who were all done with what they needed to do for the day.

"Detectives, do you still need any of us?" Erin asked.

"Thanks guys, but we are done for the day," Alison said and turned to Gabriel. "Tomorrow at eight?"

Gabriel nodded. "See ya then."

They parted ways. Once out of ear shot, Faith eyed him, "Problems?"

"Sean is a jerk. He was really out of line talking to Mandy today. If I'd known he wouldn't treat my contact with respect, I would have just brought Alison," Gabriel commented.

"Why doesn't he like us?" Erin asked.

"Fear," was all Gabriel said.

"How so? He seems kind of like a tough guy to me," James said.

"Sean is tough. He's seen a lot of combat in his day," Gabriel answered.

"Did he tell you that?" James asked.

How could Gabriel explain this to the others? Faith was the only other one who had seen any action at all. Even so, her experience wasn't vast. Not like Gabriel's; not like that of any Ark.

"It's just something you pick up, James. I couldn't tell you how, but you can just sense it in others." He glanced over at the rest of the group, his gaze lingering for just a moment longer on Faith. "I really hope none of you ever see enough bloodshed in your life to know what I'm talking about."

Out of the side of his eye he saw Faith look down and James take her hand.

They were a good distance from the station now. They stood together, reaching down inside themselves for Vis. Gabriel closed his eyes and let the energy run into an amulet. It connected with one at their house. Gabriel felt warmth as the spell worked. A moment later he opened his eyes back at home.

Gabriel took in the mansion before him. To most Humans, the dwelling would seem excessive and overly large. But it was no different than many of the team homes Mages occupied. The entirety of Gabriel's team lived under the same roof. They would have kids in the house and raise their families here for years. They would stay together until they decided to no longer take on any Pactums.

Gabriel and the others walked up a stone path leading to the granite house. They passed by statues like that of the Greeks and Romans, though the ones at the Decor house were more aggressive-looking. They looked like knights from medieval times, all holding shields, swords and axes. They were Guardians; just one more layer of defense against attack. Gabriel felt with his Vis, checking the wards he'd placed on the property. Nothing was amiss. Still, after his fight the other night he thought it a good idea to beef up security.

"James," he said.

"Yeah?"

"I would like to make some more Guardians."

James looked confused. "Really, why? We have twenty around the property and another ten in the cellar."

"Yeah, but most of those are stone," Gabriel hedged.

James shrugged. "But they are enchanted; the stone can take a lot and it's not like a Human force could even find us, let alone pass by the other defenses in place."

This was true. Faith also had many wards on the property along with that of Mages for generations. Only a handful of Seekers could find them when at home, and even then they would have to look hard. This was all standard, but still Gabriel thought he might need a little something extra.

"I know James, but I just have a feeling. Any chance you could make a few for me?" Gabriel asked again.

FAITH PENN eyed her brother. They were almost to the house. The outside was elegant and refined, hearkening to long-lost architectural style.

She spoke to James. "Honey, can we make the Guardians?"

"Sure, sorry," he said.

She took his hand. "Don't be sorry, dear."

"If anything, I should be sorry, James. I know it's a lot of work," Gabriel supplied.

James smiled. "Yeah but they are kind of fun to make."

"Do you mind if I make a request?" Gabriel asked.

"Request away," James said beaming.

Faith squeezed his hand, feeling happy. James loved Gabriel, and idolized him in so many ways. She knew James would be game for anything that Gabriel asked for.

"The ones we have now are for defense; I want the new ones to be offensive."

Everyone stopped. Faith's feeling of happiness vanished.

"Why do we need offensive Guardians?" Erin asked timidly.

Gabriel looked down and then back up, his normal carefree attitude absent. "I just have a feeling is all." With that he walked up to the heavy oak wooden door and entered the house. Faith, James, and Erin lingered outside. Erin looked worried. *As well she should be.*

Faith looked intently at her husband. "We need to make those Guardians a priority."

"But what about other Pactums we have; won't Heidi get upset?" James asked.

"Still do your regular work, just get these done sooner rather than later," she said. Then, reading the concern on his face added, "I'm sorry; it's just the last time my brother had a feeling was ten years ago."

James nodded and Faith looked over at an uncomfortable Erin.

"There hasn't been a need for offensive Guardians in fifteen years, Faith," Erin said. "This case can't be that big of deal, could it?"

Faith shook her head. "No Erin, I don't think it is." Faith backtracked; worried she'd frightened Erin and James. "Look, Gabriel was attacked by two Mages who weren't on Pactum. I think he is just being careful. I mean after all, if they attacked without a Pactum, then maybe they will try to find us."

Really Faith? That was the comfort you decided on? She again tried to backpedal. "Not that we are going to get attacked…"

Erin dropped the subject and walked in the house. Faith followed James, wishing she could hit Gabriel for freaking everyone out.

HEIDI DECOR walked into the library in the west wing of the house. Gabriel was sitting on a couch in a pair of sweats, reading a book. Heidi plopped down next to him.

"So?" she said.

He put down the book. "So what?" he asked, trying to dodge her question.

She rolled her eyes. "So why did you scare Erin so badly today?"

Gabriel sighed. "I wasn't trying to scare her Heidi; honest. I should have waited until later to ask James about the Guardians."

She could tell he was sorry. "Look, don't be hard on yourself. But try to remember that just because you own this house doesn't mean that everyone here is a Decor; the Penns are healers and builders mostly." She looked down. "They aren't like us…"

Gabriel was looking at her. "You mean they don't live waiting for constant attack?"

"Yeah," it was true. Heidi married into the Decor family. She'd grown up not fearing attack, not thinking about the dangers of the world. Most Mages didn't think about those things, they took security for granted; most living the way humans did, knowing the people around them and not waiting for an attack. "Do you remember when we were kids, and we just played and had fun? For you and Patrick - learning how to be a Seeker and how to be a Paladin were just games we played…"

Gabriel tensed. "I remember…"

Heidi wondered what it was like for Faith and Gabriel growing up. She'd known the family well; she grew up with Gabriel and his cousin Patrick, who'd later be her husband. She thought she understood the family, but now wondered. The Decors were a line of Paladins and Seekers. Faith and Gabriel never really had a choice. Gabriel could fight so he became a Paladin and Faith was good at Seeking. Families like the Decors lived a different lifestyle than the rest of her kind, a lifestyle she thought she'd never really understand.

Gabriel got up. "I'll go apologize to Erin."

"That's a good idea," Heidi said half-heartedly.

Why had she brought up their childhood? It was a mistake. Patrick was dead, and Heidi knew that Gabriel blamed himself for it every day. Heidi knew Gabriel wasn't to blame;

everyone but Gabriel seemed to know that. Heidi pushed her conversation with Gabriel from her mind. She got up and went back to her own wing of the house to get some work done.

SIX

ALISON KAUR woke with a jerk, sitting upright in bed. She turned off her alarm and thought about going back to sleep. Instead, she got up and got ready for her day. When she made it into the station, Gabriel, Faith, and Sean were already there.

"Morning, sunshine," Sean said as Alison placed her bag on her desk.

"I haven't had my coffee yet, Hughes," was her simple warning.

"Love you, too. OK, I have the address for our latest vic."

Gabriel cleared his throat. "Perhaps the conference room would be better for this…"

"Oh, right," Sean said irritated.

Alison picked her bag back up and followed Sean into the conference room. Once inside, Sean looked at the door. "Do we need to close that?" he asked.

Faith answered him, "No; sound can't leave this room."

"Right…"

He put a picture of Hannah Davis on the white board. "Our latest victim is Hannah Davis. She's a twenty-four-year-old female. The address at the DMV has her living in Highlands

Ranch. We don't have much other than that. We don't have any known relatives and when I ran her prints, nothing came up."

"You don't look all that surprised, Gabriel; why is that?" Alison asked, taking in his passive demeanor.

He shrugged. "Most Succubi have a fake Human ID. Most of them are runaways or have changed their names. That will go for any Mutari who was born in a Human family."

Alison didn't question Gabriel. "Why, if she lived in Highlands Ranch, would she be hooking downtown…" Alison wondered aloud.

"That's also not a surprise," Gabriel said. "Succubi need to take Vis from people to live. Being a Hooker allows them to get in close to people and take Vis without being noticed. Therefore, Hannah would be looking for Johns who are in their twenties or early thirties because they produce more Vis. And downtown because there is more potential clients."

"Right, college kids or young professionals," Sean said.

"What do you know about these Troll clubs that protect the Succubi?" Alison asked Gabriel.

"There are two types of clubs. The first runs more like a gang and they are made up of individuals. These types will take all sorts of jobs, though most are illegal in nature. The next is Troll clans. These are groups of families who run the organization; they have a lot of similarities to the way Mafia families are run. Clans will often contract out work to the smaller gangs like clubs of Trolls."

Alison sighed. "It's like a whole other society living in our own," she breathed. "Do they always work in crime?"

Faith answered this time. "No; as a rule they don't necessarily. Like normal Humans; only a handful of Trolls are criminals. Most families run many businesses in the clear. You will find many of them working in construction and other manual labor type jobs. Also, many of the families will work security for Succubi and other Mutari."

Gabriel spoke. "The thing to remember about Trolls is that when they use Vis, they are stronger and tougher than Humans. If they wanted to, most Trolls could lift a car. It's for that reason that so many prefer manual work. A day on a construction site for a Troll is no work at all. Also, being a bouncer is easy, along with any other type of security."

Sean laughed. "They should play sports."

Gabriel shook his head. "They are stronger, but not faster. Many Trolls never have to learn how to run fast or how to push themselves in competition. Also, for years they were kept out of society just like all Mutari and Mages. Had a Troll started down the path of becoming a pro athlete they could have exposed everyone. Trolls have their own competitions - sometimes inside clubs or other clubs will challenge each other. But all of these are kept far from the public eye."

SEAN HUGHES was mildly interested in learning more about the Trolls, but decided to drop the subject. Instead, asking a question that could help him in the near future, "Are they hard to kill?"

Alison gave him a look but Gabriel and Faith didn't look bothered.

"What, Kaur? If we have to set one of these things down, don't you want to know how?" Sean asked Alison.

"You are right to ask," Gabriel said. "The Trolls we will be dealing with will likely be violent. If we are lucky they will be from a club that is not family based, as those tend to be very well run and organized. What caliber of firearm are you using?"

".40 with hollow point plus P rounds, why?" Sean asked.

Gabriel nodded sagely and Sean was impressed the Mage knew anything about guns. "Those won't kill a powerful Troll, but if you move over to full metal jacket you might be able to hurt one. Keep in mind if the Troll is not using Vis, they will be as weak as any Human. Still if you have a .45 I would use that instead. I know the stopping power isn't all that much stronger, but every bit counts."

Sean nodded. "Right, I have a 1911 I can use."

Alison piped up, "Ditto, I can get mine at lunch."

"Gabriel, do you know where any of these clubs are?" Sean asked.

"They aren't hard to find; why?"

"We should start canvassing to see who knows Hannah Davis," Sean said.

"Don't you want to wait to see what Mandy says?" Gabriel asked.

Sean smiled, not unkindly. "You guys don't work without Vis much, do you?"

Faith shrugged. "Not really."

Alison picked up the thread of what Sean was saying, adding, "This is how we do our work; you have to get every angle of a case. So where are these Trolls going to be?"

Faith scrunched her face. "I could look for large pockets of them if you like?"

"No," Sean said. "We don't want to know where every Troll in Denver is, we just want to know where a club that might betray a client might be. You said there are some that are more like gangs, right?"

"So a group that doesn't belong to a family..." Gabriel mused. "Well, I would think they'd be in a crap part of town. Family clubs have controlled areas for generations."

"And someone will need to go to Hannah's apartment," Alison pointed out.

Gabriel nodded. "I'll go with whoever is looking for Trolls; that will be dangerous. Faith, you take the apartment."

"I'll go with Faith," Sean said. If he had to spend the day with a freak, he at least wanted to spend it with a hot one.

"Gabriel and I will start in Five Points, it's a rough area" Alison said and then asked Gabriel, "Can you find Trolls without Faith?"

"Yes; I have a higher than basic grasp of Seeking, just as Faith has a higher then basic grasp of being a Paladin. But if we are going now, I must insist that you get your other gun first." Gabriel looked apologetic. "Forgive me, but if we get attacked by a large group of Trolls it may take me a moment to kill enough of them before I can protect you."

ALISON KAUR tried not to show her discomfort at Gabriel saying he might have to kill the Trolls and that it would only take him a moment.

"Do you think we will run into trouble?" she asked, a little worried.

"I don't know. It's so rare for something like this to happen. Trolls never break a Pactum. If the group we are looking for ordered one of its members to kill Hannah, then we will very likely be attacked if we get too close."

"What if they are hunting down the member of their group, wouldn't they attack us then? To try to save their reputation?" Alison asked.

Gabriel shook his head. "No, if they want the Troll responsible dead, they won't help us but they would never attack a Mage."

"Why is that?" Sean asked.

Faith responded, "Because even an undertrained Paladin would be able to take out several Trolls before being taken down."

Alison was done talking; she had work to do. If Gabriel thought she needed a higher caliber gun then so be it, "Come on Gabe, let's get moving."

She left the station with Gabriel in tow, getting into her car and driving home. When she parked she looked over at Gabriel, deciding if she was comfortable with him in her condo. She wasn't scared that he would do anything to her; but her home was hers. It was the place she could let down her guard and she didn't want that space violated.

"Wait here," she said, making up her mind.

Alison unlocked the door of her condo, dashing into her study and kneeling down at her desk to fetch her 1911 and ammo. She heard a creek from the door. Alison jumped up reflexively, bringing up the now loaded 1911. She lowered her weapon upon seeing Gabriel fiddling around with the doorjamb, "I could have killed you!"

He was looking at the doorjamb when he answered. "Unlikely," was all he said.

"I thought I asked you to stay in the car?" she demanded.

"The enchantment in your key alerted me; someone was trying to get in here."

Alison went rigid. Someone tried to get into her apartment?

Gabriel looked at her lock and muttered something. Lavender Vis flowed into the lock, coming back out in the shape of a key. She watched him walk across the sidewalk and place the Vis key in her neighbor's lock. The Vis vanished after a moment and he straightened.

"Sorry Alison, false alarm. It looks like whoever lives across from you went to the wrong door. Does that happen a lot?" He asked.

Alison breathed out. "He's a drinker, so sometimes, yeah. The lock will know if someone else's key was used? And I thought I was supposed to know if someone came in the house."

"You would know if they managed to enter. James made it so that anything stuck in the lock would trigger a notification to us. The other Mages could try to get around our wards by not using Vis. Once again, sorry; I'll go back to the car."

Gabriel turned but Alison stopped him, telling him to sit on the couch while she reloaded the gun with the correct shells.

FAITH PENN sat on the firm leather seat of Detective Hughes' car. She eyed the fancy electronics set in the black dash. Everything in the car was black; even the windows were darkly tinted. She looked over at Sean, one hand on the wheel, his other arm resting out the open window. With his sunglasses, she thought he looked even more conceited than usual.

"So how many cars have you been in?" he asked like he was talking to someone from a third world country.

"Oh not many, I mainly stick to my broom," Faith said sarcastically.

"Really?" he asked.

Faith wasn't all that skilled at using Vis to read emotions, but she thought he was being serious.

"No, we don't ride brooms. To be fair; we don't drive often, either. In recent years, though, many Mages have taken to converting cars to run on Vis," she explained.

This seemed to interest him. "Do you have one of those?"

"James converted one a few years back."

"What did he convert?" Sean asked, amused.

"Ummm, I don't know really -- it's just a car." she admitted.

Sean turned the radio on to some station Faith didn't care for. She closed her eyes and tuned out the music. Being a Seeker was all in one's head. Faith spent hours on end meditating and learning how to focus. She didn't notice the music anymore. An invisible aura of Vis extended out from her. In her mind's eye, she could see the world around her. All living things had Vis auras of their own and the non-organic objects reflected the yellow of Faith's Vis. She could see all this with her eyes closed. In this way, even a blind Mage could see what was around them.

The car turned up an on-ramp to I-25 and Faith decided to get some work done. She focused Vis into ten orbs in front of her face. None of the Humans nor even most Mages would be able to see the orbs. *Invenire ostendere Mutari,* she thought to herself, refining the spell before releasing it. She moved her eyes back and forth under her closed lids. The city rushed by, the orbs flying out around the car. She kept them close and always moving with the car. In the distance, she saw a shock of gold from one of the orbs. The spells resonated inside Faith: *Succubus.* A moment later another orb found a Goblin and then a Vampire; but no Trolls or anything dangerous. Finally, as they passed a Home Improvement store, an orb found several Trolls.

"What are you doing? Are you sleeping?" Sean asked as he turned off I-25 and onto Lincoln.

"I'm looking for Mutari," she said, opening her eyes and releasing the spell.

He stiffened. "Did you find any?"

"There are thousands in the Denver area, so yes, I found many."

He looked confused. "Was there something specific you were looking for?"

She shrugged. "Trolls. I thought maybe if I found some large pockets of them, we would know where to look later, but Seekers are always sweeping areas we pass through."

"Why's that?"

Did she tell him? He seemed sincere. "What Mutari have you heard of?" she hedged.

He looked back at the road, thinking. "Let's see...I know of Trolls, Werewolves and Succubi obviously, but also Goblins, Vampires and Banshees, I think. Are there Pixies too?" he jabbed.

Faith was impressed. "No, not anymore; the Pixies died out. Sadly," she said, enjoying his look of surprise before she continued, "You missed a few and it's no surprise. The list you gave is accurate, but there are also Shape Shifters, Elementals and Wraiths. All of these are rare, with the latter being rare in the extreme."

He looked serious. "I kind of thought the Vamp and Banshee thing was just a myth. Are the others dangerous?"

Faith smiled. "Every kind of Mutari can be. Elementals can control one element like air or fire. Shape Shifters are like anyone, some are good and some are bad but most fall somewhere in between."

"But that's not the case for Wraiths, is it?"

"No," Faith said. "Wraiths are always dangerous. They can't help it."

He nodded. "What can they do? Or are you not allowed to talk about them?" he asked, his curiosity taking on the edge of a detective.

"I can talk about whatever I like." Faith wasn't sure if she was going to tell Sean or not; did he need to know? *Gabriel has a bad feeling,* she remembered, making up her mind. "They can fly, for one thing. They are hard to see and harder still to kill. They are lethal and only think of killing. When a Human becomes a Wraith, they slowly lose their mind. Most people know what's coming and they kill themselves."

"And if they don't?" he asked.

Faith looked away from him. "We do it," she said softly.

"So you just kill them when you find them?" Sean asked, though it was missing the tone of judgment Faith had assumed would be there.

"Like I said; they can't control themselves. They are a danger to all, so yes when we find one, we kill it."

"How?" Sean asked.

"It doesn't bother you that we just kill them?" she asked, looking over at him.

Sean looked at her. "You said they kill without thinking. Faith, sometimes some things just can't live. So how do I take one out in the event I see one?"

Faith spoke quickly. "You don't, Sean; you run and you run fast!" she said firmly making him jump. She didn't overly care for Sean but she wasn't going to let something bad happen to him.

"I can handle mysel-" he started.

"You can't kill them with bullets, or at least not easily. Even Mages have a hard time with Wraiths. The only ones of us who attack them are Paladins. If you see a Wraith; you run and you call Gabriel."

Sean looked taken aback and then he smirked. "But what if our Pactum is up?" he poked.

Faith shook her head. "Still call. It's every Seeker's duty to find Wraiths and every Paladin's duty to kill them."

Sean pulled into an apartment complex.

SEAN HUGHES pulled into a space and turned off the car. He sat for a moment looking at the dash, his mind a blur of thought. He didn't want to sound like an idiot, but there were obviously things he didn't know.

"So…are any of the old legends true?" he asked.

"What do you mean?" she asked.

"You know, like silver and stakes to the heart, stuff like that," he said.

Faith nodded her head. "Yes, there is some truth to the old legends. For example, silver can disrupt Vis flow."

Sean breathed out. He wasn't sure what to make of what she said. He wasn't sure if he was ready to hear that there was some truth to the fairytales he'd heard as a child. "What do you mean about silver affecting Vis flow?" he asked.

Faith took a moment. "Are you sure you want to know now? Aren't we supposed to be looking at Hannah's apartment?" she asked.

They were supposed to be doing that, but now that Sean was learning so much about this other side of the world, he didn't want to stop. After all, what if there were some Mutari waiting for them in the apartment? Could Faith take out a Werewolf or Troll?

"Yes; I want to know. How do I know we won't run into anything in the apartment…" he started, hoping she wouldn't question him.

She didn't. "Metals can affect how Vis flows, similar to electricity. Gold, for example, conducts Vis rather well; silver, on the other hand, has a disruptive effect. Some Mutari are allergic to silver; Wolves generally are, for example. It won't kill them, but it disrupts Vis flow in the area where the silver is and causes a great deal of pain."

"So if I shoot a Wolf in the heart with a silver bullet, would that kill it?" Sean asked.

"Yes," Faith said, "if you managed to hit its heart. When they use Vis their bones become very strong." And then she added, "Don't worry; there aren't any Mutari around here now."

"You're sure about that?" He asked, skeptical.

Faith replied by getting out of the car.

Sean stepped out of the car and looked up at a row of white apartment buildings. He started walking toward Hannah Davis' building. They walked up the stairs to her third floor apartment. Sean pulled a bag from his pocket, handing Faith a pair of latex gloves. She eyed them.

"This is a crime scene; we can't taint any evidence," Sean explained snapping on his own gloves.

He knelt to pick the lock. Faith touched his shoulder, "Let me."

She pressed her hand against the lock and it clicked. Faith opened the apartment door. "After you, Detective," she said warmly.

His feet made no sound as they tread on thick carpet. Vaulted ceilings gave the apartment a roomy feel. He walked by a dining room table where a vase of flowers was starting to wilt. The air smelled of flowery air freshener and home-cooked meals. Sean had been in the apartments of many whores whose pimps had killed them. Hannah's was different from the others. Hannah wasn't like those girls. The apartment didn't show signs of neglect, and he suspected that there wouldn't be an illegal drug anywhere. No, Hannah was not just some street corner whore.

"What are you thinking about?" Faith asked.

Sean shrugged. "Whores."

Faith looked confused.

Sean explained. "You see, not all whores are the same. There are different types. There's your street corner whore; she'll jump in your car for a twenty. They ain't pretty and are almost always druggies. Those girls die of disease or violence. Then you have high class whores like Hannah. She goes to bars and hotels; Hannah's clients pay a lot more money. They don't want outside attention, so they don't beat up the girls. Then there are your really high class girls and they…well, they work on referrals only and they keep secrets."

"You seem to know a lot about them," Faith observed.

Sean shrugged again, opening the fridge. He was pretty sure they weren't going to find anything of use in the apartment. Hannah was no moron and Sean figured none of her Johns even knew where she lived.

"Cops use whores as informants. They know the criminal world like no other. And when you figure that they are willing to sell their bodies for a few bucks…they don't really keep secrets, if you know what I mean," Sean said.

"Then why do you hate them so much if they help cops out?" Faith asked.

He was brought up short.

After a moment Faith walked away from him and into the bedroom. "I think I have the location of her lock box."

ALISON KAUR finished asking yet another woman if she'd ever seen Hannah Davis. Just like everyone else she'd talked to; the woman hadn't seen Hannah. Alison put Hannah's picture in her bag and cracked her neck. She wasn't in a good mood. They'd been walking around for a while now and all she had to show for her work was a few blisters on her feet.

She looked over at Gabriel in his heavy overcoat. He didn't look hot or uncomfortable at all and for some reason, this irritated Alison even more. He looked over at her. "Can I use Vis now or would you like to wander around for a few more hours?"

Alison bristled at the question. It was true she had been very adamant that Gabriel was not to use Vis to find Trolls. She wanted to prove that Human ways of finding people were just as effective as that of Mages. She was going to say no; that she didn't want him to do anything when a blister on her right foot popped. She winced, giving in.

"Fine, but I need to sit down for a bit," she said making her way over to a taco place.

Gabriel didn't fight her on sitting down, but she did notice just a hint of smugness in his countenance. She sat at a small table with a slushy drink and a taco.

"So do you know where to look yet?" she had bypassed civil and gone straight to sardonic.

Gabriel nodded to a small alley. "There."

She looked at a group of three men standing nearby talking. To the untrained eye, that's all they were doing – talking; but

Alison wasn't untrained. "You mean the dope dealers?" she said.

"They aren't dealing in drugs Detective, but yes; them. The small one walking away is a Goblin, the other two are Trolls," he explained.

Alison watched as the young man walked away from the two bigger ones. "Do you think the Goblin was buying? And what were they selling?"

Gabriel shrugged. "Maybe the Trolls are the buyers; it's hard to tell. They may not have even been dealing at all; that Goblin could have been from a guild, just there to change out money."

Alison wondered what Mutari would deal in. "That didn't answer my question about what they could be selling."

Gabriel looked back at her. "Anything really, but if they are selling, I would say they are selling objects imbued with Vis or Vis-altered items. It's not uncommon for Trolls to do this. It's possible that the Goblin is using the Trolls to sell."

"Because someone would be stupid to try to steal from a Troll, right?" she said.

Gabriel smiled. It made sense. Alison had figured the men were selling drugs or maybe even pimping girls. She thought they were either ballsy or morons for not leaving the area once they made her as a cop. But it wasn't illegal to trade in enchanted objects, so why leave?

"Do they know what you are?" Alison asked him.

Gabriel took his time answering. "I don't think so. Trolls aren't like Succubi or Vampires. They can't read Vis; they'd only be able to tell if someone was another Troll like they are."

Gabriel stood to leave. "They won't stay on that corner forever; we should go talk to them."

Alison followed him out of the restaurant, unsure why she was letting him take the lead. He walked with a confidence that she had to admire; he felt no fear approaching the Trolls. For her part Alison was also unconcerned. She didn't think it was because she was law enforcement or because she trusted Gabriel; no, Alison knew that she was unconcerned because of a lack of understanding. She didn't have any real world experience with Trolls. She thought back to Hannah Davis and her caved-in face. Alison picked up her pace, passing Gabriel. This was her case.

"I'll do the talking, Gabriel," Alison said.

The two Trolls turned, walking into an alleyway. The men were tall and muscular. Alison knew that even without their abilities, they would make for perfect thugs. One of them was bald and wore a white wife beater. He looked over his shoulder, eyeing Gabriel and Alison.

Alison was in the alley now, the space around them becoming dark with the shadow of the buildings.

The bald one tapped his companion's arm. They turned around, waiting for Alison and Gabriel to approach them.

The other Troll had shaggy black hair and a rough face. "It's not a good idea to follow people around," he said in a gruff voice.

Alison held out her badge while talking, "My name is Detective Kaur, and I need to ask you some questions."

The Trolls looked at each other and smirked. This time the bald one spoke. "Like you've been told; it's not a good idea to follow people around, Detective."

Alison was used to dealing with dirtbags but there was something different about these two.

"Why don't you piss off before you end up on the news?" This from the bald one.

Both Trolls turned to leave.

"We know you're Trolls," Alison said, earning a look from Gabriel.

The Trolls stopped for a moment and then turned, the black hair one sneering. "You know what; you are getting on my nerves. Maybe you need to learn some respect."

"And maybe you need to remember you are talking to someone in law enforcement," Gabriel said stepping forward.

Alison saw him rest his hand on Iram. Two Humans would have laughed at Gabriel but the Trolls didn't look so sure.

"And what are you?" they asked.

"A Paladin," Gabriel said flatly.

The Trolls backed up a bit.

The bald one spoke again. "A Mage comes to visit the lowly Mutari…well, aren't we honored. I will tell you the same thing as your filthy Human friend here; piss off!"

Gabriel paused for a moment. "No; you're going to answer her questions."

An uncomfortable silence filled the space before the bald Troll looked up, his eyes flint. "You know what? I don't like your attitude!"

Alison stepped back in shock as the Trolls' skin took on a slight green hue. The bald man roared, lunging forward. Alison felt the air leave her lungs and her hair blow in the wind. Her feet scraped along the pavement as she and Gabriel flew back ten feet. They stopped and Gabriel put her down. She realized that it wasn't the Trolls that moved them, but Gabriel.

GABRIEL DECOR set Alison down. She looked disoriented and a little afraid. He looked back at the two Trolls. From the moment the two had turned around to talk to Alison, Gabriel had known they weren't going to cooperate. He looked them over. They weren't scared of him. *They're from Human families.* Any Mutari born and raised as Mutari would know better than to square off with a Paladin. *Maybe they aren't dumb...* he wondered if they had backup.

Vis pulsed from Gabriel as he looked for other Trolls...there weren't any. *OK, I guess they are dumb.*

The black haired one came at him holding a pipe he'd found in the alley. Gabriel poured Vis into his body, augmenting his natural abilities. Gabriel sidestepped left as the pipe whizzed past the right side of his body. He pivoted on his left foot, turning right and avoiding the bald Troll's fist. He grabbed the Troll's wrist as it passed by, pulling the man off balance. As Gabriel moved, he smashed the palm of his right hand into the Troll's shoulder where the arm met. The Troll's body was stronger with its own Vis. Gabriel flexed his own. The man bellowed in pain as the joint made a wet snapping sound.

Gabriel used the momentum of the bald Troll pulling him around to send the fellow into his companion. Both crashed into the alley wall. The black-haired Troll tottered for a moment before coming back at Gabriel with the pipe, swinging it at Gabriel's head. For Gabriel, time seemed to move slower with his mind and body filled with Vis. It was simple for him to reach up and grab the pipe. He used it to fling the Troll over his head and to the ground with a crash. With a twist of his hand, the pipe came free from its owner. Gabriel spun, hitting the bald Troll in the head with the pipe. The metal bent as it hit the

Troll's Vis-strengthened skull. Still, the Troll's head snapped to the side and he fell to the ground, unconscious.

Gabriel looked back down at the black-haired Troll. He crawled away from Gabriel toward a wall, obviously defeated.

"My friend has some questions for you; will you answer them?" Gabriel asked in a polite tone.

The Troll sat against the alley wall, his chest heaving. He couldn't seem to catch his breath. He looked up at Gabriel, who wasn't even slightly winded. The Troll looked to his fallen companion and back to Gabriel again.

"Yeah, I'll answer her questions," he said.

ALISON KAUR tried not to look shaken up as she approached the Troll on the ground. She fished a picture of Hannah out of her pocket and held it in front of the Troll.

"Do you know her?" she asked.

The Troll looked the picture over for a moment, then back to Alison. "Yeah I do, her name is Hannah. Why?"

He seemed concerned.

"She's dead," Alison said.

The Troll sat up sharply. "How?" he demanded.

Gabriel offered the man his hand. "The name's Gabriel."

The Troll looked at the hand for a moment before taking it. "Miguel," he looked back to Alison, "What happened to her?"

Alison could tell by the look on his face that not only was Miguel not going to be a danger to her right now, but that he had nothing to do with Hannah's death. "Her head was caved in by a Troll," she said reading Miguel's reaction.

Miguel swore, clenching his fists. His skin shone green and he punched a dumpster. The metal buckled and groaned as the dumpster moved a few feet away, a fist shape indented in it. Alison looked at Gabriel. When he'd fought the two Trolls, Gabriel hadn't looked like he was pushing himself at all. *How powerful is he?* She wondered.

Miguel came back to his senses, breathing deeply. Alison was about to talk when Gabriel placed a hand on her arm, "Give him a moment to calm down."

The green of Miguel's skin dissipated. "Sorry," he said. "I'm a little hot-headed if you can't tell." He breathed deeply again. "I'm better now; sorry."

"Don't be," Alison said. "So how do you know Hannah?"

Miguel's head bobbed and he ran his hand through his shaggy hair.

"Hannah used to be a client of mine. I was her guard until about a month or so ago," he explained.

"What happened then?"

Miguel frowned. "Said she was going to use a different service. I asked her what I could do to keep her business but she said that her new guards could get her clients as well as protection. So I told her good luck."

"A pimp?" Alison clarified.

Miguel nodded. "Yeah, something like that."

"And you didn't want to offer her that service?" she asked.

"Nah, we don't do that. We run guard duty. If we started pimping, we would lose business and let's face it; Succubi are great clients," Miguel said honestly.

"What makes them so great?"

"They pay well and don't get into trouble. We mostly just guard them when they are moving gold and silver to or from a guild. I mean, yeah; every now and then we get a call saying they need some kind of help, but Succubi can take care of themselves."

"How is that?" Alison was curious now.

Gabriel answered. "Succubi can use Vis to make themselves look younger; they can also make themselves much stronger and faster. Most keep themselves in their twenties and use just a little extra Vis for energy and vitality, but making themselves strong takes a lot of power, so they can't do it long."

Miguel pointed at Gabriel. "Like the Mage said. Hannah couldn't make more Vis like I can, but she could use it in a quick fight; maybe throw some people through a wall or something, but she'd use up a lot of her Vis and that would mean she'd need more clients."

Alison understood. Succubi had to be judicious with the Vis they used. "So have you seen her since she stopped using your service?" Alison asked, moving the conversation back on topic.

"Nope, Hannah never came to this part of town anyway," he looked at his bald friend who was starting to stir.

Alison looked at the man. "We don't need to take any more of your time. Thank you, Miguel. Is there a way to contact you if I have more questions?"

"Yeah, I'm always down here; if you need to know anything else about Hannah you let me know." He leaned over, helping up his friend and then added darkly, "Or if you need help taking down whoever killed her; I'm game."

"Thank you," Alison said.

Gabriel pulled her from the alley. "I don't want to knock out his friend again."

SEAN HUGHES watched Faith fish her arm under Hannah's bed. There was a flash of yellow and she pulled out a long flat lock box. Faith hefted it onto the bed and muttered something. The box glowed and the lock clicked.

Sean stopped her, holding a gloved hand. "Evidence, remember?"

Faith rolled her eyes but moved away from the box. Sean opened the top and his mouth fell open. The box was full of gold and silver coins, along with a few other random notes and odds and ends. He heard a glove snap.

Faith moved him aside. "Well, it looks like she had an OK amount of gold," she commented.

"OK?" Sean asked. "Faith, there has to be forty grand in gold here and probably another two in silver."

"She's a Succubus, Sean, this is her entire life savings and just on Mages she'll spend that alone this year," Faith said, moving around the contents, "and probably another ten for Troll clubs."

Sean was confused. "Mages?"

Faith looked exasperated. "Yes Mages. Succubi pay to have enchantments put on them, curing them of diseases and also making them immune to them. It's like health insurance for hookers. Hannah and her friends will never get sick."

"Even from HIV?" Sean asked.

"That or even a cold; they won't get sick." Faith looked back to the box. "She was using a Goblin guild, here's her card and there are a few fake IDs in here, but nothing about the club she's using."

"Isn't it a little dangerous to have this much gold here?" Sean asked.

Faith shook her head. "No, this box has minor enchantments on it. Most Mutari have them. Only the owner can find the box, but it's easy enough for Mages to find the box and break the enchantment."

"Would this have her client list in it?" Sean asked.

"It might," Faith said.

She rummaged around until she found a flash drive. "Do you think it's on here?"

Sean took the flash drive from Faith. "It might. Whatever's on the drive, it has to be valuable information."

Sean left Faith to the box while he looked around Hannah's apartment. He was still waiting on phone and financial records to come in. There wasn't a phone on Hannah's person when she was found and Sean wasn't seeing one in the apartment.

"Pay dirt," he said.

"What does that mean?" Faith asked.

Sean walked to the other side of Hannah's bed, reaching for the corner of a laptop peeking out from under a pillow. He pulled out the machine.

"This could be the break we've been looking for," he said.

"How so?"

"Well, if Hannah had a smart phone, all of her contacts would have backed up here; also her email and the web pages she goes to. In short, this will hold Hannah's life in it." Sean pulled his phone out and called the station, asking for CSIs to be sent to scrub for anything else of use. Sean was hoping that Hannah had a boyfriend or someone they could talk to, but he wasn't optimistic. Everything in the case up to this point had pulled up dead ends, but now that he had a laptop... *There's no such thing as the perfect murder,* he thought.

SEVEN

SEAN HUGHES looked at the contents of Hannah Davis' lock box on the conference table. Neat rows of gold coins made up around thirty five thousand in gold bullion, depending on what the rate of gold was for the day. There was also several thousand in minted silver.

Jesse Sanderson, the department's IT guy was looking over Hannah's laptop and flash drive. Sean liked Jesse; the man was always to the point but wasn't a dick about it.

"Did you catch the game?" Jesse asked.

"Nah, I was here; did you watch it?"

Jesse looked up from the laptop. "Hell yeah I did, and why does that always surprise you?"

Sean shrugged. "I don't know, you're a computer geek; aren't you supposed to be online slaying dragons or something?"

"Do I look like a geek to you?"

He didn't. Jesse was a six foot tall, two hundred and thirty pound black man who looked like a linebacker. Sean laughed. "I guess not."

"That's stereotyping Sean, and I don't appreciate it," Jesse said looking back at the computer.

"So, were your online buddies busy…" Sean asked.

Jesse looked up. "Man, the guild's gone to crap ever since school started and a few of our guys got married; it just ain't right."

Sean laughed. Gabriel and Faith came in the room and Jesse perked up. "Well hello there dear, you must be the lovely Mage I've heard about," Jesse crooned.

Faith smiled. "Thank you, and you are?"

"He's a nerd who's supposed to be finding information about Hannah Davis," Sean said.

Faith gave him a dirty look.

"Don't listen to Sean over there; he's just scared of people who can count past ten. You know in one of my role playing games, I'm a Mage too," Jesse said winking at Faith.

She laughed blushing. "I'm sure you're a very powerful one."

Sean shook his head. Faith really did have a thing for nerds, as if her husband wasn't proof enough.

"Have you found anything out yet?" Gabriel asked Sean.

Jesse answered for Sean, getting down to business. "Yes, we have. Hannah may have had a lot of gold on her but she also had a bank account and several credit cards. She didn't look to be in any financial trouble, and her spending seemed to be pretty steady. She was also taking a few online classes from what I can tell." He looked at his tablet. "Looks like she was learning about finance." Jesse paused for a moment. "Your Hannah doesn't seem like a standard hooker at all."

"She wasn't," Faith said. "She was a Succubus. Hooking was just a means of getting the Vis she needed."

"Why take the classes? She had to know that this was going to be her life." Gabriel wondered aloud.

"Is there anything else?" Sean asked.

"I'll know more in a bit. She did have a smart phone. I've got all the contacts running through the system. I'll let you know if anything pops. Also, I'm pulling records; let's hope she texted a lot," Jesse reported.

"Why would that help?" Gabriel asked.

"When you text someone it goes over the cell networks. We'll be able to use the cell towers or GPS tagging to figure out where Hannah was at any given time," Jesse said. "With younger people who text a lot, it's like a map of their life."

Alison came in the room. "I found Hannah's parents," she announced. "They filed a report of Hannah running away when she was seventeen and they haven't heard from her since."

She glanced over to Gabriel. "Have you heard from Mandy?" she asked.

"We can go talk to her today and see what she's found. After our talk with Miguel, we know a bit more about who Hannah was working for. Maybe Mandy will have heard of a group like this," Gabriel said.

"Right," Alison said. "Sean, do you want to stay here and chase the paper trail?"

"Yeah I'll hold down the fort, you two have fun with Mandy," Sean said.

Sean figured that Alison just didn't want Sean to talk to Mandy again.

ALISON KAUR left the station with both Mages. "Where do you think she'll be at this time in the morning?"

Gabriel was playing around with a cell phone. "We can meet her at Cup of Joe's on Fifteenth."

Instead of driving, they walked to the coffee shop. This was one of the things Alison liked about working downtown. The morning was just cool enough to make the walk to the shop refreshing. Upon entering the shop, Alison saw Mandy at the counter. The woman was put together and ready for her day. This surprised Alison a bit. It wasn't early in the morning, but in Alison's experience most escorts weren't up and ready for their day by this hour.

Mandy noticed Alison and her group and waved them over to a table. She greeted Alison with a handshake and Faith with a hug. When it came to Gabriel he leaned down and kissed her. Alison turned away, embarrassed as Mandy gave a small groan. Alison looked at Faith who didn't seem bothered at all.

"Thank you," Mandy said as Gabriel pulled away.

Mandy looked keyed up as she sat down. She eyed Alison and smiled. "Detective you look mortified; are you really that embarrassed?"

Alison opened her mouth to say something rude but then changed her mind. "Just not used to the warm welcome Gabriel gives you," she said.

Faith snickered, placing her hand on Alison's arm. "Alison, they weren't kissing; you know that, right? I mean, their mouths are together but Gabriel was just giving Vis to Mandy."

Alison's face flushed, of course she knew that. "I know…it's just unusual to me is all."

Mandy smiled at her. "I don't blame you." She turned to Gabriel. "You said you had some more questions for me?"

Gabriel pointed at Alison, who spoke. "Yes, we do. We found Hannah's old guard and he said that she left him for a group that would not only protect her but also get her clients. Have you heard of any groups like this?"

Mandy pursed her lips and was silent for a moment. "About six months ago I was approached by someone asking me if I wanted to change services. They said they could find me clients and that I would get more work and all that."

"But you turned them down," Alison said.

Mandy nodded. "Yes. There is a reason why we do things the way we do. I don't need someone to find me clients and I don't need to be indebted to that person or group. So I told them I wasn't interested at that time."

"Did they push you at all?" Alison asked.

"No, I think they would have but I had protection in the area that came by to pick me up," she said.

Alison sat back in her seat. "You were that uncomfortable?"

Mandy paused. "The man who approached me had been watching me most of the evening. I knew what he was and called my guard, just in case I needed them. Even if the man had just been a client, I would have had my guard around. Trolls can be dangerous when they get too excited," she said emphasizing the excitement.

Alison could believe that. What she saw the day before was proof enough. "How did you know what he was?"

This time it was Faith who answered. "Mandy is a Succubus; they can read Vis flow in all living creatures. Trolls, like Mages and every other Mutari, have a very distinct Vis flow."

"So you know when someone isn't Human, gotcha," Alison said.

Alison filed that information away for a later time. She could see just what a wonderful informant a Succubus could truly be. They had all of the information any other hooker had but also could keep a lookout for Mages and Mutari. From what Alison had gathered, most of the Succubi weren't drugged out either, they seemed like normal girls…aside from the selling themselves for sex part.

Before she could stop herself, Alison blurted, "Is there a male Succubus?"

Mandy's eyes went down to the table for a moment. "A male is an Incubus. And yes; but there aren't many Incubi," she said softly.

Alison could see she struck a soft spot with Mandy. She wanted to know more, but decided to just drill Gabriel about it later.

"Sorry Mandy I did not mean to upset you," Alison said. "Do you know the name of the group that tried to recruit you?" she said getting back on topic.

Mandy shook her head. "No I don't; they didn't say," she paused and then looked at Gabriel. "Are you going to find the people who did this?"

"Yeah Mandy, I will," Gabriel said sincerely.

Mandy moved in her seat obviously agitated, her eyes turning red. "It's bad enough what we are, but…"

Faith moved closer to Mandy, putting an arm around her. "It'll be OK."

"We've taken enough time Mandy; will you let us know if you find anything?" Gabriel asked.

Mandy nodded again. "Yeah, I will."

Alison had a lot more to ask Mandy but wasn't going to push anything with Gabriel's informant. Once out of the shop she decided to ask Faith and Gabriel more about the Succubi. To her annoyance, they didn't share too much information, saying it wouldn't be helpful to the investigation. This made her mad.

It wasn't Gabriel's or Faith's place to say what would or would not help in the investigation.

"So what do you two think we should do?" Alison asked, annoyed.

"Faith, what's your take?" Gabriel asked.

Faith looked thoughtful. "Well, there is a Seeker blocking us, BUT, if I can get close to the Troll that's being hidden from me I should be able to find it."

"Yeah, and how do we do that?" Alison asked.

Faith stopped walking. "Easy; we find a pimp that's a Troll."

Alison laughed. "Yeah, not so easy, there are a lot of pimps in Denver. You may not think so, but every city is full of them."

"Yes, but almost none of them will be Trolls. Like Succubi, Mages can read someone's Vis flow, so unless the Seeker protecting our Troll is hiding his Vis flow, we should be able to find him."

"Will that work?" Alison asked Gabriel.

He smiled approvingly at his sister. "Yes, it will. A Troll pimp would be very rare, so if we can find one, we will be able to get in close enough to figure out if it's our perp."

"How do you know it won't be a Human pimp?" Alison asked, trying to make the Mages see all the angles.

Faith shook her head. "A Succubus wouldn't go for that. A pimp is also supposed to protect and a Succubus wouldn't use a Human for something like that. Also, a Troll can't read Vis flow so we can get in close to him and I could figure out if it's our guy."

FAITH PENN stood in front of a full-length mirror in her bedroom.

James sprawled on the bed behind her, reading a book, his eyes occasionally glancing up at her. Faith gave herself a last inspection. She wore glossy black heels, too tall for most women to even walk in, and a black form-fitting dress. The skirt of the dress came halfway up her thigh. She turned around, watching herself in the mirror. The thin fabric would be nice and cool, meaning that Faith wouldn't have to use Vis to stay comfortable. Something she was looking forward to.

"You are going to turn a lot of heads tonight," James said from the bed. "I thought this was an undercover operation?"

Faith was going to turn heads and she knew it. The Decor family was known for three things; producing world class Paladins, Seekers, and beautiful women. Faith knew this was the case for most Seeker or Paladin families. Both jobs required physical dexterity. As a result, most Seekers and Paladins were health nuts and worked out daily. Faith was no exception; she and Gabriel worked out constantly, pushing one another, and Faith had the body to prove it. As for the grace and style that went with her body, she gave her mother's constant prodding credit.

She looked up at her husband and smiled, "We are undercover. Alison and I are playing the bar-hopping friends, looking for Trolls who are pimping."

"And when you find one, what are you going to do? Arrest him?" James questioned.

She walked over to the bedside table, putting on earrings and looking down at her feet. "No, not in these things," she accused the heels. "Gabriel will come in, make a deal with the Troll and confirm that he's the one that killed Hannah."

"Is Gabriel going to have Iram?" James asked worried.

She'd been hoping he wouldn't ask that question. "No he

won't; he can't very well walk around with an unconcealed sword if he's supposed to be undercover."

She sat down on the bed, pulling the book from his hand. "I will be OK," she insisted, looking into his eyes.

James looked down. "Will you? And will Gabriel? You aren't the one picking a fight with a Troll unarmed."

This was true. If the Troll got violent, Faith would be on the other-side of the room and could cloak herself and Alison before the Troll realized that Gabriel had friends. No; if anyone was at risk tonight, it was Gabriel.

"Why are you worried about Gabriel?" she asked.

"He's like a brother to me, and Trolls are dangerous…"

Faith knew that James looked up to Gabriel and honestly she didn't blame him. Gabriel was an Ark, a legend in the Mage world, but James had never seen him in action. Faith hadn't really either. During the war, Heidi's husband Patrick was Gabriel's Seeker; not Faith.

"He's an Ark." It was all she could think to say.

There was a knock at the door and Faith looked up to see Gabriel. He too was undercover in a pair of slacks and a button-up shirt. He looked like a young traveling business man, done with work for the day.

"Do I look like some schmuck who's on a trip and wants to pay for a good time?" Gabriel asked.

James and Faith chuckled.

"Always," she said.

ALISON KAUR looked at herself awkwardly in her bathroom mirror. She just didn't feel confident. *Come on Alison,* she chided herself. It wasn't that Alison had trouble in social situations, but for some reason she just felt naked standing in a skintight dress in front of the mirror. What was wrong with her? She'd been undercover countless times; heck, when she was on vice she'd even played the part of a high-end hooker on a few occasions.

There was a knock at her door. Alison walked to the door and there stood Faith Penn, Alison understood her lack of confidence. One look at Faith in her tight black dress with low neckline, and Alison knew that if Sean were present he'd about pass out. For Alison's part, she felt what was left of her self-confidence flee for safety. That's when it hit her; when she knew why she'd been feeling so inadequate as of late. Before meeting the Mages, only her social life was something to be embarrassed about, but now standing with Faith; Alison felt so much more. This woman not only put most Hollywood starlets to shame; she could use Vis on top of that. How was Alison to compare to her? Faith could do in an hour what it took Alison a week to do.

"Hello Alison, is everything OK?" Faith asked.

No! How could it be? Alison composed herself. "I just feel a little exposed without a gun and a van full of cops backing me up, is all."

Faith nodded. "I can see that. Here," she said handing Alison a tennis bracelet and a vial from her clutch. "Drink the vial, and put on the bracelet; it will allow us all to talk and hear each other tonight," Faith said.

"What's in it?" Alison asked, wary to drink whatever the clear liquid was.

"Erin made it. It will burn off alcohol so you don't get drunk. I figured if we are going to be acting the part of party girls going from bar to bar, we should at least drink."

Alison downed the vial, which tasted of peppermint. "That was pretty good, actually. I really can't get drunk?" she confirmed as she put on the bracelet.

Gabriel's voice boomed in her head. "Not for at least ten hours." His voice got softer. "Sorry if I was loud when you first heard me. The bracelet will adjust its volume to make sure we can always hear each other. Faith, let me know when you find a Troll pimp and otherwise…you ladies have a nice evening."

"He knows we're working, right?" Alison said to Faith who just rolled her eyes.

Alison and Faith drove downtown. Alison figured a Succubus would want a John who was young, for his Vis, but also had to have the money to pay a hooker, so she made a mental list of hotels with bars and a few clubs that catered to higher end clientele. It was around five so she decided to start with a few of the high-end clubs and then move over to the hotels. She parked her car off Speer and they walked down Market Street.

Faith took in the clubs. "Which one are we going to?" she asked.

Alison pointed to a place that already had a small line forming outside the door. Alison went to the end of the line but Faith took her hand. "I don't like lines," she said, pulling Alison up to the bouncer. When they got to the front of the line, the bouncer eyed first Alison and then Faith, smiling and letting the two of them pass.

Alison looked back at the door. "I've never had that happen…" she said, her self-esteem taking another hit at Faith's results.

Faith laughed. "Alison, I used Vis on him. I was reading his emotions as he let people pass and trust me; we could look like we were Aphrodite's twins and that wouldn't have done anything for him, if you know what I mean," she said with a wink.

The place was high-end and nice. The men were in slacks and button-ups or even sport coats. The women were in dresses like Faith and Alison. At the bar, Alison picked out a high-end hooker with her spot claimed. In the corner, someone was passing off a bag of coke...

"Are any of these people Trolls?" she asked softly.

Faith leaned into her. "No, there are no Trolls here, but there is a Vampire and a Goblin."

When Faith said 'Vampire', a man in his twenties at the bar with short blond hair turned to look in their direction. Faith gave a small smile and nod. The man did likewise and turned back to his companion.

"How does he know what you are?" Alison asked, uncomfortable. The man looked completely normal and the sun was out. *Shouldn't he be burning?*

"Vampires are like Succubi and can read Vis flow, remember? But that aside, they have amazing hearing and he heard us and still can," Faith explained.

"So he knows what you are?"

"Undoubtedly. I may be masking my Vis flow but just by me being able to label him as a Vampire, he knows I'm a Mage, a Succubus or a Vampire myself and since he can't see my Vis flow..."

"He knows you're a Mage."

Alison ordered a drink which, as promised, did nothing to her. They then started a three-hour bar and club-hopping trip, in which both Faith and Alison got hit on a lot. Alison thought the Mage was some sort of 'getting picked up on' good luck charm. Men went for both of them equally and for the first time in years, Alison felt like she might not actually be a total failure when it came to men. She made a mental note to call her mother. Alison could almost imagine how her mother would latch on to the small ray of hope that her little girl might not die alone, as she'd so often worried aloud to Alison.

Finally they sat down at a table in a hotel lounge. Despite herself, Alison was having a wonderful time and all but forgetting that she was supposed to be working.

"My feet are killing me," Alison said. "Yours have to be hurting too."

Faith smirked and Alison said, "Vis," before Faith could.

Now that Alison was relaxing around Faith she found that she actually really liked the girl a lot.

Alison was about to ask her a question when Faith's eyes shot to the corner of the room "Troll," she said softly.

All of Alison's levity left as she looked at a man in a suit sitting alone, reading on his tablet and having a drink. They watched him for an hour as a few men went up to the bar and then to the Troll. The Troll would talk to each man and then play with his phone, and a moment later the man would place cash under a napkin and give it to the Troll.

"That's a pimp for sure," Alison said. "Do you think it's our guy?"

"Don't talk to him; I'm on my way," Gabriel said in her ear.

GABRIEL DECOR walked into the hotel lounge. To his right he could see Faith and Alison at a small table, sipping on drinks and acting like they were having a good time. Gabriel ignored them and walked to the bar, flagging over the bartender.

"What can I get you?" the bartender asked.

"I think tonight is a Manhattan kind of night," Gabriel said trying to make himself sound tired with a long day of work.

The bartender chuckled. "Rough one, huh?"

"Tell me about it - this trip has been a nightmare so far." Gabriel took the drink and brought it straight to his mouth in one fluid motion. He hoped he looked convincing as he took a big gulp. "Hmmmmm, but nothing a stiff drink and some action can't fix."

The bartender chuckled again. "Well I can help you with the drinking part."

Gabriel raised an eyebrow. "Do you know anyone who can help with the action part, then?"

The bartender looked around. "I guess that depends..."

"On?"

He shrugged. "What you're looking for..."

"Not any work, that's for sure. I don't want to waste time trying to pick some slut up, if you know what I mean," Gabriel said.

The bartender nodded to a table in the corner of the lounge where a big man sat alone in a booth. Even sitting, Gabriel could see that he was over six feet with a sturdy build. He had wavy dark brown hair and a firm jawline with a few days' worth of carefully trimmed stubble. Gabriel looked at the man using Vis. He could see that he was a Troll and was armed with a gun on his left side. He also had a knife tucked behind his back and a pair of brass knuckles in his right pocket. *Wow, paranoid much?* Gabriel turned back to the bartender, putting a twenty on the counter. "Thanks for the drink."

He walked over to the man, who looked up at him sternly.

"May I join you?" Gabriel asked.

The man waved his hand at the seat opposite him.

"So what brings you to my little corner of the world?" the man asked, his dark eyes cold and hostile.

"An itch. I could use some entertainment for the night if you know of anything," Gabriel supplied.

The man nodded, "Couldn't we all." He looked Gabriel over, "What kind of entertainment are you looking for?"

"I don't know, something brunette sounds nice."

The man smiled. "People say blondes get all the action, but I tend to disagree. Well, I think I can help you out. It will cost you three hundred."

Gabriel nodded. "Works for me…I've been here before and knew a girl, maybe she is one of yours?"

The man frowned. "Maybe, what's her name?"

Gabriel thought for a moment. "Her name was Hannah I think, real pretty girl, dark brown hair…have you heard of her?"

The Troll shook his head. "Never have, but I have some very nice ones for you."

Faith's voice buzzed in Gabriel's head. "I'm reading his emotions, he's lying!"

Gabriel nodded his head. "Yes, let's do that then," he said.

He pulled out a Gold Eagle from his pocket. He held it between his thumbs and spun it on the table between them. "Are you sure you don't know Hannah?"

The Troll looked at the coin spinning on the table. When he spoke, it was in a low deadly tone. "I've got a gun; don't be a moron," he said.

Gabriel looked up from the coin, all hints of his act gone. "I'm a Paladin."

The Troll sat back in his seat in shock. Gabriel figured he wouldn't do anything dumb now that he knew he was dealing with a Paladin. And then a moment later, the man grabbed under the table as his skin tinted green. The table cracked free from its base which was bolted into the floor. Gabriel pushed Vis into his body, pushing the table out of the way. The Troll was up. He grabbed a screaming woman and threw her across the room. She flew over the tables, screaming at the top of her lungs. Gabriel swore and yelled, "Prohibere!" The woman stopped midair and lowered to the ground, still in hysterics.

The Troll bolted for the door. Gabriel saw Alison begin to make a move, only to be grabbed by Faith. The two of them vanished from sight as Faith cloaked them.

Gabriel tore for the door. Trolls were not any faster than most Humans, but their strength and toughness allowed them to jump and leap great distances in comparison. As Gabriel got outside, he saw the Troll run across the street and jump to a third story ledge. He continued to make his way up, jumping several stories at a time. This was something Gabriel had hoped wouldn't happen but he'd planned for in any case.

Gabriel used Vis to rocket himself up, following the Troll. He knew that engaging a Troll in public would be a bad idea. He needed to steer the Troll to a place of his own choosing.

"Mico," he said, sending a ball of bright lavender Vis to a ledge next to the Troll. It flashed with light and the Troll moved away from it.

Gabriel continued using the same harmless spell around the Troll, making it seem as though he couldn't hit him. The Troll jumped off a roof into an alley between two office buildings. Gabriel landed behind him and the Troll bolted toward the street. Gabriel stopped and waited as his trap was activated.

The Troll tried to slow, but he inevitably touched a gossamer-fine purple thread between the buildings. Instantly, the alleyway lit with thousands of strands of the same color. The Troll twisted as the strands converged into ever bigger threads, turning the web into a perfect net. The Troll yelled as he was lifted up in the air, the cords around him glowing brightly as he struggled. Finally, he couldn't move more than a finger and stopped struggling.

"I'm going to take it you know Hannah then," Gabriel said as if he was out for a stroll and hadn't been jumping around on buildings.

EIGHT

SEAN HUGHES arrived at the hotel where Alison, Faith, and Gabriel had found the Troll. A uniformed officer told him how to get to the alleyway where the evening's events came to a close. As he entered the alley, he passed by more officers talking in hushed tones. He sidestepped piles of refuse littering the alley from the many bums in the area. He found Alison and the others standing in front of the oddest thing he had ever seen.

In the air was a large man who looked to be tangled in a glowing spider web from some B-rated horror flick. The dark-haired man was grunting and thrashing around in his glowing net.

Sean turned to the others and then saw Faith. "Wow honey, how much for you?" he asked.

Faith gave him the finger.

"Knock it off, Hughes," Alison said. "As you can see, we found our guy. Faith was able to confirm this is the Troll who killed Hannah."

Sean looked up at him, smiling. "Nice to hear, did you get his name?"

"No," Gabriel said. "I have him tied down pretty tight and his wallet is too hard to get to right now. He did a bit of a number on the hotel lounge, though," he said, wincing.

"Nah, he just messed up a table. That won't be much for the city to pay for, if they pay anything at all," Sean said, grinning. "After all, a hotel employee was referring guests to a pimp, wasn't he?"

"What about the woman the Troll threw?" Gabriel asked.

Sean wasn't sure on that one. "I'm sure she'll be fine with a little therapy," he said, trying to sound confident. In all reality, he was pretty sure getting thrown by a Troll across a hotel lounge would at least give someone a small tick for a few years, if not the rest of their life.

"Can you un-gag him?" Sean asked Gabriel.

Gabriel waved his hand and the cords around the Troll's mouth moved out of the way and he instantly started yelling.

"THIS IS EXCESSIVE FORCE! PIG, I WILL SUE!" the Troll bellowed.

"Actually, the law is still kind of fuzzy about whether Mutari and Mages are Human, so I think you're screwed, buddy. Besides, a cop didn't capture you; a Mage did, and they operate completely out of our control. I've seen this guy in action and let me tell you; you are lucky, my friend," Sean jeered.

The Troll spat on him and Sean asked Gabriel to gag him again.

Gabriel had to use more Vis to tie down the Troll until Erin could come and give him something that made it so he couldn't use Vis. Even after he was back to being a 'normal person' it took three cops to wrestle the 6'4" man into a squad car.

AFTER ALISON KAUR changed into her work clothes, she walked out into the station. Faith and Gabriel were still wearing the same thing, though Gabriel now also wore his signature black coat.

"We need a confession," Sean said as she walked up.

Alison nodded. "I can get one. Gabriel, Mr...." she looked at a folder on her desk with the Troll's information, "Javier Davison seems to react strongly to you. Would you mind joining me in the interrogation room?"

Gabriel said he was fine with that. Faith assured Alison the room they were going to had been swept for bugs so she was free to say whatever she liked without worry of being overheard.

Alison opened the door to the room, followed by Gabriel. Javier Davison sat at a stainless steel table with his cuffed hands on the cold smooth surface. Davison glared at her when she walked in. Alison took a seat in front of him. Behind her, Gabriel leaned against the one-way glass.

Alison opened the folder of information about Javier.

"It looks like you know the drill around here Mr. Davison," she said, reading. "I see you did three years in Canyon City for B&E and assault. Did you make a lot of friends there?" she asked.

"What's it to you?" he spat.

Alison shrugged, closing the folder. "I just hope that you have friends to go to. After all, once you're convicted for the murder of Hannah Davis and conspiring in the murders of Ramon Tabor and William Lanner, you're going to be looking at a lot of time down there. Maybe even the death penalty if the DA plays his cards right."

Javier grunted a laugh. "That was four years ago sweetie, that was before Vis was out in the open. I ain't going back to prison; you don't have one built that can hold me."

"It did four years ago," Alison pointed out.

Again the Troll laughed. "A little hard of hearing, aren't ya? Like I said, that was before Vis was out; I couldn't very well break down a jail cell without getting whacked by some Mage, now could I?"

Gabriel stepped forward, speaking coolly, "Don't worry, a Troll breaking out of prison now will still earn you the same fate."

Davison's cocky attitude faltered a bit and he leaned away from Gabriel. Alison looked at Gabriel. He wasn't the same… she could see that the slightly goofy but kind man she'd associated with Gabriel was gone. He was replaced by someone cold and confident…a killer.

Gabriel went on, "Your death can still be arranged if you'd like."

Alison was about to speak when Faith's voice spoke in her head. "Don't; you can't intimidate a Troll. Gabriel can. He won't work with you until he's scared."

Alison rubbed at the tennis bracelet she still wore.

Javier was looking less confident by the moment. But could she let Gabriel threaten him? *Yes*, she thought, she could. Like Sean had said before, Gabriel was not tied down by the laws that she was; he could make threats.

"Are ya gonna un-cuff me before you kill me? Huh Mage? Or are ya gonna keep me tied up?" the Troll stabbed.

Gabriel smiled a deadly smile. "I'll untie you, Troll. You see, I made a promise to a friend that I'd get to the bottom of

Hannah's death. So, you'll have plenty of time to fight. After all, I can't kill you until I get the information from you I need…"

Davison blanched, and for a moment Alison believed that Gabriel would torture the man.

Once again, Faith's voice intruded. "Keep looking worried but don't worry; Gabriel is acting right now…I think."

Gabriel leaned over the table and spoke softly. "Answer the lady's questions."

Davison looked at Alison. "What do you want to know?"

"Hannah Davis? What happened?" she asked bluntly.

"Aren't you supposed to ask me where I was on the night in question?" Davison asked and then shrugged. "Fine, but what happened is a pretty broad question, ya know what I mean?"

"Did you kill her?" Alison asked.

The Troll looked over at Gabriel and then back to Alison. "Yeah, I killed her."

"How?" Alison asked. She wanted to make sure Javier wasn't just confessing because he thought that's what Gabriel wanted.

"I hit her; one punch was all it took. She trusted me, so she wasn't using any extra Vis to make herself strong, see." Javier leaned in. "Her skull felt like an eggshell breaking, and it was about as messy as an egg too," he said smiling evilly.

He was trying to get a reaction out of her. Alison had too many years of dealing with monsters in the Human world; this Troll wasn't going to shake her.

"Why did you kill her? We know she was responsible for the draining of Ramon Tabor."

Javier nodded. "Yeah, she was. Dumb slut was only supposed to make him weak enough for a Human to knock him off, but she got greedy and your lot found her then."

"We would have anyway," Gabriel said.

"Yeah, but she wouldn't have been a suspect, right? Succubi whores drain other Mutari all the time. It's how we pay them," Davison said.

Alison glanced at Gabriel who nodded. "It's true, the same goes for Mages. They pay with Vis, not money."

"Anyway, we knew the cops would find her and no one wanted that," Javier said and then more to Alison, "Trust me sugar, even you don't want that. So I took her out and dumped her body."

"And why did you kill Ramon Tabor?" Alison asked.

"I didn't kill him," Javier said. "But he was killed because he got a little carried away taking out Billy Lanner, didn't he? Had that dumb dick done his job right, Hannah would have her legs spread for some prick right now and I would have money in my pocket and not be down here getting threatened by a Paladin." He shook his head. Alison couldn't see an ounce of remorse for his actions; he was just annoyed.

"Why was Billy killed?" Alison asked.

"Nope; not gonna happen," Javier said. "You can set your Mage on me if you want, but I ain't talkin' 'bout that until we talk deals."

"You have a Seeker, don't you?" Gabriel asked.

Javier looked uncomfortable.

"Don't worry, we swept the room for bugs; it's clean. You have one, don't you? That's how you were able to hide Hannah's body for so long and keep us from tracking you down," Gabriel said.

The Troll looked at him and spoke, serious and quiet. "Then you know why I want a deal and maybe a little protection here."

"Gabriel," Alison said. "Can I see you in the hall?"

Alison left the room, meeting up behind the one-sided glass with Sean and Faith.

"Sorry, Alison…" Gabriel started.

"Don't be; you got him talking. I want to know your opinion. Is he in danger?" she asked.

Gabriel looked back at Davison in the interrogation room. "Yes, he is. We know there are Mages involved; at least two Paladins which we've already met, and now it looks like at least one Seeker."

Sean scowled. "We need this prick; I'll talk to the DA and see what we can do. Gabriel, will he be able to use his powers anytime soon?"

"No, not unless he's given an antidote for what Erin gave him," Gabriel explained.

"Right," Alison said.

She walked back into the room, this time without Gabriel.

"I need to talk to the DA. For the time being, you get to spend the night here in the station. We'll talk more in the morning," she said, leaving the room.

SEAN HUGHES watched as Javier Davison was taken in cuffs to a holding cell. They all walked into the conference room and sat at the table.

"We're going to have to put him down if he doesn't work with us," Gabriel said.

Alison rounded on him. "We can't just kill people Gabriel, that may have been how things were in your world, but it's not how it works here!"

"Alison," Faith said, "he's right. Your jails can't hold him and he knows that. If we don't give him the deal he wants, he'll just break out."

"I thought he was worried about a Mage coming and getting him?" Sean asked.

Gabriel shook his head. "That was before we confirmed that he's working with Mages. All he has to do is get out and provided whoever he's working for doesn't kill him, he'll be protected." Gabriel breathed out. "It would have been so much simpler if he was just paid to kill Hannah. Honestly, that was what I figured the case would be, but instead he's part of some group and not just hired help."

"That doesn't matter; we aren't killing him Gabriel, we can just keep giving him whatever it is that stops him from using his abilities," Alison said sternly, trying to close the subject.

Faith shook her head again. "Actually we can't. The potion he was given suppresses his ability to produce excessive amounts of Vis but it's also poisonous over the course of time."

"How long until he gets sick?" Sean asked her.

Faith frowned. "I'd have to ask Erin, but maybe a day or two. He'll get real sick and then die."

Sean pinched his nose. "We really don't have a choice on this, do we? We have to get him the deal so he'll stay of his own accord."

Or have Gabriel kill him, he thought. He knew that Alison wasn't on board with the whole killing a suspect thing, and normally Sean would agree. In this case, however, he wasn't sure there was a way around it. There was no way for them to hold Davison if he didn't want to be held. But at the end of the day their opinions didn't matter; Davison was a ward of the state now, which meant unless he got the death penalty, Davison was not going to be killed.

"Aren't there some chains or something James could make to hold Davison?" Sean asked.

"Yes of course he could, indeed we could even build a jail cell to hold him but then what? Do you keep him in his cell forever? I don't think your laws would allow for that, and if you wanted something like that built, the cost to the city would be outrageous," Gabriel said.

"So we should kill him because it will save us a buck!?" Alison spat.

Gabriel looked at her, a torn expression on his face. "Alison, I have no desire to kill anyone, but I learned a long time ago to do what had to be done. Javier has killed in the past and will again in the future; I'm sure of it. Not to mention, you and Sean will now be targets for arresting him and interfering with his life. I may be obliged to kill Javier just on the grounds of our Pactum alone."

Alison sat back. Sean watched her skin flush and a vein on her neck pulse. She was pissed, but he didn't think it was completely directed at Gabriel. She leaned forward to say something when there was a rumble and the floor shook. An alarm sounded, triggering Sean and Alison to shoot up from their seats. Sean ran out of the conference room, his hand on the grip of his service weapon. Alison and the Mages were right behind him. Gabriel already had Iram unsheathed. They ran out of the office, seeing dust fly from the stair well.

Sean ran into the stairs amidst the clatter of the alarm and people yelling orders at one another. Running down the aisles of cells, he made it to the holding floor, coming to one with a hole in the wall. Sean swore loudly and stared out into the space between the station and the building next door. Javier Davison was gone.

Sean and Alison walked into the cell.

"I thought he couldn't use his powers for a few hours?!" Sean bellowed.

Alison leaned over and picked up a bottle from the ground. "Hughes," she said.

Sean looked at the bottle. Faith came up and waved her hand over the bottle. "It's an antidote."

GABRIEL DECOR scanned the perimeter of the police station, trying to see if he could catch the trail of the Troll, but neither he nor Faith had any luck. The Troll obviously had the protection of a very skilled Seeker.

Alison's voice buzzed in his head. "Did you find anything?"

"No, we didn't," he said angrily.

"The Sergeant is in; come back up if you can," she said.

Gabriel made his way back to the office. Inside the building was a flurry of activity, cops were rushing to check the rest of the building for breakouts and doing their best to secure the place.

Alison, Sean, and Faith were in the Sergeant's office when he got there. Sergeant Montoya gave him an icy glare. Gabriel was sure he and Faith were going to get fired.

"How did this happen, Decor?" Montoya demanded.

"He had help on the inside. We found a vial of antidote in his cell," Gabriel explained.

Sean spoke. "We checked surveillance from the cell block and it cut out about five minutes before Mr. Davison broke out."

Montoya hit his desk. "This case is pissing me off!" He swore loudly. "We get bugged, we have people killing off leads and now we have someone inside our building letting crazy Trolls punch holes in the walls?!"

Montoya leveled his gaze on Faith. "Have you found him?"

"Not yet," she said, frustrated.

Montoya calmed down. "I can tell this has you two just as pissed as I am," he said, and then looking again at Gabriel and Faith added, "OK, maybe you two are a little more pissed. I take it this doesn't happen a lot?"

"I'll find the Troll," Faith said, teeth gritted.

Gabriel put his hand on her shoulder. She shook it off, getting up and leaving the room.

Gabriel addressed the Sergeant. "Sorry about that."

Montoya shook his head. "Don't be; that's the first time I've seen that girl show any emotion at all. Why are you so calm about this?"

Gabriel breathed out. How did he explain the years of experience he had, how could he say he'd learned to bide his time, learned how to stalk his prey.

"Years of doing this. We'll find him, this could work out better in fact; if truth be told," Gabriel said.

"That's right," Sean said, animated. "We know who he is now - Alison and I can track him down and he may have gone to ground. We might just be able to find his whole organization."

"Decor, can you handle a group of Trolls?" Montoya asked. "I don't mean to question you, but that man went through a concrete wall. You're my people now, and I don't like my people getting hurt."

Gabriel was flattered. He could tell Montoya wasn't lying; he and Faith really were his people.

"Most of them won't survive sir; I can't use the same restraint as I did with Javier tonight."

"Will you need back up?"

Gabriel looked down. "I don't think that would be a good idea. Troll clubs only have a handful of members and I don't want your people to get hurt. I can handle them and leave at least one or two survivors."

Montoya nodded. "Fine. OK, everyone get to work. I have to go explain to the Captain why there is a hole in the building."

Alison told Gabriel to leave for the night and to come back early the next day.

Gabriel found Faith in the parking lot of the station, sitting on a bench, her shoulders hunched over, all of her anger spent.

"Are you OK?" he asked.

She looked up at him, her eyes glassy. "Yeah, sorry for being rude back there."

He sat down next to her. "It's fine, I'm pretty mad about this too."

"But you didn't have a tantrum," she pointed out.

Gabriel shrugged. "This isn't the first time I've lost."

She looked at him and then back to the ground. "Yeah, I forget about that." She sat up. "It's just that I can't find anything from this guy, the Seeker is so good. Better than anyone I've ever dealt with."

"Patrick used to get upset like that too, during the war…" he paused. Gabriel didn't talk about Patrick often but he didn't want Faith to keep living in his shadow. "Faith, you're a good Seeker, one of the best. Whoever this is has to be working hard to block you. Just give it time."

She chuckled without humor. "I'm an OK Seeker. Mom is a good Seeker and Patrick was your Seeker during the war. I'm just…"

Gabriel put his hand on her shoulder. "My sister and my Seeker."

"Yeah, but you're so good; you're an Ark, for crying out loud," she said.

Gabriel squeezed her hand. "Faith, I work so hard because I have a purpose," his voice got thick. "Patrick is dead because of me, Heidi a widow because I wasn't good enough." He made her look at him. "I am as good as I am because I will not fail my family again and because the day will come when I will find the one who killed Patrick and I will not lose again."

"And that's why I have to be better, Gabriel, don't you understand? Worthy or not, I am your Seeker and when that day comes that you get your revenge, I'll be fighting with you," she said.

Gabriel couldn't argue that point. It was true. The day would come when he'd find Marcus Vies and when Gabriel found and fought him, Faith would have to deal with Marcus' Seeker and wife Angelica. Both of the Vies were incredibly skilled and powerful.

Gabriel decided that he didn't want to think about the evening any longer. "Come on Faith, let's go home, tomorrow we'll worry about our missing Troll."

NINE

GABRIEL DECOR squared off with a statue of a medieval knight. James had been working on new Guardians that were more offensive and this was one of his test models. The knight was made of a solid piece of bronze, its shield held in front of it with its left arm. In its right hand was a sword. Like most Guardians it was large, standing over nine feet tall. Gabriel held Iram off to his side, circling the statue. Gabriel was in the back yard of the house, the rest of the family on the patio watching with excitement.

"What can it do?" Gabriel asked James.

"Nothing special yet; right now the only thing making it different from a standard defensive Guardian is that it won't stay in a specified area," James explained.

Gabriel nodded; that was good. In general Guardians were a lot like robots. They couldn't really think, only react to things around them and most could only function in a small area. That the Guardian could function and stay locked onto a target in any place was a credit to James.

"Can you make it do more?" Gabriel asked.

"I don't think so. It's using a lot of the Vis I stored in it to figure out its surroundings. I think if I put in any offensive spells, it would run out of juice too fast. But I can enchant the shield and blade to give it an edge," James said.

That was good enough for Gabriel. Without warning the guardian lunged, swinging at him. Gabriel smiled, looking forward to playing. He ignored his family, pushing Vis into his body, moving faster and faster as he tested the Guardian. It didn't look to be matching his pace. Gabriel frowned in disappointment. He didn't want to hurt James' feelings, but this thing wouldn't work. Gabriel moved to the side of the Guardian, slicing at its exposed side. The Guardian blurred and Gabriel had to move fast to block its giant sword. Gabriel backed away, impressed.

"HA didn't see that coming did you?" James taunted.

Gabriel laughed. "I've never seen a Guardian do that before! Good work, James."

Again the Guardian came at Gabriel, raising its sword high in the air. At the peak of its swing, the statue stopped moving and froze. Gabriel was careful; he wasn't sure if this was one of James' tricks.

"Dangit!" James yelled, trotting down to the Guardian.

He placed his hands on the metal body, muttering spells. After a while, he stepped back. "It's fried. Sorry Gabe," he said.

Gabriel sheathed Iram. "This was your first attempt at a new design, and I liked it."

"Thanks," James said.

"Come on Gabriel, we need to go," Faith called from the patio.

"Let me know when it's ready again," Gabriel said to James as he left.

SEAN HUGHES sat at his laptop in the conference room that was now starting to feel like home to him. In front of him were Javier Davison's credit card records and other financial information. Sean also had map software up and was doing his best to map out the man's life. Sean was listing the more common places Davison went to on a regular basis, like grocery stores and gas stations. If he was lucky, he would be able to canvass those areas and pick up some leads on where Javier was now. The thing that was bothering him was that Sean couldn't find a current address.

Alison came into the conference room. "Have you found anything?"

Sean sat back, stretching. "Yes and no. I've gotten ahold of all of Davison's credit cards and even his banking information. We are still waiting on phone records to come in. I don't have a current residence for him, but I'm getting an idea of the area he lived or worked in. Any news from the tech guys?"

Alison frowned. "No, I had them pull street cams from the area around the station and they all went blank at the same time as our cameras. I'm still waiting on ATM cameras to be pulled, but I'm not hopeful."

"Why is that?" Sean asked her.

"I don't think the cameras were shut down from the inside... think about, it if they were, how did all of the street cams go down too?"

"What, so you think it was a Mage who did it?"

Alison took a sip of coffee. "Yes, I do. I think whoever that Seeker is who's giving Faith a hard time was waiting and blocked out all the cameras in the area."

"Is that even possible?" Sean asked.

He was answered by Faith as she came in. "Yes, it is. It would also explain why Gabriel and I were unable to find a trail last night. But that aside, there still has to be someone on the inside as well. Had the Seeker tried to influence the cameras inside the station, they would have been blocked by our wards."

"How so?" Sean asked.

Gabriel answered this time. "If the Troll had someone inside your building working with him, they would have been able to tip off the Troll's Seeker long before we even got him back to the station. They would have had hours to set up and get ready for Davison to escape."

Sean thought about it for a moment and it seemed logical. By waiting until Davison was in holding, it meant that no one would have to deal directly with Gabriel. Sean stretched again, looking back at his laptop. "Ya know Decor, your kind is really starting to get under my skin."

"Have you guys been able to find anything?" Alison asked Faith.

She shook her head. "No; I can feel that I'm getting blocked by someone, which is a good sign. Sooner or later, I'll be able to get past whatever wards are protecting Davison, but in the meantime if you can find anything on the Human side of the investigation, that might be able to get me closer to where Davison is…"

"Right, we can do that," Alison said.

Sean blocked the conversation out of his head and dug back into the records. He would never admit it, but Sean loved to

PACTUM161

do research. You could learn everything about someone from records; where they worked and shopped, and with GPS tagging, he could even tell where they went. Truly, Sean could know a person better than they knew themselves without ever having to meet them. And from what he could tell about Davison, he was a creature of habit and one who didn't leave the city. Sean figured the Troll clubs, like any gang, had territories they tended to work; so it wasn't hard to figure out where Davison did most of his business. A little after lunch Sean finally got what he was hoping for, access to Davison's phone records. The IT department had his cell phone and was almost done pulling all of the GPS information from it. By four, Sean could see everything.

ALISON KAUR flicked off the lights in the conference room. Sean was projecting his day's findings on the wall. The image was a collection of dots in all different colors, each representing things like credit card use, phone calls, or even GPS signals from Javier's phone.

Sean pointed to a spot around Park Ave and Glenarm. "This is the place it has to be," Sean said. "The building in question can comfortably hold several people and it's also where Davison spends most of his time during the day." He turned to Gabriel. "What do you think?"

Gabriel looked impressed. "That should be it; my guess is there will be several Trolls there - maybe four or five."

"Can you contain them?" Montoya asked.

Gabriel looked at the picture of the building. "No, that area is wide open. If they stay and fight, I'll be able to keep them there, but if any of them run - which is likely - I won't be able to stop them all."

"I'll have SWAT surround the place; you plan the assault, and we'll have your back," Montoya said, getting up. "Give me an hour to get everybody back here for a briefing. In the meantime, Faith, can you confirm this is the place?"

"Yeah, I'll get on it," Faith said leaving the room.

Alison stayed with Gabriel and Sean went with Faith so he could get an on-the-ground view of the building.

FAITH PENN sat in Sean's car as he drove past where they thought the Troll club was located.

"Are they here?" he asked.

Faith pushed out seeking spells to the area. "Yes," she said, concerned, "but there are more than Trolls here; I'm also picking up Werewolf vibes as well. I can't tell how many are in the house; there are wards protecting it."

Sean looked out his tinted windows. Faith followed his gaze. The building was two stories tall with chipping white paint and small windows. It was square-looking and at one point had probably been a small apartment building. Behind it was a small asphalt lot. River rocks and large chunks of concrete were piled up behind the building. In front of it was a small open field. Sean was eyeing the buildings on either side of it.

He pointed to roofs. "We can get snipers on the roofs on three sides of the building. The only thing we really can't cover is the front," Sean said.

"Gabriel can go in that way. Trust me; if anyone leaves this place, it will be via the back door," she said, thinking of the havoc Gabriel would be causing in the front of the building.

Sean didn't question her and contented himself with making a few notes about the area.

"You aren't new to this part of the job are you?" she asked.

"Nah I'm not; I was in the army before this. I've had to breach and enter plenty of buildings; though I get the impression this one will be different."

SEAN HUGHES sat in a large room with the SWAT team that would be accompanying them that evening. Gabriel was standing in the front of the room with Faith. Sean had to remind himself that while Gabriel came off as kind of a nerd, he was an extremely skilled fighter with lots of command and combat experience. Watching Decor brief everyone reminded Sean of his days in the army.

The plan was pretty basic. SWAT would cover the sides and back of the building while Faith cloaked their presence. Gabriel would go in the front and take out anyone who didn't surrender. Sean, Alison, and Faith would be behind the building with some of the SWAT guys, taking cover behind cars or anything in the area. It was pretty straightforward. If people came out the back and were hostile, SWAT would try to kill them or hold them off until Gabriel could take care of things. It was the last part that had Sean a little worried. The SWAT guys were going to be using assault rifles and would have plenty of firepower, but in Sean's limited experience with Vis users, he wasn't going to feel comfortable until Gabriel gave the all clear.

"I will be placing as many wards on you as possible, but don't let that fool you into thinking that you cannot get hurt. Those wards will only protect you from Vis attacks. It's unlikely there will be Mages here today, but we want to be safe as Mages could be in the area. Do you have any questions?" Gabriel asked the room. He waited for a moment and then said, "OK let's move!"

GABRIEL DECOR played with the microphone in his ear, listening to the babble of the people around him. Everyone was in place and ready to go. He strolled down the street and walked up to the white house, its wood exterior starting to show through the chipping paint. His jacket flapped loosely around him in the hot, dry summer air as he walked up the creaky steps of the house. He reached with his right hand, wrapping his fingers around Iram's grip.

Gabriel's eyes darted back and forth, looking for anything out of the ordinary. He reached within himself, feeling the well of Vis inside him bubble up to the surface. His muscles became taught with energy and time seemed to slow.

He pulled on Iram's grip, the blade coming free and slashing in the air. "Decido!" he barked.

Iram glowed amethyst as a ribbon of Vis stretched out from the edge, cutting through the old wood door. "Ventus." A gust of air blew bits of the door from its hinges. Gabriel swept into the house. On the right, a man with long hair looked to him in shock, falling back in a recliner. Gabriel looked left to see another man who had yet to infuse his body with Vis swing a lamp at him. Gabriel sidestepped, lashing out with Iram. The blade jerked and blood sprayed the wall. The man fell to the floor, his abdomen gushing blood and soaking the old shag carpet. Gabriel ducked another blow from a different foe. This one's skin shone green with his power. This time Iram took a leg.

"MAGE!" someone called as the rest of the house realized what was happening.

Gabriel struggled to sense anything in the house around whatever wards the Seeker had placed on it. From another room a figure entered, moving fast. Its body covered in fur, the Werewolf features a blur with its speed. Gabriel moved to his left, his side burning as claws cut into his flesh. Gabriel didn't pay the pain any attention, instead using Vis to fly across the room away from the Wolf.

Gabriel waved his hand in front of him. "Ventus." Little lavender strands flew around the room, cutting everything in their wake. The Wolf dropped to the ground, avoiding the spell. Gabriel thrust Iram into the floor and then flew across the room over the Wolf before it could rise. Vainly, it tried to move out of the way before Iram cut it in half. There was a crunch of wood and Gabriel heard gunshots from outside.

They must be trying to flee. He moved more quickly now, into the next room. His vision flashed purple as wards stopped what would have been lethal hits to his head and abdomen when he entered the kitchen. Gabriel crouched, avoiding another one of the Troll's swings.

He swore. "Faith, I'm fighting blind!" he called out, frustrated.

Faith didn't respond.

Gabriel clenched his teeth as he kept avoiding the Trolls' wild swings. He pushed more Vis into his body, making time seem to all but stop. The looks on the Trolls' faces were that of terror and determination. Gabriel had to give them credit; they had guts. He removed the head of one and then stabbed the other in the chest.

ALISON KAUR listened on the radio as Gabriel entered the building. There were a few yells and what sounded like wood being torn to shreds. A moment later, someone burst from the back door out onto the pavement. The man was green and one of the officers yelled an order to fire. Alison tried to stop them but she was too late. The air was rent with the sound of assault rifles. The Troll tried to move back to the house as its body was riddled with bullets. Alison stood in shock, seeing how far it made it. Then her shock turned to horror as a bronze statue jumped out of a window.

The statue made all pause for a moment.

"GUARDIAN - TAKE COVER!" Faith roared.

The statue reached down and picked up a chunk of concrete the size of a bowling ball. It looked to where Alison stood, took a half step and flung the block in the air. The wind was knocked out of her lungs as Sean slammed into her. A moment later there was a crash as the block of concrete tore through the brick wall behind her. Again, the officers shot. The statue lit up as sparks flew off its body from bullets that did nothing. Faith spread her arms as waves of yellow washed over the officers. The statue started throwing rocks and concrete at them. Alison noted that its aim wasn't as good now.

Faith's voice boomed over her headset. "It can't see you; hold your fire or it will figure out where you are!"

The officers didn't listen to her. Alison watched as cars and other objects the police were hiding behind were demolished by projectiles. There were screams of pain as men were hit. Faith cursed and ran from behind cover. Alison reached up to stop her but missed. The Guardian somehow was able to see her and focused on her tiny form. Alison tried to reach Faith as a rock flew at her. Faith stood tall as an orb of yellow Vis surrounded her. The rock hit the orb, shattering. Alison didn't fight back against Sean's grip anymore. Faith's crystal ball was in her hand and shining bright.

She yelled something and yellow Vis flew at the Guardian. Its metal skin flashed green and it fell back. It stood and ran at Faith. Again she shot Vis at it, knocking it down.

From the back door a figure in black emerged. The officers fired at the figure. It lit up purple as wards activated.

"IT'S GABRIEL! HOLD YOUR FIRE, HOLD YOUR FIRE!" Alison and Sean roared.

Gabriel didn't seem to notice the bullets hitting his wards as he ran. The Guardian spun and charged Gabriel. Gabriel's path didn't change. Right before he hit the statue, he jerked to the side and slashed with his sword. The metal of the blade burned bright with power, cutting the Guardian in two. Its pieces hit the earth, no longer moving.

Gabriel looked around the area and then lowered his blade. "It's over," he said, turning and walking back in the building.

SEAN HUGHES rushed into the building with several SWAT guys on his heels. Gabriel hadn't been kidding; it really was over. There was blood everywhere, along with bodies. None among them was Javier Davison. The kitchen was the room downstairs that seemed to fare the best, with only a few chairs being knocked over. On the kitchen table were bags of coke and weed along with scales and wads of cash. *So much for just being pimps.* SWAT cleared the upstairs, not finding anyone up there.

Alison came in from outside, boasting a scrape on her arm from where she hit the sidewalk.

"How's your arm?" he asked.

She looked down at the scrape. "I didn't even know I had it…" she said.

Sean chuckled. "Well ya do now."

Alison surveyed the inside of the house. "We have six bodies total, one our guys took out and the others Gabriel finished," she said picking up a bag of coke with a gloved hand. "So, we have a group of drug dealing, murdering pimps."

"Decor should get an award for today," Sean said. Alison didn't disagree.

Sergeant Montoya came into the building. "Where's Decor?" he asked.

Gabriel came in the kitchen from the front room. "I'm here."

Montoya looked him up and down. "You hurt, son?"

Gabriel shook his head. "I got a few dings, but I had spells in place that healed me before the fight was over."

Montoya shook his head. "You managed to take out five of these monsters and whatever the hell that thing was outside, and you aren't even hurt." He shook his head again in disbelief.

Gabriel didn't look happy.

"What is it?" Alison asked.

"That thing I took out was a Guardian. We use them for defense; there shouldn't have been one here," Gabriel said.

"How so?" Sean asked.

Faith came in the back door, answering. "When Gabriel says 'we', he means Mages. Mutari don't have them; it takes an Enchanter to make one. Nor should there have been a Wolf here, either. Strictly speaking, Troll clubs and Wolf packs don't mix."

"So what are you saying? There's a fourth Mage and more Wolves?" Montoya asked sternly.

"At least," Gabriel said. He looked at the drugs. "And more Humans. Trolls and Wolves don't sell drugs; in fact they don't even use them. Drug use is a bit of a mystery to Vis users."

Before anyone could ask why they didn't use drugs, Faith supplied an answer. "Their bodies are too strong and drugs mess with that. Once they take something, their body will produce more Vis which in effect gets rid of the drug. Indeed, most Trolls and Wolves can heal from almost anything within a few days; they don't need medicine. This is the case for most Vis users."

"So what's that mean?" Alison asked.

"It means that the Mages are likely running things. That's the only way you would have a Guardian and Mutari in the same house. And plus, with Humans doing some of the killing and there being drugs and prostitution…" Gabriel said.

"It's an organized crime ring," Sean said.

He looked at the building in a different light. Before they'd thought they found some group's headquarters, but now he saw it for what it was, just a location, and probably only one of many. It was going to be a long case.

"This is just what I need," Montoya said angrily. "I'll call the feds and see if they are tracking anything like this," he said leaving the building.

Gabriel looked at Sean, confused.

"The murders are our jurisdiction, but if this is a crime syndicate, they will probably be in several states doing the same thing. If we are lucky, the FBI has a line on them and can tell us more. But at the same time, we might not get lucky. If they have a line on the group, we may have to back off or start working with another agency. It's a pain; I'll be honest with you." Sean slapped Gabriel on the arm. "Well, I hope you like working with us because this is going to be a long process."

After that, Sean turned to the task of telling officers and CSIs what they needed to do and he resigned himself to a late night.

TEN

ALISON KAUR walked through the wreckage that was once a front room. There were two bodies on the floor, one of them split in two. Blood oozed from the corpses, dripping through holes in the floor made by Gabriel's Vis. The gore didn't bother her; if anything it was a comfort. Mangled bodies were par for the course for a homicide detective. They were something she understood and could handle, unlike a bronze statue throwing rocks at her. Cameras flashed all around her as CSI techs worked to document the scene. It was getting late in the evening now, but Alison could still hear the deep, gruff voice of one of the uniformed officers out front telling the media to go away.

She looked out of the window at several news vans and reporters. Up to this point, the media hadn't really gotten into the case, but that was long over now. Some kid had posted a video online of the Guardian hurling debris, and it had gone viral. By morning, Alison knew that every network in the country and even some overseas would be playing the video and running crackpot interviews with supposed witnesses.

"So what happens now?" Gabriel asked, walking up next to her.

Alison looked over at him. He watched the reporters outside with an air of curiosity.

"It has really hit the fan. There's footage all over the Internet of you taking out that thing. Mage supporters will say that you are a savior and those who fear Vis will demand more control over Mages and Mutari," Alison explained.

Gabriel chuckled. "I know that. I meant what about the case? How does this affect us now?"

She glanced at him. He really didn't care about what the rest of the world thought of Vis users.

"There are pros and cons. We can give stuff to the news services and that could help us track down Davison. On the flip side we will be watched on the street and will have to step lightly now that everyone knows who you are."

"That won't be a problem," Faith said joining them. "I'll take care of making sure no one pays us any attention."

"How?" Alison asked doubtful.

Faith shrugged. "It's pretty simple. I already have spells on Gabriel and myself that make it so that people notice us when they see us but forget about us right after. This is how Mages have lived in your society for years. We went to the same stores and restaurants as you, but you never remembered seeing anyone out of the ordinary. Now, I will add spells to you and Sean as well as Gabriel and myself that will make it harder for people to recognize us. Friends and family won't have a hard time - they know you well - BUT the average person who doesn't know you would have a hard time telling if they had even seen you before."

Alison was dumbfounded. What Faith was describing would all but make someone invisible; it would also mean that they could now use all of the benefits of the population knowing about the case without any of the pitfalls. Alison smiled, for the first time excited about Vis being in the investigation.

"Faith, I'm starting to like you more and more," Alison said brightly.

Faith beamed up at her, wrapping her arm around hers. "I like you too, Alison. Now come on - I've found where the Trolls' lock boxes are. I'm sure once I get them open, there will be all sorts of stuff you'll want to see."

Alison allowed herself to be led off by Faith, upstairs and into a cramped office. The space was littered with junk mail and newspapers along with what looked at first glance to be a general ledger for a company. Alison ignored the ledger on the desk, knowing that it would be a decoy with the real ledger hidden away. Faith knelt down in front of a waist-high safe and pointed.

"Wow Faith, good job with that," Alison said good naturedly.

Faith stuck out her tongue. "Not the safe, there's a compartment behind the safe with Vis," she explained.

Alison raised en eyebrow. "Faith, I don't think they would put their books in such a hard-to-get-to place."

Faith rolled her eyes. "Alison, this thing only weighs a couple hundred pounds and this is a house of Trolls; this safe wouldn't be much to them."

"Oh…right," Alison said, chiding herself for forgetting about how strong Trolls were. *How many Troll houses have been searched over the years,* she wondered, *and how many searches have come up clean just because no one would think to move a two hundred-pound safe?* "Do I need to call Gabriel?"

Faith didn't respond, instead she extended her right arm and said, "Concio," with her hand pointed at the safe. It glowed a light shade of amber and lifted from the wood floor, floating over a few feet before Faith set it back down. Behind the safe were plain wood walls. Faith put her hand on the wall and frowned.

"What is it?" Alison asked, slightly concerned.

"This isn't your standard enchantment. I'd bet a Seeker and Enchanter built this right into the wall," she shrugged. "I suppose it should be no surprise with there being a Guardian here and all."

Faith started to mutter to herself. Alison watched her as she worked. After a while, she decided to leave Faith to her work and sweep the room. Alison pulled out a recorder and mic that she kept on her. She clipped the mic to her collar. She liked to record what she observed in a crime scene. Later she'd have her computer transcribe her observations. She walked around the room, picking up random slips of paper and making comments.

"I'm not seeing any delivery receipts here," she said. "That suggests the perps kept a low profile." She thumbed through the pages of the fake ledger on the desk, seeing entries for construction items. "It looks like the Trolls were running a small contracting service as a front," she observed, and then using her bracelet, spoke to Gabriel. "Do you think it's possible for the Trolls to be running a legitimate front company?"

He answered almost at once. "I'm sure they were running one; remember hard labor is easy for a Troll, so it's also easy money."

Alison continued her inspection for a bit longer when Faith finally huffed. "There! Got it!"

Alison went back to where she was. "OK, what do we have?"

Faith pushed on the wall and the wood popped out, revealing a hidden compartment. Inside there was a small top shelf with paperwork. Underneath that were several small boxes and a few stacks of Dollars, Euros and Yuan. Faith turned to the safe next to her and with a wave of her hand the safe spun to face her. With another wave the door opened. Inside, in neat rows, was more money. Some of it in paper currency, but for the most part there was a lot of silver and gold. Alison could make out gold and silver coins from the US, Canada, and others.

"Where are all these coins from?" Alison asked.

Faith frowned. "That's what's odd. For the most part, we deal primarily in gold and silver from the US and Canada, but I'm seeing not only US Eagles and Canadian Maples but also Austrian Philharmonics and China Pandas as well. I'd expect to see those overseas where they are more common..." she picked up another coin. "This is a Gold Krugerrand, from South Africa," she sighed.

"But it's easy to get gold from other countries; you can get it online," Alison said, not understanding Faith's apprehension.

Faith shook her head. "I know, but that's not the point. Eagles and Maples are standard currency for Mutari and Mages on this side of the globe. Most Mutari won't work for other types of currency; you see they know the look and feel of Eagles and Maples and their silver counter parts. It would be like taking money from a country whose currency you'd never seen before," Faith said.

Alison still wasn't sure if she got what the problem was, but decided not to question Mutari society at the moment. There was a footstep behind them and Alison looked to see Gabriel peering into the safe, his face becoming calm for a moment.

"What is it?" Alison asked.

Gabriel looked at her questioningly. "You looked all calm, which means you aren't," Alison said.

Faith chuckled. "She's figuring you out."

"Faith is right; the only Mutari who would be comfortable with minted bullion from another country would be Goblins, and they keep a tight lock on what is being used in the Mutari world."

"Why is that?" Alison asked.

"Simple really, they've made a system where you have to use them and convinced Mutari for generations that they can't trust coin that hasn't been checked by Goblins. Maples and Eagles are common, but if you wanted to trade in – say, Pandas, you'd go get the coin's gold checked out by a Goblin, who'd charge you," Gabriel said.

Alison nodded. "Right, so don't trust other coins, but what does this have to do with our case?"

"It means that either we are dealing with Mages from another country, as Mages can validate gold amounts, or more likely there are Goblins involved."

"And Goblins are a problem why?" Alison asked.

"They are the business people in the Mutari world. It supports our organized crime theory and makes it worse. If Goblins are in on this, then they'll have them working with Human crime syndicates and the Trolls will just be pawns," Gabriel said.

Alison rubbed her temples. "Trolls, Wolves, Goblins, Succubi and Gangsters; how wonderful," she said leaning over to the compartment in the wall, taking out the paperwork to bring back to the station. "What an awesome case, guys." She got up with the paperwork and walked out of the room.

Hours later, Alison walked up to the door of her condo. The night was still warm and she could hear snoring from her neighbor's open window. She looked down at her phone, *Three AM*. She sighed and opened the door, her body tired but mind awake. She made her way up the stairs of the dark condo, flicking on a light in the kitchen. Her place felt oversized to her. She knew it wasn't a large condo, but it was just herself; she didn't even have a cat.

She got ready for bed but still wasn't tired enough to sleep. She made her way back to the kitchen, plucking a wine glass out of a cabinet. She poured herself a glass of Merlot and sipped the dark liquid, relaxing just a bit. Sitting at her computer, she decided to check and see what the rest of the world was up to. She clenched her teeth upon seeing that Jake Rowley had gone from being "single" to "in a relationship." That prick, they had gone out not too long ago.

"We went out what, like…" she opened the calendar on her phone, flipping through the dates to find 'night out with Jake'. She paused, looking at the date. "We went out like two months ago…"

Had it really been that long? He'd asked her out again after that but Alison was in the middle of a case and said she'd call him. *And ya didn't think to call, did you?* Her mother's voice echoed in her head. It had been hard to find Jake, but she could surely find another person to go out with. Alison took a long pull on the wine and checked one of her online dating profiles…no messages.

The building creaked, making Alison tense for a moment, but there was nothing there. Just her, just Alison Kaur, alone in her condo like always. *If you were married, you wouldn't jump like that… or if you weren't a cop; instead you insist on dying alone, leaving your mother without grandchildren,* her mother's voice sounded again. Was that true? Was she going to be alone the rest of her life? She thought about it. For years now, those thoughts popped into her head. When she was young, she wanted a career and didn't have time for men; she was her own person. But now all of her friends were married with kids and lives. Alison had kept herself so busy most of her friends didn't even call her anymore. Her night with Faith was the first night out she'd had since Jake. Alison turned off the computer and downed the rest of her wine, depressed. Trying to push the thoughts of her life from her mind she went into her room and slipped under the sheets.

She lay in her dark bedroom, looking up at a smudge on the ceiling. The flat ceiling acted like a movie screen as memories of the day played again and again in front of her. She saw the Guardian throwing things at people and at her. At the time she wouldn't let herself think about what had happened. There were things she could handle. Getting shot at she could do. It wasn't fun, but it was normal. Some perp taking a swing at her, that she could also handle…but a statue coming to life and hurling rocks and concrete?

SEAN HUGHES was off to a late start and he honestly didn't care. He was at the building where they'd taken out the Mutari until past three in the morning and his reserves of giving a crap were on E. Alison was already in when Sean got to his desk.

"How'd you sleep?" he asked.

She looked up at him from paperwork. "I had a dream I was in the art museum and the statues started chasing me," she said.

"Nice, so you took some acid from evidence again, huh?"

Alison just flipped him off. Sean laughed as he made his way to the conference room. Only Gabriel was in the conference room when he got there.

"Is Faith sleeping in?" he asked.

Gabriel raised an eyebrow. "She still hasn't gone to bed yet," he said, and then added, "We spent the rest of the night trying to take care of any other dangerous spells left at the house and now Faith is trying to find Davison again."

"How are you so perky then?" Sean asked.

Gabriel smiled and pushed a little bottle across the table to Sean, who picked it up, peering at the sickly brown liquid. "Erin made one for Alison too, drink up."

Sean looked at Gabriel to see if he was joking.

"If you're too scared, I get it…" Gabriel said.

Sean bristled, unscrewing the top. "Don't be a moron Decor, I'm not scared of a drink," he said, downing it in one gulp.

Whatever it was tasted pretty nasty and warmed his gut like a shot of hard liquor. The warmth spread throughout his body and Sean felt a bead of sweat roll down his neck. Then the heat went away and with it, all of his fatigue.

"You can't drink that too often, but liquid sleep is handy," Gabriel said.

Sean looked at the empty bottle, feeling like he'd had the best night's sleep of his life. "Wow that's amazing man, how does she make it?"

"Magic," Gabriel said, sarcastic.

Alison came in the room holding a box before Sean could say anything to Gabriel. She placed it on the table.

"Here is all of the paperwork recovered from the bust last night," she said rummaging in the box. "We should have an idea of the perps sometime soon."

Sean got up and started to look inside the box.

"Looks like these guys ran a pretty tight shop when it came to their finances," Sean said, looking at a general ledger. "None of the guys Decor got yesterday looked like the accountant type. Do you think this is where William Lanner comes into the picture?"

Alison looked thoughtful. "Most likely," she said.

"How would that help? Don't we already know who killed Lanner? Or I should say who had Lanner killed," Gabriel asked.

"This helps tighten down what Davison said. For all we know he was lying to us that night, we need to get a case around evidence. Plus, if we can connect Lanner to the group we found last night, that may lead us to whoever's running this show," Sean said. "I'm kind of amazed they didn't try to destroy all this stuff when you busted down their door."

Gabriel didn't look all that surprised. "They probably didn't think we would find their hideout with Javier Davison not being there, and with the wards on the building."

"That was dumb; how could they not think we could track down where they live?" Alison asked.

Gabriel smiled tightly. "When Mages get involved, sometimes Mutari get sloppy in thinking that the Mages will make sure everything is OK. I doubt they even took the time to think about how a Human would find them; all they were worried about was Faith and she was supposed to be blocked."

That made sense to Sean; if the tables were turned he wouldn't take Mages into account.

"This is good news then, maybe we can use this weakness to our advantage," Sean said.

With that, Sean delved vigorously into the files they had taken. Sean had pulled a handful of prints from the building and in the afternoon, a match came in on the prints.

"We got a hit on Lanner's prints on the paperwork from the Trolls' hiding spot," Sean said to Alison as she looked through her own stacks of paper.

"That's fantastic," Alison said. "I'm about to see if the ME has IDs yet on the perps."

ALISON KAUR left the conference room and made her way down to the morgue. The brightly lit room was cold and smelled of medical supplies and the slight scent of death. Dr. Partington sat on a small stool in front of his computer, clacking away at the keyboard. He turned to take in Alison.

"Disappointed to see me?" Alison asked, reading the disappointed look on his face.

Partington smiled wanly. "I was hoping you were Erin. I haven't seen her in a while, and I must admit that I miss seeing her. She is rather knowledgeable, but don't worry Detective, you are much nicer on the eyes," Partington said warmly.

Alison's face flushed at Partington's awkward compliment. "Um…thanks…ah, do you have IDs on the perps?"

Partington perked up. "Why yes, I do! All of them had driver's licenses that checked out." He walked down the line of bodies pointing. "This is Derek Kinderman, he's a Troll, and then we have Edgar McDonnell and James Rindfleisch, also Trolls. Followed by Cyriak Kuchejinski who is a Werewolf, and last Mr. Charlie Olszanska who is a Troll." Partington turned back to her. "I will have to have Miss Penn's assistance with the autopsy, I dare say, though I think it's pretty clear that our Paladin friend was the cause of death," he finished smiling.

Alison wondered if all MEs were as strange as Partington. She figured working with dead people all day would probably make anyone a little screwy.

"Right, thanks Doctor, I'll tell Gabriel or Faith to have Erin come and help you," Alison said, making her way out of the morgue.

Sean greeted her when she got back to the team's conference room. "How was Partington?" he asked.

Alison shook her head. "There's something just not right with him," she said and started writing the names of the perps on the white board along with their driver's license numbers. Jesse was able to use the numbers to start getting information on the Mutari. For her part, Alison spent a few hours doing background checks on the Mutari. Other than a lot of address changes, none of the other Mutari had criminal records.

"Do you think they are changing their identities?" Alison asked Gabriel.

"Not likely; that's not really how Mutari work. Remember, they don't generally need to go through the hoops that Humans do." Gabriel explained, "If they think a cop is onto them, they generally can either buy enchanted objects to cover their trails or hire Mages to cover their trail for them. In fact, cases like Davison's arrest are rare because most Mutari have a hard time keeping what they are under wraps."

"Meaning?" Alison asked.

Gabriel shrugged like it was obvious. "If a Mutari had exposed themselves prior to Vis coming out into the open, they'd have been killed by Paladins. Even now if a Mutari were to run rampant, there would be a high chance that a Mage would take them out."

Alison thought about that for a moment. "Hmmm, well I suppose we could look through old unsolved cases to see if we've been onto the Trolls before…"

"I don't think we'll need to do that," Sean said. "I've got phone records up and I'm seeing that one of the phones we found hidden in that house only ever called one number. I'm doing a trace on that number now," he said.

SEAN HUGHES tapped away at the keyboard, tracing the number the Mutari called. An address popped and his jaw tightened a bit.

"Corey McLoughlin," Sean said.

"No way?!" Alison exclaimed.

"Who's that?" Gabriel asked.

Sean sighed. "Corey McLoughlin is a pain in the neck is what he is. He's a small-time crime lord here in town; no one's ever gotten anything to stick on him. He spends some of his time with drugs, but can you guess what he's known for?" Sean asked Gabriel.

Gabriel's face darkened. "Prostitution," he said.

Sean rubbed his face. "Yep you got it, but McLoughlin isn't your small-time pimp; he managed to avoid human trafficking and loan shark charges about a year ago," Sean said. "This guy is as slippery as they come, but word on the street was he'd stopped forcing girls into prostitution and was sticking with the doped out and otherwise willing variety."

"Is there that much to be made in prostitution?" Gabriel asked.

Alison nodded her head. "Yeah there's money; but hookers also make some of the best drug dealers, or their pimps do."

This was why Sean hated whores. He just couldn't bring himself to trust anyone who sold themselves for a few bucks. The girls they were talking about now were street whores. They spent their evenings jumping in the back seats of cars for twenty bucks, and then sold some dope while at it. Most were strung out on drugs themselves, food and shelter being their payment for what they did. Most of them kicked the bucket fairly young.

"Hughes," Alison said.

"What?" Sean asked angrily.

"Be smart. We'll nail him this time," she said.

Sean nodded, thinking back a few years ago to when McLoughlin slipped through his fingers. He wouldn't this time. McLoughlin was the vilest of criminals. He forced young girls into prostitution, getting them hooked on drugs or by threatening their families. In Sean's mind, girls who chose to be whores had whatever death they got coming, but those who were forced into it? That was different. Sean still kicked himself for not killing the bastard when he had the chance.

GABRIEL DECOR watched Sean fume. He knew the look on his face all too well. It was the same look that Gabriel wore when he thought about Marcus Vies. Corey McLoughlin was Sean's Marcus; something Gabriel could empathize with.

"If this guy is running with Mutari now, he'll be more dangerous," Gabriel pointed out. "Faith and I won't be able to get too close. I'll have Mandy ask around and see what she can find out, now that we know who is in charge. Then we can make our move."

Gabriel left the station and sought out Mandy without Alison or Sean.

"This is getting to be pretty common," Mandy said when she saw him.

Gabriel sighed. "Sorry Mandy, I know you have work to do."

He leaned over and touched his lips to hers, flexing his Vis. He felt it drain from him, flowing into her. She gasped slightly and pulled away.

"With all the Vis you give me, don't worry about it," she said.

"Have you been cleared of diseases lately?" he asked.

Mandy was fine with Vis as payment, but for Gabriel it wasn't enough. She could hold about a week's worth of Vis, which was nothing for him.

She looked down. "Gabriel…" she started.

He placed the palm of his hand over her heart, releasing a spell that would cure every disease she may have had. Along with it, he placed a ward on her, preventing other illnesses. The ward would last almost a month.

"There. I'm not as good as a healer, but that should work," he said.

She looked up at him and smiled. "Thanks. What can I do for you?"

Gabriel explained what they had found and asked her to ask around and find out what she could. She said she would and Gabriel left her, returning home.

ELEVEN

SEAN HUGHES sat at his desk, working on a few side cases that needed to be closed up. It had been a few days since anything had happened with the Troll case and Sean was starting to feel antsy about it. It wasn't good when a case became stagnant. On the bright side, he wasn't stuck in the conference room anymore. The office was clearing out, everyone leaving to enjoy Friday night.

"Excuse me; Detective Hughes, right?" a woman's voice said.

Sean looked up into the blue eyes of Mandy Stafford, Gabriel's whore informant. She was in a short black skirt, contrasting with her smooth ivory skin. Her blue shirt was skin tight with a plunging neckline, showing a decent amount of cleavage. *Hmmmm 36B if I had to guess,* Sean thought to himself. He didn't hide that he was checking her out. Sean figured if this slut was going to sell herself like an object, he could look at her like one.

"What do you want?" he asked curtly.

To her credit, his hostility and ogling didn't seem to affect her.

"Is Gabriel here?" she asked.

"Does it look like he's here?" Sean asked, like she was a moron.

She shifted uncomfortably. Sean thought that was funny.

"What do you need?"

"I have my report for him. I can come back tomorrow," she said turning, to leave.

"I'll take it," Sean said.

She turned back to him. "Umm, Gabriel told me to only give it to him or Faith…"

Sean felt a flash of anger; who did this whore think she was?

"Look, I'm a cop and you have information on a case I'm working. You have two options here; you can give me the information you have OR I can throw you in jail for obstruction or solicitation, I'll let you pick the charge," he said smiling sarcastically.

Mandy stuttered, "O-OK, I can give it to you. Should I sit down?"

Sean was fine with the view he was getting now. "I didn't offer you a seat."

Mandy stood for a moment before speaking. "I was able to find out more about the organization you're looking for. They are running out of a hotel downtown. I think they have a few other high-end locations. I talked to one of their girls and she said it's not a bad gig. A pimp waits in the lobby and then sends Johns up to the girls' rooms. She wasn't sure if the hotel was in on it or not. They are also moving drugs and they have a few motels around town they are running."

"Are Mutari at all of them?" Sean asked.

"I'm not sure yet. I'm sure they are out of the higher end places, but out of the motels, I wouldn't think so."

"And why is that?" Sean asked.

"Succubi walk a line of finding Johns who have a lot of Vis and can pay a decent price," she explained.

"Fine, give me your number in case I need more information," Sean said.

Mandy didn't argue as she wrote down her number on a piece of paper, handing it to him. He didn't say anything to her, going back to what he was working on before. After a few moments Mandy left the office.

The next day Sean didn't say anything about Mandy coming in.

"I got a tip about McLoughlin's group. They are working out of high-end hotels," he announced.

No one questioned where he got his information from, and within an hour Sergeant Montoya was in the conference room.

"Good work, Hughes," Montoya said. "What is your plan?"

Alison spoke. "We are going to set up a team of people to watch the hotel along with Faith."

"I'll be watching for Mutari," Faith said. "With it being a hotel we are watching, it's unreasonable to think that we are going to find any of the Johns, but if we can figure out which Mutari work there, we can hopefully track down the rest of the organization."

Montoya thought for a moment. "That's a good plan. Don't move in on the hotel until we know what's going on, I won't lose a chance at Corey McLoughlin again. The last time we went after this prick we got our dicks in a bind, and the DA won't move on this without concrete evidence…so get some," he said getting up to leave the office.

As they didn't have enough evidence for the DA thus far, Sean and Alison were unable to obtain a warrant for tapping the hotel's phones or to place bugs in the building. To Sean's frustration, they were even denied letting the Mages place any bugs in the hotel.

"Why is the city being so difficult about this?" Gabriel asked.

"We aren't Mages Decor, we have law and order!" Sean spat taking his frustration out on Gabriel.

"Sean!" Alison said sternly. "Cool it." She addressed Gabriel. "If we had a room number or something like that, we might be able to get a warrant. The issue is that if we bug the whole hotel we will be violating a bunch of people's rights. The city won't take a chance on getting into trouble with that. We have to get solid evidence so a judge would be willing to sign a warrant."

ALISON KAUR sat in her car across the street from the hotel they were watching. Next to her sat Faith, reading a book.

"What are you reading?" Alison asked, trying to alleviate her boredom.

"It's a history of the Succubus," Faith said.

"Are there Vis bookstores or something?" Alison wondered.

Faith nodded. "Yep, most are run by Goblins, of course, but we have them."

Alison looked at the book. It was modern-looking like any book she'd read. It was nothing like what movies would have had her believe. Alison peered at the text, noticing it wasn't written in English. "What language is that?"

"Latin; almost all Mages speak it. You could say it's the official language of Vis users - even most Mutari are passable with Latin," Faith said.

"Why is that? Do you need it to use Vis?" Alison asked.

"No…it's not that. We don't need to speak at all when casting a spell; it just helps your mind focus. The more trained you are, the less words you have to speak. For example," she said, holding out her cup of coffee, "Usque." The cup of coffee lifted from her hand with a slight hue of yellow tinting it. "You can see that the cup lifted up like I told it to. That was all I needed to say to focus my mind on lifting something. If I was new at using Vis, I might have to say 'Levare calicem usque' so my mind could lift the cup up. Does that make sense?"

Alison thought for a moment. "It does…it's not the words doing something with the Vis; it's your mind, right?"

"Correct," Faith said brightly.

"OK, but why Latin? It seems like it would be hard to learn how to use Vis and learn a new language at the same time," Alison asked, going back to her original question.

"That's a good question," Faith said. "We learn Latin at the same time we learn whatever the native language is where we live, but generally we only use Latin when using Vis. In this way, when we speak in that language, our mind is used to focusing on Vis. You can use any language you want. For example, Italian is so close to Latin that in Italy, many Mages cast spells in Greek. Since almost all Mages know Latin, most books are printed in it."

Alison was happy to be getting more information about the Vis world.

"So, is that book interesting?" she asked.

Faith shrugged. "Yes and no. It's a history of when the Succubi had their own government. They had a Queen and King, along with a whole system of governing. In their time, they were powerful. They didn't need to work as hookers back in their heyday. In fact, that's when the relationship between Trolls and Succubi came about; the Trolls served Succubi."

"That is interesting," Alison said.

"Troll," Faith said, softly ending their conversation.

Alison focused back on what she needed to and snapped pictures of the Troll as he walked into the hotel.

FAITH PENN finished with a map of the hotel, showing where the Mutari were in it. She was about to hand the map over to Alison when it occurred to her that she didn't know if the Mutari in the building were guilty of any wrongdoing.

"Alison?" she asked.

"What is it?" Alison asked.

"I have a map of where all the Mutari in the hotel are..." she looked at the woman, "is it right for me to do that?"

Alison paused. "How do you mean?"

Faith looked down at the map. "Ya know, they could just be staying at the hotel; we don't know that all of these people are bad guys, right?"

Alison looked thoughtful. "No; it's not right," she finally said. "Can you watch to see if one of the rooms has Humans cycling through it? Maybe in a roundabout way that doesn't affect people's privacy?"

"Yes I can...I know the parts of the building Mutari are in...I can look to see if they stay put but have a lot of visitors," Faith said, feeling slightly better about what they were doing.

How did Humans do this? For Mages, finding a person was simple, you used Vis and found what you needed to. That didn't mean Faith didn't stumble upon the innocent at times, but there weren't stakeouts for Mages. She saw why Humans had their due process, they didn't have Contractors who could read your every emotion and tell if you were lying. Faith wondered how Alison and those like her ever found the truth.

ALISON KAUR sat in her car with a mostly silent Faith.

"How do you do this job, Alison?" Faith asked.

"I know stakeouts are a little dull, but it's not always like this," Alison said.

"No, I mean live this life? With Vis things are so much more black and white for Mages, but for Humans…" Faith asked.

That was easy for her to answer. "I see everything," she said. Then, reading the confusion on Faith's face added, "You're right; we can't use Vis. I had to learn how to read people, and to be honest; to always distrust those I come in contact with. You had to notice when you first met me how much I distrusted you."

Faith nodded. "I did, but I thought that was just because I'm a Mage."

Alison laughed without humor. "I wish it was," she shook her head. "Honestly, you being able to use Vis did make me that much more wary of you at first, but I don't trust anyone. No cop does. We deal with the trash of our society. We're also supposed to protect people, but a lot of times things aren't black and white." Alison was about to share a story about a case she had, but stopped herself. She looked over at the woman next to her and decided that if she wanted Faith and Gabriel to trust her, she had to give them the same respect.

"I had to arrest a lady who killed her husband once…" she started, "he beat her. We had medical records but she never pressed charges on him. Then one day she snapped and killed the guy."

"He had it coming," Faith said.

"Maybe," Alison said. "Everyone who's worked this job has that same story; it runs in movies, books, and TV for so many years that people don't even get affected by stories like that anymore. But when you work a case like that…"

"It changes you, I'm sure," Faith said.

"You don't always know the innocent and the guilty, and sometimes you just get so numb you stop caring and see everyone as scum," the words spilled out. "That must make me sound awful," Alison said.

She went on, "I can't even get a cup of coffee without sizing up everyone in the shop as a threat. We are trained to spot lies and as a result we see just how much the average person lies every day. I can't go on a date without trying to take the guy apart." She shook her head and laughed. "It's like an interrogation," she chuckled, "even when some poor bastard tries to be polite, I can tell that he's just acting."

"That sounds lonely," Faith observed.

Alison looked out her window, feeling tears well up in her eyes. "And the things I've seen…sometimes I don't know what I was thinking picking this job. It's like a curse; on the one hand I tell myself that I'm doing good, but on the other hand, no matter how hard I work there is still more evil in the world." She looked at Faith, breaking. "And what do I have to show for it? I'm a workaholic with no social life; I'm a decade from being the Cat Lady."

"What's a Cat Lady?" Faith asked, confused.

Even though Faith fit in with Humans well, she wasn't one. She would have no idea what a Cat Lady was. Alison started to laugh, at Faith's confusion of the situation, and that she was spilling her guts to someone who five years ago she didn't believe in.

As she laughed, tears ran down her cheeks. "Sorry Faith, I should be able to keep control of myself."

"Don't be ridiculous; everyone has worries and if your social life is as bad as you claim, then you probably don't have a girlfriend to confide in," Faith said.

"That I don't," Alison said. "But really Faith, I apologize. I'm sure you don't want to hear this."

Faith put her hand on Alison's arm. "Don't be sorry Alison; truly. I know what it's like living a stressful life. If I didn't have James, I don't know what I'd do…" Faith looked out the window for a moment and then smiled. "It sounds like you need a night out," Faith said.

Alison shook her head. "Really Faith, I'm fine now; I don't know what came over me."

Faith was obstinate. "Nope, not going to happen. I will pick a night and we will all go out and not talk about the case," Faith said and then added, "You should know Gabriel and I will have no problem kidnapping you and forcing you to have a night on the town," she said, looking sternly at Alison.

Alison wanted to argue, but a small part of her perked up at the idea of a night out where she didn't have to worry about the case. Also, if she was being honest, Faith was becoming a friend; which was something Alison didn't have a lot of.

Alison rolled her eyes. "Fine, now can we get back to work?"

SEAN HUGHES sat in a crap restaurant looking at the seedy hotel across the street from him. Days of surveillance

had produced a fair amount of results. Faith had managed to
identify a handful of pimps and whores. As a result, Sean and
the others were now aware of five locations that were running
girls and drugs. The only thing that was bad was that even after
finding everything they had, they still had no idea where the
group was based.

Sean tensed up, moving away from the restaurant's window.
Corey McLoughlin was making an appearance at the motel.
That was something rare. *What are you up to, Corey?* A few years
back, Sean would have walked up to the man and tried to rattle
his cage. He resisted the urge now. Sean figured with Mutari
guards, he would only be in danger.

Sean's pocket vibrated. He pulled out his cell and read a text
message from Alison telling him the Sergeant wanted to meet.

"Another time," Sean whispered in Corey's direction.

He left the restaurant, being sure to avoid McLoughlin's
view, making it back to his car and the station without being
spotted. Montoya, Alison, and the Mages were already in the
conference room waiting for him.

"Find anything?" Montoya asked.

Sean shrugged. "McLoughlin made an appearance tonight,
but that's about it."

Montoya didn't look happy. "It's been almost a week, people
and we don't have dick! Kaur, any thoughts?"

"Not many, sir. We have enough to justify getting warrants
on the locations that we know of, and a few of the Johns,
but in the grand scheme of things? I'm not sure that's a good
plan," Alison said.

"Decor, Penn, how about you?" Montoya asked.

Gabriel spoke first. "We could bust the locations we have
now. Succubi are very rarely caught. They make it a business

of being careful; arresting them could shake things up a bit."

"That may work; we could hold them for a night and then claim we don't have enough to hold them on and let them go," Faith said.

"Or we could book them and get them to flip on their bosses," Sean said tersely. "I don't think taking a bunch of drug-dealing whores off the street is such a bad thing, but that's just me."

Faith narrowed her gaze on him. "Good plan Sean, and then what happens when the Succubi die from lack of Vis or start a rampage in the jail? Oh yeah, and how do you plan on keeping them and the Trolls behind bars?" she asked coolly.

Sean quavered a bit under her look. "Have Erin give them some of that junk to make them not use Vis."

"That won't work, Sean," Gabriel said calmly. "Remember, in essence it's poison and in the case of the Succubi, it would kill them within a few hours."

"Still, that's just a few less freaks out there," Sean said, his pride not letting him admit defeat.

"Well Hughes, too bad for you we won't be killing random suspects today," Montoya said. "Penn, how would letting them go help?"

Faith looked back at the Sergeant. "This group offered the Succubi protection; if we arrest them they aren't being protected. In most cases, the Succubi will just walk away from the group and not even give them the time of day. However, the Trolls and some of the Succubi will want answers or will want to hide, and the organization will have to do something to keep from losing all their Succubi."

"You think they'd lead us back to their headquarters?" Alison asked.

Faith shook her head. "I doubt they know where it is."

"Then what does that do?" Montoya asked.

Gabriel laughed. "Good thinking, Faith." He turned his attention to Montoya. "They would have to use their Mages to make the Mutari feel safe; that could mean exposing their Paladins to me, or if we are really lucky; their Seeker."

Montoya didn't look convinced. "Would that turn into a fight?"

Gabriel deflated a bit. "Yeah, it probably would."

Montoya smiled. "Gabriel, you are an amazing fighter, but the last time you fought other Mages, the city was picking up cars someone threw at you. Maybe we should give the regular investigation another few days before we make the news again."

Gabriel's face flushed with embarrassment. "Yes, that sounds like a good idea."

"What if we got that Mandy girl to go into the group?" Sean said.

Gabriel didn't look stern but his calm seemed to be phased a bit. "No, I won't ask Mandy to put herself in danger like that," he said.

"Come on, Decor…" Sean started.

"The answer is no, Sean!" Gabriel said firmly.

Sean left the meeting pissed off about the course of action they were taking. He went back to his desk, tapping his pen and thinking. They needed to get someone on the inside. Then he remembered that he had Mandy's phone number. He stood.

"I'm done for the day," he said to the others.

He left the station, pulling out his phone and texting the girl. She responded and he told her to meet him nearby. Sean made sure he was a good distance from the station and right along the border with another county. He heard someone walking and turned to see Mandy approach. Like the last time, Sean didn't hide that he was looking her over.

"What do you need?" Mandy asked timidly.

"You're going to infiltrate that group and find me their headquarters and get me whatever information you can on them," Sean said curtly.

Mandy looked shocked. "I'm sorry Detec-"

Sean cut her off. "You will be sorry if you don't," he said menacingly. He reached in his pocket and took out a listening device. "Look, you just wear this when you aren't screwing people. Save the money you make; it will be evidence."

"And what do I get out of this?" Mandy asked, no longer sounding timid.

Sean laughed. "You get to finally be a help to society. I saw how much cash your friend had, so a few weeks of not getting paid won't hurt you." Sean held up his phone. "By the way, if you're thinking of not taking my offer, there's a friend of mine with Jefferson County just around the corner to take you into holding for a bit…like a week or so…"

"What does Gabriel think of this?" Mandy asked, her face drained of color.

That brought Sean up a little short but he decided he didn't care what Gabriel thought. "This is between us and it will stay that way, got it?"

Sean knew he had her where he wanted her; there was no way she could back out.

"Look," he said, softer, "You aren't going to be in any danger. I know this organization, they aren't going to hurt merchandise and let's face it; you're top shelf as far as whores go. Do this and I won't bother you again, OK?"

Mandy dabbed at her eyes. "Yeah, because I have a lot of choice," she said. "I know where to find them." She held up the recorder. "Did an Enchanter make sure this won't be found?"

"Yep, sure did," Sean lied. "Call me when you get something," he turned around and walked away.

As he walked, he felt a little bad about lying to her about the recorder, but he figured she would be fine. The device was small and he assumed no one would think to look for Human technology. Soon, Sean wasn't thinking about how he'd bullied Mandy into working for him; all that was on his mind was the big fat promotion busting Corey McLoughlin could get him.

TWELVE

MANDY STAFFORD was covered in sweat as she exerted herself. Beneath her, the client moaned slightly. He was in town on business and had wasted no time in finding entertainment for the evening. Mandy was thankful for that. Many of her clients spent a few hours getting tipsy or full out drunk before talking to her pimp about something to do for the night. The man she was on top of now - Ben was his name - was sober. His body wasn't fighting the effects of booze and as a result Mandy could see his body flowing with uninterrupted Vis.

She watched as Ben came closer and closer to finishing, the Vis in his body glowing ever brighter. This was the only thing that made bearable what she was forced to do. As a Succubus, high amounts of Vis captivated her. Her body craved the Vis, but she had to be patient. If she drew it from him now, Ben wouldn't finish and could possibly notice his life force leaving him. Mandy looked down his chest and torso, following the Vis as it collected in his lower body, pulsing with energy. Mandy tapped the Vis she had stored in her body. Her fatigue abated and she didn't feel as worn out.

Ben cried out. His Vis exploded in him, flooding every cell in his body. Mandy leaned forward, locking her lips on his. He kissed her back and she pulled with her abilities. Her lips and mouth tingled with the most wonderful feeling, as Vis left Ben and went into her. Her body warmed and flushed as it accepted the Vis, her muscles tensing with power. She wanted so desperately to drain him of power, to take ever last bit of it, but she didn't. It was a fight she and every Succubus had each time they took Vis from someone. The more she took, the stronger the urge to take more was. Mandy lifted herself, wiping lipstick from his mouth with her thumb.

"How was that, baby?" she asked, slipping into her role.

He closed his eyes, breathing hard. "You're amazing; you know that?"

Mandy giggled, hating the act. "How long are you in town?" she said, rolling off him.

He looked over at her in wonderment. "I leave in the morning," he said.

She made a pouty face.

He leaned over and kissed her again. This time she didn't pull Vis from him. "Well, it was fun, but I need to get to bed."

She watched Ben get dressed and leave her room. It was an odd sort of feeling, not being the one who collected the money. Mandy's face lost the look of a happy, love-struck girl and relaxed into no longer having to act for anyone. She got out of the bed, stripping the sheets. The group she was with had an arrangement with the hotel, meaning that Mandy had a closet full of sheets for the bed. She swapped out the sheets, remaking the bed. *That was number four for the day, so I'm done,* she thought.

Her phone buzzed on the nightstand. It was a text from the Troll in the lobby. "Are you ready for another?" he asked.

Mandy typed a quick response, saying she was done for the night. He tried to convince her to take one more client, but she said she couldn't take on any extra Vis for the evening. For a normal pimp, she suspected saying no wouldn't work, but the Troll said he understood and left her alone.

Still undressed, she walked into the bathroom and turned on the shower. She could smell Ben on her and wanted to be washed clean. She stepped under the water, scrubbing her body, though no matter how much she scrubbed, she never felt clean. In her head, she catalogued the last few days she'd been with the new group. She knew the crew of Trolls they used and even knew a lot of the Succubi as well. She was compiling a mental list of names and faces. She'd met a few other Mutari. Even in a few days, the others had a respect for her; she was one of the oldest and most experienced Succubi on the crew. Most of the girls weren't even twenty yet, even though they looked to be in their early twenties.

This was what happened to Succubi without enough Vis. They aged quickly. Mandy worked with the young girls, teaching them how to wait for a John to be at the peak of Vis production before taking it from him, and how to best use the Vis they had. Some of the girls were picking it up and she was happy to see their youth coming back to them. Mandy kept herself in her mid-twenties, matching her current age. She found it gave her an edge with clients who wanted someone young, but not someone inexperienced.

Now that she was done hooking for the night, she turned her attention to what her real purpose was. And that was finding out information for Detective Hughes. Just thinking of him made her face flush with anger. He wasn't literally holding a gun to her head, but it was there. If she were left in jail for a week like he'd promised, she would run out of Vis. When that happened, Mandy would get sick and die within a few days, or go on a killing rampage, draining other inmates. If the latter happened, Mages would come for her. *Don't think about that Mandy; just get him what he wants and then see if Gabriel can get you into another state.*

It didn't take Mandy long to make friends with a girl named Leslie and ask more about the group she was in. She found out they called themselves Trinity. Leslie said that it was a combination of Mutari, Mages, and Humans.

"How did you find out all this?" Mandy asked.

Leslie brushed her long blond hair behind an ear. "I gave one of the Mages a freebie once and he told me a bunch of stuff," she said.

"Really? Who was he?" Mandy asked.

"His name is Keith. He's come back to me a few times, but he's a real jerk." She shrugged. "But he always makes sure my disease wards are fully charged, so I'm not going to complain."

"Do you give a lot of the staff freebies?" Mandy asked.

Leslie looked down. "Yeah I guess so…they say I need the practice…"

Mandy resisted getting angry. "Do they ask that of a lot of the girls?"

Leslie looked up. "Yeah; I'm sure at some point you'll get asked too, but I seem to be asked a lot."

"Well at least Mutari are good for Vis," Mandy pointed out.

"They say I'm not allowed to take Vis from them so they don't become weak."

Mandy looked at her, anger flaring. "What!? Leslie, you do not work for free; they are paid to protect you. If some Mutari wants you to do something to them, they pay with Vis."

Leslie looked worried. "Come on Mandy, I'm not going to do that…you heard on the news about that Hannah Davis they found dead, right? She was a Succubus and worked here; I knew her."

"I knew Hannah, she was a friend of mine," Mandy said. "I doubt that she was killed for not putting out. Trinity isn't going to risk losing money by killing a Succubus." Mandy changed the subject. "So, where do you live?"

"Oh, I live with some of the other girls. Trinity provides places for us to live if we don't have a place of our own. There are some Human girls there too, are you looking for a place to stay?" she asked.

Mandy was about to say no when a thought came to her. *If I can find someplace they are using to keep people, I might be able to get Sean what he needs and get him off my back.* "You know what, I am looking for a place; my lease runs out soon. Would you mind showing me where you live?"

Leslie smiled and Mandy felt her heart drop. She was putting this girl in danger by having her lead her to where the group's command could be, but she had to get Sean what he needed. Mandy told herself that she would take Leslie from Trinity when she left. The girl was clueless to how the Vis world worked.

Mandy went with Leslie to where she lived. The building wasn't all that different from the one Mandy had seen on the news that Gabriel had taken out. The difference being that this one was far larger and at one point in time had been an apartment building. Mandy tapped her Vis reserves, heightening her senses. Naturally she was able to read Vis flow and could tell if someone was a Mutari, Human or Mage. Mandy, like most experienced Succubi, could even tell what type of Mutari someone was.

A man sat playing on his phone on the front steps. Mandy could see Vis radiating from his heart to the rest of his body. This only occurred in Wolves and Vampires. *Wolf* she thought, reading the flow. A woman walked out of the building, passing the Wolf without a second glance. Her liver shone bright. *Goblin*. Mandy and Leslie passed the Wolf without comment, entering the building. The entry hall was dirty and old. At least ten doors lined the hallway, and at the end was a staircase. A few people walked in and out of the rooms. None of them had excess Vis flowing from just one organ, meaning they weren't Vampires, Werewolves, or Goblins. Most of them were other Succubi with a few Trolls scattered about. She even noticed a Banshee and…

"Is that an Elemental?" Mandy asked Leslie softly.

Leslie glanced over to where the Elemental stood talking to a Succubus. Leslie giggled. "Yep, we even get a few vamps here," she said.

Mandy looked at her. "Are people working here?"

Leslie shook her head. "Not really; upstairs and in the basement they do some stuff, but this is just a meeting spot for Trinity. Come on, let me show you around."

Mandy didn't feel comfortable at all in the building. It wasn't being around so many other Mutari so much, but rather the diversity and that all of them were likely engaged in illegal activity. What Sean was looking into was far bigger than Sean had let on to her. Mandy had only seen one Elemental in her life; they were among the rarest of Mutari.

Mandy tried to remember names as Leslie took her around the building. She chatted with a few of the people, some of them even being Human; though they seemed subdued somehow. They ended up going to the top floor where Mandy met a man in his forties with a scruffy goatee.

"The name's Corey; who are you?" he asked.

"Mandy," she said, shaking his outstretched hand. "It's good to meet you."

"No; the honor is all mine. From what I've been told, you've been quite an asset in just the few days you've been with us. For some reason, most of the seasoned Succubi in the city aren't willing to work with us. Do you know why that might be?" Corey asked.

He looked like he was honestly curious, so Mandy decided to answer him honestly. "Most of us keep a fine balance with our Troll protectors; it's been this way for years."

He smirked. "Yeah, since the Succubi kingdom fell in the thirteen hundreds, right?"

Mandy's mouth fell open and Leslie spoke. "We had a kingdom?"

Mandy snapped her head to look at Leslie. "Yes; didn't you know that?" she was horrified that one of her kind didn't even know her own people's history.

"Yep, you sure did," Corey said. "It was the Vampires that brought it down, wasn't it?"

Mandy was impressed. Corey was obviously scum but he at least took the time to understand people. "Yes, that is why there has been a division between our races ever since. I suspect that's why I don't see any here tonight," Mandy noted.

Corey's phone beeped and he looked at it before responding. "That's correct; you lot don't seem to mix well together," he seemed distracted and then returned back to normal. He added, "Well, if you decide to stay here, be sure to let us know." He handed her a card. "And by all means, if you ever need anything; just ask," he said, glancing up and down her body.

Mandy could tell that he wanted to do a lot more than help her. She made a mental note of that. If she needed to, she could exploit his desire at a later time.

"Isn't this place great?" Leslie gushed.

Mandy tried not to roll her eyes. "Yeah, it is," she lied.

As she looked around the room, she could see drugs and guns lying out in the open. The people running this place weren't even remotely concerned about anyone finding out what they were up to.

Leslie noticed her gaze and nudged her. "Ya know, if you want to make a little more, you can sell the clients stuff."

Mandy looked from the drugs to the girl. "I don't sell drugs, Leslie."

"Why not? You don't have to use them and it makes the clients happy. Plus, you can sell them more than drugs…geez."

"Like what?" Mandy asked, glossing over Leslie talking about 'making the clients happy'.

She shrugged. "You name it really, but mostly guns. I don't sell them, but if someone says something about wanting one, I just tell the Troll in the lobby and they take care of them. They take care of anything they need and we get a cut of it. You'd be amazed at how many Humans want magical objects."

"Vis," Mandy said.

"What?" Leslie asked.

"Vis objects; not magical."

"Same difference," Leslie said. "Anyway, if you want to move more stuff just ask a Goblin and he'll fill you in."

ALISON KAUR smiled at herself in the mirror. She was in the ladies' room at the station, Faith next to her dabbing at her makeup.

"This is going to be so much fun, Alison," Faith gushed.

Alison smiled despite herself. "I think it will be," she said.

As Faith had promised, they were going to have a social night. They were going to a sports bar downtown and Alison was looking forward to a night off the case.

"So what do you want me to be?" Faith asked.

Alison looked at her, confused. Faith looked at her like she was a moron.

"What do you mean?" Alison asked.

Faith shook her head, rolling her eyes. She put an arm around Alison. "As your wingman, what do you want me to be? I can be the dumb girl, the mean girl, the flirt…Ya know, whatever you think will help you seal the deal."

"Wingman? Are we going to be fighting someone tonight?" Alison said, trying to avoid the subject with humor.

It didn't work. "No Alison, tonight you are to have a good time. Additionally, if there is anyone at the bar not married who is to your liking, we are going to get you some action," Faith said, beaming.

Alison blushed. "I don't need action, Faith…"

Faith laughed. "We all need action, Alison, and since I watch your house and no one comes by…I'm going to go out on a ledge and say it's been a while."

Alison sputtered. It had been a while since she'd even been on a date.

"Don't worry," Faith said, taking her hand. "It's like a bike; once you get back on you'll know what you're doing." She winked.

"Faith!" Alison said blushing deeper.

"Fine! Fine!" Faith said. "If you're that concerned, you're gonna suck then we'll just have to get him drunk."

"Faith, I don't suck," she blurted, and then embarrassed added, "Not that I have too much experience...I mean, I've just been told. Oh, you know what, it's none of your business," Alison said, trying not to sound too embarrassed. Faith just chuckled.

Faith hooked her arm in Alison's. "Come on, let's go," she said dragging Alison from the bathroom and into the hall.

They were met by Gabriel who was just in a pair of jeans and button up shirt. Alison really hadn't noticed it before, but Gabriel was pretty cute when he wasn't in the overcoat. Erin was also present in a polka dot dress. Next to her was a hulking man who had to be over six foot and all muscle. He had wavy hair and a short beard. If it weren't for the big smile he wore, he'd have been very intimidating.

"Alison," Erin said. "This is Guy, my husband." She pointed to the man.

He reached forward to shake her hand. Alison thought her hand was going to vanish in his. His blue eyes were friendly as he spoke, "It's so good to meet you, Erin talks about you all the time."

"Good to meet you too," Alison said.

Also present were James and Heidi.

Sean joined them a moment later. "Are we ready to go?"

"Yep, is the Sarge coming?" Alison asked.

"Nah," Sean said.

They left the station and made their way to the bar.

Alison knew the place well; it was often frequented by cops and she knew the barkeep. It was loud when they entered, and Alison felt herself relax for some reason. Big screens showed sporting events from around the world with pool tables in some places and a few poker tables scattered about.

"I thought you couldn't gamble in Denver?" Gabriel asked.

"You can't open a casino in Denver, but people will do whatever they want. The people playing cards don't have to play with money, but still most do." she explained.

They made their way to the bar. Faith ordered for Alison, insisting she wasn't going to drink anything boring. The Mages all got drinks and sipped at them. Erin was watching the poker tables.

"Do you play?" Sean asked her.

Alison knew the look he had on his face and she didn't like it.

"Oh no, Mages don't play...what is it?" Erin asked embarrassed.

"It's fun and it's called poker. Come on, I know the people at that table - we'll teach you," Sean said with fake warmth.

Erin let herself be led off to the table, smiling brightly.

Alison made to go after them but stopped at Faith's touch.

"Faith, you can't let her go; Sean's a shark and so are all the guys over there. They'll take her money!" Alison said.

Guy clapped a hand on Alison's shoulder, turning her back to the bar. "Just so long as she has fun," he said.

Alison watched as Erin listened to the men at the table and lost a few hands. She turned away, telling herself she'd make Sean give Erin back the money tomorrow.

No one approached them, which was just fine with Alison, and she found that she loved all of the Mages. They joked with each other just like a regular family. Gabriel was more goofy than normal and she found that the quiet Heidi was hilarious.

"Interior design, really?" Alison questioned Guy.

He nodded his head, taking a deep pull on his drink. "Yep, it's a passion of mine. Alison, I've seen pictures of your condo and I really wouldn't mind doing your drapes. I'm telling you, new drapes will bring that place together."

"I don't know what's wrong with the ones I have now," she jabbed.

Guy acted appalled. "What isn't?"

She just laughed. "How are none of you drunk?" she asked.

"We use Vis," Faith said.

It had been a few hours and Alison had forgotten about Erin. Worried, she looked for the girl and saw her at the table. Sean was still there, but a few of the original people had been replaced. Erin looked ecstatic, and to Alison's amazement, she had a stack of cash in front of her. Sean looked worried as did a few of the others.

Alison turned at Guy's deep laugh. "Sorry about lying to you earlier Allison, but I was worried you were going to stop her from playing."

"She's cleaning them out!" Alison said.

"Oh yeah," Gabriel said. "Just wait until she plays pool."

"Seriously," Heidi said adding, "I bet she walks out of here with ten grand tonight."

"Bu-but but," Alison sputtered.

"You thought they were going to take advantage of her didn't you?" Gabriel asked.

"Well yeah…"

Gabriel laughed. "Erin may seem all sweet and nice but she's a diehard gambler. We only let her go out and play a few times a year." He laughed again.

Alison watched as Erin played, acting like a flake. But now that Alison was paying attention, she could see the girl getting the guys loaded. Then to her amazement, when Erin went to the pool table, she unbuttoned the top few buttons of her blouse.

Alison joined the Mages laughing. "Tonight was worth it just to watch Sean lose a week's pay."

An hour later, Erin came bouncing back to them with a wad of cash. She lay some on the counter. "Will this cover our tab?"

"Sure will," the barkeep said.

She took a drink of Guy's beer and hopped up on a stool. "So, Faith tells me we are getting you a boy tonight."

Alison turned red. "Um yeah, no we aren't," she said, uncomfortable.

Erin ignored her and pointed to a guy sitting with his friends having some dinner. "How about him? He's hot."

Alison wasn't sure who she was talking to; Erin never acted this way.

"Ah yeah, I guess so," Alison said.

"Great!" Faith said. "Target acquired! There's three other guys with him. HEIDI!" she called. "We've got some work to do!"

Alison was dragged to the table, the whole while being told not to worry; that Heidi would make sure the guy's emotions were compliant. Alison got lucky, the guys were from out of town so she was able to keep from any real awkwardness, and she had to admit that she had fun.

They left the bar without Sean. He'd tucked his tail between his legs in defeat not long after Erin took his money in poker. They walked back to the station where their cars were.

"I need a cab," Alison said.

Erin bounced up next to her, placing her hand on her chest. Alison saw a glow of pink and then she felt clear-headed.

"Now you don't," Erin said as she counted her money.

"Thanks…"

"So baby, how much did you get?" Guy asked.

Erin grinned. "I won enough for that cruise and then some!"

Gabriel laughed, shaking his head.

"So Alison, are ya gonna hang out with us again?" Heidi asked.

"You better believe it," Alison said without hesitation.

MANDY STAFFORD dialed Detective Hughes' number. After a few rings he answered. "What do you need? It's late," he demanded.

Mandy thought he sounded tipsy but wasn't positive. "I have everything you need on the group. I met some guy named Corey tonight; I think he's running the show."

It was quiet on the other end. "Are you there?" Mandy asked.

"What did you see?" Sean asked.

Mandy told Sean about everything she'd seen and been told.

"Look, I won't be able to do this much longer; they'll figure me out," Mandy said, worried.

"Have you been wearing the wire?" Sean asked.

She hadn't been. "No I haven't; it's kind of hard to do when you aren't wearing clothes."

"A jury isn't going to take the testimony of a whore; you need to wear the wire," he said.

Mandy gritted her teeth; she was getting tired of being called a whore. "I can-"

"You can and you will!" he said angrily. "Call me when you have real evidence." Then he hung up.

Mandy put her phone in her purse, trying to control her temper. She was in a gas station bathroom about a mile away from Trinity's safe house. Mandy went out to her car and got the bag with the wire in it. She clipped it to her underwear, wrapping the cord for the mic up her body and under her bra. *Fine, just get Corey to spill his guts,* she thought. She could do that.

Mandy made her way back to the safe house. She paused when she got there, seeing a black conversion van outside. The doors opened and a few girls lead of out of it, being pulled by their hair around the back of the building. Mandy used her ability to see if the girls were Mutari. They weren't, but the two men pulling them along were Trolls. *Dammit. I thought those Human girls didn't seem right.* Mandy figured the girls were being forced into being hookers. It wasn't the first time she had seen that. She pushed the girls from her mind, telling herself that if Sean was able to make a bust, they'd be freed.

Mandy walked up to the building, this time the guy sitting on the steps stood up, giving her a stern look.

"I work for Trinity," Mandy said simply. "You saw me a few hours ago…"

"Mandy!" a voice called.

Mandy cringed as Leslie bounded down the steps toward her.

"She's with us," Leslie said, leading Mandy inside.

This wasn't good; she didn't really want Leslie to be seen with her. Not while she wore a wire. At least Sean said it was enchanted, so Mandy shouldn't be found out.

"Is Corey in?" Mandy asked Leslie.

"Yeah he is, why?"

"I just wanted to talk to him...ya know about getting a place," Mandy lied.

"OK," she said taking her upstairs.

When they got to the top level, Corey wasn't alone. There was a man in the room with him. Mandy's gut clinched as she read his Vis; he was a Mage. He was blond with a haughty expression. He smiled at Leslie.

"Mandy," Corey said warmly. "This is Keith Spencer, one of our Paladins," Corey explained.

One? Mandy fought her fear at knowing Trinity had more than one Paladin.

"Good to meet you," Mandy said to the man, who only grunted.

"Come on, Leslie," he said, taking her hand.

Leslie's face flushed and Mandy figured she saw it a privilege to service a Mage.

Once Keith and Leslie were gone, Mandy sat down across from Corey.

"What can I do for you?" he asked.

"I was thinking of moving in and maybe getting a little more involved with things," Mandy said.

"Oh yeah, how so?" Corey asked.

"Well," she said trying to sound a little uneasy, a tone that was all too easy to do with a Mage in the building. "I saw the drugs and I've heard from some of the girls that some enchanted objects are being sold...I can't be a hooker forever and..."

"You want a retirement," Corey said sagely.

"That's what I like about Succubi. Most of the Human girls we get don't think long term; they are just in it for some dope or maybe a few bucks. Sure, we have a few smart ones but not many. You Succubi however," he indicated toward her and continued, "you think in the long term and I like that." He took a sip of something. "Yeah, we can do that for you; you don't need to ask. The Troll in the lobby of the hotels you're working should have already told you that, but you are new so he probably didn't get around to it yet."

"Right, so what do I need to do for that?" Mandy asked.

Corey was about to speak when the door to the room opened. A woman walked in wearing a white coat that matched Keith's. That coupled with her Vis flow and Mandy knew the woman was a Mage who worked with Keith. She was in her late thirties with her blond hair pulled back into a ponytail. She was very pretty. Her brown eyes focused on Mandy and then back to Corey.

"Someone here has some sort of recording device," the woman said. "I thought you told your girls not to bring in tape recorders?"

Corey looked surprised. "I do…where is it coming from?"

Mandy's blood ran cold; the woman was a Seeker.

The woman closed her eyes and to Mandy's horror, her shirt glowed red in a line with the wire. Both Corey and the woman's faces snapped to where Mandy sat.

THIRTEEN

MANDY STAFFORD felt her heart stop for a moment as the Seeker and Corey looked at her. In the next moment, the Seeker turned to call for a Paladin. Mandy tapped the Vis she'd stored up in her body, pulling on her reserve harder than she ever had. She stood from the chair she was in and sprinted for the window. They were on the third story but that shouldn't matter with the Vis she was using.

Mandy dove at the window, ripping the curtains and breaking the glass. The August night air was hot as she fell from the building. Time moved in slow motion for her as she tucked herself into a ball, flipping in the air. Her feet hit the pavement first, but she lost her balance and toppled over. She rolled four or five times before standing up and sprinting. She needed to contact Sean. That was her only chance at surviving the night.

It was past midnight but a few people still walked the street. They cried out as Mandy blew past them. She made it a few blocks in mere moments but she was in trouble, she could feel her Vis reserve being quickly depleted. She ran into an alley, diving into a dumpster and closing the lid over herself. She rummaged in her purse, which she had managed to keep. She found an amulet inside. It looked like a throwing star. Mandy drove one of the sharp points into her leg, feeling her skin stretch. She relaxed her Vis and stabbed herself again. This time without Vis helping her body, the metal pierced her with ease. Mandy tried to keep from yelping in pain. Instantly, she felt Vis leave her body as the amulet pulled power from her, holding the Seeker at bay.

With her other hand she pulled out her phone and dialed Detective Hughes.

"What do you want?" he said groggily.

"You need to get me - I've been found out," she pled in a whisper and then worried that he wouldn't help her she added, "If they catch me they'll find out you're on to them…"

She hoped that would get his attention.

It seemed to as he quickly said, "Where are you?"

She went into her phone's map app and sent Sean her location.

"Got it, I'll be there as fast as I can," he said urgently.

"Bring the Mages," she said but Sean had already hung up the phone.

Mandy sat back in the filth filling the dumpster, praying that no one would find her. She knew the amulet wouldn't hold off a Mage for long but hopefully Sean would have Gabriel with him.

* * * * *

Sean Hughes raced down the street in his car, ignoring stoplights at this late hour. He looked at his phone, seeing that he was right near where Mandy was supposed to be. He came to a stop by an alley. He got out of the car and ran down it.

"Mandy!" he yelled.

A dumpster opened to his right and Sean went for his gun. Mandy came tumbling out of the dumpster covered in sweat, blood oozing down her leg, her makeup running in streaks from tears. Sean grabbed her hand. "Come on!"

"I don't think so," a voice said.

Sean turned in time to see a man with a slight green glow swat at him. Sean's side exploded in pain as the Troll hit him. He felt himself lift from the ground and fly back as Mandy screamed. He hit the asphalt hard, rolling to avoid a foot as the Troll kicked at him. Sean rolled again, grabbing his gun. He lifted it at the Troll; BAP BAP BAP! He fired three rounds, hitting the Troll's chest and gut. The Troll backed away grunting in pain, his shirt crimson, but Sean could tell he was only hurt.

Sean tried to get up, the stabs of pain in his side almost dropping him back to the ground. He gritted his teeth and swore. Mandy was at his side, trying to lift him. Despite his opinion of what Mandy was, years of training and conditioning kicked in.

He batted her hands away. "GET OUT OF HERE; I'LL HOLD IT OFF!"

"I'm not leaving you; you can't hold a Troll," she said.

"Mandy!" he shouted.

She spun, avoiding the Troll's hand. Mandy crouched down and grabbed a brick. She lunged forward in a blur. There was a crack as the brick broke and the Troll flew back, holding its face.

"Come on - I don't have enough Vis to do that again!" she said lifting him.

Sean watched as the beast came at them again. Behind him a man covered in fur was growling and next to him was yet another Troll. They were going to die.

The Troll swung a fist at Sean's head. He didn't close his eyes; he would meet death looking it in the eye. The air around them flashed yellow. The Troll backed away in shock. A figure in a dressing gown and black overcoat landed in front of him and Mandy.

Faith threw her hands out to the side, a yellow crystal ball pulsing in front of her right hand. "IGNIS!" Three balls of energy left the crystal ball, streaking toward the Trolls and Wolf. There was a concussion as the balls exploded and Sean felt a flash of intense heat. Faith turned back to them, coming in close to wrap her arms around both himself and Mandy. There was another flash of yellow and then Sean collapsed onto soft carpet.

His head was fuzzy and he looked around, wondering if he was dreaming. He was in a small room with two beds. Mandy sat on one looking tired. Sean tried to get up and winced.

"Are you injured?" Faith asked concerned.

"I'm fine," he started.

She ignored what he said and knelt down next to him placing her hand on his side.

"Ahh," he groaned.

"Fine, huh?" she asked sardonically.

She muttered something and his side glowed yellow. Instantly the pain in his ribs vanished.

"They were broken; I'd hardly call that fine. What happened?" she demanded.

"I called him for help," Mandy said. "I was found out by a Seeker and Sean came to save me…"

"What?" Faith asked in shock. "Why would a Seeker be looking for you?"

"I had her undercover getting info on McLoughlin," Sean said, standing.

Faith snapped her head to look at him, her eyes flint. "You sent her to do what? What part about Gabriel telling you Mandy wasn't to be put in harm's way confused you? And why did you come without backup? Did you want to get killed?"

"Keep your panties on, Penn-" he started to say.

"Keep my panties on!" she bellowed. "You could have both been killed, don't you get that!?" she rounded on Mandy. "What would make you of all people do something this stupid?"

Mandy looked at Sean, anger in her eyes. Sean made to stop her, but Faith held up her hand.

"He made me," Mandy said. "He said that if I didn't do it, or if I told Gabriel or you, that he would make sure I got arrested in another county so that you guys couldn't find out. He told me to wear a wire and he said that you guys had enchanted it so a Mage couldn't find it." Mandy's eyes filled with angry tears. "And now there is a Seeker after me."

"Look..." Sean started again.

"You threatened to kill her?" Faith asked in a deadly whisper. "Think wisely about how you answer Sean Hughes; I know Mandy isn't lying to me."

"She wouldn't really die..."

"Yes, actually she would have, or other inmates would have," Faith spat. "Gabriel will be here soon," she said and then to Mandy, "how much Vis do you have left?"

Mandy looked thoughtful. "I have about a day before I start getting sick."

Sean felt his gut clench; Mandy was telling the truth. If he'd locked her up, she would have gotten sick. His disorientation was starting to wane. "We need to go back there and round up those people," he said.

Faith eyed him again. "No Sean; we are going to wait for Gabriel. Once he's here, we will ask Mandy about everything she saw, so we don't go half-cocked into combat."

Sean wanted to argue with her but chose not to. A moment later, Gabriel came in the room.

"What happened?" he asked, looking at Mandy.

Faith filled Decor in. His normally kind face turned to Sean, his eyes cold as ice.

"I did what I had to do!" Sean blurted without thinking.

Sean stepped forward and stopped as the cold sharp edge of Iram rested against his neck. Gabriel had drawn it so fast, Sean hadn't even seen it.

"I should kill you," Gabriel said calmly. "Pactum or not; I should kill you, Sean Hughes."

Sean's heart raced, he could see that Gabriel was considering it. "You really want to go to jail for killing a cop, Decor?" Sean asked with more authority than he felt.

Gabriel laughed once without humor. "Do you really think I would ever even stand trial? Do you think any Mage would contract with your department to hunt me down?"

Sean felt sweat roll down his forehead. Gabriel was right. He was a legend in the Vis world, he would lose his Pactum with the city, but that would be it. Gabriel removed the blade from Sean's throat and sheathed it. He glanced at Faith, who looked just as angry as Gabriel was. Finally, Gabriel's gaze rested on Mandy.

"Forgive me, Mandy; tonight must have been horrible for you," Gabriel said.

Sean knew in that moment that Mandy's presence had saved his life. He figured the only reason Gabriel hadn't just killed him was because he didn't want the girl to have to witness or deal with anything else.

"Tell me about the Seeker," Gabriel said calmly.

Mandy described the Seeker and Sean listened silently. Gabriel and Faith both tensed. Gabriel pulled a folded picture from his pocket, handing it to Mandy.

"Was this the woman you saw?" he asked, still calm.

Mandy looked at the picture for only a moment. "Yeah, that's her! Who is she?"

Gabriel clenched his hands into fists and Faith blanched.

"Her name is Angelica Vies. She's the wife and Seeker of Marcus Vies," he said.

The name rang a bell with Sean but he wasn't sure from where. Mandy must have known the name because she paled. "The Vies'? No, no, no, no, no not them, no not them!" Mandy became hysterical.

"What is it?!" Sean asked, starting to worry.

Mandy locked eyes with him, terrified tears running down her face. "YOU KILLED ME! YOU KILLED ME! YOU BASTARD, YOU KILLED ME!" she screamed.

"What are you talking about?" he asked, backing away from the girl.

"You sent me into that horrid place and now I'm being hunted by an Ark Seeker!" she wailed.

Sean looked at Gabriel, who was looking at the wall with a rage-filled expression. Gabriel was an Ark Sean knew this but he didn't know what was going on; the Arches were supposed to be the good guys.

"Decor?" Sean asked.

Gabriel looked at him. "Marcus Vies was my former captain; he betrayed the Arches and killed my last Seeker and cousin, Patrick Decor. He defeated me ten years ago and I have been looking for him ever since."

Sean couldn't wrap his head around what he was hearing. Gabriel had been defeated ten years ago? And his cousin and old Seeker was killed?

Faith winced.

"What is it?" Sean asked.

"She's looking for her," Faith said. "I can hold her for now…"

Faith looked concerned.

Gabriel's face softened. "You can beat her Faith; I know you can."

Faith spun. "No Gabriel, I can't! I'm no Ark! I'm not Patrick! I'm not Mom! I won't be able to leave Mandy's side if I want to keep Angelica at bay; never mind the fact that I will have to keep her off of Sean and Alison now!"

Gabriel looked down. "How long will the wards here hold?" he asked.

Faith thought for a moment. "Not long; not without me here, but back at the house we would be fine."

Gabriel nodded. "But only if you were there, hmmmmm."

"What do we do?" Faith asked.

"There's no chance of being discovered right now?" Gabriel confirmed.

Faith shook her head.

"Very well, I will see if our parents would like a house guest." And with that he left the room.

ALISON KAUR woke with a jerk. Someone was pounding on her front door, calling her name. She recognized Gabriel's voice. She stumbled her way to the door and opened it.

Gabriel stood in the doorway, tense and in his overcoat. Alison instantly perked up.

"We need to go," he said.

She didn't question him but let him in her condo. "OK, let me put on some clothes. Do you want to tell me what's going on?" she stopped and watched as Gabriel took her phone charger from the wall and started packing up her laptop.

He turned to her. "Pack a bag; we are taking you and Sean into protective custody for at least a few days."

"What? I'm not going into protection! Gabriel, what is going on?" she demanded.

Gabriel stopped packing and looked at her seriously. "Alison, please, you are in danger and I cannot protect you here anymore, Sean has kicked a hornet's nest. We have him and Mandy in a safe house; I need to get you there so that Faith and I can come up with a plan. Now please trust me and pack a bag."

Alison decided not to question him and went into her room, changing and tossing a few things in a luggage bag. When she came back out, Gabriel was looking out her window.

"What is it?" she asked.

"Vampires," he said, "two of them. Trinity moved faster than I thought they would."

Alison felt an involuntary twinge of fear at the word Vampire. Gabriel had his hand resting on Iram's grip. "Is there anything in here you don't want found?"

Alison thought for a moment. "Yes, there is."

He nodded. "Grab it if you can; I will do what I can to protect your place from Trinity."

Alison went to a firebox under her bed and grabbed it and brought it with her. Her living room was alight with Vis. Strands of purple Vis clung to ceiling, wall and floor. Objects in the room glowed and little balls of fire popped in and out of existence. The whole time, Gabriel stood with his eyes closed muttering in Latin. Finally, he stopped.

"That is the best I can do for now," he said, walking over and taking her hand.

"Are you going to have to fight them?" she asked.

"No, we are jumping to the safe house."

Before Alison could ask what jumping was, she saw a flash of lavender. When the light subsided, she was standing in front of a dingy wooden door in an even dingier hallway. Gabriel opened the door and she walked in.

Faith was there, along with Mandy and Sean. There were two other people in the room Alison didn't know. A woman with long auburn hair turned and greeted Gabriel with a hug. "Your father and I came as soon as we got your message." she said. *So these are Faith and Gabriel's parents. Something big must be going on.*

Alison stepped forward, extending her hand to the woman. She took Alison's hand in a firm yet still soft grip. She was stunningly beautiful and Alison could see where Faith got her looks from. "Alison Kaur," Alison said.

"Melinda Decor," the woman said, her brown eyes warm and kind. "This is my husband Edward," she indicated the man next to her.

He was a bit shorter than Gabriel, with the same dark hair and eyes, but both only looked to be in their forties at the oldest. Edward shook her hand. "A pleasure," he said. Alison noticed the pummel of a sword glint from Edward's belt and she knew instantly what his job was. *So being a Paladin is a family thing,* she thought.

"Excuse us," Melinda said politely and Alison followed her gaze to where Sean and Mandy were sitting on a bed.

Alison was surprised she didn't resist the courteous dismissal Melinda had given her. She went and sat next to Sean. "What did you do?" she accused.

Sean's face hardened and he explained the string of stupid decisions he'd made over the last few days. Alison was irate. "Why would you do something like that?"

"He's a moron; that's why," Mandy gave him a dirty look and then added, "What? Are you going to arrest me for accosting an officer? Go for it; better to die starving of Vis in jail than die being tortured by Trinity."

Alison placed her hand on Mandy's knee. "Mandy, I'm so sorry," she said.

Mandy sniffed. "It's not your fault Detective; you didn't do anything."

Sean made no move to defend himself.

"What are they talking about?" Alison asked Mandy.

Mandy looked at the three Mages in a calm but tense discussion.

"I don't know. I'm low on Vis so I can't improve my ears but I would say they are talking about what to do about Angelica," Mandy explained.

"Will she be that big of problem?" Alison asked.

Mandy looked at her like she was an idiot.

"OK, what can you tell me then," Alison asked.

Mandy gestured to the Mages. "You need to know more about the Vis world. The Decor family is known for many things but two of those are that they produce high quality Seekers and Paladins." She pointed at Edward. "Edward is a top-rate Paladin; he's no Ark but he trained several of them, including Marcus Vies. Melinda is a world class Seeker; she is up to Ark standards and trained Angelica Vies. During the war years ago, Marcus was the Captain of the Arches; his wife Angelica by virtue of being Marcus' Seeker, was in charge of the Ark Seekers. Marcus and Angelica betrayed the Arches in the last battle of the war. Marcus turned on his second in command killing him and then managed to kill Gabriel's Seeker, who was his cousin Patrick Decor before defeating Gabriel."

Alison was shocked. The thought of anybody even being able to hurt Gabriel seemed impossible; let alone defeat him. "So why didn't he kill him?" Alison asked.

"Marcus was badly wounded and the other Arches were coming to assist Gabriel, or at least that's what I've been told. I wasn't there," Mandy said.

"So their parents taught them. Is that why they are here then?" Alison asked.

Mandy shook her head. "No. You see, Mages run the Vis world. It doesn't matter what Goblins or Trolls tell you, Mages run things and those Mages are essentially ruled by powerful families. Edward Decor is the head of the family and Gabriel is the heir to the Decor family."

"Like royals?" Alison verified.

Mandy looked unsure. "No, not like that. They are very wealthy and powerful. They have many Mutari that have sworn loyalty to their family generations ago. Also, all of the families' cousins or branch families, as they are called, answer to the head family. It's like a clan. The branch families will pay a tribute to the head family and do whatever they are told."

"Wow," Alison said. "They sound like the Rockefellers or Vanderbilts."

"That's a good comparison. Though families like those in America still have a lot of money and a little power, the Vis world's large families have a lot of control. Mages have never had a formal government; each family acts of its own accord," Mandy said.

Alison jumped as Gabriel cleared his throat.

"Sorry…" Alison said.

Faith made a face. "Why? For asking how our world works? Don't be; you need to know as it will affect you now."

"What's going on, Gabriel?" Alison asked, taking a business tone.

He sighed. "We have been looking for the Vies for ten years now, and tonight is the best lead we've gotten. The problem is we don't know if Angelica is working on a Pactum or something more."

"Would it matter?" Alison asked. "I thought large Mage families were powerful; why would the Vies need Humans?"

Melinda shook her head. "The Vies are not a prominent family. Indeed, if they were, we'd have been able to deal with them ten years ago. Not all Arches come from powerful families. If Angelica is on Pactum, then that's one thing. But if she and her husband are using the Mutari and Humans, that will be different."

"I'm sorry, Alison," Gabriel said. "You will need to stay with a Mage at all times until we get this sorted out. What we need to figure out is how to best hide you, Sean, and Mandy from Angelica."

"So what do we do? Stay here?" Mandy asked.

Melinda turned her gaze to the girl. "No my dear, you will be coming and staying with Edward and I. You have nothing to fear with us; Angelica cannot best me."

"Thank you ma'am, but I can't afford that," Mandy said looking down.

Melinda took a seat next to Mandy, placing an arm around her. "Our years of filling Pactums are over. You will be a guest."

"But won't Angelica see this coming? Wouldn't she know where you live?" Alison asked.

Edward answered confidently. "The wards protecting our house will not fold so easily; indeed we would be lucky to have them attack. By the time our defenses fell, Gabriel, I, and the branch families would be waiting."

"Sean, you will also be staying with my family," Gabriel said. "Mandy, as soon as one of my team can spare some time they will come and give you Vis." He turned to Alison. "Alison, you will be staying with Faith and me."

"Are you going to notify the remaining Arches?" Edward asked.

"Yes I will. Would you be willing to involve the branch families?" Gabriel asked.

Edward smiled. "Gabriel, this is battle and you are the ranking Paladin; you're in charge here. If you want the branch families, they are yours," he said proudly.

Gabriel smiled. "Thank you father, but you are still the head of the family."

"For now," Melinda said warmly, beaming at her son.

"What's your plan?" Edward asked.

"During the day when working, Faith and I will stay with Alison and Sean. So long as a Seeker is present, they shouldn't be spotted. At night when protected by the house's concealment spells, Faith will search. Angelica may be the only Seeker working with Trinity or she could have a team of Seekers; we don't know."

Edward nodded. "Keep what they are looking for close and make them stretch their resources," he observed.

"Correct," Gabriel said.

"Faith, what are your orders?" Melinda asked.

Faith looked uncomfortable. "I don't know...you would know best."

Melinda shook her head. "Gabriel is the head Paladin; therefore, you are the head Seeker."

Faith's face reddened and Alison realized that she was intimidated by her mother's abilities.

"But I'm not as good as you or as Angelica..." Faith had shame on her face.

Melinda stood, walking to her daughter. "You are good enough for this. Now, what would you have me do?"

Faith looked to Gabriel and then back to her mother. "Please, keep Mandy on the property at all times. I need you to stay on the property with her." Faith got some of her confidence back. "You are more skilled than Angelica and know her well. Keep Mandy concealed but not so much that Angelica gives up the search for her. I want Angelica focused on thinking she can find Mandy, Sean, and Alison so that she doesn't keep up on everything that she has to hide."

Melinda smiled proudly at Faith. "Of course, and I agree this will give us the best chance of beating her."

"We need to head out," Gabriel said. "Alison, we will contact the station tomorrow, but I think it best to take a few days off so Faith and I can make arrangements."

Alison stood, feeling tired. "That's fine with me."

Mandy and Sean left with Melinda and Edward. Alison hung back with Gabriel and Faith. The still-too-silent Faith hooked arms with her and smiled slightly. Suddenly, her vision flashed lavender and they jumped from the safe house.

FOURTEEN

ALISON KAUR'S lungs filled with sweet mountain air. Gabriel and Faith let go of her. Alison stood before a massive house. Her eyes looked down either side of it and she decided it wasn't a house, but rather a mansion.

"This is where you live?" she asked, unable to hide her amazement.

The house's exterior was white granite, making the building seem to almost glow in the early morning darkness. Alison looked around her, seeing that there were no other houses in sight as the property stretched forth. Statues peppered the area. Alison reflexively backed away from the closest one, bumping into something firm. Gabriel placed a hand on her shoulder as she ran into him.

"They are what you're thinking, but don't worry they won't hurt you or even move. They will only become active if the house comes under attack," Gabriel said.

"So they are like a security system?" She asked.

"No," Faith said. "The property has several layers of defense. The first one is a security system; if it is attacked we will know trouble is coming. These Guardians will only become active if our primary defenses are breached." Then in a reassuring tone, "Don't worry about them, Alison. Nothing is going to make it past our first lines of defense."

Alison didn't feel comforted. Faith hadn't said that nothing was going to attack the house; just that nothing would make it past the first line of spells. Gabriel led them through a massive wooden door and into the entryway, and Alison's jaw dropped at the splendor of the house.

"I take it you approve?" Guy's voice called.

Alison saw him and Erin coming down a winding staircase.

"Did you do this?" Alison asked, not believing him.

Guy laughed. "I helped on the inside a bit, but this house has been in the Decor family for years."

"So you all live together?" Alison asked, changing the subject.

Erin answered this time. "Yes, it is very common for teams of Mages to live under the same roof during their Pactum working days. That is why this house is so large; it has to accommodate up to six families in it at one time and any staff they may need for a job."

"Six?"

"Yes, remember a Pactum team is made up of six Mages, though not all of them are married to each other as in our case. Most Mages live in normal homes when they are done with Pactums," Erin said.

"Yep." Guy said. "Actually in some Pactum groups, instead of one large house for all the team, there will be a large property with five or six houses close together."

"So who owns this house?" Alison asked.

"Technically I do," Gabriel said. "It is my family's; we have several of them around the country for different Pactum groups. In most cases, part of the payment of every Pactum goes to the family who owns the property, though in our case - because this house is mine - we don't pay tribute to my parents."

"Why would people do that instead of building their own houses?" Alison wondered.

"This much land isn't cheap; we still have to buy it from Humans so they don't try to build something on it," Guy said.

"Also, there are defenses that have been here for decades, plus concealment spells," Gabriel said.

"It's true," Erin said. "We are able to jump here because we are welcome, but only Faith and Gabriel know the actual location of this property. In this way, Pactum teams minimize their risk of being found."

Alison shook her head, deciding it was too late and had been too long of a night for her to try to understand the Mage world.

"You know what; it doesn't matter…where am I staying?" she asked.

"My wing of the house tonight," Gabriel said. "Tomorrow we will move you into one of the unused wings, it will be like having your own home," he said.

She followed Gabriel as he led her to her room. It was large with its own bathroom in it.

"Gabriel," she said.

"Yes?"

"What happened?" she asked.

"Tonight? I thought we told you," he said.

She looked down, not sure how to broach the subject of Gabriel's connection with Angelica Vies. After a few moments she decided to be direct. "With you and the Vies? I'm sorry

Gabriel, I don't want to pry into your personal life, but I need to know everything; this is still my investigation." She was worried she'd been too direct, but Gabriel didn't seem bothered.

"You are right to ask; before tonight my past wasn't any concern to your case but in light of recent events, that has changed." He looked into her eyes. "Are you sure you aren't too tired for this conversation?"

She was too tired but she needed to know everything.

"Look," Gabriel said. "We will need to take a few days to plan our next steps. In that time I will answer any questions you have, but as for tonight we are all tired."

She agreed a little grudgingly. "You're right, but tomorrow we need to have that conversation."

Gabriel smiled. "Of course. Now please make yourself at home and go ahead and sleep in tomorrow, we will all need to be at a hundred percent in the coming days and weeks."

With that, Gabriel left her in her room. He seemed like a different person to her now; he had the air of someone who is used to command and is good at it. She wondered if up to this point, Gabriel had just been drifting along, moving wherever Alison and Sean had directed. She was starting to realize that in reality, Gabriel was a leader and one who had at one time commanded a great deal of respect.

SEAN HUGHES rolled over in bed, the soft sheets feeling good. He opened an eye. A line of sunlight ran across the room from a gap in the shades. His watch showed it was past ten in the morning. He decided to get out of bed. He showered and changed into some clothes the Decors had loaned him.

He left his room to find the house empty. The house was

big but not ostentatious, with a couple of guest rooms. He sauntered into the kitchen and saw a note telling him to help himself to whatever he liked, and that if he needed anything; Melinda and Edward would be working in the orchard. He looked out a bay window, seeing rows of trees. He enjoyed a quiet breakfast when a thought occurred to him. *Where is Mandy?*

He went to what he assumed was another guest room and knocked on the door.

"Come in," a weak voice called.

Sean entered the room to find Mandy still in bed and looking sick.

"What's wrong with you?" he asked.

"I used more Vis than I thought last night," she said, and then winced and grabbed at her belly.

Sean rushed over to her. "Are you ok?" he asked.

She looked up at him, her eyes surrounded by dark blotchy shadows. "Do I look fine, Detective?"

He sat on the bed next to her. "Do you need anything?"

She coughed a laugh. "Yeah, Vis. Don't worry, I'll be fine for the day. When Melinda gets in, I'll ask if she can call Gabriel."

He looked her over, her once glowing skin gray and dull. He felt bad for her; she looked like she was dying.

"What?" she asked. "Do I not look pretty to you anymore?"

Sean made a face. "Nah, I was just thinking you look like you're dying."

"I am."

"Oh come on Mandy, you just said…"

"That I need Vis," she said firmly. "Vis is life-force Sean, and my body doesn't make any of it so yes; I'm dying right now. I always am. You know this."

He did know it, but he wasn't sure he really understood until now. She had to have Vis to live.

"Why do you think I work so much," she said.

That got Sean's attention. "How does being a whore factor into this? I know you take Vis from your clients."

She nodded. "Yeah, or this happens…or worse…three a day is what it takes for me to live."

"You have to sleep with three guys a day to not die? Right," he said, sarcastic. He wasn't going to listen to some BS from a whore justifying her life choices.

"Yeah," she said sternly. "If I take too much Vis, the client will not only know but could pass out or even die; that's what my kind used to do, ya know. A healthy Human body holds about a week's worth of Vis in it. But I can't take that without killing, I can only take enough to make you feel tired."

"That is a pretty common side effect of sex," Sean said, light-hearted. "So why don't you just pay people for Vis?" he asked. He knew this would be the question that stumped her.

She just laughed. "What, from a Mage or Mutari? I couldn't do that with a Human. Up until a few years ago we were just a myth, remember? And as for the Mutari or even a Mage, it isn't cheap."

"Right like how not cheap?" he asked, giving her enough rope to hang herself with.

"Four or five grand," she said.

Sean scoffed. "Come on!"

She looked serious. "Think about it, what would you do? Someone comes up to you and needs your life-force, she needs it so bad or she'll die. How many people do you think are gonna give that for cheap? Now think if a girl in, say her twenties, came up to you and asked, what would go through your head?"

Sean paused, he knew what would go through his head, and he knew the prices he could charge. It would be like bartering with a drowning man, he'd pay anything. Sean thought back to every time he'd checked out Mandy and he instantly knew what clsc would pop into his mind. A small pit in his gut began to form.

"Why isn't there any guy Succubus?" he asked.

"Incubus; and male hookers aren't as in demand," Mandy said. "They don't…they don't make it long."

"How old were you when you figured out what you were?" he asked.

She looked down. "Eighteen. I would get sick, I mean really sick. Being a Succubus doesn't kick in fast; it takes time. I started to age faster, by nineteen I looked like I was in my mid-twenties."

Sean didn't believe her; Mandy looked like she was twenty-four at the oldest.

She read the expression on his face. "We can affect how young our bodies are. Anyway, I was at school and that's when I started seeing Vis flows," she chuckled. "It freaked me out. See Succubi try not to breed; we don't want our children to have this curse, so my parents are normal Humans…anyway a guy found me…Josh was his name." Her eyes looked far off. "He was twenty-three when I met him. He was working as a janitor at the school but he looked like he was fifty.

"You see, men have a hard time, they will save and pay people for Vis if they can, but for the most part, they either go on a rampage and a Mage finds and kills them or they starve. Josh, he was starving slowly, the part of him that was an Incubus wasn't completely active yet so his body was making just the hint of its own Vis." She shook her head. "He brought me in the loop of the Vis world and that's when everything changed."

"How so?" Sean asked.

She shrugged. "Well, I tried to stay in school but as I got sick…I worked a few jobs, but the more you work the more Vis you use and I wasn't producing much at the time. I was fighting becoming a hooker. The thought of selling myself made my skin crawl…"

"But?" Sean prodded.

"But one night I had a one-night stand." She looked ashamed. "I took Vis from the guy, whose name I still don't know. I didn't take enough to kill him, but he passed out. I saw him on campus a few days later and he looked sick. I knew I had made him sick." She looked at Sean. "I took too much."

Sean felt his own sense of shame well up in him. He'd looked at Mandy as some bit of filth that clung to society; looked at her like vermin, but she was no villain. No, Mandy was just like the girls that Corey McLoughlin used to run, she was a slave forced into this life.

"What were you going to school for?" he asked, his voice shaky.

She smiled "I was going to be a doctor. I had the grades for it. My dad was a doctor." She looked down.

"Do you not talk to them anymore?" he asked.

She shook her head.

"Why not?"

She looked at him with tears in her eyes. "And tell them what? That their little girl is a monster? Or better yet that I'm a whore? That I gave up a promising life to sleep with random men? Or how about I just try to explain why I don't age anymore?"

Sean's sense of guilt was building in him. This girl was a

victim, someone who should be being protected and he had put her in danger for his own selfish goals. How was he any different from the people he put behind bars? He wasn't. Sean pinched the bridge of his nose. "Mandy..." he had a hard time forming words. "I am so sorry."

"What? For my life? It's not your fault. Getting me hunted down by Angelica is your fault, though," she said in a flinty voice.

Yes, he was sorry for all those things and so much more.

"Are all Succubi like you? Ya know, do they hate what they do?" he asked.

"Most of us do. It would be one thing if we chose to live this way, but we don't. It's not about money; it's what we do to stay alive, and the first time you take a week off you die. We are slaves," she said dryly.

Hannah Davis' face flashed in Sean's head; she was just like Mandy. She was forced into a life of selling herself and likely forced into doing what she had to with Ramon Tabor. And what had it gotten her? Killed. Sean's guilt began to be tinted with anger. Not just at himself but at everything around him. He was angry with the people of Trinity for killing someone who he now saw as innocent. He was mad at himself for thinking the way he did and treating Mandy so poorly, and for the way he had viewed Hannah. He looked over at Mandy as again she grabbed her gut, a pained expression crossing her face.

"I'll be fine," she said to him.

"No you won't," Sean said. "You need Vis...take some from me," he said, making the decision in a second.

She looked at him. "Sean..."

"Take it," he said looking at her intently. "You take whatever you need," he said with conviction.

"You're serious…" Mandy was amazed and looked at him completely differently.

In that moment, Sean saw the world differently. He wondered…how many other victims hadn't he protected? That was his job, wasn't it? Wasn't that the oath he'd taken? To protect and serve.

"Take it; I don't care how sick I get," he said again.

"OK," Mandy said softly. "I need a fair amount; it's going to make you pass out so lay down on the bed."

Sean did as he was asked without argument. Mandy placed her hands on both sides of his head and one last time asked, "Are you sure?"

Sean lifted his head up and locked his lips with hers. At first Mandy didn't seem to know what to do, and then he felt her lips open. The strangest sensation came over him as he felt energy leave his body and flow into her. At first it felt wonderful, like the buzz of just one too many drinks, but soon fear crept in. He couldn't move his arms or legs. Sean felt himself dying; he could actually feel his life leave him. Terror seized control of his mind. Was Mandy going too far? He wanted to throw her off him, but couldn't move and then everything went black.

FIFTEEN

SEAN HUGHES forced his eyes open. His vision was blurry and every part of his body was sore. He felt sick, weak and a whole mess of other unpleasant things. His mind was clouded, like he'd been drinking all day long. He tried to turn his head but it wasn't responding, so he just tried to move his eyes. There was a bright light with a fuzzy silhouette. Sound rumbled in his ears and his ability to hear; like his sight, was slow to focus. After what felt like a few minutes, sounds and images focused back to normal.

Melinda looked down at him with a passive expression that softened. "He's awake," she said.

Sean pushed hard with his arms, barely able to lift himself from the bed. What had he been doing? Melinda helped him up.

"Careful, don't rush yourself," the sound of her voice rattled inside his head, making it hurt worse. He gave a small groan and that too hurt.

He remembered where he was and what he'd been doing. "Mandy?" he asked feebly.

"Here," she said to his left.

He looked over at her. No longer did she look sick and pale. Again she was the beautiful girl he'd first met.

"How many days was I out?" he asked.

Mandy giggled. "Try minutes, and you were out for about thirty of those."

"What? That's not possible, I feel like I've been running for three days straight."

"That's about as much Vis as she took from you," Melinda said and then reading the confusion on his face, "three days' worth; let me help you to the bathroom, you'll want to vomit, I'm sure."

Sean tried to stand from the bed and found himself putting almost all his weight on Melinda's arm. He noticed a blue mist in front of him. He looked up at her. "Are you using Vis to hold me up?" he asked, sounding pathetic.

Melinda smiled apologetically. "You're holding most of your own weight. I do apologize; I don't want to sound rude but that Vis is there in case you throw up prior to getting to the bathroom. Sorry; it's new carpet."

Sean bobbed his head dumbly. "It's really soft carpet," he pointed out.

She led him into the bathroom, the cold tile feeling harsh on his bare feet, and it clicked with his slow mind that she kept talking about him throwing up.

"Melinda why do you thin-" he started to ask and then spun.

It never failed to amaze him that no matter how hurt or immobile you were, the moment you knew you were going to puke, you would travel great distances with amazing agility to make it to a toilet. Sean landed on his knees and wretched violently.

Melinda patted his back gently. "There you go, out with the bad."

"Hey, that was my breakfast," he said in his stupor.

Oddly he felt better. He slumped onto the tile curling up into a ball. "Can I just lay here for a while?" he asked.

Melinda smiled maternally at him. "Take as long as you need, dear."

"Thank you, Mrs. Decor," he said, laying his head down. He heard Melinda ask Mandy if she'd like anything to eat and then Sean fell asleep on the cold hard tile.

ALISON KAUR sat at a small table in the back of the house, though she'd decided it was more of a compound with its size. Next to her, Guy was reading a book.

"So what is it exactly that a Builder does?" Alison asked.

Guy put down the book. "It's pretty simple, really. We build things using Vis, but we also learn how to make stuff grow, like plants and whatnot."

"You make plants grow?" she asked intrigued.

"Yep, well, not into anything special. For instance, we can make a flower grow faster. So in that way, we used to be what kept a Pactum group fed for the most part. But I tend to just stick to sprucing up the flower garden when it comes to using Vis," he explained.

"So how do you use Vis to build?" she asked.

He shrugged. "I can make a lot of the raw building material needed and I can form things using Vis to do construction. For example, I could build a two thousand-square foot house in about a day. If you gave me all the wood and whatnot, I could do it in half that time."

Alison was shocked. "That's amazing; do you go on a lot of Pactums? Sorry, I don't mean to pry."

Guy laughed good-naturedly. "You aren't, it's only Paladins and Seekers who keep mum on what they do. Builders do a lot of work in the Vis world for other Mages. Most of us don't even work on Pactum teams, but Human governments will make Pactums with us after disasters or wars to help rebuild, or to drill wells, or canals. You name it. But normally when we do work with Humans, a Healer will also be contracted as well; that's how Erin and I met."

"Oh yeah?"

"Yep," Guy said. "We were both new to the whole Pactum thing and Erin and I were on the same project working together and one thing led to another."

Before Alison could say anything, she heard Gabriel call. "Alison! Sean and Mandy are here."

She got up. "Thanks for keeping me company," she said to Guy and made her way inside.

Melinda was in the entryway with Mandy, who looked much better than she had the night before and...

"Sean? What happened to you?" Alison asked.

Sean looked like death had washed over him. His skin was pale and eyes dark. He winced when she spoke.

"He gave me Vis this morning," Mandy said.

"Hi Alison, can you not talk so loud?" Sean sounded like he was drunk.

"His head will clear if Erin can give him something, but otherwise right now he is in a mixed state of being intoxicated and very hung over," Melinda said sweetly. Melinda led Sean into one of the kitchens, plopping him down in a seat.

"Oh, I see," Alison said and then something in her twitched, and she smiled wickedly. "So you mean if I talk loud, it hurts?" she said, loudly.

Sean winced away from her and Alison grinned. "DO YOU REMEMBER WHEN I WAS SICK A FEW MONTHS BACK AND YOU KEPT YELLING AT ME AND PLAYING RAP MUSIC REALLY LOUD IN YOUR CAR?!"

Sean put his hands over his ears. "Alison I'm sorry; please stop," he moaned.

Alison didn't take pleasure in hurting people, but Sean had it coming. Alison laughed and turned to Mandy. "Thank you Mandy, you are an angel."

"Is someone's head hurting?" Faith asked loudly, walking into the room. Sean flinched away from her. "Good morning Mandy, good morning Mother, how are you two?"

"Faith, this man is in pain…" Melinda said, looking at Alison and Faith disapprovingly.

Faith looked down at Sean. "I know," she said, looking at Alison and smiling.

Erin came bouncing into the room with a cup of tea. "Drink this," she said brightly.

Sean eyed the drink but complied. At first, he just took a small sip and then he started to drink faster and faster. His skin began to pink up again.

"Thanks Erin, what is this?" he asked.

"It makes your body produce more Vis," she said.

By the time she was done speaking, Sean was done with the tea and sitting up. "Wow, that's amazing; I feel a hundred times better. So Mandy, is what happened to me pretty common?"

Mandy nodded. "Yep, that's what it feels like to have your life sucked from you."

Sean looked serious. "Hmmm, sucking the life out of me, huh? You really are like a normal woman," Sean said.

Alison gave him a look and heard someone snicker. She saw Faith shoot her husband a look that made him quail. "You find that funny?" she demanded.

James cowered. "No, well yes, but mostly no…I mean," he stammered.

Sean saved James. "Hey Erin, do I need to drink this stuff before, or after Mandy takes Vis from me? And how do I get it?"

This stopped Faith and James. Everyone in the room looked at him and Erin looked at Sean seriously. "Sean, you can't take this very often. It's like the potion I used to keep Javier Davison from using his abilities. It's poisonous with repeated use."

Sean looked concerned. "So I'm just going to get sick every time?"

Alison could tell the thought didn't make him happy but didn't seem to have an impact on whether or not he was going to give Mandy Vis again. *What happened to you, Sean?* Alison wondered.

Mandy spoke. "Sean…you can't; your body can only give so much before it burns out. I can take a little here and there, but that's it."

Sean looked like he'd had the wind knocked out of him. He looked at Mandy. "But I promised you…"

Mandy walked over and sat down in the chair next to him. "That is very kind of you. I know that you meant what you said, and I appreciate that even the prospect of making yourself sick every few days doesn't seem to affect your decision; but I won't do that to you."

SEAN HUGHES sat in the chair trying to wrap his mind around the fact that even if he sacrificed himself, Mandy would still be forced to live the life she had. At that moment, Gabriel came in the room. Sean got out of the chair, still a little shaky. Gabriel eyed him coolly. Sean ignored the look and walked up to the man.

"Can we talk alone?" Sean asked.

Gabriel considered him for a moment and then gestured for him to follow. Gabriel led Sean into a medium-sized room lined with bookshelves.

"What, Hughes?" Gabriel asked, irritated.

How was Sean supposed to begin? He decided to just say what came to mind. "Gabriel, I'm sorry for behind your back with Mandy; it very nearly got her killed…but I need your help."

Gabriel looked at him like he was nuts. "You want my help?" he spat. "And why would I help you?" he said through gritted teeth.

"Mandy can't go back to the life she had."

"That was your doing, if you recall."

"I know, I know I messed up, but I don't mean like you're thinking." Sean braced himself. "She can't be a hooker anymore. I won't let that happen." He looked at Gabriel, determined. "I'm gonna do whatever I have to do to keep her alive and away from that life."

Gabriel was taken aback. "What are you asking, Sean?"

"Can I make a Pactum with you…I'll give you everything I have in my savings and retirement, you can have it all, and I'll pay you as much as I can every month."

"To do what?" Gabriel asked, dumbfounded.

"To give Mandy Vis, just what I can't give her," Sean said.

Gabriel looked at Sean like he'd never seen him before, and then understanding showed on his face. "She told you about her life, didn't she?"

Sean nodded and Gabriel softened, placing his hand on Sean's shoulder. "You are forgiven for last night. I will not make a Pactum with you, but I will give you my word that we will find a way for Mandy to not have to live how she has up to this point. She really got to you, didn't she?"

Sean felt a weight lift from his chest as he nodded. "If I had only known..."

"I should have told you more about the Succubi, maybe if I had made their situation more clear to you and Alison..." Gabriel said.

"No, Decor," Sean said firmly. "You do not take blame for what happened; you did explain to us why the Succubi did what they did, and I just chose not to believe you. None of this is your fault; I carry all of the blame."

Gabriel didn't question Sean, instead telling him that they needed to go back and talk to the others.

ALISON KAUR sat at a table in the kitchen, waiting for Sean and Gabriel to come back. When they did, they were joined by the rest of Faith and Gabriel's team, along with their parents. Gabriel sat at the head of the table. Erin, Mandy, Guy, Heidi, and James stood away from the table, leaning against the kitchen counter.

"Aren't you going to join us?" Alison asked those not seated.

"No," said Heidi. "None of us are combat Mages."

Combat Mages? Alison looked at those at the table a bit differently. There were Edward and Gabriel, both top Paladins and Melinda and Faith, their Seekers. She and Sean were law enforcement.

"We have a lot that we need to discuss. First off," he said, turning to Heidi, "we need to suspend all active Pactums we have excluding the one with the Denver Police Department."

Alison always thought Heidi ran the show with the Mages. From her understanding, that's who set up Pactums, but it appeared that when the team was in danger, the Paladin took command.

"When you two were attacked by the other Mages, I stopped taking on new Pactums. We should be fine. The only open one we have is for the health department; I'll have it closed by the end of the day." Heidi said.

"Do you need to go to their office?" Gabriel asked.

Heidi said that she did.

"Very well, I will go with you when you do that. From this point on, no one is to leave the property without my father or myself," Gabriel said. "Our Seekers will stay with Sean, Alison, and Mandy."

No one argued with him.

"Father, have the branch families been notified?" Gabriel asked.

"They are in the loop," Edward said.

"Mother, is Angelica looking?"

Melinda nodded her head. "Yes, rather hard at the moment."

Alison noticed Mandy grow tense.

"I have notified the former Arches. Even though the Arches were disbanded ten years ago, all have said they will assist if we find anything concrete," Gabriel explained. "Now Alison, I owe you and Sean an explanation, don't I?"

"Yes, please," Alison said.

"I trust that Mandy has filled you in enough about Mages to know that we do not have a government. However, in times of crisis, prominent families will assign leaders and create special groups. Fifteen years ago, one of those times came. War broke out in the entire Vis world. What Mandy may not have told you is that there are Vis cities. These are places where Vis has always been in the open. I'm not going to go into detail about them for the sake of time, but suffice it to say that during this war, many of those cities were destroyed."

Alison felt herself going cold. How much of the Vis world had Humans not been able to see? The thought of a war happening with no one knowing anything about it bothered her.

Gabriel went on, "I was fifteen when the war started. Mage and Mutari fought side by side on each side of the war. Our side's leader created the Ark squad. Arches are the most powerful of Mages, and the squad has only been created a handful of times in history. That war was one of those times. There were twelve Ark teams. Each team consisted of a Paladin who is in command and that Paladin's Seeker.

"At the time, my Seeker was a man named Patrick Decor. He was my cousin and would later be Heidi's husband."

Alison couldn't wrap her head around what Gabriel had said. *He was in the top twelve in the world by age fifteen? Who is this guy?*

"I was the Arches' third seat," Gabriel said. "Meaning I was the third most powerful/skilled Paladin. An Arch's seat or even being an Ark at all, has nothing to do with the skill or power of a Paladin's Seeker, but Patrick was my equal. We were commanded by a man named Marcus Vies. He was our captain and a lifelong friend of the Decors. My Father trained Marcus and my mother trained Angelica.

"During the five years the war raged on, Patrick and Heidi married, Marcus even preformed the ceremony. A year after that, the war came to a head. The enemy had powerful Mages, even a group that was equal to the Arches in many ways, but there were more Arches and the enemy's strongest Paladin was only equal to our fifth seat." Gabriel looked pained. "It was the last battle of the war…the enemy fought heroically, even managing to kill several Arches. I myself was badly wounded in the fighting, but we had won; after five years we had won… or so we thought.

"Marcus betrayed us…I don't know when or how it happened, but Marcus turned on our Second in command, killing him and his Seeker before they even knew Marcus was an enemy. It was the same for Patrick and me…" Gabriel's face was a mask of shame and sorrow. "When Marcus came up behind us, I didn't give him a second thought…neither did Patrick. It wasn't until Marcus attacked Patrick that I reacted. But I was too late to save him…too slow and weak. Without a Seeker to aid me and with my wounds, Marcus thought he had an easy victory. In a way, I suppose he did…"

Alison heard a sniff and looked to a red-faced Heidi. Gabriel went on, "Before he was able to kill me, the remaining Arches had figured out Marcus was a traitor. They came to my aid and he and Angelica fled. No one has seen or heard from them since then. We have all looked but found nothing…we don't even know why he turned on us," Gabriel admitted.

Ten years, Alison thought, *ten years Gabriel and Heidi's family had been dealing with this, had been hunting.* And now Alison's investigation had given them a lead.

"Are you going to be able to keep a level head about this, Gabriel?" Sean asked.

"Yes, I want to kill Marcus and Angelica Vies, but I've had ten years to calm down. I won't be planning my strategy based on emotions. It's important to note that Marcus was the head of all military actions during the war. Both he and Angelica are master tacticians," Gabriel said.

Edward leaned forward in his chair. "First, we need to look at the possibilities for why Angelica is here."

"This could simply be a Pactum," Melinda said. "They have been hiding for years and their money has likely run out. Heidi, what kind of a take could Angelica get from a job like she's pulling now?"

Heidi thought for a moment. "Well, if she is the only Seeker or at least is in charge of Seekers over a group covering a whole city…hmmmm, for a few months, that would run you at least one hundred G.E."

Alison did the conversion in her head. G.E. was Gold Eagles, and each of those was an ounce of gold putting the dollar value at…"Even on a short term basis, there's no way a small organization could afford that. One hundred G.E. would be almost two hundred grand, and you said that was just for a few months." The Mages didn't question her; after all Alison was the Human expert.

"She may not be running the show," Sean said and then after getting a look added, "Oh come on guys, think about it. When that Tracy and Keith attacked us, they said they didn't have a Pactum, right? So that could mean that Angelica wasn't hired by McLoughlin. I know this guy, and he isn't going to shell out all kinds of money for keeping out of the eye of law enforcement."

"It's true," Alison said reading looks of skepticism. "McLoughlin has run in this town for years and no one has been able to touch him. He has too many people in his pocket to even see the inside of a courtroom."

"So then, what do you think this is?" Gabriel asked Sean.

"Simple; he brought Tracy and Keith on. They are young, powerful, and have access to something McLaughlin hasn't had in the past…Vis users. But Tracy and Keith aren't Seekers, right? And they know now that someone is on their case…"

"So they made a Pactum with Angelica," Edward said. "That sounds more probable than her having one with McLoughlin."

"Could they afford to do that?" Alison asked.

Heidi spoke again. "They might. Tracy and Keith don't follow standard Mage protocol do they? No guild or Pactum team would openly give the Vies the time of day, but people who are on the fringe might give them a job, and if they are needing a quick buck…"

The pieces seemed to fit for Alison but…"There's something missing here," she said.

"Like?" Melinda asked.

Alison stood pacing around. Finally, she was in her element with the conversation. She didn't know much about Vis or Pactums, but she was good at figuring out people's motives.

"She might be looking to double cross them," Alison said more to herself.

Sean heard her and picked up her thought. "Right, of course, Tracy and Keith sound like good marks." He looked at the confused Mages. "Look, Tracy and Keith are not working the way other Mages do. That will be for one of several reasons, but the most likely is they don't understand why Mages work they way they do. This suggests that they are disconnected from most of the Mage world. Someone who is as good as Angelica isn't going to work for beer money; not unless she sees something in it for her. So she comes in working with a couple of morons for a few bucks and figures out where McLoughlin's group keeps all their money."

"And cleans them out," Gabriel said. "The Vies aren't known for being loyal. But what are other reasons Angelica can be here?"

Alison was a little surprised Gabriel discounted her and Sean's idea. She was also a little miffed about it.

"Option two," Faith said, "is that they are partners with McLoughlin, splitting earnings and helping him tap into new markets and new employees."

"No," Edward said, "that can't be; Marcus and Angelica would never work side by side with Humans. They don't respect them enough. What about if they were hired by Mutari? I could see Goblins hooking up with the mob."

The group of Mages chattered for a while longer. Sean and Alison didn't add anything now that the conversation had moved out of their arena. Finally Gabriel sighed. "So I think we can agree Angelica is planning on double crossing this Trinity group."

Alison looked up from her tea. "I thought you didn't like that idea?" she asked.

Melinda smiled at her. "No dear, when you presented it there was little doubt in my mind that you were correct. However, when dealing with an enemy of the likes we are now, you must explore all possible outcomes. We think that Angelica will betray Trinity but we don't know what she has told them. We also don't know when she will betray them or what her goal is. We know she doesn't want their money; she could be looking for something else. Also, we still don't know if her husband is involved or not."

Alison could respect that. "So what now?" she asked.

"We need help," Gabriel said. "We need Mutari of our own to assist us; it will be evening soon so tomorrow we will go on a little trip to find some allies."

From there the meeting fell into side conversations and Alison found herself thinking of Gabriel's past, wondering what his life must have been like. When she was fifteen Alison's biggest problem was her parents telling her she was too young to go out with Kyle Lazowski. But at about that same time, Gabriel was one of the top warriors in the world and fighting a war.

SIXTEEN

GABRIEL DECOR found himself in command; a role he slipped into without effort. It had been years since he'd last commanded people and he didn't really enjoy having to do it again, but that was one of the responsibilities of being a Paladin. Around the table he assessed the skills and people he had to work with. The team would not be able to lean too heavily on his parents; they were retired and busy with the prospect of keeping Mandy hidden. Faith didn't look confident, and he didn't really blame her. He could tell Faith that she could take Angelica Vies any day of the week, but he knew that was a lie. Faith was skilled enough, but until she believed in herself, Angelica would be able to mop the floor with her. Also, Angelica had years of experience fighting in war, and for some of those years keeping herself and her husband hidden from the entire Mage world.

He listed off the skills the two Humans had. Mages looked at Humans like they were weak. Gabriel wasn't going to make that mistake; Alison and Sean had just as much value as others.

Alison was sharp and good with people; she had a keen eye for things and for the most part kept her cool in sticky situations. Sean on the other hand, had shown that when a fight broke out, you wanted him by your side. Gabriel knew that Sean had spent time in the army and even commanded small groups. He understood tactics and he didn't seem to be afraid to make hard decisions. *But how to use that?* James sneezed, causing Gabriel to glance up at the Enchanter, and an idea came to him.

"What are you thinking, son?" Edward asked.

"We need a team to help us find wherever Angelica is hiding and to help us take over wherever that place is," Gabriel said.

"We've got lots of SWAT, but we need to avoid major action if we can. This is a criminal case, Gabriel, not a war," Alison pointed out.

Gabriel shook his head. "Sadly Alison, this is a war," he read the look on her face and added, "but not the way you are thinking. Trinity will hold ground like your gangsters of old did, and they'll do it with Humans, Mages and Mutari. And just like the old days we will have to match that force. We need to gather a group of Mutari to help us with this. With any luck, when we move on Trinity, we can quickly subdue them."

Alison still didn't look happy. "Will Angelica let you subdue her? Or the other Paladins?"

Gabriel made a sad face. "No Alison, when I say subdue, I mean the Human and Mutari might give up when they see they are outnumbered. As for Angelica and the other Mages…well, I would very much like to keep Angelica alive so that I may find her husband." This last part was important to him. Angelica would make perfect bait for Marcus. Gabriel continued to outline his plan. "We will use our team and Mutari along with Human SWAT," he looked at Alison and Sean. "I would like to try something with the two of you." Sean gave him a quizzical look. "I assume that both of you remember all too well the Guardian we encountered the other day."

"I keep seeing that thing throw stuff in my head," Alison admitted.

Gabriel smiled to himself. "How would you both like to control some of those?"

"What?" Sean asked dumbfounded.

Gabriel turned to James. "Can you do it?"

James smiled broadly. "Easy, what can I get for ya? Some of those offensive ones you've had me working on?"

Sean and Alison still looked confused, but Gabriel continued speaking to James. "Six offensive, and I think fifteen or so Shields and a couple Hurlers."

"What are you talking about, Gabriel?" Alison asked nervously.

"Guardians can work on their own as you've seen, BUT you can also make them to be directed by a third party; in this case you and Detective Hughes," Gabriel told her, smiling.

"Umm I don't think so…" Alison said warily.

Sean looked like a kid getting a toy. "So wait a second, you mean I get to make one of those things throw junk?"

Gabriel tried to keep from grinning at Sean. "Yes, but more than one. You will have a team of them. Guardians work best when they only do a handful of tasks. Shields are slow, lumbering Guardians that normally hold a large enchanted shield; they are good for hiding behind. The Guardian you saw the other day was generic and capable of doing a wider range of tasks, though it wasn't very good at any one of those tasks."

Sean nodded. "Right, right, that makes sense. So what are the other ones you were talking about?"

This time James spoke, excited about his new task. "Offensive Guardians will be fast and be armed; the Hurlers are very strong and what they do is basically throw stuff."

"Stuff like?" Sean asked.

James shrugged. "I don't know; whatever - rocks, cars, dumpsters maybe."

Alison blanched and Sean looked like he was going to explode.

"Sean," Gabriel said. "You have combat experience and I would like you to take control of the majority of the Guardians. You'll be using your Shields to give your SWAT and our Mutari cover; the other types of Guardians will assist you in this."

Sean got serious. "Hold the line; got ya."

"I understand that we will have to run all of this by your department, but based on our last encounter with Trinity; I don't see the city minding if Faith and I take control," Gabriel said. "I would like to find some Mutari to help us tomorrow. They will be able to assist us in tracking down Trinity. Prior to taking any action against Trinity, I think it wise that Alison and Sean are trained more in dealing with Vis users."

"They'll need to practice with the Guardians anyway," James said.

"And what about the SWAT guys?" Sean asked.

Gabriel thought for a moment, not happy about what he had to say. "Sean, I am sorry but until we know who in your department is helping Trinity, I don't think it's a good idea to share anything of our plans, except with Sergeant Montoya…"

Sean and Alison didn't look happy and it was the latter who spoke. "I wish I could say that I disagree with you, but you're right. And while I'm not thrilled about how we are looking at handling all of this, I think it's a good idea to be prepared for the worst."

ALISON KAUR sat listening to Gabriel outline his plan. She didn't care for it. Not that Gabriel was planning something; she'd learned to trust his abilities as a leader, but she wasn't happy with what he was planning on happening. It was one thing to think about the shootouts between the cops and gangsters back in the thirties, but that was back then and this was now. Things didn't work that way anymore. Already the DPD was going to be coming under a lot of media scrutiny with just the few incidents that had already happened, and now they were planning a large-scale raid... *There has to be a way around this,* she thought. She refused to think that there would be a need for everything Gabriel was asking for. *But doesn't he know this world better than you?*

Melinda and Edward watched their son intently, even taking notes. It was amazing to her how they looked at him. It wasn't the look of a parent humoring their kid, but one of respect and not for the first time Alison wondered what Gabriel was to the rest of the Mage world. Sean seemed to respect him too, his normal cocky attitude absent as he asked questions. She thought Sean could be a jerk, but he'd been her partner for a few years and she trusted his opinion. So she listened to Gabriel and considered what he was saying.

"Alison, do you have any thoughts?" Gabriel asked her.

"Yes actually," she said. "I want us to remember this is a police investigation," she held up her hand, forestalling comments. "While the Mages may fight us there will be Humans who will go into custody, and one of those will be Corey McLoughlin.

We need to have an actual case against him before we do anything. Our department cannot afford to let him get away from us again. Furthermore, we will have to get warrants when needed for all this, and if you want to come in guns blazing, a judge will need a strong case to sign off on that."

Sean sat back in his chair. "Alison is right; we can't be dumb about this. I know this is a big catch for you Gabriel, but Alison and I have a job to do."

Gabriel was silent for a moment. "I understand," he said. "We will make sure that you have what you need for this." He looked embarrassed. "I forget that we are in the open now and we cannot work the way Mages once did. I'm also used to being in command; forgive me. Detectives, what course of action would you like us to take?"

"We are running this case, but we would be wrong to not listen to you," Sean said. "I personally like your plan. I hope we won't need everything you think we will, but there is something to be said for being prepared. When it comes time to make arrests, we will take your lead, Gabriel. But if there is a way to get McLoughlin without having to go to the extent we've been planning, that would be preferable."

Gabriel said that he understood and moved on with the meeting. "There is a town I would like to go to tomorrow to recruit Mutari to help us out; would you be open to that Detectives?" Gabriel asked.

Alison wasn't sure how she felt about yet more outsiders being involved in her case, but up to this point Gabriel had proven apt at whatever he did so she decided to trust him on this. "That's fine, but I would like them to be on a need-to-know basis."

Gabriel smiled warmly. "Yes, of course." He stretched in his chair. "Well I think we are done with that." He looked over to Sean who, despite sounding fully recovered from Mandy, looked a little beat. "I think rest would be the best course of action for the time being. Well..." he added looking at James.

James frowned. "Right, you guys rest and I'll get to work."

Melinda and Edward disappeared with Sean and Mandy, leaving Alison alone with Gabriel and his team. They all departed to different parts of the massive house. Alison turned at the sound of a refrigerator door thudding closed. It was Gabriel, taking a drink from a milk carton.

Alison smirked. "My mother used to get on my case for doing that," she pointed out.

Gabriel put the carton back. "Mine still does," he said brightly. "It's one of her biggest pet peeves."

Alison laughed. "Is that why you do it?"

Gabriel shrugged and leaned on the speckled granite counter top. "When I was young, I think so but now it's just a habit." His voice was warm and friendly. "So, is there anything you would like to do today?"

"I thought we had to stay at the house?" Alison asked.

Gabriel smiled wider. "This is a big house and there's a lot to do. We have a pool and hot tub and just about anything else you would want to do. We even have a huge garden."

Alison thought about that last one, looking out the back windows of the house to the unusually gray and drizzly sky outside. It looked cool out, a change from the heat they'd been having all summer. "It looks nice outside; I like cloudy days," she said.

Gabriel straightened up. "Shall we?" he gestured to the door.

"You know you don't have to babysit me. I won't try to leave the property," Alison said good-naturedly.

"I know, but you are our guest here. I don't want to be a bad host, unless you would rather be on your own?"

She thought about it for a moment. "No, I think company would be nice."

Gabriel led her out the back of the house and down off the deck. There was a pool in the back of the house, and connected to it was the promised hot tub. Alison thought that later she might have to soak in it for a while. They walked across a well-manicured lawn, coming up on a tall hedge. Then they walked through it and Alison gaped. In front of her were rows of masterfully planted flower beds. Fountains dotted the garden, along with benches and trees.

"This is amazing," she breathed.

"Be sure to tell Guy that," Gabriel said.

"Guy did this?" Alison asked in disbelief.

Gabriel nodded. "He sure did, landscape design is a bit of a hobby for him. Builders learn to use Vis to build things but they can also help plants grow faster as well. This garden took him a while to do, but we haven't had a lot of work for him so he's had time," Gabriel said.

Alison walked around the garden, Gabriel at her side. "Where did he come up with the design?" she asked.

"He and Erin honeymooned in Europe; I think that's where he got the idea from. Although, this property has always had a large garden for as long as the family has owned it." Gabriel explained.

That got Alison thinking about the Mages and their families. "Do you have a lot of houses like this one?" she asked and then added, "If you don't mind me asking."

"You're fine," Gabriel said kindly. "We have several, yes; though not all are being used for Pactum teams at the moment. It just depends on how many younger people the family has, or who need a place for their team to stay."

Gabriel led her around the garden, explaining how his family was very old and had been producing Mages for hundreds of years. He told her how some Mages worked in Pactum groups while others lived like Humans. Alison found it fascinating. She thought of her own family. She'd done some genealogy work a few years back, trying to find a hobby but the exercise hadn't produced anything of interest. But hearing about Gabriel's family made her want to look into her own again. After the garden, Alison spent her day resting in her room, even taking a small nap. She hadn't been so unproductive in years and part of her wasn't happy about it, but another part of her reveled in the day of relative nothingness.

The following morning she rose early, her patience for waiting and resting gone. Gabriel, Faith, and James were in the main kitchen when she came down. Alison was put out to see that they were not in their standard overcoats and white button-up shirts.

Something of her thoughts must have shown on her face as Faith smiled. "We are going to talk to people today; we don't need unwanted attention," Faith explained. That made sense and Alison relaxed a bit. Gabriel handed her a plate of eggs and bacon. She took the dish of food and thanked him. She sat next to James at the table, resting her plate on the oak's smooth lacquered surface. She ate in silence for a while before asking him what he was planning on doing with his day.

"Working on those Guardians mostly; I should have something for you and Detective Hughes to try out tonight," he said between bites.

Alison felt a little apprehensive about the prospect of controlling living statues, but for the moment she tried to focus on what they needed to do for the day. She'd called into the station the night before, bringing Montoya up to speed. The life of a detective was a careful blend of autonomy and following orders. Most times she was able to complete cases as she saw fit, provided she stayed within the bounds of the law and basic rules. Working with the Mages almost felt like a violation of those rules and codes that she lived her life by. *Maybe not a violation,* she thought but rather that some of the rules had been tossed out of the window. Gabriel and Faith operated with little in the ways required for Human law enforcement, and really, why should they? Her laws were for her people; Mutari and Mages had lived carefully within the system for years, not out of a sense of belonging but necessity. How much longer would they do that now that they didn't have to hide themselves from Humans?

"What's got you so concerned?" a voice asked.

Alison turned. Not only had she missed that Heidi had come into the room, but she was unaware that Heidi was sitting next to her and almost finished with her own breakfast

"Nothing," Alison said.

Heidi made a face that said that she didn't believe Alison, but she didn't push the subject. *She's a contractor,* Alison thought, *which means she specializes in reading people's emotions.*

A question popped in Alison's mind. "Heidi?" she said. "How do you know if a Contractor is messing with…ya know, your emotions?"

Heidi put down her fork. "For one, any Mage can mess with your emotions, Vampires also have that ability," she warned, "but it's not an easy skill to master. If you notice a sudden change in how you feel you'll know someone is trying to influence you. Paladins use this a lot in combat to make their enemies feel fearful. They don't need to be subtle; they want their foe to know that they have no control over their own emotions."

Alison thought about that for a moment. "Can you show me?" she asked. Alison didn't like the idea of anyone having any control over her, let alone her emotions, nor did she really want to expose herself to Heidi. But she thought if she understood it personally, she could fight it better.

"Sure," Heidi said nonchalantly.

Alison sat still waiting for a moment, and then a wave of sadness hit her. She could feel waves of sorrow wash over her body. In an instant she knew what Heidi had meant about knowing that you were being messed with. She felt sad, but her mind fought the emotion, not letting it control her. Then she felt overly happy. For some reason, this emotion was harder for Alison to fight. Then she gasped, her blood running cold, her body tensing up. A primal fear gripped her. The sadness had been one thing, almost like a fog. She could see past it and function. The happiness was like wading in a pool; she could walk but not without effort. Fear, on the other hand was chains. The rational part of her mind vanished, leaving her paralyzed, sweat beaded on her brow and her heart pumped fast. For the life of her, Alison felt as though she couldn't scream even if she wanted to. Never had she felt such fear. Then…nothing, her mind was clear.

She breathed out. "Whoa, you were right, I could tell you were messing with me," she said, looking at Heidi who was smirking with pride. Alison ignored the urge to make a sharp comment. What kind of person would enjoy making someone feel that much fear? Why hadn't she just made Alison happy, that would have been enough to prove her point. "How good are you, compared to other Mages?" Alison asked tartly.

Heidi shrugged. "Pretty good," she said with a cocky smile.

Why was her smile so annoying? Alison opened her mouth to make a comment and stopped, feeling her body like she was patting herself down.

"You're still doing it, aren't you?" she asked in amazement.

Alison's irritation vanished. "Yep," Heidi said, as Alison felt a chill run down her spine that she knew wasn't Heidi's doing.

"If I wouldn't have been thinking about you affecting me, I don't think I would have caught on…" Alison said.

"You wouldn't have," Gabriel said from the kitchen.

"Unless you ask us to, it is a violation of a Pactum to affect your emotions. When you are with Gabriel, Faith, or me, you won't have to worry about other Contractors," Heidi assured her seriously.

"Can all Mages do that?" Alison asked.

"Yes," Heidi said. "But like I said before, changing people's emotions without notice is no easy skill to learn. All but Contractors are fairly bad at it, and you'll know if they try."

Two more people walked into the kitchen, ending the conversation.

"Hughes," Alison said in greeting and then to Mandy, "How are you feeling?"

"How is she feeling?" Sean asked. "I was the one who was sick yesterday."

"I'm fine," Mandy said warmly.

"Are you coming today?" Alison asked wondering why the girl was with them.

"Yes she is," Gabriel said. "We are going to a town of all Vis users, the Vies won't make a move on us there."

"Yeah," Faith said, "No way we'd get that lucky. Still, it will piss them off being able to find Mandy so easily but not being able to do a thing about it."

"Why can't they do anything?" Sean asked confused.

"In an all-Vis town, there are only a handful of locations you can use Vis to jump to. They would have to jump into town, come to us, kill Gabriel and myself and then try to make it back to a jump location before everyone in town tried to stop them," Faith said smirking. "They just aren't that stupid." She hooked arms with Alison. "Ready?"

SEVENTEEN

FAITH PENN hooked arms with Alison and Mandy as her mind locked in on the town center jump site in Domum. Vis filled her and rushed out, casting the area in yellow for the span of a heartbeat, and then she relaxed her grip on their hands. Surrounding her was the town of Domum. Instantly, her Seeker senses were assaulted. She pulled back on her spells, avoiding the sudden onslaught. When in Denver or any other place dominated by Humans, a Seeker's job in many ways became simpler. Faith need only look for the touch of Vis to find what she needed. Conversely, hiding things was harder in a Human city; masking Vis was an art form. In Domum however, things were reversed. As she gazed at the city with her abilities she was bombarded with all manner of Vis. Indeed the very amount of Vis would hide most anything, it was like trying to find one specific flower in a valley of wild flowers.

Faith smoothed the light fabric of her sundress, allowing the action to clear her mind. Domum was one of the last vestiges of all-Vis society. Around her there was no need to hide what one was. Mages flashed in and out of existence at designated jump locations. Elsewhere, shops that specialized in all-Vis products could be seen. Even the town's very name screamed of Vis. Domum was Latin for home, and home it was for many Mage and Mutari.

Gabriel, Heidi, Mandy, Sean, Alison, and Faith walked from the jump site, passing by a bakery. The sidewalks were wide and dotted with pots of flowers and vines that crawled up old fashion street lamps. Faith looked at Alison, her expression one of confusion.

"Disappointed?" Faith teased. "No one is flying on brooms."

Alison looked at her, cheeks flushing. "Sorry," she said. "It's just that Domum seems so…so normal is all."

Faith smiled. It was true Domum looked like a nice town with its open store fronts and cobblestone streets. The thing that made Domum so special was the hours of time Seekers and Enchanters put into making sure that normal Humans didn't accidentally drive into it. Contractors also worked to ensure that the entire city limits was on private property with high fences keeping everyone out. There was no real security to speak of, as far as getting into town went. If a Human were with a Vis user all of the town's barrier spells would hold no sway on them and they could enter with ease. Once a Human had entered Domum one time, they could do so whenever they wanted to again. Faith was unsure of the mechanics around the spells that protected the town but she was impressed with them.

"Yes, Domum is very normal if you want to look at it that way," Faith said. "It has a town mayor and all that jazz; it's just a little lax when it comes to keeping Vis under wraps."

Alison continued to take in the sights next to her when she finally said, "It's so new looking."

At this, Faith noticed Gabriel's head turn down a bit in front of them.

Mandy spoke to Alison softly, "That is because most of the town was rebuilt about ten years ago after the war. The Nobilis destroyed most of Domum."

"Who are the Nobilis?" Alison asked, not as softly as Mandy.

"In the war, I was an Ark," Gabriel said very sober. "More specifically, the Ark Squad is what commanded our side. When you hear people talk about the war, they might say they were Ark soldiers, meaning they were commanded by an Ark. The Nobilis were who we fought; they too had a squad that commanded and fought. A member of the Nobilis Squad along with some of his forces, took Domum and ravaged the town. It took our side several years to free the town," Gabriel said and then closed the topic by adding, "We have some contacts set up at a bistro. Heidi and I can take care of recruitment for the time being. Faith, do you want to stay with Alison, Sean, and Mandy?"

"Yep, we will grab something to eat and then wait in the park. We'll stay close," she said.

ALISON KAUR was acutely aware that she had unknowingly brought up a subject that was sore for Gabriel. For that she was sorry, but she still couldn't help but wonder about Domum and the rest of the Vis world she was slowly learning about. Mandy and Sean walked together, the latter appearing to be guarding Mandy, giving passersby harsh looks when their gazed lingered on her too long. Sean was changing. He was still brash and cocky, these traits Alison felt were at his core; but now they were tempered by something else…compassion? Alison wondered if the new Sean would last long.

"Do you come here a lot?" Alison asked the two other women.

Mandy shrugged. "Not really, there are enough Succubi here to make competition too tight, but I will come up here for a night or lunch sometimes."

Sean seemed to tense at Mandy's mention of competition.

"We come here a few times a month," Faith said brightly. "We have some friends who live up on the hill." She pointed across the small valley Domum rested in to a mountain whose side was lined with houses. The further up the hill you went, the larger and more lavish the homes appeared to become. Alison noted the occasional flash of Vis.

"Can you only jump to certain spots?" Alison asked.

Faith nodded. "Yes and no. Jumping is a bit of a mystery even to Mages. We can jump to a spot if we can find it, and by find it I mean know where it is."

"Yep, that made no sense," Sean said.

Faith rolled her eyes. "OK, look at it this way, the earth is spinning right?" she said and everyone nodded their agreement. "So at any given time, everything is moving. When you jump it's like you aren't really on this plane."

"You mean like a wormhole?" Mandy said.

"Wormhole?" Sean asked her, looking dumbfounded.

It was Mandy's turn to roll her eyes. "I was an honor student, remember? And yes wormhole, like a fold in space fabric…" she said and then reading the look on his face, "I'll explain later. Sorry Faith."

"Don't be," Faith said. "So when you jump you would have to know right where the spot you are jumping to is, but also where it's going to be in a moment. Add that to the fact that the earth is orbiting the sun, which in turn is moving around the galaxy which is moving around the universe."

Alison found herself becoming very uneasy with jumping. "How on earth are you supposed to know where you're going?"

Faith smirked. "Pun intended, right? OK, so, since you can't factor all of that crap in your mind you need an anchor. When we jump we find a location that has an anchor and we move our little bubble of space to that location, so there's no need to think about all the other stuff like the movement of the world."

"So you can jump from anywhere; that's not the hard part," Mandy said, obviously following along better than Alison and Sean.

Faith pointed at her. "Yes exactly, BUT there can be more to it, like you can control who jumps to an area and all that. Also, when a Mage spends a lot of time someplace they can find it even if there isn't an anchor, like I said we don't fully understand jumping. In addition, you can have moving anchors, like the bracelet and watch Sean and Alison wear. Gabriel and I can jump to them any time we like."

"So why do Mages go to jump sites when they leave Domum?" Mandy asked.

"Because you can't jump out of Domum, it's enchanted," Faith said.

"And I'm bored and hungry," Sean said, cutting into the conversation.

Faith eyed him coolly. "We are going to a little restaurant I like, if that works for you, Detective."

Sean was unfazed. "Works for me," he said ignoring her tone and then adding, "You're cute when you're pissed, ya know that?"

HEIDI DECOR sat next to Gabriel at a small bistro sipping a glass of strawberry lemonade. Across from her and Gabriel were two Elementals; one fire and the other air. Elementals were among the rarest of Vis users and also the most powerful, rivaling that of some Mages. Alfie Crow was the fire Elemental. He was 6'5" and about two hundred and seventy pounds, the skin on his arms rippled with muscles. He was bald and black, and wore a passive expression. Heidi read his emotions, seeing that they were calm and relaxed, a trait most Fire Elementals had. Heidi, like most; had always assumed that Fire Elementals were hotheads as their element would suggest, but they weren't. Most seemed to make a point of being level-headed, as if to throw people's assumptions back in their faces.

Next to Alfie's hulking form was a waif of a girl named Makina Yamanomoto, her dark eyes darting back and forth on occasion. Makina had long, flowing black hair, her figure fine lines, her expression controlled. The emotions coming from her were that of respect toward Gabriel, but still an air of apprehension. Makina could control every aspect of the air, from how much oxygen was in the area to using it to cut metal. Heidi knew that Makina would also be able to fly, a skill all Air Elementals mastered early on in life.

"So you want us to help out the Human police force?" Alfie's deep voice asked calmly.

"Yes, though you would also be doing the Decor family a great service," Gabriel explained.

Normally Heidi would take care of negotiating a Pactum, but these were Gabriel's friends and contacts; he would know best and Heidi would take care of the details later.

Makina looked more serious. "The Vies are involved in this, correct?" she asked and Gabriel nodded. "Hmmm, that means a lot more risk," Makina thought aloud, "but it also means having the opportunity to do something worthwhile."

Alfie shrugged. "Look Gabe, you should know by now we're with you regardless of what you're doing; you don't have to sell us."

"I know," Gabriel said soberly, "but there is risk in this…"

Makina cut him off with a wave of her hand. "We're in, Gabriel," she said kindly. Then addressing Heidi, "I assume you have a Pactum for us?"

"Yes," Heidi said. "We can talk about the particulars at the house if you like."

"So you will be providing shelter during this little adventure then?" Makina asked.

"Of course," Gabriel said smiling. "When and where can I pick you two up?" he asked.

Alfie and Makina glanced at each other before Makina answered. "We don't have anything going on right now so would tomorrow work? Maybe around two back here?"

Gabriel said that would work fine.

Some of the other groups they talked to were as easy to deal with as the Elementals. The group of Trolls they spoke to said that they would be proud to honor their family's vow to the Decors. The Werewolves were not as easy nor was a Vampire Gabriel said they needed. That left them with a Goblin and a few Banshees still to talk to.

Paul Labus, a Goblin, sat across from them, his tight curly hair a frizz. He wore thick black-framed glasses and his skin was pasty, speaking to how often he didn't get out of the house.

"So let me get this right, you want me to help you with the Mafia?" he said with disbelief.

"It's not the Mafia Paul, I told you…" Gabriel said for the tenth time.

"Yeah but you see it is, it's an organized crime group with Mutari and Mages. This is some heavy junk, man, and you want me to do what, run supplies?"

"Yes, Paul," Gabriel said seeming to give up convincing Paul that they were not taking on the Mafia.

Paul sat back in his seat rubbing his chin, which was covered by a short scruffy beard. "I don't know man, this is too dang good to pass up…the mafia," he said excited.

Gabriel was about to speak when Heidi spoke instead. "I know, right, it's like a movie, isn't it?" she said brightly.

Paul pointed at her. "I was just thinking that! Yeah guys, I'm down, when do we start this?"

"I'll pick you up in the morning," Gabriel said.

"Right, right, but we better be on the low low with it, I don't want some goon to get the drop on us."

Gabriel pinched the bridge of his nose. "Right Paul, the low low."

Once Paul was gone, Gabriel turned to Heidi. "A movie?" he asked.

She shrugged. "What? It's what he wanted to hear."

The Banshees were Heidi's least favorite. In her experience, Banshees seemed to think that because when they yelled stuff got destroyed, that meant they had to be overly loud in all aspects of life. Laura Perkins and Joseph Trick were no exception to that rule. They argued with Gabriel and Heidi about the whole suggestion that they work with the government or "the man" as Joseph put it. But like most people swearing they wouldn't do something, as soon as money came into play they changed their tune.

SEAN HUGHES gritted his teeth and pushed as hard as he could. His head felt like it was going to explode with exertion, his face reddened, sweat stinging his eyes. The manic face of Guy Penn loomed over him, eyebrows knit together and Sean pushed on.

"Come on, Sean!" Guy said aggressively. "You've got this, you're a train; push it!"

Guy reached down, placing just his index fingers under the bar. Sean felt it rise a little but he still felt his muscles straining with effort.

"Keep your back down, no cheating!" Guy barked.

Sean grunted, the bar finally lifting at a steady pace.

"Come on man; that's all you, that's all you, I'm not doing anything, you got this, come on!"

Sean locked his arms straight. "Fifteen," he grunted.

Sean sat up from the bench, his tank top soaked with sweat. He got up and faced Guy who clapped his hand. "That's what I'm talking about!" he said enthusiastically.

Sean breathed hard. "I told you I could bench two eighty, didn't I?"

"Please," a sarcastic voice said.

Sean turned to Mandy as she ran on a treadmill. "You're gonna have to do better than that around Vis users," she taunted.

Sean smiled. "Oh yeah, sugar, do you think you could do that?"

Mandy slowed the treadmill to a stop. "Yep," she said confidently.

"Twenty bucks," Sean said.

Mandy laughed. "No way, how about a day's worth of Vis," she countered.

Sean thought about that for a moment. The last time she drained him he got sick. He smiled mischievously. "Deal, but if I win when you take that Vis you can't make me sick and it better be a real kiss."

To his surprise, Mandy's cheeks flushed. She walked over to him, holding out her hand. Sean shook it feeling a twinge in his gut. Did he really want to kiss Mandy? Not just because she was hot, but because he felt something for her? He pushed that from his mind as she walked to the bench.

Mandy reached up and grasped the bar, grunting as she tried to lift it. It dropped, almost hitting her chest. Sean moved forward, convinced she was going to get hurt, but she stopped it. Mandy's face turned red and she looked like she was straining. Then she looked up at him and smiled, the red in her face vanishing.

"Just kidding," she said with a wink and then tossed the bar five feet in the air and caught it, doing the same thing five more times. Sean felt his jaw drop as she got off the bench not even looking winded. "Heidi gave me Vis this morning," she winked. "You have stuff to do today but I'll be expecting that Vis before you go to bed tonight, sugar." She emphasized the sugar with a wink. She went back to the treadmill.

Guy was laughing hard, his hands on his knees. "Man, between that girl and my wife you aren't gonna have any money or Vis left, are ya?"

ALISON KAUR walked through the back door of the house, taking off her running shoes so she wouldn't dirty the Decor's white carpet. Faith was next to her in skimpy shorts and a tight shirt that was so skimpy, it really didn't deserve the name.

Faith noticed Alison scrutinizing her. Faith looked down her body and then back at her. "What? What do I have on me?" she asked, looking at herself.

Alison rolled her eyes and said under her breath, "Not an ounce of fat."

Faith cocked an eyebrow. "You're one to talk; look at you - you've got a totally bangin' bod," she said, gesturing with her hand. "If I were a single dude, I'd totally hit that."

Alison started to walk away. "Thanks Faith," she said sarcastically.

"I hate it when you leave, but love to see you go!" Faith called at Alison's retreating form.

In the hall, she passed James who gave her a confused look. Back in her room, she showered and got ready for her day. She spent a few hours looking over case files with Hughes, and in the afternoon James came up to get them.

"The rest of the team is here," he announced when he got to her room.

"Thanks James, we'll be right down."

Alison and Sean made their way to the house's entry, the size of the house now more of an annoyance than a wonder to her. There, they met with a large group of people in the entryway.

Gabriel and Faith were in the center of the group talking to people. Heidi made her way around the group of people with stacks of contracts which she handed out.

"Here they are," Gabriel said loud enough for everyone in the room to hear.

All eyes shifted toward Alison and Sean.

"These are the pigs?" this from a short girl with a petite figure, pale skin and long, jet-black hair with a streak of purple in it.

"Police officers," Sean said with authority.

A scraggily boy with shaggy, sand-colored hair turned to the short girl. "Listen to that tone. I hate that Gestapo crap, why did we agree to do this?" he said, shooting glances at Sean and Alison.

Heidi piped up angrily. "Because we paid you, that's why, Joseph! If you don't like it, you know where the door is."

"Actually, I don't know where the door in this monstrosity is. You see, this is the problem with the-"

He was cut off by a bald Latino man in his early thirties. "Híjole, I forgot what a pain in the ass Banshees are," he said, agitated.

"So that's a Banshee, huh?" Sean said.

Joseph rounded on him. "Yes. Why Officer, does that bother you?"

The Latino guy spoke again. "Yes, that's a Banshee." He turned to the Banshee, speaking loudly. "And they think because they are loud that they should be disrespectful punks that..."

"Enough!" Gabriel said.

Everyone went silent.

He pointed at Alison and Sean in turn. "This is Detective Alison Kaur and Sean Hughes. They are who we work for and we are assisting on their case, as all of you know." He started naming people off in groups pointing to a large group of people "These are the O'Flynn Troll Club: Michael, Jennifer, John, Daniel, Troy, and Rebecca…" he went around the room, making introductions.

"We all will be living under the same roof together for a while. I will be meeting with each of you individually to discuss your role in our mission." Gabriel's voice took on the tone of one who was familiar with leadership and command. "We are dealing with a former Ark. Make no mistake about it; Angelica Vies is a formidable opponent. I chose all of you in this room because I trust you and know what you can do. Work together; get to know one another, because it is very likely that one of the people in this room will save your life." He became softer. "We will be training together in case we need to coordinate an attack on Trinity. Our fine detectives here would like us to find a non-violent solution to Trinity." To this, the people in the room didn't look like they thought a non-violent solution could be found. Gabriel went on. "I hope as they do, but we will prepare for the worst. Now please make yourselves at home," Gabriel said dismissing the group.

"Dang," Sean said quietly. "Did you see how not a one of them questioned him? That's respect."

Mandy came up the stairs to meet them and looked back at Gabriel for a moment. "That is because he has commanded many of these people in battle before. James sent me to find you two."

Alison followed Mandy out of the house and to a garage that could hold several bulldozers. There James stood in front of a group of statues, beaming at Alison and Sean.

"Are you guys ready to learn how to use Guardians?" he asked.

"No," Alison blurted. "Sorry," she corrected. "Yes, I am."

James looked apologetic. "I dare say your first answer was the right one. Today I'm going to have you working with some generic models so you can get the hang of things."

He picked up two thick black cords, handing one to each of them.

"OK, go ahead and put those around your neck," he said.

Slowly, Alison complied. As soon as the rubbery cord touched her skin, it wrapped around her throat. At first she flinched, but James held her hand and said, "Give it a moment." She calmed and realized that while the cord held fast to her neck, she could breathe without issue. "Ok now, relax and say, Coniungere."

"Coniungere," they both said.

Her mind swam with two images of the room. One image came from her eyes and the other...from one of the statues! It turned its head, locking eyes with hers, giving her a sense of vertigo. She could feel everything about the statue, how much energy it had, what it was capable of feeling and even some general commands she could give it.

She looked at Sean who looked a little sick.

"The first connection is like this, sorry I didn't warn you. I thought you might not want to try this if you knew," James said shrugging. "Now you should be able to get an idea of what your Guardian can do. This is important; Guardians are limited in what they can do and what commands they can be given. If you confuse them they will make mistakes just like people. You also cannot take direct control of limbs - you can only tell it what you want it to do. So let's try it."

Alison thought to her Guardian, *Walk forward*. It complied, stopping when it came to the wall.

"They will avoid objects unless told otherwise," James informed them.

He made them use the Guardians to pick up objects and do various tasks. Alison was feeling more and more comfortable with the thing when James asked her to do one last task. The Guardian was to pick her up and then walk her back to the house in its arms. Alison was to wear a blind fold during the whole exercise. As the statue came close to her, she found herself breaking into a sweat. The Guardian's cold stone arms picked her up with ease, as she watched herself shake through its eyes. It started back to the house and she found herself relaxing a bit. She was in control and she knew that not only would the Guardian not drop her but it also wouldn't allow her to be harmed.

EIGHTEEN

MANDY STAFFORD felt herself sink into a soft armchair in Gabriel's study. A table sat between her, Alison, and Sean. Gabriel and Faith were also in the room, but a short distance away sitting on a sofa. Sean and Alison held pads of paper and a tape recorder was on the table.

"I know we've talked about what happened the night of the twenty-seventh of August before, but we need to have this on the record. Do you understand?" Sean asked calmly.

The twenty-seventh was the night Faith had rescued Sean and Mandy from Trinity. Mandy said that she understood.

"What can you tell us about Trinity's safe house?" Alison asked.

Mandy thought for a moment, bringing back memories of the building. "It was big; an old apartment building, I think. There were two stories to it."

"What do you remember about what was happening there? Who was there?" Sean clarified.

"Oh, right. There were Humans and Mutari there, also a few Mages but mostly Mutari and Humans. There were some Succubi along with a few Trolls and other types that would come in and out. The building was supposed to be a residence and headquarters of sorts. There were no clients who came there," Mandy said trying to be as clear as she could.

"Tell us about the Humans," Alison said.

"Well, they were prostitutes, but not your street corner variety. I know that Trinity had a group of those as well, but at the house the girls there were different."

"How so?" Sean asked.

Mandy looked down. This was the part of her whole time with Trinity that bothered her. "Most were in their teens; some of age but most weren't. A few were on drugs and that's how Trinity kept them around, but most were kidnap victims...you see it a lot really. Some girl is told that her family will be hurt or killed if she doesn't work and so she does...most of them don't stick around long, most groups that do that sort of thing move them around a lot."

"It makes it harder for law enforcement to track them down," Sean said. "Before, you told me about drugs and guns..."

"Yes," Mandy said nodding. "They had most of the Succubi selling drugs to Johns. I know they had some regular dealers too, but they had some of us doing that. It was our choice if we sold or not. The Succubi seemed to have about as much freedom as we wanted. Some of the drug deals turned into gun deals, but mostly it was just drugs."

"What type of clients did you have?" Alison asked.

She shrugged. "Standard. Business men and women, along with a few city workers."

At that, Alison and Sean shared a glance. "These workers, how did you know they worked for the city?"

"People talk," Mandy said. "Even if a guy has paid for sex and knows he's gonna get it he tries to brag…ya know, man up a bit. People tell you all sorts of things."

Sean wrote something down on the pad of paper. He reached over and clicked off the recorder.

"This doesn't make sense to me," Sean said.

Mandy felt bad. "I'm sorry; I'm trying…"

"No, not you," he said gently. "McLoughlin…forced prostitution is his M.O., with a bit of dope on the side, but guns?"

"And the city workers," Alison said. "When he got off last time it wasn't because he had people in his pocket, we just couldn't get any evidence on him at any of the crime scenes."

"I'm confused," Gabriel said. "Why does this matter? We know that McLoughlin is now working with another group."

"Yeah, but why is he? Corey had a pretty sweet setup going before; hookers bring in some good cash and easy drug sales. Human trafficking is a lot more common here in the States than most people think. It isn't hard to get away with, but gunrunning; that's a different story." Sean sighed, leaning back in his chair. "Gunrunners are a whole different kind of scum, and getting city workers in your pocket, well that's organized on a level that Corey can't do."

"So what, he isn't running things?" Faith said.

"Which means there's a lot bigger fish to fry," Alison said. "When we first got here we suspected as much, but hearing what Mandy is saying now, it makes me think that McLoughlin isn't even remotely in control. You just don't go from running girls to managing a whole operation."

"He seemed in charge when I was in the safe house," Mandy said. "Though Angelica seemed to have a lot of authority too."

"There is no way Corey McLoughlin can afford Angelica Vies and two Paladins," Gabriel said "Sean and Alison are right, at best Corey is running things here in Denver."

"Agreed, he's a good pick," Sean started. "Corey knows enough about the area to be able to keep the operation out of the public eye, but he doesn't know enough to try to break out on his own."

"But does he know enough to keep out of the public eye?" Faith asked. "We are on the case, after all."

Alison shook her head. "That's different. Us getting wind of this was William Lanner's doing. If he hadn't been skimming from Trinity and gotten himself killed, we'd never have known." Alison looked off into the distance. "But from what we were able to find out from Javier Davison, there has to be more to this." She huffed. "There's a lot more going on here that we just can't see."

"What makes you say that?" Mandy asked.

"They killed William Lanner, Ramon Tabor and Hannah Davis to keep us from picking up their trail. You don't put that kind of effort into something unless you have a lot on the line," Sean said. He looked at Gabriel and shook his head "I think you may be right on about needing to be prepared for the worst. I mean Davison broke out of lock up, not just broke out but knocked down a wall. He must be confident about not getting caught. Also, to break him out, Trinity had to be willing to expose a mole in the Denver Police Department."

SEAN HUGHES thought about what they were saying and everything that had happened. It wasn't easy to place people in the department who could spring a guy from lockup. And to probably expose that person was a big gamble you didn't do flippantly, unless...for a moment Sean entertained the possibility that Trinity had been building contacts for years in the department. He didn't want to think about people he worked with being dirty so he changed the direction of his thoughts.

"We need more information before we do anything else," Sean said. "We need real intel, where people are going, how many they have, if there is a paper trail, you name it, the works. I'd bet a month's pay Corey McLoughlin is in over his head on this one and he knows it. If we can get him, we might be able to get him to flip on whoever is really pulling the strings on this."

The thought boggled his mind. What they were looking at was what made legends in law enforcement. But for every legend, there were twenty other people who wasted away an entire career never getting to take down the big mob boss, and even more still that got killed along the way. Part of Sean just wanted Corey McLoughlin to be in charge, just wanted to make that one big career bust. He'd get a commendation from the Mayor and maybe even a bump in pay. He wasn't sure he wanted to be involved in something as big as they were looking at now. Sean wasn't even sure if he could be, he was just a cop in Denver. Hunting down organized crime groups was the FBI's job, not a homicide cop's.

"What are you thinking?" Sean asked Gabriel.

"I think we should use our Mutari wisely. I want to have Makina trail some people and find out where Trinity's real base of operations is in Denver. Also, I have a fairly well-connected Vampire asking around."

"Do you think he will be able to find out anything?" Sean asked, not caring to know who the contact's name was. Sean figured after the incident with Mandy he wasn't going to ever do anything directly with any of Gabriel's contacts again.

Gabriel didn't look optimistic. "It's hard to tell really; it will depend on how long this investigation takes. If Makina or Faith find Trinity, then he may not be of much use. However, if this investigation runs for a few months or years, he will be indispensable."

"And what's in it for this informant?" Alison asked.

"Vampires live the longest of all Vis users, seconded only by Mages. They live on the topmost crust of society, almost never getting directly involved. Theirs is a game of plotting and planning. My contact owes me some favors, but helping House Decor is in his best financial interests as well as putting him in a place to possibly topple other Vampires or Goblins."

Alison didn't look all that thrilled with Gabriel's answer, but didn't push the subject. Gabriel invited Makina into the room, her long black hair seeming to hang unnaturally in her wake.

"Makina," Gabriel said. "We need you to follow some people."

She gave a quick nod of the head. "Who would you like me to follow?"

"Mandy can give you a description. When you find out where Trinity is based, please tell me," Gabriel said.

"Would you like me to investigate the area when I do find it?" Makina asked.

"Sorry - not to sound rude, but wouldn't it be safer for Faith to do this?" Sean asked.

Makina gave Sean a stern look, and then he felt a breeze touching his cheek. Makina's hair floated up around her and she lifted out of her chair, her shirt flapping in a wind that only she could feel.

"Right…I stand corrected," Sean said.

Makina floated back down to her chair.

ALISON KAUR convinced Gabriel that she needed to go back to the station, but Faith was unavailable, so now Alison walked into the office with Melinda trailing her. Sergeant Montoya flagged Alison down and she followed him into the conference room.

"Who is this?" he asked, looking at Melinda.

Melinda extended her hand. "Melinda Decor," she said regally.

Montoya didn't seem to know how to respond so he gently took her hand, looking flustered. "Oh, well um, it's a pleasure to meet you," he said respectfully.

Then he turned his attention to Alison. "What the hell is going on?" he asked not so respectfully.

Alison breathed out, launching into the last few days' worth of information.

"I don't like this Kaur, you going out on your own like that and not coming in to report to me directly!"

"Sir I know but-"

"I don't want to hear it! This whole case has been a nightmare from the word go. And now come to find out our nice little murder investigation is delving into an organized crime ring of

Trolls that break out of jails, Succubi that drain the life from people and Wolves that eat you!" His face was red, and the longer he talked the louder he got.

"Don't forget Mages and Humans," Melinda said sweetly.

Alison winced for Melinda, knowing that a rebuke was coming. Montoya looked at Melinda, about to snap at her but seemed to deflate. "Yeah, those things too," he said more subdued. "Look Kaur, just wrap McLoughlin up in a nice little bow OK? I'm gonna see if the FBI or ATF are tracking Trinity. God willing they are, and when Corey is taken down we can go back to our old happy lives of drug dealers who knock off their competition," he said leaving the room.

"How did you do that?" Alison asked Melinda.

"Do what?" Melinda asked.

Alison gestured to where Montoya had been. "That. He didn't even yell at you."

She smiled slightly. "Ah that, well it's all in how you hold yourself, my dear. Also, putting on a bit of makeup can make a difference too. Most men have a hard time keeping their confidence around a put-together confident woman."

Alison thought back to her morning. She wasn't wearing a dab of makeup, it just hadn't occurred to her to put some on. She was going to be in the station for an hour tops. Faith made little comments like that all the time too, and after seeing how Melinda could curb even Montoya's anger with a mere glance, she thought she might take a page out of their book.

MAKINA YAMAMOTO rested atop an old church's tower, the tassels of her shifter playing in a slight breeze. The night was pitch black, the moon obscured by clouds. Makina looked down at the street, her eyes aided by a pair of enchanted glasses. She leaned over the building's stone edge, watching her quarry. Her shifter was a ghillie suit similar to that of Human Special Forces or hunters. Instead of colored strips of burlap, Makina's was made of a light fabric with long strips that gently moved in a breeze she kept constantly moving. The fabric was enchanted to change to the colors around it, thus breaking up her form and hiding her better than any Human-made ghillie suit ever could. The shifter would be ineffective in broad daylight, but where she stood now in the dark of night only a Seeker would be able to find her easily.

Makina was very patient, not bothering to wonder at how long she'd been in the same spot watching the small group below her. She wasn't sure if they were Human or not; unlike Vampires, Mages and Succubi, Makina was not able to read Vis. She could, however, read the air current, could sense the pollen, dust and pollution in the air as it rode thermals from the hot asphalt of the street. This was why she could stand here for hours. The air in the city told a story, a story that only Makina and a few other people in the world could listen to.

The group on the street moved and she focused on them. They were leaving the bar they'd been at all night. She watched as one of the men took the tip off of another table and pocketed it. They moved north away from her. Makina stood, padding along the roof of the church. On her feet were slippers similar to those worn by ballerinas. Her steps were lighter than that of any animal as the air around her supported her. She moved quickly to the edge of the roof and jumped, the air around her lifting her into a graceful arc across the street. She landed soundlessly on the building where the men had been eating. She could fly if she wanted to, but Makina liked having the extra cover of the buildings, so she followed the men to their car by leaping from building to building.

Once they were in the car she was forced to fly, still trying to use the buildings for cover. People wouldn't have known it from her stern and serious demeanor, but Makina loved to fly. And who wouldn't? There was more than freedom in it, there was power and perspective. Each time she flew it felt much as it had the first time. Following the car was more of a game to her than it was work, and she had to force herself not to get carried away and be seen.

The car drove into an abandoned rail yard and Makina stopped in the air, her gut telling her not to enter the grounds. If Angelica Vies had protected the property, Makina could be in grave danger if she tried to fly overhead. She watched the car bounce along the rough ground of the yard. She pulled off her glasses to look with her own eyes, finding that the car was not just hard to find, but missing. She put the glasses back on, seeing it parked but starting to fade. Yes, the rail yard was definitely protected.

Makina pushed at an enchanted ear piece. "Faith, this is Makina," she said softly, using the breeze to mask her voice.

"Yes? What have you found?" Faith asked immediately.

"I've found a rail yard; it has protection, and I don't think it would be wise for me to travel any closer to it," Makina explained.

"Or away," Faith said catching her off-guard. "Sit tight in case she has a detection spell looking for Mutari leaving the area. Where are you? I'll come get you."

Makina told Faith where she was and stopped using her Vis just in case Angelica was able to find her.

FAITH PENN walked quickly down the dark streets of Denver. Vis cloaked her, making her invisible to the few people left out and about in the late hour. She found Makina atop a building looking out over the train yard. Old, rusted-out cars still sat on tracks, mounds of rubbish and train wheels scattered throughout the yard.

"There hasn't been much in the way of activity," Makina said once Faith was next to her.

Faith enveloped both of them in a transparent sphere of amber Vis. The bubble rose in the air with Faith and Makina until they hovered a few hundred feet off the ground. Not even Angelica would be able to see them in the bubble and Faith used her senses to inspect the area.

She closed her eyes, seeing only with Vis. She let power flow into the air around them, covering everything in gold. A dome appeared in front of her and Faith focused on it. The yard was well cloaked. Not to the same level as a Mage home like the one she lived in, but Faith would have been hard-pressed to find the train yard on her own.

"It has far more shielding than the other Trinity safe houses we found," Faith said absently.

"So this is the headquarters, isn't it?" Makina asked.

Faith figured it was but didn't want to say for sure. "It would seem so but for all we know, it isn't." She opened her eyes. "I will have to come back with Gabriel so he can check out its defenses," she breathed out.

Makina seemed to understand. "Yes, it will not be easy getting the evidence that the detectives need."

Faith smiled, happy to be around someone who understood how the world worked. Makina was skilled at surveillance; she would know that the train yard would be nigh impossible to get into without raising an alarm.

"We should be able to figure out what is coming and going at least," Faith said.

GABRIEL DECOR hovered next to his sister, watching the train yard. From all indications it was well guarded.

Sean's voice buzzed in his ear. "So what are we looking at?"

"A lot of passive wards. From what I can tell, anyone can come and go as they please. I would suspect that once an intruder is found that the yard will lock up pretty tight. In the meantime they can't have every Human and Mutari coming and going setting off the alarm," he mused more to himself than to Sean. "I see two points of entry. There are high fences along the perimeter with old train cars blocking the rail entrance. There's a warehouse/office building on the north side that I would guess is where their HQ is. From the west is the main entrance. It has a clear path to the office building."

"Yeah, but you know it won't be a picnic to use that route," Sean said.

Gabriel liked working with someone who had a basic idea of strategy; it made his job a lot simpler and meant that he didn't have to spend hours on end explaining why he wanted to do something. "Agreed," Gabriel continued, "but we won't have a choice, if we don't hold the main entrance, Trinity will be able to get away." He looked to the south at a chained-up service entrance. "To the south there's a small gate that looks like it hasn't been used in years."

"Flank 'em, right," Sean said. "So main team from the west coming in hard and fast-"

"And a small team moving in silently from the south," Gabriel finished.

"I like it; how long do you want to wait?" Sean asked.

Gabriel shrugged. As far as he was concerned, they could move in once he thought his team was ready. "That depends on you and Alison. You're gonna need a warrant to move on this place. How much time do you need for evidence?"

Sean didn't talk for a moment. "We should have enough for a warrant already, but I want a tight case so let's wait a few days, I don't want these pricks getting off again."

ALISON KAUR busied herself managing the Mutari, when she wasn't learning how to use the Guardians. In the few days she'd been working with the Mutari, they'd come together a lot. The Banshees were still obnoxious but did as they were asked. Alison had a network of Trolls watching Trinity's common locations, along with the Banshees. Her biggest help was Makina. The woman didn't give Alison any lip and was hands down the best at tailing people she'd ever seen.

Next to her sat the Goblin Paul Labus, clacking away at his laptop and talking on the phone in Latin. Paul was on the team to get anything they might need but Alison soon learned that he also had many other skills.

"Compello vos laxus," he said hanging up his phone. "Right, so I just got off the phone with a guy in my guild." he said, then reading the look of confusion on her face added, "Not like an online gaming one, like one for companies and stuff... anyway, I asked around about enchanted merchandise on the move and he said there wasn't much to talk about, but when I asked about gold and silver, he perked up."

"How so?" Alison asked, worrying that Paul may have tipped off a possible Trinity informant.

Paul smiled. "I told him I was seeing a lot of foreign coins come my way. You see I don't do a lot of banking, but most of my clients do. Goblins take gold in whatever form we want because we can tell if it's pure or not right," He said with animation. "Get this, he said that the banking system has been seeing a crapload of this stuff; he even reported it to the Head of the guild."

"What's important about that? What did they do?" Alison asked.

"Nothing, they told him they were aware of the issue and to go about his day," Paul said.

"And…" Alison said still confused.

Paul shook his head. "We are the banking system, Alison. Our guild not caring about a massive influx of foreign gold in Denver is like the Fed not caring about an influx of foreign currency."

What he was saying clicked with her. The Fed would investigate anything like that, it would be a telltale sign that something fishy was going on in the area. "So Trinity is using gold to keep the local law enforcement from finding out, and the guild is in on it."

"At least at the city level," Paul said. "Someone heading up Denver has to be on the take, there's no way the guild itself has been corrupted."

"Why not?" Alison asked.

Paul didn't look like he had an answer.

"Don't worry about that now," she said not wanting him to lose focus. "Just see if you can find me the contact in Denver."

"Right," he said, though he seemed shaken.

NINETEEN

ALISON KAUR tilted her head to the side with a satisfying crack. She was convinced she finally had what she needed to make a conviction on Corey McLoughlin and most of his crew. However, Paul was still unable to make headway with the Goblin guild.

"What have ya got?" Sean asked her.

Alison read off a list. "We have eight different safe houses we've found thus far. We've got documentation of drug deals and also black market arms deals. From Javier Davison's short time with us, we have him confessing to being a part of the murders of William Lanner, Ramon Tabor and Hannah Davis. Provided we can take Javier into custody, I'm sure he will flip on McLoughlin." Alison held up a finger. "But on the chance he doesn't, we have enough to not only place him at six of the safe houses but," she held out a picture of Corey threatening two girls, "we have him here with Julia Whitmore, eighteen from Provo, Utah; and Kathy Servas, twenty-one from Gillette, Wyoming. Both girls were reported missing several months ago. There are a few other cases like Julia and Kathy."

Sean shook his head, no humor or bravado coloring his tone. "Drugs, murder, prostitution, gunrunning and human trafficking. Disgusting. I can't believe someone like this has been able to make it by all these years."

Alison gave him a knowing look. "Yeah, but this time it won't matter who's in his pocket," she said confidently.

Alison turned to Gabriel who sat quietly in the room with Faith. "Are you ready?" she asked him.

"Yes, you and Sean will do well as will the rest of the team, but you should know we only have the manpower to take care of the train yard. The other safe houses will be on their own," he said.

Alison wasn't thrilled about that part but figured that without a commander, the rest of Trinity in Denver would have a hard time running, and with the information they had on hand they would be able to hunt down many in the group.

Alison stood and gathered her papers. "I'll call the Sergeant," she said, taking out her phone and dialing the office.

GABRIEL DECOR hefted a heavy box, infusing his body with just a hint of Vis. *What the heck does she have in here?* He wondered. He, his sister, Alison, and Sean with his own box, were walking into the police station.

"Seriously Kaur, there are these things called computers," Sean grunted. "You see they hold stuff in them like evidence and documentation," he complained.

Alison rolled her eyes at Sean. "Gabriel's fine, what's your problem? And I like paper, it feels real to me."

"Well Gabriel's some super soldier, isn't he? But you've got a point though about paper feeling real; the pain in my lower back feels real real right now."

They rode the elevator up to the office and made their way into the conference room. Jesse, the lab tech, sat at the conference table eyeing the boxes.

"What are you doing in here, Jesse?" Alison asked.

"Working. Since you made it impossible for other people to get in here, I spend a lot of time enjoying the quiet." He pointed at the boxes. "Your computers broken or something?"

"I like paper, OK?!" Alison said sharply.

"And the rainforest likes you too, Detective," Jesse said, closing his own laptop, making to leave. "I know my cue when I hear it," he said, grumbling out the door.

Alison procured a file with a summary of their findings. "Let's go see the Sergeant and get a warrant."

They left the conference room, making their way to Sergeant Montoya's office. Alison knocked on the door and Faith twitched.

"What is it?" Gabriel asked her.

His question was answered as the door opened and he walked in. Sergeant Montoya sat behind his desk, across from him a man in his late forties with a balding head. Next to him sat a woman with long silver hair. Gabriel didn't need Faith for him to sense that she was a Mage. The woman turned her head, a small smile on her face, her red eyes calm. She stood, bowing slightly to him.

"It's been a very long time, master," she said with respect.

"Master?" Sean said.

"Madison," Gabriel said as she came out of her bow. She'd changed over the last...what was it? Six years? Her straight silver hair hung to her hips, her skin fair. She wore tight black leather pants and a thin leather jacket, showing off a fair amount of cleavage. A katana hung from her belt. Gabriel felt his heart race as he took in her glossy red lips. "You've grown up," he said.

The corner of her lip twitched up in a smile. "Good of you to notice," she said.

Any air of coolness she was trying to portray vanished as Faith wrapped her in a bear hug, knocking the wind out of her. "Oh Maddy, it's been too long! How are ya? You've turned into a dish!" Faith noted.

"I'm good, thanks," Madison said blushing.

Montoya cleared his throat. "This is Agent Alesbury with the FBI and I take it you know his associate."

Madison stepped forward and shook hands with Sean and Alison. "Madison Beldame."

Sean and Alison introduced themselves, seeming wary of Madison.

Alesbury spoke in a gruff voice. "We understand you are looking into Trinity?"

Alison glanced at Faith who said, "The room is safe."

"Yes sir," Alison said. "We believe we have enough for a warrant, we have found several safe houses and what we think is their head command center for Denver."

"This is the FBI'S case," Montoya said, "but they would like to work closely with us." He addressed Gabriel. "As you can see, the FBI has Mages of their own, so you will not be needed any further."

"Of course," Sean said stiffly.

"Madison," Gabriel said. "Respectfully, it would be unwise to change leadership at this time."

"Look, son…" Alesbury started.

"What is it?" Madison interrupted him, concerned.

"Angelica Vies is involved…" Gabriel paused as Madison composed herself. "She is protecting their primary facility."

Madison nodded. "Do you have an attack plan?"

"For the main buildings; yes we do, and we have a team of Mutari and Guardians. For the eight safe houses we found; no," Gabriel said.

Alesbury started talking, "Look, that's fine and dandy and all, but this is our case and therefore the end of your Pactum. Now I don't want to sound ungrateful for what you and yours have done, but we have this covered."

Madison was silent for a moment before she turned to a frustrated Alesbury. "Angelica Vies is an Ark; I do not have the ability to defeat her husband, nor does my Seeker have the ability to defeat her. Gabriel and his team must be the ones to take the main target."

It was a sign of how much Alesbury respected Madison when he said, "Are you sure you want to give control to this man? Do you trust him?"

Madison looked into Gabriel's eyes and nodded. "To the end of the world."

Alesbury paused, thinking things over "Very well, but we can't just take care of one target," he said.

"If I may make a suggestion," Madison said to Gabriel. "I could work with the FBI on the other safe houses while you raid Angelica's location."

Gabriel smiled. "I think that would be a very good idea." He turned to Alesbury. "Forgive me; I don't mean to overstep my bounds."

Alesbury smiled grimly. "Don't apologize; I dare say I was the one who overstepped. What do you need from us, son?"

"And the Denver police department, too," Montoya said gruffly. "You do work for us after all."

"Tomorrow my mother will go with one of you to get a warrant. At the same time, both of you will call in your SWAT teams which will not be told of anything until tomorrow. Madison, you and your Seeker cloak them and make sure Trinity doesn't get word of an attack. Faith will do the same for the DPD. Madison, once we begin our assault on Trinity, you will begin to raid safe houses. My father and mother will be with the Denver group, along with Erin and Guy to take care of any injuries." He looked at Madison. "Do you need any assistance in planning the raids on the safe houses?"

"Just some basic intel about what to expect on the ground," she said.

"Fine," Alesbury said, "until tomorrow then." He started to leave the room, Madison in tow.

"Should I come by the house later?" Madison asked Gabriel softly.

Gabriel felt his stomach flutter. "Um yeah, does eight work?"

"Sure does," she said, leaving with a wink.

As soon as Montoya's door closed behind Alesbury and Madison, Alison rounded on him. "Who was that?"

Gabriel felt sheepish.

"That was Madison Beldame," Faith said like Alison was an idiot. "She told you." She turned to Gabriel. "She's grown up a lot and she's a Paladin," Faith said, nudging him.

Gabriel just looked at her flatly.

"Oh come on, the Decors and Beldames have been allies for centuries, it's about time there was a union between them," Faith said.

Gabriel laughed. "You have us married already?"

Faith scowled, taking a different tack. "She's a Paladin and it's your duty."

"What kind of screwy crap is going on here, Decor?" Montoya asked.

Gabriel felt self-conscious. "Forgive me. I've known Madison her whole life; I trained her for a short time after the war…her sister was an Ark…she didn't make it."

"What's with the hair and eyes?" Sean asked. "Not that it wasn't doing it for me and all."

Alison gave him a look.

"Is there a time you don't think with your prick, boy?" Montoya asked.

Sean grinned. "No sir; you taught me well!"

Montoya cracked a chuckle "Fine. But what is the deal with that?" he asked Gabriel.

"The Beldames are like the Decors - we are known for our Seekers and Paladins. They feel that battle is more than just fighting; that one's appearance can lend a hand. Every Beldame Paladin I've met has their cornea colored red; they do this at a very young age. Also, they change their hair color. For the men it's to inspire fear, and for the women to inspire deadly beauty." Gabriel chuckled. "Her sister Stella had blue hair. They use Vis to do that. Stella would shock almost everyone she fought; it gave her an advantage. The Beldame's keep you off-balance. Madison was fourteen or fifteen the last time I saw her."

"Seems like a pretty big difference in age if you were in the war with her sister," Montoya mused.

"Well, Madison was what you would call a bonus," Faith supplied.

"Got ya, can we trust her?" he asked.

"Without a doubt," Gabriel said, faster than he should have.

Madison popped back in his mind and his gut fluttered again. *Your sister liked to do that to me too,* he thought. Stella was gorgeous, a trait shared by almost all of the prominent families. Stella was almost thirty when the war ended. She'd died trying to take back Domum. And in a way it was sad to see Madison as an adult Paladin. Would she share her sister's fate? At least she'd been level-headed about letting Gabriel lead the assault on Angelica's strong hold.

SEAN HUGHES took a drink of the smoothie Mandy had made for him. The two of them were back at Gabriel's parents' house, his meetings done for the day. In a way, he wished they weren't waiting until the morning to attack the train yard; he wanted to go now and be done with it.

"What are you thinking about?" Mandy asked.

He sighed. "Just about tomorrow," he said. Her blue eyes held his, twisting his insides.

"You'll be OK," she said.

Sean wasn't worried about his own safety, he really wasn't. He'd seen enough action in his day to not worry about his own well-being until it came time for it. Sean worried about the thing every commander did. He worried about those he led. He would be in charge of a group of SWAT guys and a good number of Mutari.

"You going to be OK tomorrow?" he asked Mandy.

She looked down. "I'm coming along more to help Alison and Gabriel identify people, but I suppose I'm a little nervous," she admitted.

The front door opened, ending their conversation. Gabriel strolled into the living room where Sean and Mandy were talking.

"Good evening, how are you two?" he asked.

"Peachy," Mandy said. "What brings you here?"

"Madison and I are going to talk over the plan for tomorrow," he said.

The doorbell rang and Gabriel turned to answer it. Madison Beldame walked in wearing the same getup she had on earlier. Sean shifted in his seat. Madison greeted Gabriel and then Mandy.

"Detective," she said coming to Sean.

Her hand was soft and her perfume intoxicating. Sean's heart picked up a bit and as Madison turned away from him he saw a look of annoyance cross Mandy's face. "What?" he mouthed at her.

"Madison my dear, how are you!" Melinda's voice called.

Melinda hugged Madison then held her at an arm's length, inspecting her. "You have grown up into a very fine lady," Melinda said warmly.

"Oh thank you, that's so sweet," Madison gushed.

Madison hugged Edward, quickly adding, "My father sends his best."

"How is your family?" Edward asked. "Can we expect them to be moving back out here anytime soon?"

"And you, for that matter," Melinda asked.

"My mother does want to come back to the States, so it's a possibility. As for me, I'm out here on a Pactum. Once we are done here or the Pactum ends I haven't decided. I don't have anything tying me to one area," she admitted.

Melinda shot a glance at her son who rolled his eyes.

"Well, we won't keep you from what you need to do. Are you staying for dinner?" Melinda asked.

"I would love to, thank you," Madison said.

"Sean, can we borrow you for a bit?" Gabriel asked.

Sean rose from his seat and walked over to Gabriel and Madison. They went into the small study where Gabriel laid out a map of Denver. Stickers indicated known safe houses and their known strength.

Madison became serious, looking the map over. "You've found a lot," she noted.

"Is Trinity in other cities?" Gabriel asked.

"A small town in Utah rooted them out. We think they were expanding into the area. It was a small operation but enough to garner the FBI's attention," she said.

She pushed silver hair behind her ear, crimson eyes scanning the map. She was like something out of a movie, unearthly in a way but also powerfully beautiful. It was this that Sean thought gave her an edge. Her scarlet eyes would make any foe wary. Her nonstandard beauty would captivate any enemy. As Gabriel said, people would be distracted and off-balance.

"What do I need to watch for?" Madison asked him.

Sean pushed her appearance from his mind and went to work giving Madison all the information he had about the area.

"What kind of numbers do you have?" he asked, thinking back to the one safe house they'd taken out.

"We've contracted with several Troll clubs. If these safe houses have Guardians, they shouldn't pose an issue," she said. "May I ask what your plans are?" she asked Gabriel.

Gabriel smiled, replacing the map of the city with one of the train yard.

He pointed to the west entrance. "Our main assault team will enter here," he said.

Madison leaned over the map to study it. "They will be met with heavy resistance," she noted.

"That they will. Sean here will be in charge of that team. I'll be leading another team from the south," he placed his index finger on the south entrance, tracing a path to the office building.

Madison looked up at Sean with those ruby eyes. "What are you hitting them with?"

"Twenty SWAT, six Trolls, two Werewolves, two Elementals and about sixteen Guardians. Oh, and two Banshees," Sean said.

Madison nodded approvingly. "What type of Elementals?"

"Air and Fire."

Madison's lips formed a half smile "Makina and Alfie?" she asked.

"Yes, and the O'Flynn's," Gabriel said, matching her smile.

Madison winked at Sean. "Don't worry, with that bunch, none of your men will get hurt," she paused. "Well, not by Trinity at least; just tell your men to watch their tongues around Jennifer O'Flynn and Makina."

Madison stood up straight. "Well, I think that's all I need. Do you think dinner is ready?"

MADISON BELDAME tried to come off cool and relaxed but she was pretty sure she was only managing cocky. She took in Gabriel's friendly face. How many times had she dreamt of that face over the years? But back when he knew her she was just a teenager; did he see her as a woman now? He looked much the same as he had back then, though with age he had become more handsome. Their two families had been close for many years; Madison's parents respected the Decors a great deal. She needed to represent her family well.

Melinda and Edward were in the kitchen with the Succubus Mandy, putting dinner on the table. Old memories flowed into her mind as she sat at the oak table. How many times had she stayed here as a kid? Melinda sat Gabriel next to Madison, making her tense again. *Why are you so timid? It's not like he's going to bite you.* She chided herself. She was a Paladin now, possibly even powerful enough to be an Ark. She shouldn't feel like a little girl around her first school yard crush.

"So Madison, what have you been up to since we saw you last?" Melinda asked.

"Training and a lot of Pactums. When Vis went public, I was working on a Pactum in D.C. where I met Agent Alesbury. I've been working with the FBI ever since," she said.

"That's a long Pactum; do you like it?" Gabriel asked.

She shrugged. "It's nice having steady work and getting to build a relationship with people. Do you not work long Pactums?"

Gabriel shook his head. "No; this is my longest."

She felt self-conscious; was it bad that she'd only had one job for the last three years?

"But I have to admit I like it," Gabriel said. "It looks like this Pactum will turn into something more permanent. I'm looking forward to not having to always get used to new people, and to have some sense of normality."

* * * * *

Sean Hughes smirked. "Yeah, you might even be able to settle down," he interjected, earning a sharp kick under the table from Mandy.

Gabriel turned red. "Um, yeah I suppose so…"

Madison looked down at her plate.

Melinda looked at Sean sweetly. "That's a very good point, Sean. Madison how about you, are you seeing anybody?"

Now Madison turned as red as her eyes. "Er…well no, not really…I keep busy with work. Not that I'm a shut-in or anything, lots of guys like me…" her eyes widened in horror. "Not that I'm running around or anything, it's just that…"

"You're a talented young woman with goals and you aren't going to throw your life away for some jerk," Mandy said coming to her rescue.

"Yes, that's right. Thank you, Mandy," Madison said.

Sean wasn't about to let this opportunity go. "Well Madison, after all this is said and done, maybe you could use some downtime. I bet Gabriel would be happy to take you around the city."

"What a fantastic idea!" Melinda gushed, winking at Sean. "Yes Madison, you should take a vacation after this case, won't you stay for a few days?"

Madison looked like a cornered animal. For his part, this was the highlight of Sean's day.

Gabriel stood up. "That was a great meal. Thank you, Mother," he looked to Madison. "It's been ages since I've trained - would you care to join me?"

Madison took to Gabriel's offer like a caged animal shooting up from her chair. "Yes, that's a good idea. With a job tomorrow, we want to be in top condition," she said, making her way with Gabriel out of the room, waving at Melinda. "Thank you Melinda, dinner was lovely."

As soon as they were out of earshot, Mandy rounded on Sean. "You are such a dick," then looking at Melinda. "Sorry, Melinda."

"I think it went well," Melinda said. "Thank you, Sean."

"He didn't mean what he said in a nice way; he was trying to make them uncomfortable," Mandy said glaring at him.

"What?" Sean said innocently. "I didn't, honestly," he tried to lie. "Edward, you're with me, right?"

Edward Decor laughed heartily. "Son, I've been married long enough to know when not to argue. I'm sure you two will figure it out."

"Us two?" Mandy said.

"That's right," Melinda interjected. "You are getting to an age where you should settle down Detective, and you and Mandy are so cute," she said.

"Oh no," Mandy said holding her hands in front of her. "We aren't together; he just almost got me killed!"

"Something he can spend the rest of his life making up to you," Melinda said brightly.

Sean knew Mandy would make him regret it later, but he put his arm around the back of her chair. "You know what, Melinda? I think you are onto something…" he said, grinning at a red Mandy.

TWENTY

ALISON KAUR sat in the back corner of a large room. Gabriel was up front outlining the raid on the train yard to a group of fifty or so police officers and the Mutari. Faith sat next to her mother, muttering nervously while Erin worked her way down a checklist. The only Mage in the back of the room who didn't appear to be distracted in one way or another was Edward, who sat next to Alison. He watched his son with an air of respect and reverence. Here was a father confident in who his child was. Yet his expression was grim at the same time.

"Are you worried?" Alison asked him softly.

Edward frowned. "No, not worried." He looked at her. "Are you?"

"A little, but I think that's normal. I won't feel right until everyone is back home safe and sound," she said. Then reading the look on Edward's face added, "You don't think everyone is coming home safe and sound, do you?" The concern in her own voice surprised her.

Edward shook his head. "No dear; everyone is not coming home today."

"Do you mean the men and Mutari who work for Trinity will be dying today?" she asked.

Edward gave her an 'are you kidding me?' look before saying, "Today, some of our own will not make it. My son has done his best, but not even he can prevent everything."

Alison looked over at Erin as she checked her list. She was to be back in the staging area to take care of the wounded. Alison only now started to realize that she wasn't just here to be on the safe side; Gabriel knew she would be needed and so did she.

Sean walked in front of the group of men and Alison saw it on his face too. Was that the look every commander had going into a battle they knew they could lose people in?

"There are going to be two teams," Sean said. "Team one will be with me; we will be taking on the west gate of the yard. We will come in fast and hard, but don't expect to make it far before we encounter resistance. Team two, you will be with Gabriel."

Sean looked down. "We know that Trinity has infiltrated our office…this was plain to see when Javier Davison escaped a few weeks back. We also have reason to believe that Trinity has the ability to listen in on a lot of what takes place here. For that reason, we must ask that you not make any phone calls from here out." Sean paused as a few people grumbled. "We can't afford to lose the element of surprise."

Gabriel stepped forward. "I must echo what Detective Hughes has said. I know that many of you were there when we took down that Guardian," he said, letting his words sink in with the group before continuing. "Can you imagine what that encounter would have been like had the enemy known that we were coming? I can say to you now that what we face today is far greater a threat than what we've faced before, so please do not endanger yourself or your brothers and sisters here in this room."

Alison smirked. Gabriel was going to try to fire up the troops. She almost gasped as she felt her sense of honor and determination bolster. The touch on her emotions was subtle, but after Heidi had shown her what it was like, she could feel Gabriel's touch. The people in the room sat up taller in their chairs.

"Here we have a mockery of people who think they can spit in the face of society, who believe they are above what is good and right." With his words, Alison felt anger. She resisted the emotions and then decided to let herself be carried. "Four years have Vis users and Humans tried to build a relationship of trust and respect and Trinity laughs at us, trampling that which we've worked for." Gabriel paced the room, looking angry, and Alison caught a fleeting glimpse of what he must have been like during the war. He didn't see the men and women before him as public servants but soldiers. He continued to speak, his words flowing faster and with more and more emotion. Despite her knowledge of how he was affecting her emotions, Alison wanted to jump from her seat; she was so infused with feeling.

"My brothers and sisters, today I go in harm's ugly path, to death or victory I do not know. Who of you will stand with me?!" he asked.

"I will!" Alison said along with everyone else. It felt like fire was coursing in her veins and she liked it.

The Mutari she'd met all seemed willing to follow Gabriel to the ends of the world, a sentiment that up until this point Alison hadn't shared, but now she did. She knew that she would follow wherever Gabriel went and told her to go, as would any of the other people in the room. Was this what it was to be an Ark?

She looked to his father. "Was he like this in the war?"

Edward smiled proudly. "Every time he readied men to fight, he made them feel as though the world depended on them and that there was no way they could lose. There will not be a single person in this room who doesn't believe to their core in what we're fighting for."

FAITH PENN knelt atop a SWAT van as it headed down I-25. She was cloaking herself so that no one could see her; she also cast a veil over the procession of vans and squad cars, keeping onlookers from thinking about the vehicles. They exited the highway and entered a dilapidated industrial section of town that had died long ago.

The yard was surrounded by a high fence of corrugated steel, chain link, and barbed wire. The metal of the fence was dark and rusted with splashes of graffiti providing color. The van came to a stop by the south gate of the yard. Her mother was with the group bound for the west entrance. Faith leapt down from the van's roof next to Gabriel and Alison. Police poured out of the vans, gathering around Gabriel. With them was a small group of Mutari including two Trolls: Tory and Rebecca Coutler.

ALISON KAUR wrapped the cord around her neck that would allow her to control her Guardians. Instantly, her mind was flooded with information coming from the Guardians. It had taken her some time to get used to the feeling, but now she could keep them in the back of her mind without being distracted. Alison had five Shields and two Attack Guardians. She connected with them, making them pay attention as she looked at every member of her group and telling the statues not to kill any of these people in the coming hours.

"Are you ready?" Gabriel asked her.

Alison didn't think she looked worried, but the Guardians reacted to her pang of apprehension by moving around her protectively.

Gabriel eyed them. "Yes," he said to himself, and then to the rest of the people, "We are going to wait for Officer Hughes team to breach the west gate, and then we are up. Move fast and silently. Let the Shields lead the way whenever possible. The west gate will likely not have Vis webs on it if they could hurt Trinity staff. That will not be the case for us; we will encounter more aggressive wards. Follow my instructions and watch each other."

SEAN HUGHES gave his equipment one last check. His mind was connected with the Guardians and he moved the ten Shields and four Attackers into position by the west gate. Away from Sean's position, Erin waited with an ambulance and Gabriel's parents. The cops, along with the Guardians, moved along either side of the gate; the lead officer on each side signaling Sean when they were in position.

Sean directed his thoughts to the two Hurlers they had with them. They were short statues with arms that hung to the ground. Next to each was a large stone ball that James had enchanted to spring any wards.

"Do we have the go?" Sean said in his radio to Sergeant Montoya.

"You have your warrant," Montoya said.

Sean spurred the Hurlers into motion, each hefting a stone ball. They started to spin around, building momentum. Sean told them where to aim and one let go of the stone ball. It hurled through the air, slamming into the gate with a crash. The gate flew open from the force of impact as the second Hurler let its ball go. Sean watched the stone bounce down a dirt roadway. The area flashed with orange and green Vis.

"GO! GO! GO!" Sean called to the men and Mutari.

The Shields moved at the speed of a slow jog into the yard. Cops rushed inside, moving to piles of debris that littered the area, some taking cover behind the Guardians. Sean moved in with them, John and Michael O'Flynn on either side of him. The two men had a slight green hue, and carried iron rods as thick as baseball bats. *Take our flanks; move forward,* Sean thought to the Attackers. They moved with lighting speed around the group. Sean clapped his hands to his ears as the air was rent with a siren from inside the yard.

Ahead of them were two large piles of metal and a few rail cars. Sean's team moved to them, trying to make it past the natural bottleneck they made before Trinity showed up. There was a sound of metal on metal and Sean watched in horror as a train wheel bounded on the ground toward them. *Form a line,* he thought to the Shields. They moved in the wheel's path, hefting giant square shields. There was a deafening clang of metal as the wheel hit a shield. The Statues held fast; the train wheel popping up in the air and coming down toward the men.

The Banshee Laura rushed forward, her face upturned. She screamed and Sean thought he felt his eardrum rupture. The air in front of Laura distorted into waves with a slight yellow tint. The waves crashed against the wheel, and it flew back away from them.

"They're, here!" the rough voice of Alberto Doyle, one of the Werewolves called.

He growled, his clothes ripping away and gray fur covering his body. His face morphed, taking on the appearance of a Wolf; his hands twisting into long, clawed fingers, arms growing long. He howled, kicking off his shoes and running forward around the Shields, his companion Hector alongside him. They jumped in the air, being met by two other Wolves. As the air filled with the sound of gunfire, the four Wolves hit the ground, unfazed by bullets flying past them. The animals' muzzles and paws were quickly covered in scarlet.

GABRIEL DECOR unsheathed Iram as he heard the alarm sound from the west end of the train yard. Faith, Alison, Mandy, and a small contingent of Mutari followed him as he loped to the south gate.

The tall gate was held closed by a thick rusty chain. He held Iram's edge close to the chain pulling on Vis. "Perseco," he said. There was a small flash of purple and the chain fell from the gate.

He looked to Faith, who nodded. Gabriel motioned for the two Trolls to come forward, their Vis aura strong. Troy and Rebecca pushed on the gates, as Faith used a spell to silence the groaning metal. The gates shuddered and started to move.

Alison's Guardians moved in first, the five Shields taking the lead as her two Attackers moved to keep their flanks clear. Gabriel followed them inside with the rest of his team. He took the lead, not using the Guardians for cover. He poured Vis into wards and down into Iram. He breathed a mist of Vis in front of him. About five feet away, a gossamer-fine thread appeared with an emerald glow.

"Tracy Hope," he said to Faith softly, recognizing the color of the other Paladin's Vis.

Faith moved back, hissing, "Take cover and stay still."

The others did as told and Faith cloaked them as Gabriel assessed the yard's defenses.

They hadn't been discovered yet, but that would change at some point. He filled the area with Vis mist, watching the threads come into view. Vis webs were made of multiple parts. Some strands were just to trigger others that would capture or kill whatever they ran into. If that was all a web had in it, Gabriel could deal with it in a moment; it would be equally simple if he knew the Mage who made it to be a novice. He came close to a strand, inspecting it. It was thin, suggesting Tracy was halfway decent with webs. That meant that some strands would sound an alarm or passively alert Tracy that they'd been activated.

In the distance he could hear gunfire. He could hear the radio from Sean softly in the back of his head, though he wasn't paying strict attention. From what he did notice, Sean's group was encountering heavy resistance. How long until Mages were deployed to the west?

"Faith, do you have a line on any Mages?" he asked her over his shoulder.

She shook her head. "I'm blind; Angelica is here for sure, and has the place buckled down pretty tight."

Faith looked and sounded like she was exerting herself pretty hard. *Angelica is looking for us,* he thought. *And until you find me you aren't going to do anything dumb like sending out Paladins.*

Unless…he spoke to his mother, "Do you have the area secure?" he asked her.

"Yes," she said. "No communication is getting in or out of here."

Gabriel felt at one of his own spells. Upon arrival, he'd used Vis to make a perimeter around the yard, blocking anyone trying to Jump in or out. The ward wasn't perfect, but he doubted that Angelica or even Marcus, if he was onsite, would be able to break it anytime soon or without him knowing. *Hmmm, she'll probably assume that we are coming in the south.*

"Makina," he said over the radio. "Have you entered the fight yet?"

"Per your orders, I am holding back," she responded.

"Good, I want you to fly to the east end of the yard, find a weak place in the fence and attack it like you were trying to sneak in. After you do that, let me know and head back to the west gate to assist Sean," he ordered.

She acknowledged the command.

Gabriel worked quickly, clearing a path for his team to follow amongst the web; making sure not to activate the web but rather push strands to the side for people to walk by.

"Move where I do," he told them.

Everyone followed him and once they were past the web, he heard an alarm in the east.

"Done," Makina said. "I assume you wanted the alarm to sound?"

"Yes I did; thank you Makina."

SEAN HUGHES hunkered down, the air around him a buzz of bullets. His line of Guardians was moving slowly forward, men and Mutari using them for cover. Sean sent orders to the Hurlers who continued to send a steady barrage at Trinity. He looked across an open space separating him and the other half of his people. The earth trembled and Sean braced himself. Trinity had an Earth Elemental that was wreaking havoc on his people.

"Makina!" he yelled at the Air Elemental. "Anything you can do?"

Her voice floated on the breeze, sounding in his ear like he was only a few feet away. "Alfie and I can disorient them, but it's up to you to capitalize on the opportunity."

"Good enough for me."

Sean directed two of his Attackers to move in from the flanks and to the front line. His other two were fighting other Guardians. He could sense what damage they took and the energy they were burning. *I need the upper hand.*

Alfie ran in the open, Makina on his heels.

"COVER!" Sean yelled.

The cops all jumped into action providing cover fire for Makina and Alfie, pushing back Trinity's group of Humans and Mutari. Alfie knelt down on the ground and for a moment Sean was worried that he was hit. Fire burst around the man, swirling angrily. Makina leapt above him. Sean pitched forward as wind buffeted him, moving toward Makina. He got lightheaded as the air thinned. The air around Makina exploded into a fireball and Sean felt his mouth drop open. She was high above them, pulling all of the oxygen from her surroundings. A fireball the size of a few buses flew toward Trinity, scorching rubbish and people who didn't get out of the way.

Sean took advantage of the moment, spurring his Attacker Guardians forward and yelling to his units.

"Forward! Forward! Forward! Come on!" he yelled.

MANDY STAFFORD crept inside a warehouse connected to the office that was their target. Rusted equipment lined the walls and dust hung in the air. Across the large expanse was a door leading into the offices. She moved slowly near the rear of the group. Faith paused for moment, signaling for the others to stop.

"HEADS UP!" she yelled.

The warehouse vanished before their eyes, replaced by a large patch of dirt, at the end of which was the real building.

"Stay put!" Gabriel barked but too late; some of the Humans were already moving for cover.

Orange and emerald threads flashed into existence all around them. They'd walked right into a Vis web Angelica had been hiding. Men screamed as the web collapsed in on them, the strands cutting flesh and bone, killing them. Mandy yelped as web encased her. She flexed her Vis reserve, making her strong enough to hold off the web. Men hunched by Alison's Shield Guardians who held the web back with ease. Gabriel shouted a spell and ribbons of lavender Vis sliced the web.

Mandy relaxed her Vis, feeling fatigue. The dirt around her feet exploded with bullets. She ran for cover, jumping through the window of a shack. She rolled on the ground, clutching at her side. Outside there was more gunfire, accompanied by the war cries of Trolls. Mandy was shaking. She looked to her side, horrified to see hot blood soaking her shirt. The sensation of life draining from her was alarming. As she looked at her wound, she felt the pain exploding. She tried to use Vis to heal herself but had very little left after the web, and what little she had could only stop the pain.

The shack door opened. Mandy rolled behind some rubbish as several people entered.

"Come on, take cover and shoot through the window," one of the voices said.

Mandy was getting cold and lightheaded. She needed to do something, needed to act or she was going to die. She could see one of the men in the room. He was Human; his Vis pulsing in his body; excited. Instinct roared in Mandy, telling her to attack, to take the Vis and live. Her Vis was failing and pain started to radiate in her side. She stifled a gasp but twitched, knocking over a tin can. The men in the room froze.

The one she'd been looking at turned, saw her on the ground, blood pooling around her. He came over to her calmly, pointing a gun at her head.

"Don't worry; this will help the pain," he said.

Mandy's hand snapped up to the man's wrist, gripping it. Her instincts were finally in control. What little Vis she had left flared in her as she wrenched the man forward, her other hand grabbing the back of his head and slamming their faces together painfully. He tried to pull away but Mandy pulled on his Vis. An intoxicating energy filled her, warming and soothing her wrecked body. The man struggled weakly as Mandy's muscles became stronger with Vis. She sucked on his life force as hard as she could, his body going limp with death.

She arose from the ground, her wound no longer hurting. Vis was like a drug for Succubi, a drug that clouded her mind with an instinctual need to feed and survive. One of the other men saw her and Mandy bounded forward faster than any Human ever could. She grabbed him, dragging him to the back of the shack as his companions shot at her. His punches felt like a child's to her. She twisted his mouth to her own; draining him. She felt her side finish healing as another Human came around the corner. She had more Vis than her body could hold. *May as well use it*, she thought in her altered state.

He swung a bat at her. She ducked, pivoting away from the bat but moving in closer to the man. She shot her hand forward like a knife, her skin and bone strengthening to that of stone. She hit his ribs, the force of her thrust punching her fingers through skin as her hand followed easily. Her arm dug deep into his upper body, his organs a slimy mush around her skin. When her elbow entered his body, her fingers breached through the other side and poked out above the back of his shoulder. Mandy pulled her arm out of the now dead man with an audible slurp. She spun at a sound, her hand stopping an attack. She read the Vis flow of her attacker as she leaped back.

He didn't go after her but kept an eye on her. "You can't keep using Vis like that for long," he said.

He was right; Mandy would need to attack. But doing so hastily would get her hurt. An idea came to her. Strictly speaking, she didn't need to drain someone from their lips; that was just the most ideal spot. Mandy darted forward, headed for the Troll but changing direction at the last second. He swung a metal rod at the spot she should have been in. Mandy came up from behind him, biting down on the exposed skin on the back of his neck, using Vis to make her jaw strong enough to hold on. He twisted Mandy, but she was connected to his back like a rabid dog. She pulled on his Vis. She was only able to pull enough to counter the amount she was using, but that was all she needed.

She groped for the arm he was holding the rod with, pulling it back. He shoved himself backwards, ramming her into the cinder block wall. She grunted, letting go with her mouth and falling back. The Troll turned, grabbing her leg before she could move it. He threw her across the room over tables covered in metal equipment. She tried to stand, pain in her knee sending her to the ground. Before she could use Vis, the Troll was back on her, raising a fist. She flexed her Vis in time to stop his fist from caving in her skull. Instead, she felt the bone below her eye crack. He hit her again and again making her eyes swell and sting with blood. Mandy struggled, feeling her Vis again leaving her. She was going to be beaten to death.

Her hand stung as something cut it. Her mind flashed back to awareness. She groped for what had cut her, finding it on the ground. She jammed it into the Troll's leg. He wailed in pain and Mandy burned her Vis in a moment, taking advantage and going for his lips. She bit down on his lower lip and pulled. Her body surged with power. He tried to push her off but she dug her finger into his eye. He tried to lurch back from her, but she was attached to his lip. Had he not been a Troll, the lip would have come off but as it was strong with Vis, she held on. The Troll was becoming weaker as she felt her wounds heal and her muscles clamp onto him. She'd never pulled Vis like this before and it felt amazing. She was in a state of euphoria as the Troll died.

She stood from his body, Vis surging in her. There were no more enemies. She let her Vis drop back to a normal level lest she waste it. As soon as her mind cleared from her frenzy and awareness came back to her, Mandy stumbled. It was as if she'd awakened from a horrible dream to find out it was true. Blood covered her arm and torn clothes. Three Humans and a Troll lay dead on the ground; three of them she had drained and one of the Humans she had mutilated.

Mandy shuffled back away from the bodies until she was in the corner.

"What have I done," she moaned, slumping to the floor, tears clouding her vision.

ALISON KAUR held fast behind a Shield Guardian. The firefight appeared to be over for the moment, but she wasn't about to let her guard down. Gabriel jogged over to her, Iram gripped tightly in his hand, crimson running down the blade.

"How are your Guardians doing?" he asked.

Alison paused, feeling with her mind to the group of statues. All were in good condition, not having taken much damage from the ambush. "Fine," she said. There was a yellow glow and Faith came into view, dropping her cloak. She and Gabriel started to talk.

Alison let her attention drift to those in her group. She saw three men dead, cut to pieces by the Vis web. She clenched her jaw as she recognized faces of those she knew. The Trolls with them were relatively unharmed and only a few other officers were hurt. Something seemed off to Alison.

"Where is Mandy?" she asked aloud.

Gabriel and Faith stopped talking and looked at her. She repeated her question and Faith's face scrunched. She turned and pointed to a small shack. "She's in there," Faith said.

Alison moved to the shack to fetch Mandy. *If you let anything happen to that girl, Hughes is going to kill you.*

She peeked in the door, her gun up, not wanting Trinity goons to get the drop on her. The room was trashed, blood spattering the walls and pooling on the floor around a torn-up body. Alison walked slowly, hearing the muffled sound of sobs. She saw three other bodies.

She found Mandy sitting in the corner of the room, her knees held tightly to her chest. Alison carefully holstered her weapon. Mandy was covered in blood; her own or others', Alison wasn't sure.

She spoke softly, walking slowly to the girl. "Mandy, are you hurt?"

Mandy didn't say anything. Alison came up closer to the girl, seeing her shaking with what she presumed was shock. Mandy didn't look hurt. *Did she kill these people on her own? And what of the man with a hole through him?* Alison wondered in horror. She sat next to the girl, trying to put her hand on her shoulder. Mandy flinched away. "Don't touch me, I'm a monster!"

So Mandy had killed the men. All right, Alison could handle this. Mandy had defended herself and the team, she'd done nothing wrong.

"You did what you had to," Alison said. "It's going to be OK."

Mandy didn't respond but she didn't pull away from Alison's touch either.

Alison put her finger to her ear. "Gabriel I think you better come here."

A moment later, Gabriel and Faith came in the shack, taking in Mandy with speculative eyes. Gabriel looked to Mandy and then the bodies. "She drained them, that's how she was able to do this," he said, kneeling down next to her.

Mandy's trembling subsided as Gabriel came closer. "We need to get her out of here," he said to himself.

He called for an officer to come in.

"I need you to take her to Erin," he said, and then leaned down to Mandy, speaking softly in Latin. Mandy's head slumped with unconsciousness. Gabriel turned back to the officer. "Can you carry her?"

The officer smirked. "I think I can manage carrying a hundred pound girl, sir."

Gabriel lifted Mandy, giving her to the officer.

"We need to move out," he said as Alison and Faith followed him out of the shack.

The group continued their steady push toward the warehouse/office building. Two tall steel doors stood slightly ajar, leading into the warehouse. Alison nudged a Shield to move forward, pushing open one of the doors. They entered silently, knowing that Trinity would have people inside.

"Keep sharp," she said softly. "We didn't take too many down when we got ambushed, so expect them here."

The warehouse was empty save a few crates in a line by the entrance. Alison heard a footstep in front of her and to her left. She jerked, holding her gun up, ready to shoot…nothing. There was no body where the sound came from.

A hand rested on her shoulder. "Angelica," Faith said in a whisper. "She's here."

Alison felt a pit in her gut. "How do you know?"

"You heard something that wasn't there, right?"

How had Faith known that? Alison looked at the men as they too looked quietly about, readying to fight a nonexistent foe.

Faith spoke again. "We Seekers hide things Alison, and sometimes the best way to hide a single footstep is to hide it amongst the sound of a thousand footsteps," Faith explained as Alison grew more nervous. "Or what if you make a thousand footsteps but muffle the one real footstep," Faith looked at Alison. "This is one of many ways we fight. When a Seeker is present, you cannot trust any of your senses; not your ears, your nose, or even your eyes. Let me show you."

Faith pointed and Alison looked to see Sean walking toward her. Alison made to wave to him, but then Sean turned into Gabriel, who turned into Faith, who turned into herself. Alison swallowed hard.

"Get your people out of here," Faith said.

Alison motioned to her men. "Fall back, let the Ma-"

She was cut off by a cocky voice. "You haven't done so well this time, Ark," Keith Spencer said.

Alison watched the young man walk into the warehouse, his white jacket flapping around his feet. He wore a hateful expression as he took in Gabriel. Alongside him was Tracy Hope, her long blond hair in a bun atop her head. Between the two was a Mage Alison hadn't seen before.

"To whom do I have the privilege of meeting?" Gabriel said to the new Mage.

The Mage drew a broad sword, inclining his head at Gabriel "Eric Hague, and my blade is Power. And you?"

By this point, both Tracy and Keith had their swords drawn. Alison couldn't take her eyes away from the Mages as Gabriel drew his own. "Ark Third Seat Gabriel Decor, my blade is Iram."

"So you've decided to stay, huh?" Faith said to Alison.

Alison looked to Faith. She stared at the other Mages unflinchingly. Alison's men and Mutari had fallen back as ordered, leaving Alison alone with the Mages.

"Yes I have," Alison said.

Faith nodded. "You stay with me and control those Guardians; don't interfere with the Paladins."

The room lit-up with lavender, orange, emerald, and brown light. Alison looked to the Mages, each one wrapped in a column of light. Gabriel's shone the brightest. Faith placed her hand on Alison's shoulder. Instantly they were in a sphere of yellow, hovering high in the room. Yellow Vis rippled out like waves crashing into the walls of the room, met by red Vis as the Paladins attacked.

GABRIEL DECOR pushed Vis out in all directions as he had the first time he'd fought Tracy and Keith. This time, however, Angelica's presence made him unable to predict their moves with the technique. He infused his body with Vis as he moved forward toward Eric. Eric sidestepped Gabriel, swinging his sword at Gabriel's side. With a flare of Vis, Gabriel avoided Eric's counter attack with ease. Around him, the room shifted as Angelica and Faith tried to throw the other Paladins off. From what he could tell; Faith was losing, which meant that Gabriel was going to have to fight smart.

"Calor!" Keith said, making the concrete floor glow bright orange.

Gabriel countered Keith's heat spell with a freezing spell of his own. The floor cracked and broke as its temperature fluctuated. Gabriel landed on the ground amidst chunks of gray. He raised his hand. "Usque." The floor ripped free in pieces. Gabriel pushed on the concrete forcing it out and away from him on all sides. Keith used Vis to deflect a chunk the size of his head. Eric and Tracy didn't waste energy but rather wove around the projectiles. Gabriel didn't give Keith a chance to recover. He moved in fast, slashing with Iram. milliseconds before Iram would have finished him, Keith's blade met Gabriel's with a clang. Gabriel rolled away, sweeping Iram behind his back and guarding from any attack. Eric sent a wave of brown Vis at Gabriel. He jumped, avoiding the wave and landing hard, barely getting Iram up in time to stop Tracy from taking his head. *Where did she come from? I didn't even see her.* Faith was not holding Angelica well at all. Gabriel was having a hard time focusing on his opponents. One of his wards flashed as Gabriel cartwheeled back in the air. He threw a shielding ward all around him, pumping mass amounts of Vis into it; not knowing who had made the last attack.

Almost at once, the ward was tested as Gabriel spun from Tracy to Keith to Eric; each trying to outflank him. Gabriel was surrounded; he needed to get the upper hand. He ducked away from an attack and faked a jump. Eric took his bluff and Gabriel dashed below him as the man jumped. Eric landed, swearing as Gabriel came upright, the three Paladins in front of him. Something wet ran down his fingers, soaking into his grip on Iram. *When did I get hurt?* Gabriel wondered in surprise as blood dripped from his hand. He lessened the pain wards he had, causing a burning pain to erupt in his right arm. Tracy nodded at him, a glint of crimson on the tip of her sword, Dolor.

Gabriel inclined his head to her giving her credit for drawing first blood. The four Mages stood apart from one another circling the room, around them a din of conflicting sounds and images. Keith's form flickered. Gabriel twisted, fear clenching at him as he realized he'd been seeing a projection of Keith and not Keith himself. Too late Gabriel was able to find the real man, who thrust his sword at him. Gabriel clenched his teeth, pain wards draining him. Gabriel felt other wards being tested as they shielded vital organs, moving them around Keith's blade. The hilt of the broad sword hit Gabriel's right side shortly after the tip of the blade ran through his left. Gabriel tapped his Vis, pushing out on Keith. The room lit with a blinding flash of lavender as Gabriel pushed.

Keith flew back crashing to the ground.

FAITH PENN yelped in pain as a spell reverberated back on itself. Her sphere of Vis was collapsing. Vis buffeted her as Gabriel pushed away Keith. Blood was pouring from his gut where he'd been stabbed. The blood stopped as his wards activated.

"GABRIEL!" Alison called out next to her, "Faith, do something, he's losing!"

But Faith couldn't do anything. Angelica was too good, she was too powerful. It was all Faith could do to keep Gabriel from being a sitting duck in the middle of the room. Ruby Vis lapped at her sphere. Sooner or later, Faith would lose the fight and when she did she would be visible to all in the room. With the number of Paladins Trinity had, Faith had no doubt that one would attack her and in that moment Gabriel would lose for sure. *Come on Faith!* she goaded herself.

"Faith, a little help," Gabriel said, ever calm.

"I can't beat her," Faith admitted, feeling like a failure.

Tracy hit Gabriel again, and then he was hit by a wave of Vis from Eric. Faith reached her hand out, watching as her brother was being slowly killed.

GABRIEL DECOR landed hard on the ground, blood gushing from his neck. Sealing wards stopped the blood flowing from the artery Eric had nicked. He pushed himself across the only remaining patch of concrete that was still intact. Getting up, his body screamed with pain, but it wasn't the worst he'd ever had. Faith could beat Angelica; Gabriel knew that, but Faith didn't and until she believed in herself, Angelica would win. *Fine,* Gabriel thought.

Seekers were hard to find and therefore harder still to kill. Making it even more difficult was the fact that Paladins protected their Seekers with wards, wards that had to be breached in order to hurt the Seeker. Gabriel needed to find Angelica and hurt her so she couldn't help her people, and he also needed to get past all of the wards protecting her.

Gabriel lowered Iram, causing the other three Mages to pause.

"I don't suppose you are ready to give up?" Gabriel asked.

Eric shook his head grimly.

Gabriel nodded, delving down deep inside himself and pulling on his Vis.

Angelica's voice rang in the room, panicked. "Attack him now! He's going full power!"

Eric and the others lunged at him but too late; Vis exploded inside Gabriel, flowing out his body in a flood of lavender light.

"Adolebit," Gabriel said.

The Paladins raised their hands; Vis shields blocking an

amethyst ball of fire that engulfed the room. Gabriel felt their wards strain against his burning spell and in the corner of the room he felt a ward fail. Gabriel let the Vis go spinning to the corner of the room where Angelica Vies stood wrapped in a cocoon of ruby, shielding herself from Gabriel's attack.

They locked eyes for one moment and Gabriel felt a primal rage take control of him. "VIS!" he yelled sending a ball of pure energy at her. Keith cast a ward in front of her that shattered when Gabriel's spell hit. Angelica managed to turn away from the ball. As it passed her Gabriel said, "Extendo." The ball expanded in all directions in a flash, throwing her against the wall and knocking her out.

As she slumped to the ground, her spells failed. The room filled with Vis and Gabriel sensed Eric's attack. He dodged the attack, pushing himself back and away from the other man. Gabriel came in low to the ground and rushed forward at Eric. Gabriel used a burst of Vis for speed at the last moment, catching Eric off guard. Iram came across the man's chest, catching on bone and flesh, slicing through protective wards. Gabriel jerked the blade free, dropping the man to the ground.

He turned to Keith and Tracy, the prior carrying Angelica Vies from the room. Tracy stood still for a moment. Gabriel made to attack when he felt the spell he'd placed on the area preventing jumps crumble. And in that moment, Tracy Hope vanished in a flash of emerald Vis.

TWENTY-ONE

SEAN HUGHES ran forward, chasing down one of Trinity's men. Once Angelica had been defeated, Trinity split in a hurry; giving up for other fortified locations. Sean panted as he ran after the man who was making a break for the office building. Sean rolled to the ground at the staccato RAT TAT TAT of gunfire. He turned as one of the cops returned fire on a man, dropping the perp to the ground, clutching at his leg. Sean resumed his chase of the other perp who hadn't given the gunfire a second thought.

As they rounded a corner, Sean grew irritated with the chase, sensing one of his Attacker Guardians in the area. He directed the statue to where he thought the perp was going.

The perp, a big burly man who could run astonishingly fast, didn't even see the statue. The Guardian slammed into the man like an NFL lineman, sending them both to the ground. Sean barked a laugh. He came to a jog, stopping next to the figure on the ground. The Attacker stood awaiting another order. Sean leaned down to the man on the ground. Sean hadn't taken into account that the Guardian was made of bronze when he'd ordered it to ram the man. Sean checked for a pulse and found one. He fished the man's wallet out of his pocket.

"Well there…" he pulled out his driver's license. "Travis Mathews, I would tell you you're under arrest and read you your rights, but I'll save that for when you wake up," Sean said.

Jennifer O'Flynn, one of the Trolls, made it to Sean, her brown eyes taking in the knocked-out man.

"Did you kill him?" she asked.

"Nah he's alive; I just forgot that those Attackers are made of bronze," Sean said.

She didn't question his mistake. "Do you want me to take him back to the squad cars?" she asked.

Sean almost made a comment about a five-foot-nothing girl like her not being able to pick up a tall, thick man but then he remembered she was a Troll and could probably throw a dumpster. "Sure, if you don't mind."

She shrugged, leaning over and slinging the man over her shoulder like he was a toddler. "It's not a problem if he wakes up while I'm on my way back; I'll get a kick out of him freaking out about being carried by someone who still has to shop in the junior section to find clothes that fit," she said, walking off.

"Sean where are you?" Alison's voice buzzed in his ear.

"Not far away; why what's up?" he asked.

"We found Corey McLaughlin."

ALISON KAUR looked down at the corpse of Corey McLoughlin. She wasn't mad at the situation; just tired. Next to him was Javier Davison, also very dead, along with a contingent of other people, some Human and some not. Corey and the others were found in an office. The offices next to theirs were full of drugs, guns and a handful of kidnapped girls. In a big way, this was a win for Alison and Sean. They'd stopped Corey and his gang for good. But in the same way it was a loss, because now not only would McLoughlin never see the inside of a jail cell, but he was a murder victim. Someone was going to have to track down his killer, though Alison doubted that would be her responsibility. That task would go to the FBI.

Sean came into the room and swore. "Got off lucky again," he said.

The raid hadn't been a bust, however. Many of Trinity's people were captured, and when Alison got back to the station she found Madison Beldame talking with Gabriel.

Alison didn't find her red eyes and silver hair to be as off-putting as the first time she'd encountered the woman.

"Congratulations on solving your case, Detective," Madison said.

"Thanks for taking care of all those safe houses," Alison replied. "I take it your team will have a lot of work to do with Trinity now."

Madison looked down for a moment.

"Kaur, Hughes, get in here!" Sergeant Montoya called, though without his normal sharpness.

Madison and Gabriel followed Alison as she joined Sean, Montoya, Agent Alesbury from the FBI, along with…"Heidi?" Alison said when she came in the room.

Heidi Decor sat in a seat in front of Montoya and Alesbury, a pair of reading glasses perched on her nose. Faith came in the room, not commenting on any of the attendees. Alison worried about Faith. Angelica had beaten her and it had gotten

Gabriel hurt. Alison knew that Faith was taking her loss hard and hadn't said much since the train yard.

Agent Alesbury spoke. "Now that we know we are dealing with a much larger and more complex enemy than we thought; the FBI felt it would be prudent to bring on the DPD's Mage team."

Alison was about to zone out. They were going to lose Gabriel and Faith. She wasn't surprised; both of them would be invaluable assets to the hunt for Trinity, and given the Decor's past, Alison thought it unlikely that Gabriel and Heidi wouldn't do everything in their power to fight Trinity.

"But that does not work with the Pactum we have with the Denver Police Department," Heidi said, making Alison perk up.

"Right," Alesbury said. "So since you two," he said motioning to Sean and Alison, "have done such an upstanding job, we'd like to bring the DPD on as consultants."

"Really?" Sean said, surprised.

Alesbury nodded his head. "We know this isn't standard by any means, but to be honest neither are Mage, Mutari and Humans working so close together. We have reason to believe that Trinity will not stop working in the Denver area or in Colorado, for that matter. They were moving a lot of guns and drugs. Denver is the only major city in the middle of the country that can facilitate that kind of traffic. Plus, and I mean this with no disrespect; Denver doesn't have the same experience with organized crime as say, Chicago."

"The mid-section of the country also has the highest amount of Vis users," Gabriel said.

Alesbury nodded. "That is also correct. Anyway, how does it sound? You'd be working for the DPD like you do now, but also answering to the FBI"

Montoya looked at Alison and Sean.

"I'm in," Sean said smugly.

"Me too," Alison said.

"Does this work with our Pactum?" Montoya asked Heidi.

She smiled. "Yes; our Pactum's primary agreement is that we protect Detectives Kaur and Hughes. Also it is stipulated that our team will assist in investigation and arrests. Since the Pactum does not limit us to which government agency is in charge, everything should be in order."

Sean chuckled. "What about paperwork? Does your Pactum cover helping out with that?"

Gabriel winced, rotating his hand. "Ooo sorry, I've got carpal tunnel."

Faith sighed. "Sorry Sean, but I can't read, so I guess we won't be of much help."

Sean shook his head. "Can't read my foot, didn't I see you with like ten different books at your house?"

Gabriel shrugged. "She likes the way the letters look on the paper."

Alison smirked. It was good to see Faith making comments again, even if they were lies so she didn't have to fill out paperwork.

MANDY STAFFORD couldn't believe what she was looking at. Before her was a Pactum with Heidi Decor's signature on it.

"So what does this mean?" Sean asked her.

Mandy smiled. "I'm free. Heidi agreed to give me the Vis I need every week, or to have another Mage do it in payment for getting a lead on the Vies."

"So what are you going to do now?" Sean asked.

What was Mandy going to do? She could finally do whatever she liked, no longer having to hook to survive. "I'm not sure," she admitted. "I guess I could go back to school. I'm just not sure; I have a lot of money that I've made over the years, so I'll be fine for a while in that regard." She knew it was going to take some getting used to not having to rush everything in life.

"And how are you doing about what happened at the yard?" Sean asked.

Mandy looked down. To that she wasn't sure. It had only been a few days since she'd killed the people there, but she was sure that it would haunt her for the rest of her life.

"I think it will always be with me…but when I was like that it was like being really drunk, ya know?"

Sean smirked. "I know really drunk." He got serious. "But really I know what it's like to take a life and you need to get help…I have the name of someone if you like. I was a real mess at one point, and talking to someone helped."

She considered him for a moment. Sean was a dick, but only on the surface, and not to her anymore.

"I think I'd like that. Can I talk to you about it?" she asked.

"I still owe you whatever you need after what I did to you…" he paused.

Mandy decided to change the subject. "So what is happening now with the case?"

Sean perked back up. "We are still on it, so on Monday it will be back to hunting down Trinity. If I have any Mutari questions, can I call you?"

"Of course," she said, warmly.

Melinda Decor entered the room. "Are you two ready to leave?" she asked.

Mandy looked at her bag, making sure she hadn't forgotten anything from her stay.

"I have everything. Thank you again so much, Melinda," Mandy said.

Melinda smiled warmly. "You are welcome anytime, and thank you for giving us a line on the Vies." She became serious. "The Decors don't forget things like that, and now that we have a lead on the Vies, we will finally be able to seek justice."

Mandy and Sean were ushered out of the house to where Edward waited for them. Mandy took his hand and he jumped with her back to her home.

EPILOGUE

ANGELICA VIES walked quickly down the hall of a grand house, her shoes clacking loudly against the tiled floors. Her shoulder still hurt from her encounter with Gabriel Decor but she was faring well, all things considered. Next to her walked Keith and Tracy, *the latter showing skill and brains when it came to fighting, the first being more of a liability than a help.*

She came to a closed oak door.

"Wait here," she told the two Paladins as she entered.

In the room at a table sat her husband with two other people. Marcus was calm and collected, sipping at a glass of scotch. Omar Gloom, a Goblin, also looked fine, but the Human named Vicente Saucer did not.

"We now have the FBI and the DPD on our asses; how could you have lost so badly?" Vicente spat at Angelica.

"Do not take that tone with my wife," Marcus said, taking her side. "She was up against an Ark, and let us not forget that they caught wind of Trinity by your mistake. Had you not trusted William Lanner, none of this would have happened."

Vicente waved his hand. "Bah, I didn't hire the boy; Corey did." He turned to Angelica. "Will Corey be a problem?" he asked.

Angelica sat next to Marcus, his arm draping around her shoulders, her hand on his knee. They were a team through and through. "No; anyone with knowledge was either extracted or killed," she said. "But Gabriel is going to be hunting us again," she said to just Marcus.

"That is to be expected," the Goblin said. "How much inventory did we lose?"

Of course that's what the Goblin cared about, how much money was lost.

"Not much," she said.

"How much do they know?" Marcus asked, concerned.

Angelica smiled. "I left enough evidence for them to go in the wrong direction."

He nodded to her. "Very well; it seems that we need to move up our timetable. I vote to moving on to the next stage."

Omar nodded. "Agreed."

Vicente looked confused. "What next stage?"

"Interficiam," Marcus said with a casual flick of his hand.

A gold ribbon of Vis flashed out and sliced Vicente's neck, blood spraying the table and dappling the carpet with crimson droplets.

"The stage that doesn't include you, Human," Marcus said, turning to Omar and continuing the meeting.

SAMPLE OF SEEKER
PROLOGUE

BRYAN HARLEY stood quietly in the night air, observing the house before him. It wasn't terribly late at night, but still many of the windows nearby were dark. Bryan was a Shape Shifter. At the moment, he was naked, kneeling behind a bush. The evening air was getting crisp as Fall came into its own. Bryan didn't care to be cold, but it was necessary; after all, he needed to hide. Bryan was exceptionally skilled at hiding. Shape Shifters or Shifters as they are called, are rather adept at not being spotted. Bryan could not turn himself into a couch or any nonsense like that, but he could change his skin tone to whatever he liked. He changed his skin, rippling his flesh and breaking up the pattern of his body, defusing his form. Bryan couldn't become a couch, but he could turn himself into any other human shape he wanted, even changing his voice to that of the human he copied.

The downstairs lights went off in the house. Bryan paused for a moment before creeping to the front door. He had a key given to him by Angelica Vies. She was Bryan's employer. He looked around before slipping the key into the lock, and then turned it with a soft click. Carefully, he opened the door of the house and stepped inside. A bristly welcome mat brushed the soles of his feet, tickling them. He looked around the entryway. Above him, the sound of a shower started.

Good, he thought. *That should keep him from hearing me.*

Bryan made his way up a narrow staircase, the small amount of carpeting on each of the stairs making his approach even softer. He turned his skin off-white to match the wall he was next to, just in case his quarry wasn't in the shower. Bryan only held a small syringe clasped in his hand, hidden from view. The staircase wound up to the second floor. Bryan padded down the upstairs halls and peeked through the gap of a bedroom door. The room was bright, making his eyes water for a moment. Bryan moved around a queen-size bed and pressed himself against the wall next to the bathroom door. This is where he would wait.

While the movies made it seem like shower ambushes were the best, Bryan disagreed. It was one thing if you were planning on shooting the mark, but didn't work so well when you wanted them alive. No, he couldn't kill the mark -- he would need information for months to come -- and he didn't fancy wrestling a slippery, soapy man to the ground while also trying to stick him with a needle. Instead, Bryan waited and thought back to when he'd started all this Shifter stuff.

1972 was when Bryan figured out what he was. He was in junior high at the time. He'd just been caught taking a candy bar from the gas station. Bryan was an accomplished thief but had been caught this time, so he bolted, hiding under some trash behind the station as the clerk ran out back looking for him. Bryan had heard of the clerk, some guy who did some time for breaking into houses. Bryan figured that's how he'd been caught. Thieves know their own. He also knew this guy was going to kick his ass. The clerk had been clear about that, yelling it at the top of his voice and thirteen-year-old Bryan was on the verge of pissing himself. He just wanted to not be found, he wanted to blend in with the trash. The clerk searched for a solid ten minutes before giving up, passing Bryan by several times. It wasn't until Bryan stood and looked down at his hands that he saw why he hadn't been seen. His hands were black and shiny like the trash bags.

Bryan stood against the wall smirking, thinking back on the memory. After freeing himself from the trash, he'd had to spend a day getting his hand back to normal.

Bryan didn't truly start to come into his abilities until he was seventeen. He sighed, remembering the year. Britney Wamble had shot him down when he asked her out. She wasn't rude about her rejection in any way, but Bryan was still pissed as hell. Who had she been to say no? He'd gotten her back and that cocky little prick Richard Hicks, too. Richard was one of those good-at-everything, never-made-a-mistake kind of guys. Bryan hated that type. He remembered the night well. He'd discovered if he concentrated when he touched someone, he could mimic their appearance perfectly. Later he'd learn to find scars and learn a mark's personality, but in 1976, Bryan hadn't progressed that far yet. Still he thought he'd made a pretty decent Richard.

He'd tracked Britney to a small shop where she worked and followed her home. Bryan closed his eyes, relishing the memory, oh the lesson he'd taught her. Bryan smiled at the thought; she was one of many. Bryan hadn't done his homework and when she told the authorities it was Richard Hicks who had raped her, Richard was able to alibi out. He'd apparently spent the week with his family in Portland.

Bryan shrugged. *You were young and dumb.* He didn't make mistakes like that anymore. Now he knew what he was doing, knew how to mimic people to a T. After his failed attempt with Richard, Bryan had doubled his effort at mastering his craft. He caught his reflection in the glass of a picture on the wall. It was a picture of the mark and his wife. Bryan was currently taking on the appearance of someone he'd run into at the airport. Bryan couldn't even guess to what his real appearance was anymore, it had been decades since he'd been himself. He reached out to get a closer look at the picture, looking at the mark and his wife. She wasn't anything to write home about, but from his recon, he'd only have to screw her once every few weeks.

Families were the quickest thing to blow a job. Pulling one over on someone's co-workers was hard enough, but convincing a mark's spouse that you were their loved one was something else. Bryan spent weeks watching people, seeing how they worked together and how they played off each other. He'd also have to get little details from the mark, things like family trips and the like, things that kept someone's mind at ease when a loved one didn't seem right. In this regard, it was easier to be a woman; men rarely picked up on the little things.

The shower stopped. Bryan focused, gripping the syringe tightly in his hand. He held his breath as the bathroom door opened and a figure came out in a towel. Bryan rushed forward, wrapped his arm under the mark's chin, and pulled back as he jammed the needle in his throat. The man jabbed an elbow into Bryan, but Bryan held fast and waited for the tranquilizer to take effect. As it did, the man's body went limp in his arms. Bryan lowered him to the bed and pulled off the towel. He placed his hand on the man's chest, his own flesh rippling as it took on its new appearance. Bryan began methodically inspecting the mark's body for tattoos or scars, finding only a few. The wife wouldn't be home for two days. Bryan made the skin on his belly split open, revealing a plastic bag with a phone inside. He turned on the phone and dialed Angelica.

"Did you get him?" she asked, not even bothering with a greeting.

"Yeah, I've got him. Where do you want to store him until we're done?" Bryan asked.

About the Author

Nicholas was born and raised in Denver, Colorado. He didn't want to write until October of 2007. While he was driving around with a friend and said "hey, I wonder if I can write a book." So he thought he would try and write outline and see what happens.

www.NicholasTaylor.co